GAY SALUTE

GAY SALUTE

by

NORMAN TUCKER

Norman Tucker.

JOHN LONG

ARS LONGA BREVIS VITA

LONG

LIMITED

LONDON : NEW YORK : MELBOURNE : SYDNEY

TO
RUTH AINSWORTH
WITH GRATITUDE

THIS BOOK IS PRODUCED IN COM-
PLETE CONFORMITY WITH THE
AUTHORIZED ECONOMY STANDARDS

MADE AND PRINTED IN GREAT BRITAIN
AT GAINSBOROUGH PRESS, ST. ALBANS,
BY FISHER, KNIGHT AND CO., LTD.

CHAPTER ONE

THE SOUND ON THE WINDOW CAUSED ANN TREVOR TO TURN IN HER sleep. She looked curiously small in the great four-poster bed with the half-curtains drawn to keep out the draught. And there were draughts in Plas Mawr, the rambling old house which looked so sturdy and stately when viewed from the park. The sound was repeated. Ann drew the bed-clothes closer about her pretty ears and snuggled more cosily into the pillow. Hail! she mused. Hail on the first day of April! The harshness of the elements made her bed appear the more comfortable. The tattoo on the window-pane sounded again, a hard, clear-cut sound. Surely hail could never be so insistent. Ann sat up in bed and listened. The room was in darkness so no one could see how fair she looked with her cheeks flushed, and her eyes big with surprise and her dark wavy hair tumbling in silken disorder. Again the tattoo rattled on the casement, an eerie sound in the stillness of the night. There could only be one explanation. Someone was throwing gravel at her chamber window. Curiosity got the better of her. She lowered her feet and groped for her slippers. Tossing a shawl about her, she moved cautiously across the floor and flung back the curtains. Her room, which had been so dark, was now bathed in a pale ethereal light as the rays of a full moon streamed in. Somewhere in the encircling woods an owl hooted. Ann fumbled with the fastening and threw open the window. As the night air greeted her she was conscious, not of its coldness, but of its freshness, as it caressed her heated cheek. On the gravel drive was a figure in bold silhouette; a man in a caped riding-coat who stood with booted feet apart, gazing upwards towards her room.

As she looked out he swept off his tricorne hat with a gay salute and she was able to see his upturned face more clearly in the light of the moon. A handsome face, assuredly, with a touch of reckless bravado about it; the face of a complete stranger.

"Come down," he commanded. His voice was low but distinct. "Come down and let me in."

"Why should I, pray?"

"Egad, Frances, this is a cool reception after all these months. You do not recognize your wandering lad, eh?"

"If it is Frances Holt you seek she is not here. My father, Squire Trevor, bought this place from the Holts twelve months since."

"The deuce!" The man's assurance ebbed from him disconcertingly. He clicked his heels together and bowed. "Madam, your pardon for thus rudely disturbing your slumbers. I am no gay serenader, I beg you to believe. The mistake was genuine. I did but seek a meal and a few hours' sleep. Forgive me for troubling you."

He replaced his hat. Ann saw that it bore a white cockade. Before

5

he had taken a couple of paces her voice checked him. "Stay. You wear the white cockade. Are you for the King across the water?"

"Why, yes. I'm for King James the Third and his bonny son, the legitimate Prince of Wales."

"Bide awhile. You shall have food and rest. Go to the side door and wait. My father sleeps in the front of the house. I will not be a moment."

Ann's hands trembled so that she could not manage the flint and steel. She abandoned her task and set about struggling into some clothes by the light of the moon. She opened her door and listened. The stertorous breathing from her father's bedchamber showed that the squire, fortified by his last bottle of port, was sound asleep. The leaded window at the end of the landing cast a pretty pattern on the uneven boards as she made her way towards the stairs, pausing anxiously whenever the dry wood creaked. Her progress was comparatively noiseless but not rapid. When at length she slid back the bolts and unloosed the chain from the side door, she found her nocturnal visitor waiting with a stoicism which indicated that he had a proper appreciation of the length of a feminine moment. To her surprise Ann experienced no qualms about admitting the stranger to the house. She closed the door behind him.

"We will go to the dining-room," she said softly. "This way." Even as he followed, Ann was struck by the noiselessness of his step. It was as though he was accustomed to move by stealth.

The dining-room was still warm, and heavy with a sickly pungent smell of wine and tobacco mingled with the acrid smoke from a slowly dying log in the wide fire-place. She brought candles but again her hand shook when she fumbled with the tinder.

"This is quicker," said the stranger, thrusting the wicks into the embers of the fire.

He held each candle aloft and scrutinized his hostess. Ann instinctively drew her shawl about her, but returned his gaze fearlessly.

"Golden eyes!" he said softly as though in soliloquy. Indeed there was a quality about Ann's eyes which arrested attention for the pupils were large and dark and seemed to be encircled by pure amber. She flushed, and he apologized.

"My rudeness is inexcusable. I fear I have travelled so much alone that I have acquired the unfortunate habit of speaking my thoughts aloud. Accept my thanks for your kindness in offering me hospitality."

"You ride for the Prince?" she asked eagerly. "I was expecting some of his messengers. It was for that purpose that we planted the Charlie Trees close to the lodge entrance."

"Charlie Trees?" A puzzled expression crossed his face.

"Yes. Little groves of Scots pine. Prince Charlie Trees we call them. They are put so that Stuart supporters who may be wandering homeless may know where to find a welcome. Do not say that you did not know."

"Now that you mention it, I have heard something about the practice, though not by that name. A kindly thought, egad. No,

I did not notice your Charlie Trees, I am afraid. Can you give me something to eat? Something cold. Anything."

"I am sorry. Of course you must be starving." Ann opened a cupboard in the mahogany sideboard and took out a partly-cut veal-and-ham pie. This she placed on the table and turned to get a plate and cutlery but her guest was impatient and, breaking the pastry between strong fingers, he began to eat without ceremony. He did not talk, but his eyes roved the room.

Presently he spoke. "New. All new. Hardly know the old room but for the fire-place."

"You used to know the house, then?"

"Before I went away, yes." His tone was succinct. The pie proved more engrossing than the room. He paused in his eating to hold up a candle so that its light fell on a picture. "So you have kept the Lely. I am glad. An ancestor of the Holts."

"Yes. Mr. Holt said that it was too big to carry away and sold it to Father. I am afraid I persuaded him to spend his money on it—I like the scarlet coat; it brightens this dark room so."

"He was an admiral of sorts, I believe, under Charles the Second. I had his virtues extolled often enough when I was a lad, though I always fancied he must have been a gay dog off duty."

He brushed the crumbs from his waistcoat which, though worn, was sprigged and brocaded. When his eyes caught sight of the decanter they brightened. Ann read his look and picking up a glass, she poured the amber liquid with a steady hand. He took it eagerly but had the grace to bow before he drank. "To your bright eyes, Hostess," he said gravely.

It was fine old sherry and the girl expected a word of praise, but to her consternation he tossed off the wine at a gulp and turned for more. Ann forestalled him.

"No. No. I would not appear inhospitable but Father will miss it. He keeps a closer watch on the sherry than he does on his purse."

"You are right," he said slowly. "And I am better without it. How goes the time?"

"Half an hour after midnight."

"I must be away by six. That gives me five hours' sleep. Have you a boot-jack?"

She fetched him one and he divested himself of his spurred boots as coolly as if he were at home. She picked them up. The leather was warm to her touch. They were worn and spattered, but of a good quality. He loosened his cravat. She thought he looked less dignified now that his boots were removed. Her thoughts did not trouble him. He was busy looking to the priming of his pistols. Both these he laid on the hearth-rug with his naked sword beside them. He flung down a few cushions and stretched himself beside the embers.

"Get back to your bed, Hostess," he commanded, "and leave me to my repose. I have ridden far to-day."

Instead she fetched a couple of rugs to spread over him. "Are these weapons necessary?" she asked curiously. "Is it really so dangerous?"

7

"A hanging matter if I am caught," he said lightly.

Ann seated herself in a high-backed chair. "Then I'll stay and keep watch," she said firmly.

"Better seek your bed; you'll catch cold."

"I'm not sleepy."

"Well, I am." He burrowed his head into the cushion and pulled the rugs about his shoulders. "I shall probably snore." Ann sat very still. The embers threw a cosy glow; occasionally a spot of resin in the wood would flare up, lighting the features of the slumbering man. She studied them closely, endeavouring to analyse them. He was not unhandsome though the dark stubble on his unshaved chin detracted somewhat from his appearance. The face was weathered and tanned. There were dark lines under the eyes but she could not determine whether they were caused by weariness or dissipation. Still, it was a strong face; a reckless face. Who could he be? He knew the house; he knew the Holts; he knew Frances Holt well. He might be her cousin. There was some talk, she recollected, of a love affair which had not run smoothly. Whoever he was he was serving the Prince. Perhaps he had actually seen his Royal Highness. She must ask him when he awoke. The candles flickered. Ann wondered whether she had been amiss in not putting a bowl of water on the table before he drank so that he could toast the King over the water. It was customary; but he seemed too weary to bother about ceremony, so perhaps he had not noticed her omission. Ann dozed. The grandfather clock which stood in the hall near the foot of the stairs solemnly struck one and Ann stirred. Was it, she wondered sleepily, one o'clock, or was it half past something? It did not really matter but she wondered. She glanced at the recumbent figure on the hearth-rug. The man slept heavily. He was a better colour now. Perhaps it was rest he needed. The candles were guttering. She snuffed one of them and stood it close to her hand with the tinder-box within reach. The fire was low but the room was still warm. Ann yawned. Why had she imposed this vigil on herself? She would be more comfortable in her bed. Still, it was not every night one was roused by a messenger from Prince Charlie, and she could make up for lost sleep another night. It was rather fun playing sentinel.

The pistols and the drawn sword added a real spice of excitement. Almost she hoped that some Hanoverian search-party would come crunching up the drive. She fetched herself another cushion and a rug and settled herself more comfortably in the chair. Sleepily she blew out the remaining candle. After all, there would be no harm in just dozing; the night hours seemed interminably long.

*　　*　　*　　*　　*

How long she slept she did not know. The room was cold when she awoke. Her first conscious thought was that her neck was stiff. She rubbed it tenderly and then, bewildered by the darkness, groped for flint and steel. They were near her hand, just where she had laid them. The sparks flashed in the dark room. She had the candle alight. The sound of the chiming of the old clock caused her to start.

8

She paused to count the strokes. Six! It was time to arouse the messenger. Her gaze turned to the hearth-rug and she gave a gasp of amazement. The rugs were neatly folded on the cushions. Of the man and the pistols and the drawn sword there was no sign. For a moment she wondered whether the house had been ransacked but the room seemed as orderly as usual. He had disappeared. Ann was conscious of a sense of disappointment. She could have cried with vexation. After her befriending him he might at least have bade her farewell, given a word of thanks. She had wanted him to carry away her expression of loyalty to the Prince. But he had gone; stolen away silently in the stillness of the night while she slept; vanished with never a sign. Ann bit her lip and stood up. Something tumbled to the carpet. She stared, stooped and picked it up. The colour flooded her cheeks. The messenger had left her his white cockade.

CHAPTER TWO

ANN WAS NO LIE-ABED. WHEN SHE OPENED HER EYES SHE WAS FULLY awake, and awake, she was consumed with restlessness. She wanted to know what was going on in the world about her once the never-palling miracle of dawn had come to pass. Accordingly the servants were not surprised to see Ann fully dressed when they began their duties. She wore an air of dignity and casualness which was so obviously assumed that it would have deceived no one but an adoring servant. Ann, stifling a yawn, prided herself on her astuteness. It had not been easy putting the room in order and then going upstairs to complete her attiring before anyone was astir. Yet she had managed it commendably. Ann surveyed the room with complacency; nothing was amiss, save, alas, the level of the sherry in the decanter. For one brief moment Ann thought of restoring it to its former height by the addition of water but firmly she put the impious suggestion from her mind. This was prompted less by scruples of conscience than by her knowledge of her parent's discriminating palate. No, the sherry must be left to take its chance; after all, her father might not notice. Again she yawned, and took herself to task. She must check herself. A yawn was most incriminating. No one had ever seen Ann yawn in the morning. Fresh air would cure it. She flung wide the front door and stepped into the porch. The fairness of the night had departed with the going down of the moon. A fine rain was falling, typical April rain which made the land seem greener, yet failed to check the vocal ardour of the vociferous thrushes. She donned a hooded cape and walked forth into the still, fresh world. Instinctively she broke into a run. She often ran, not because she was in a hurry but out of sheer exuberance, just as a child will skip. Soon she paused to regard her little shoes critically. It was wet under-foot and gave promise of becoming more so. Ann was as fastidious as she was neat. Returning to the house she put on her pattens. The light clatter of these sounded not unmusically as she walked the slate-flagged path which crossed the garden to the rear premises. The

9

A*

path skirted a cluster of trees and Ann had to pause before a clump of daffodils to shake them daintily because she loved to hear their silken rustle. Ann loved flowers. She was, had she but known it, a human flower, redolent of fragrance and delicacy. She gladdened lives by being just herself.

It was towards the stables that she picked her way. She was a frequent visitor for Howells, the head groom, had been her devoted slave since he had taught her not to tumble off the Welsh mountain pony which had been her father's present on her seventh birthday. That was so long ago that Ann positively felt mature when she looked back down the long vista of thirteen years.

Howells's voice was uplifted angrily from the stables. The delicate arch of her eyebrows indicated Ann's surprise. Howells took a pride in the immaculateness of his stables; someone had transgressed. She saw Hughie, the stable-boy, with his back to the wall and Howells facing him with a leading-rein wrapped about his gnarled right hand. The light of relief leaped to Hughie's eyes at Ann's appearance. Howells lowered the strap and looked sheepish.

"Just giving this here lad a piece of my mind," he explained hurriedly.

"Piece of your mind?" echoed Ann, glancing at the strap which the groom was endeavouring to conceal from her quick eyes.

"Now, Mistress Ann, don't go standing up for these lazy young rascals or I'll never get no work out of them. A bit of strap won't do Hughie no harm. He's got to learn to keep the stables clean. There's been a horse in the loose-box and he swears he knows nothing about it——"

"Nor do I," burst out the stable-boy. "Honest, Mistress Ann——"

"Silence," thundered Howells, raising the strap.

"Oh!" ejaculated Ann apprehensively. She took a deep breath. The Prince's messenger! Of course he had a horse. Why had she not thought of it before? "Now, run away, Hughie, and don't you get into Mr. Howells's black books again!" she exclaimed. The boy obeyed, anxious to please his young mistress; more anxious to get beyond reach of the leading-rein.

"Let's go to the harness-room. I want to talk to you," said Ann, and led the way. Howells followed with the docility of a well-bred hound. Ann would have been horrified had she been called an autocrat but never was a tyrant's sway more absolute. The roughest, toughest men on the estate were slaves to her sweet imperiousness. The harness-room was her favourite haunt, dearer far than her boudoir. She loved the sight of the hanging bridles with their bright bits, the saddles placed on pegs, pieces of whipcord, tins of harness-polish or saddle-soap, the warm smell of horseflesh mingling with hay, the rhythmic crunching which sounded through the half-open door. Howells placed a folded yellow horse-blanket on a chair for her; Ann ignored it and sat on top of the worn wooden corn-bin swinging her dainty feet. This might have been a ritual. Ann invariably sat on the corn-bin; Howells never forgot to offer the chair.

The weather-tanned groom shook his grizzled head slowly at his

10

mistress. "'Tain't right, Mistress Ann, spoiling the young rascal the way you does. How am I to keep him in order?"

"But it wasn't his fault, Howells, this time."

"This place were all tidy when I left it; it weren't his fault, you say. Whose fault, then, was it, I'd like to ask?"

"It was my fault."

"You mean to say you come here—in the night—— !"

"Don't be silly; of course I did not."

"But you said——"

"Don't interrupt, Howells, or I won't tell you. Yes, I will, too, because I must. But don't interrupt. It was a man, a gentleman."

"A man!" The groom's face was a study.

"He woke me up at midnight, throwing stones at my window."

"Mistress Ann! A man throwing stones at your window at midnight. What would Squire say?"

"His language would be shocking, so you must not tell him, Howells."

"But when a man comes throwing gravel at your window——"

"But he didn't."

"You just said he did."

"Oh, don't be stupid, Howells. He did and he didn't, don't you see?"

"Drat me if I do. He did and he didn't——"

"Do let me explain. He did throw stones at the window, but not my window. At least he didn't know it was my window. . . ."

"Mistress Ann, you haven't been and fallen in love——"

Ann laughed with the irrepressible abandon of a child. Her laughter was so unrestrained that there came a rattle of chains against mangers as each horse turned to look at the doorway through which sounded such silvery mirth. It was, of course, ridiculous. Ann had never loved anybody, because she loved everybody.

"Oh, Howells, how adorably absurd you are. Of course it was nothing so preposterous. It was a very—very serious affair. The man wore," Ann lowered her voice impressively, "a white cockade."

Howells was not awed. "Why?" he asked sensibly.

"I am nearly cross with you, Howells. You have no sense of romance. The white cockade is the badge of the Stuarts just as the black cockade stands for the House of Hanover. This man was a messenger—a messenger for Prince Charles Edward."

"And what might Prince Charlie be sending you messages for?"

"There was no message for me, nothing so exciting. I don't know what the message was, even. But the messenger was weary and hungry so I let him in."

"You—let—him—in! In the house?"

Ann nodded vigorously. "And he ate all that remained of the veal-and-ham pasty, and made crumbs on the floor, and drank Father's sherry. . . ."

"Mistress Ann!"

"And then he put his sword and pistols on the hearth-rug and lay down and went fast asleep. And I watched all night——"

11

"Mistress Ann!" Howells's face registered perturbation.

"At least I tried to, but I fell asleep and when I awoke he was gone."

"With the silver as like as not."

"I am surprised at you, Howells. This was the Prince's own messenger. Nothing was touched, not a thing; that is, I am afraid he did take another drink of sherry. It is going to be difficult to explain if Father notices. And he is so observant, suspecting the servants, quite unjustly of course. I'm sure the messenger was thirsty after his long ride. And he left me this."

Almost reverently she drew from her bosom a soiled white cockade. The groom stared with wrinkles of perplexity on his brow. "I don't like it; I don't hold with it. Drat me if I do. Such goings on. I'd never have slept a wink if I'd known."

"You mustn't say a word; not a word. Promise."

"It's my bounden duty to tell Squire."

"That would spoil everything. I have never, never been so excited before. And if you could have seen the drawn sword——"

"Stuff and nonsense."

Ann slowly slipped down from the bin and walked towards Howells. "It's a secret, my secret. You will not betray—us? You won't betray gallant Prince Charlie and our King across the water?"

Howells grunted and turned his head from the appealing eyes which gazed into his.

"You will not mention the strange horse?" coaxed Ann. "You will do this for Prince Charlie's sake?"

The groom crossed the room as though trying to escape from the mesmerism of those wonderful eyes, those golden eyes which seemed to glow with some hidden fire. He took down a whip and commenced to tie knots rapidly in the cord with fingers that trembled. "Bah! Nothing but a pack of lies and nonsense; have nothing to do with the affair, my dear. Take an old man's advice. Tell the Master; tell the old Squire, I beg you."

"Not a word. You must be sworn to secrecy. Promise for bonny Prince Charlie's sake."

"To the devil with Prince Charlie. What is he to me? Or Geordie either? Names! Names! Folks who mean nothing in my life, fine folk though they be. I'd do nothing for Prince Charlie."

"Howells!" Ann was scandalized.

"I'd do nothing for this Prince Charlie. No not for King Geordie either, but heaven forgive me, there's nothing I would not do for Mistress Ann, so have it your own way. I will keep my mouth shut, and God grant no ill comes of it. If anything were to happen to you, my little queen, it would break my heart."

CHAPTER THREE

IT WAS THE BREAKFAST HOUR, AND DOUBTLESS BY THIS TIME THE SANDS in the egg-timing glass were running their course, but the rain had stopped and an April sun was lighting up the scene, making the tender leaves glisten. All thoughts of breakfast vanished. Ann must explore the world about her for she knew that though it might appear the same old world, really it changed with every change of the weather. "Send Hughie to the house with my cloak," she commanded, tossing the encumbrance to Howells. She ran across the cobbles joyfully. At the last door of the outhouses she dropped to her knees to caress a sad-eyed, broad-backed mastiff which moved stiffly to greet her. He had been Ann's special property since puppyhood and now, an honoured pensioner, his last days were warmed by the unquenchable fire of her affections. "My adored!" exclaimed Ann. When charged with the joy of life she was all superlatives and extravagances. Her arms were about him. He accepted the embraces with the stoicism of advancing years.

Ann felt a cold nose thrust impatiently, impulsively, almost demandingly against her arm. Rip the terrier was calling attention to his presence. When Ann looked at him he became so vociferous that he almost knocked the old hound off his balance.

"Wretch! Have you no respect for age? No, of course you have not." Placing her hands against the mastiff's massive flanks she thrust him back into the room and closed the half-door. "You may get your feet wet, my sweet," she apologized.

The next instant she had forgotten him, for Rip was barking and she chased him. Down the lane which led to the road went the dog. The old mastiff might claim Ann's tenderness, but Rip's outlook on life more nearly coincided with her own. The pattens impeded her progress.

"Oh, bother the old things," exclaimed Ann, which was strong language for her. She flung the offending pattens from her impetuously. Rip pounced on one as eagerly as if it had been a rat.

"That's not for you! Rip! Give it up. Do you hear?" Ann's tone was severe but the terrier was too engrossed in his new plaything to pay attention. "You villain! Give it back to me. It was not meant for you. Drop it!" As Ann made a grab, Rip darted down the lane and vanished around the corner into the hedge-fringed road, the patten firm in his jaws. Ann raced after him.

"You rogue!" she cried. "You wretch!"

She almost collided with a man who stood near the roadside hedge; a tall man who looked gravely down into her flushed face.

"How quickly you have estimated my character!" he said, shaking his head mournfully. "Was it womanly intuition?"

Ann stared up at him. His whole aspect was dignified and deliberate, his expression pensive, yet she thought that she detected a light dancing in those grave eyes as though mirth lay not far beneath the surface. That he was laughing at her never occurred to Ann. She explained with the naivety of a child, "I did not mean you. It is Rip who is a wretch; he has run off with my patten and he will chew it to splinters."

"Luckless Rip, to incur your displeasure. My relief at finding I am not the object of your disapprobation is prodigious, I assure you, Miss——?" His eyebrows were raised interrogatively.

"Ann !" she said. "I am Ann. I mean I am Miss Trevor."

He shook his head. "Oh, no !" he contradicted. "You are Ann. You could not be anything but Ann. I positively refuse to think of you as Miss Trevor."

"Well," observed Ann after deliberation, "you need not call me Miss Trevor. You are old enough to call me Ann." She was appraising him. The man was quite old. He must be forty at least.

He made a wry face. "Yes," he said deliberately. "Old enough to call you Ann, and young enough to want to."

"And what is your name ?"

"I am Philip Yorke."

"The Mystery Man ? You have come to dwell at the old Rectory."

"Which I intend to rechristen the Hermitage, for there I shall live the life of a hermit. The Mystery Man. So that is what folk term me ?"

"I should not have said it. I am sorry if I was rude. Father is for ever reprimanding me for speaking without thinking. It is a great fault of mine."

"I have the temerity to disagree with your parent. The trait should be included among your outstanding charms. Tell me, what else do folk say about me ? I vow that I am vastly intrigued."

"All manner of nasty things."

"My back is broad, as you notice. I should survive even if I were called a rogue and a wretch."

"You know perfectly well I referred to Rip. It is unkind and unmannerly to fasten on me a fault of which I was not guilty."

"I confess my guilt and accept your reproof. How can I make atonement ?"

"By rescuing my patten. We stand gossiping while the young villain gnaws it to pieces."

"Let us seek the young villain."

They walked down the road to where Rip lay in the lush roadside grass reducing the patten to splinters. Ann's scolding and Yorke's coaxing failed to produce results and Rip, on their closer approach, wriggled through the hedge.

"The scamp is running back home," ejaculated Ann. A thought struck her. "And I must too. It is long past breakfast hour. The eggs will be cold."

"The blame must be laid to my charge."

"Never mind. They will boil some fresh ones, for me."

"I am convinced that they will."

"But I really must fly, Mr. Yorke, you will have to excuse me."

"When shall I see you again ?"

"Why should you want to see me again ?"

"That is something which I must deliberate, and time does not permit an adequate answer. Let me say that I am anxious to know why I am called a Mystery Man."

"I wish I had not mentioned it. Father is correct."

"But you did mention it, and in fairness to me, you ought to see me again and offer some explanation. That is but justice." His tone sounded serious, almost like an admonition. Ann looked up

14

quickly. He seemed to be almost frowning with displeasure, yet the little starry light persisted in dancing in his eyes.

"I suppose so," agreed Ann demurely.

"Then let us say——" He groped for his fob and consulted a gold watch. "Let us say that you will be out again by eleven o'clock. Where shall we meet?"

"I could not say. Is it really necessary?"

"Imperative if you would undo all the harm you have done."

"Very well, then. At eleven."

"Where?"

"Oh, let me see—near the Charlie Trees."

"The what?"

"The Charlie Trees. Those young Scots pines yonder."

"I see. So be it."

"Good-bye. I am starving."

As informally as a child, Ann ran back along the road and vanished into the stable yard. Philip Yorke stood in the roadway, his tricorne hat in his hand, gazing thoughtfully after her. He continued to gaze long after Ann had vanished from his sight. When Ann entered the dining-room she found her father seated at the head of the table in solitary state. He had finished his meal. This he stressed by a gesture towards the untidy plates.

"You are late!" His voice was gruff.

"Yes. I am late."

"You ought not to be late."

"Does it matter?"

"Matter? Of course it matters. Order and punctuality are the foundation of every well-run household."

"How funny. You are the most erratic and unpunctual man I ever met. I must have acquired my bad habits from you."

"I—unpunctual? Preposterous. I would have you know that my word is law. You have a most disrespectful way of speaking to your father. I must insist on your addressing me with the respect and—er—veneration that my age and rank entitle me——"

"Darling, you look so quaint when you try to appear dignified. Is that how you talk when you are on the Bench? And you are getting so grumpy these days."

"Grumpy? Is that the proper way to speak of your father?"

"I think 'grumpy' is a perfect word and so appropriate. Why do you think it your duty to be always scolding me and finding fault with me? On such a morning, too, when the sun is shining and the birds are singing."

"Why? Why? In self-defence of course. Where would we all be if I did not keep you in your place? You'd wheedle me round your finger just like you wheedle the servants. They all conspire against me. I cannot be master in my own house. It is scandalous."

"Poor Grumpy."

"If you call me that again, I'll—I'll——"

"What terrible thing would you do to me?" inquired Ann, seating herself on the arm of his chair.

"Stop making a fuss of me. Stop it, I say. Dammit, am I not to be obeyed? Gad, I pity the poor devil you marry. He'll not be able to call his soul his own."

"But he could call me his own; that would be nicer."

Her father was looking at her serene face. She noticed how blue his eyes were in the round florid face. A trifle wistful they seemed.

"How like your mother you look, Ann, when the sunlight strikes your hair. It is seventeen years since——" He sighed and patted her hand.

"Never mind, darling, you still have me to pester you, and I won't let you grow old."

"Old! old! Confound it, girl, I'm not old. There, give the bell-pull a tug and tell Morgan to brew you a fresh dish of tea."

Ann crossed to the sideboard and picked up a neatly finished tea caddy of inlaid-mahogany, and lifted the lid.

"How's this?" cried her father. "Have you not kept it locked? Demme, girl, you know the price of tea. Keep it locked, I tell you, or every servant in the place will be having a pinch."

"But why not? I am sure that a drink of tea would be an acceptable treat for them. After all, you are not so poor. I don't mind if they do taste a little. I should not call it stealing."

"No, you wouldn't. That's the trouble. You spoil 'em; spoil the whole lot of 'em. This house is going to the dogs. Can't do anything with the staff."

"What wrong have they done now?"

"Wrong? Let me see! Dash my eyes I can't think of anything at the moment, but there's plenty for a man to grumble about."

"Aren't you glad? You would be miserable without something to grumble about You know that. And you really must not drink so much sherry. It is bad for the liver. I think that is what is the matter with you. You are liverish."

"Liverish! Liverish be—that is, I don't agree."

"What is the matter, then? There is something on your mind these days. I can tell."

Squire Trevor commenced to flick pellets of bread viciously across the table while furrows showed on his usually smooth, weather-tanned brow. He sat silent while the servants brought Ann her breakfast.

"Shut the door fast," he shouted as the last servant left. "I drink too much sherry, eh? No, girl, it isn't sherry. It is, well, it is affairs in general, you know. The country's in an awful state."

"You were out in the 'Fifteen weren't you, darling?"

"What's that got to do with it? Of course I was out in the 'Fifteen. What prompted you to make that inane remark?"

"It is not inane. It is a very wise remark. You have been thinking about that rebellion and wondering whether there is going to be another. I can read your thoughts. Ever since the Young Chevalier left Rome and went to live in Paris you have been restless. Now, don't contradict. I shall not betray you. In fact," Ann lowered her voice impressively, "I shall come in with you."

The Squire roared with laughter. Ann looked pained and a trifle

16

dignified. "Oh, very well. I intended to help you but if that is how you feel I shall manage my affairs without taking you into my confidence," she said haughtily.

"You'll do nothing of the sort. I won't have you meddling with politics. A damned dirty game, eh? That is, it's not for innocent, inexperienced maids. Ann, leave it alone. I command it."

"You can't command me. I'm for Bonny Prince Charlie. Darling, I must have romance and adventure. Life is intolerably dull without them. Risk adds spice to the game. Were you very, very cautious when you were young?"

"Was I?"

Ann answered for him. "Of course you were not. You rode out for King James the Third in the 'Fifteen, and you are planning to do so again. I know you."

Squire Trevor sat drumming restlessly on the table with his fingers. "You know too much. Romance and adventure. Ah, lass, you have hit it. Do they still appeal? Or is it more mercenary motives? Bah! I am a fool. I am comfortably off, why should I burn my fingers? If I gamble and I lose, you are robbed of your patrimony. Ann, my Ann."

"What of it? You shall not hear a grumble from me. Do not hesitate to declare for the Stuart on my account. If I were a lad I'd be among the first. As it is I cannot draw blade for the Stuart, but I shall help in other ways. I'll plot and conspire."

She slipped a white arm about her father's stocky neck. "You are not really grumpy. Not really. I take it back. We are in this together, you and I. So, hey for Bonny Prince Charlie, and never heed the consequences."

CHAPTER FOUR

ANN KEPT HER APPOINTMENT. SHE WENT TO SEE PHILIP YORKE. SHE kept faith. It was entirely impersonal. She was not curious; he meant nothing to her. Her thoughts, as she walked along the road, were not of Philip Yorke—probably by this time she had forgotten his name, it signified so little—but of her nocturnal visitor. Now, she really would like to have learnt *his* name, and all about him. A messenger of the Prince. How long had he been in the country? What had been his adventures? Had he a price on his head? Ann pictured him riding out in the grey dawn. Whither? Thinking thus she recollected his horse and instinctively glanced at the muddy road surface to see if the animal had passed that way. Yes, the hoof-prints were clearly defined in the morning mud. Her quick eyes followed them as she walked. She recalled the amusing incident of the morning. That was the spot where Rip, the rascal, had vanished through the hedge with her patten; that was where she encountered the stranger who had been standing there. Why had he been standing there? Ann stopped abruptly as a disquieting thought struck her. Had he, this man who called himself Philip Yorke, been studying the hoof-

17

tracks of the Prince's messenger? A disquieting thought indeed. Ann puckered her brow. It almost seemed as if she were frowning but it was merely the result of unwonted mental concentration. She reconstructed the scene from her imagination. There was the hedge-fringed corner around which she ran so impetuously after the recalcitrant Rip; that was the spot where she had collided—or nearly collided—with the unknown man. She recollected now that he had been staring at the ground. Was he (the thought which leaped to her mind gave her a thrill of apprehension), was he a spy? A Hanoverian spy? "Oh, don't be absurd," quoth Ann aloud. She commenced to walk more briskly as though to escape from her thoughts. She saw Mr. Yorke's tall figure near the Charlie Trees. His hands were behind his back, his feet apart. He appeared lost in meditation. There was a certain sombreness about his appearance, a subdued colouring which seemed the more pronounced because Ann had been brought up among men whose gaiety was reflected in the brightness of their apparel. Mr. Yorke's wide-skirted coat with its great cuffs was of unpretentious brown, his breeches and stockings were black. Yet she noted that the broadcloth of his coat was of a fineness and richness which bespoke fastidious taste. His hair was dark, and though flecked with grey, was thick. It was tied at the nape with a broad black ribbon. The touch of silver gave it the appearance of a wig, though actually it was far more distinguished. So Ann was thinking when the sound of her steps caused him to turn quickly. He swept off his three-cornered hat with an easy bow and stood regarding her gravely. This gravity seemed part of the man, and yet Ann could never feel certain that he was as serious as he appeared. His eyes were fixed on her; deep penetrating eyes; hypnotic eyes; which seemed earnest and profound, save that a little dancing light kept twinkling in them like a will-o'-the-wisp.

"You look patient and long-suffering," observed Ann, without formality. "Does it mean that I am late?"

"Let us say that I am ahead of time," said Mr. Yorke, consulting his watch. Ann's quick eyes caught sight of the dial. "I am five minutes late!" she cried in consternation.

"The watch must be five minutes fast; whatever time you arrive is the right time."

Ann ignored the compliment. This was not due to hauteur but to indifference. Gallantries did not interest her.

"What really matters is that I have kept the appointment. I am here as I said to—Ah!"

"What is it?"

"I have really forgotten why I said I would come. How absurd."

"I have a better memory. It was to tell me why people term me the Mystery Man."

"What a ridiculously trivial thing on which to base a meeting."

"The end justifies the triviality." His words drifted into space.

Ann's fair brow was puckered. She was endeavouring to think quickly. If this man was interested in the Prince's messenger, that is, if he was likely to prove an enemy to the Stuart cause, she must be

18

on her guard. Mr. Yorke must be watched. Perhaps the cause might benefit if she cultivated his closer acquaintance. She became aware that Mr. Yorke was addressing her.

"Someone must have ridden from your stable-yard in the early hours," he was saying. "The horse passed this way obviously after the rain began to fall."

Ann felt herself colouring. The eyes which were uplifted to Mr. Yorke were large, puzzled and a little apprehensive. In her surprise Ann resorted to platitudes.

"Why, whatever do you mean?" She spoke a little sharply. It was as though the man had read her thoughts.

"I noticed that you paused to study the hoof-prints in the roadway," he said with a grave smile.

"Oh!" ejaculated Ann who could think of nothing else to say.

"They were conspicuous. I, too, noticed them. I was examining them when you burst with such joyous abandon into my colourless existence."

"You were examining them? But why?"

"I was interested. One of my secrets of happiness is to be continually interested. It may be because I have so far discovered no better way. I take an interest in my fellow creatures, in the recorded thoughts of long dead sages, in the world about me, in the book of Nature. Nature fascinates me. There seems a system of order behind all life and yet there are occasions when the system appears to go astray as though accidents of circumstance were stronger than the procedure intended."

"I do not understand."

"If you plant two acorns under similar conditions in similar ground, one may live and the other die. Why do not both respond alike if there is an infallible system?"

"I do not know. Do you?"

"No, and never shall. Still the study fascinates me; it seems the nearest we can get to the object of life. If you would learn Nature's secrets you must not merely look closely but endeavour to understand. Details of the plot of the story are often given but we have to weave them together for ourselves."

"I, too, love to watch the flowers and the birds and the wild life in the woods, but I never wonder why such things happen. So it is because you have trained yourself to study Nature that you noticed the hoof-prints?"

"I could not help seeing them. But it was from force of habit that I noticed them and wondered what they signified. I wondered for a moment whether someone had been taken ill in the night and a groom had been sent for a doctor."

Ann grew bold. "Do you wish me to tell you who it was, and why?"

"Heaven forbid. There would be no satisfaction in that. Where is the lure of the unsolved if someone gives the answer? I did but notice the hoof-marks just as I would notice the lesser celandine, or see how white the stitchwort looks after the rain."

"Shall I tell you who rode from our gate in the morning hours?"

Ann sounded almost defiant, nor could she have explained the recklessness of her mood. Mr. Yorke shook his head gravely.

"I am not curious. My dear young lady, do not interpret my interest in all that goes on in the world about me to be a desire to pry into the affairs of my neighbours. I beg of you to put all thought of such discourtesy far from you. Now let us talk of something else. Why do people call me the Mystery Man?"

"I would rather apologize for my rudeness. The expression just slipped out."

"I am not offended. A trifle amused, perhaps; a little interested. Why am I mysterious?"

"I suppose it is because you appear to be a man of means and yet do not associate with the neighbouring gentry; you are a man of culture yet your only companions are illiterate men and boys; you must have mixed with society yet you prefer to dwell alone."

Mr. Yorke leaned his arms along the top of a five-bar gate and stared at the landscape. Ann watched him curiously without speaking. He seemed oblivious of her presence; lost in reverie.

"What you say is true," he said finally. "Strange, is it not, that a man cannot do normal, simple things just because he likes to do them without attracting attention? If I spent each day hunting, each night drinking, each Sunday sleeping in a pew, I should attract no attention because I should be normal. One must hunt with the pack, or be regarded as eccentric. How fortunate it is that I care not a jot what men think of me. The average man has not the intelligence of a Hereford steer. I prefer his room to his company."

Ann tossed her head. "Yet you seek the company of illiterates."

"They at least are humble and know how little they know. They desire to learn. There is more hope for them than there is for the Squire or the parson. They hunger for food. That is my mission in life: to feed the hungry."

This was beyond Ann's comprehension. "You have them at your house to feed them?" she asked, mystified. "That is kind of you. But you do us an injustice, Mr. Yorke. We, too, feed the poor of the parish. A hungry person is never turned from our kitchen."

"Ah!" said he, enigmatically, "I do not feed mine in the kitchen."

Ann was looking up at him with an expression akin to awe. His hat was still in his hand and she could not help noticing how broad, high, calm, majestic his forehead appeared. He still stared at the landscape with dreaming eyes. The fields were fair and the skies were blue, but he heeded them not. Rather he seemed to be trying to penetrate some mystery. The mystic look passed from his face and he glanced down at Ann; still grave but the kindly light now showed in his eyes.

"You have already caused me to go back on my principles, Ann."

"I am sorry."

"You have no occasion to be."

"What have I done?"

"I wished to hold aloof from mankind, in particular, womankind. I preferred to be alone with my thoughts, but you have convinced me that a man cannot live by thoughts alone. These few minutes with you have persuaded me of the need of companionship. Life can be a perpetual giving-out of mental energy, which is as it should be. One should give out. But when can one do the taking in? The replenishing? The banking of the fires of Life? Books are not enough. One needs the relationship of another human being to strengthen the structure, to shore up the walls. Will you give that companionship to me, Ann?"

"I don't know. I don't understand. What is it you require of me?"

"A short time in your company—each day if that were possible. There is something in your freshness, your young vitality, that gives me something that I lack, something that neither books nor Nature can supply. I shall not weary you. I hope I shall not prove uncongenial. You would confer a boon on a lonely man if you allowed me to talk to you from time to time."

"That is not asking much."

"It seems much to me."

"Of course I will see you and talk to you. I do not understand half you say. You ought to have a companion who is far more intellectual than I am, but I like listening to you, and you look very, very clever."

"Good. Then we shall meet again, and I will try not to look very, very clever. We will turn over the pages of Life's book together and learn what we can. And now I must not outstay my welcome. Let me escort you to your gate."

They walked without speaking until they came to the cluster of Scots pine. Mr. Yorke paused and shook his head. "Why did you?" he asked and though he looked serious, there was a whimsical smile in his eyes. "Oh, Ann, Ann, why did you?"

"Why did I what? Plant my Charlie Trees?"

"Yes."

"I have told you the reason. It is so that any wandering or hunted follower of the House of Stuart may know that he can find shelter in that house."

"You have not known me long but will you do something to oblige me?"

"What is it, Mr. Yorke?"

"Pull them all up as soon as possible."

"Oh, but I couldn't." Ann was scandalized. "I have worked so hard planting them and they have taken root nicely. They would fail in their purpose if I uprooted them."

"Dear Little Miss Innocence," he said gently. "Cannot you perceive?"

"Perceive what?"

"That they may or may not assist a fugitive Jacobite, but of a surety they will proclaim to every Hanoverian agent that an enemy of the reigning dynasty dwells in the house. The harm they will do is likely to outweigh the good. Pull them up, my dear."

21

CHAPTER FIVE

ONCE DARKNESS HAD DESCENDED, SQUIRE TREVOR APPRECIATED THE comfort of his own fireside. Younger men might venture abroad, and if they chose to call upon him they could always count on a seat at his table, or a bed for the night, should their libations be such as to preclude their finding their way back to the place whence they came. His hospitality was proverbial, his wines famed, and the charms of his only daughter had not escaped the eyes of the young bloods of the district. Callers, accordingly, were not infrequent, but this night showed an exceptional number of horsemen making their way to his porch. The capacity of his stables was tested. The servants were busy and the long dining-table gleamed with silver. Ann herself saw that the great branching candelabra was in place, and that the silver bowl filled with water occupied an honoured position in the centre of the table. The King across the water must never be forgotten.

She entered the room wearing her outdoor garb; there were earth stains on the green material of her dress. Her father stood with his back to the hearth and looked benevolently at a slender but erect officer who wore the red tunic with blue facings of the Royal Welch Fusiliers—His Majesty's Twenty-Third Regiment of Foot. He rose and bowed as Ann appeared at the doorway.

"Why, Captain Berners," she exclaimed, "what are you doing in this country? I thought that you were with your regiment in Flanders."

"So I was, Ann, and I hope shortly to rejoin them. I was sent home with dispatches and, as my younger daughter was ailing, the Duke permitted me to return home for a few days."

"And you have found time to call on us; that was friendly of you, Captain Berners."

He smiled. It was a quiet smile and winsome from eloquent, dark eyes which seemed curiously gentle for a warrior in so renowned a fighting regiment.

"The effort was not so great as it appears. My duties carried me to Wrexham; my inclinations bore me only slightly off my route so that I could pause at your hospitable gates. I am sure my dereliction will be pardoned by all who have met Miss Ann Trevor."

"You will remain the night?"

"Not a moment longer, I fear. I have a long ride ahead."

"Then a stirrup cup ere you leave, Berners," cried Squire Trevor. Ann brought the glasses. Before he took one from her hand, Captain Berners solemnly spread a table napkin over the silver bowl which stood in the centre of the table. Ann blushed.

"I think," said the guest with simulated gravity, "that this little precaution is necessary ere a loyal officer of His Majesty King George the Second drinks a health!"

"Captain Berners, you are too observant," cried Ann.

"On the contrary, my dear Ann; in the house of a friend I am the least observant of persons. I never see what I ought not to see."

"Ah!" exclaimed the Squire heartily. "Good, demmed good, Berners. I confess that your welcome but unexpected appearance caught us on the wrong foot. As you say a bad memory is plaguy convenient at times."

The Fusilier officer raised his glass by its dainty stem. "The King," he said and kept his back to the table.

"Certainly—the King!" replied the Squire and tossed off his wine. He laughed a trifle boisterously. "Have you heard the latest toast, Berners? Subtle, 'pon my oath."

"We are out of touch with such matters in Flanders. Let me have it to take back with me."

"Very well, sir, you shall have it.

> "*God bless the King; I mean our soul's defender !*
> *God bless (no harm in blessing) the Pretender.*
> *But who Pretender is and who is King,*
> *God bless my soul, that's quite another thing.*"

Captain Berners shrugged his shoulders. "Neat, certainly," he observed but he did not smile. His dark thoughtful eyes rested on Ann a trifle anxiously, and then on her father. "Well, sir, drink your toasts, but leave the matter there and no harm will come of it. As an old friend; as one who wishes well to this dear child, don't be dazzled by Stuart glamour. The Hanover jockey has found his seat in the national saddle and will take a lot of unseating."

The Squire looked uneasy and cleared his throat. Ann came to the rescue. "How is your wife, Captain Berners?"

"Her health is good, Ann, but she is vastly depressed. She has a pre-monition that she will not see me again. She, who is usually so brave, clung to me at the parting. Do you know, Ann, the rigours of a campaign which we men have to face are trivial compared to what women go through when they sit at home and wait. She has the greater courage."

"Think no more of it, Berners," cried the Squire. "It is but a natural apprehension on your good lady's part. You will return home sound in wind and limb, I'll wager. Is there likely to be a battle?"

"It is highly probable, sir, once we leave our winter quarters." He clicked his heels together as he shook hands with his host. Ann walked to the drive with him and watched him depart.

"I wonder," she observed pensively as she rejoined her father, "whether it is possible for those who love dearly to pick up messages from the unseen. I vow Captain Berners' words have made me sad."

"Heigh, lass, think no more of it. Our guests will be here any minute now. Whip that napkin off the King's bowl; pity he should have noticed it, though he would never betray us. Never! He is the soul of honour. Bless my soul, you are not changed into your evening frock yet, and demme, what's happened to your skirt? It is all over mud."

"I have been pulling up the Charlie Trees."

"What the deuce for? It is not long since you were pestering me to have 'em planted. I thought they were to guide Stuart messengers to our door."

"They are more likely to inform Hanoverians where our sympathies lie."

23

"Bless my soul, that's not your own thought. Far too clever."

"It was Mr. Yorke who called my attention to the risk."

"Mr. Yorke?"

"Philip Yorke. He has but newly come to live in the old Rectory."

"I've heard of him; never met the fellow. Bit eccentric isn't he? I'll thank him to mind his own affairs, though demme, there may be something in what he says."

"He meant well, I am sure, Father."

"The trees are up now, any way. Pays us to be cautious. If the trees set him thinking they would have set others. Well, to your room, girl, and slip into your gown or you will be disgracing me when the guests begin to show up."

When Ann descended half-an-hour later the room was full of men who stood and chatted and drank while awaiting her arrival. Ann was in no wise abashed. She had on many an occasion presided over a roomful of men. All of these she knew save one new-comer who wore the royal blue coat which was beginning to find favour in the Royal Navy. There were some who predicted that it would in time be adopted to the exclusion of scarlet. The conversation ceased and Ann was accorded a series of bows which would have done honour to a queen. They seemed in no wise out of place so regal did she look. Her smile of welcome had the ingenuousness of a girl.

"To your seats, gentlemen, please; I regret to have kept you waiting."

"No apology is called for, Ann," said Tom Eyton. "Had we waited a week your appearance would have been sufficient reward."

"Now, Tom, don't get turning my girl's head with your silly flattery."

The Squire looked from one guest to another. "You all know my daughter, I believe; ah, no. Lieutenant Peris, this is my girl Ann. Just like her mother was at her age; 'pon my soul the likeness is so amazing that there are times when I nearly fall in love with the little baggage myself. The minx knows it and twiddles me around her finger. Ann, child, this is Lieutenant Peris, Andrew Peris, who can tell you rare stories of adventure, having circumnavigated the globe with Mr. Anson."

"But how exciting! Are you really one of the *Centurion's* crew?"

"I have that honour, Ma'am," said Mr. Peris.

"You must be glad to be back in this old country again after so long a time. What a terrible experience you must have had, and yet how thrilling. Let me see, when did you reach Portsmouth?"

"As far back as last June, but I haven't yet grown weary of good English food. Faith, we had more gold than lemons aboard the old lady, and scurvy took a heavier toll than Spaniards' shot."

"You shall sit next to me at dinner and tell me all about it, Mr. Peris. Here's Sir Watkin looking ravenous and the rest——"

"All feasting their eyes on you, Miss Ann," cried Mr. Eyton. The laugh which followed was a signal for the meal to commence. Light talk prevailed until the last course was finished, and the servants had withdrawn.

24

Ann cleared the centre of the table so that the bowl of water stood conspicuously alone. With one accord the company stood and passed their glasses over the water as they drank to King James.

"May I ask whether Mr. Peris finds it consistent with his duties as an officer of the Royal Navy to unite with us?" asked Mr. Eyton. There was an awkward pause, but Andrew Peris was not disconcerted.

"A fair question," said he coolly. "My sympathies are entirely with the Stuart. My share of prize money is sufficient to allow me to buy myself out of the service. I shall not be sorry to have a spell ashore for nigh four years aboard the old *Centurion* was enough to turn a mariner into a tailor."

"So you intend to resign?"

"I had already intended to send in my papers. Now this game's afoot the matter is as good as settled. Count me as one of you. If there is any boat-work to be undertaken I may be useful."

"Well, gentlemen," interposed the Squire, "let's to business. You gathered that I did not summon you here without a purpose. I have received word from Paris that events are moving apace. Prince Charlie is to try his hand this summer, and a messenger from him should have arrived to-day to confirm the tidings."

Ann opened her mouth to speak, but Nathaniel Pryce cut in. "We heard a similar story last year but nothing came of it."

"You are unfair to His Highness, sir," said Tom Eyton. "Luck was against him; give the lad his due, he did set sail."

The Squire reached for the decanter. "It was no fault of his that tempest scattered the transports. We'll drink to the Prince's better success this summer. Ha! Who's been at this bottle?" The ejaculation contained far more fervour than had been evoked by the Prince's project. Keen of eye he examined the decanter. "It's those damned servants again," he bellowed. "Infernal thieves, every one of 'em. I have warned them; if they tamper with my wines, I'll—Ann, summon 'em in here; fetch the lot. I'll find out who has touched my sherry."

It was the magistrate who spoke. Ann did not stir. "There is no need to summon the servants."

"No need! No need! I tell you someone has been at the sherry—"

"They did not touch it."

"Then who the devil did?"

"I did."

"Ann! You? You're mad. Why . . . why . . . now listen to me. Don't you start, Ann. Don't you get fond of the bottle. As it is I drink enough for two or three——"

"Five or six, darling; you're too modest."

"But you! Bless my soul. I can't get over it. You at my sherry!"

"Do you begrudge it me, Father?"

"Begrudge? You must not put it that way. You can have what you like: anything! What am I saying, the minx will take advantage of that. No, my dear, I dread lest you should inherit my vice . . . but it was only after I lost your dear mother, you understand. Ann, girl, promise you'll leave the bottle alone." There was something plaintive in his tone. The door opened noiselessly.

25

"I fear that the lady takes blame which is not merited," said a suave voice. The men at the table wheeled to see a man in a riding-coat standing in the doorway.

"Who the devil are you, sir? And what do you know about it?" The Squire was irascible.

"I drank your sherry, sir."

"You enter my house! You drink my sherry! Ann, girl, what are you laughing at, you baggage. You are at the bottom of this. Who is this fellow?"

"This fellow, darling, is the messenger from Prince Charles Edward whom you are expecting. He—he—made his first call this morning before you were awake. It was I who offered him a glass of sherry. Would you have me inhospitable?"

"Ha!" cried the Squire, struggling to his feet. "That's a horse of a different colour. Let me see your credentials, sir. If they be in order you are more than welcome. Meanwhile let me glance at your papers; off with your coat and join us at the meal. Ann! Ann! Where the deuce has the girl got to?"

Ann had slipped past the stranger and vanished from the room.

CHAPTER SIX

THERE WAS A SILENCE IN THE ROOM AS THE SQUIRE PORED OVER THE papers. His eyesight was not what it had been and he was more partial to field sports than to reading. The men at the table toyed with their glasses and eyed the stranger at the door who stood unabashed, almost defiant.

"The papers appear to be in order, gentlemen," said the Squire as he placed the documents on the table. Turning to the messenger he observed, "We bid you welcome, sir. Draw up a chair and join us. So you are Captain Richard Conway?"

"At your service, sir," said the newcomer quietly, making himself at home.

"Dick Conway!" cried Mr. Eyton. "'Zounds, man, come to the light. I thought there was something familiar about your mode of speech. It is years since I saw you."

"Ha, Tom," said the messenger. "So you recollect me? It is some years since I was last in these parts. There have been changes: old houses sold, newcomers settling. I could have saved myself some needless riding had I but known what I know now." He turned to the Squire. "You ask how it comes about I made such free use of your house this morning. I expected to find the Holts here, and of old I was wont to drop in upon them *sans* ceremony."

"Holt was in a bad way; I bought his place from him," said Squire Trevor succinctly.

"D'ye mind if I eat while you talk?" asked Dick Conway coolly as he set about carving a capon.

"You have news for us, Captain?" inquired young Seth Morrice eagerly. "You make your appearance most opportunely, sir."

"I have news," admitted Conway, nodding his head. "I have also an appetite. But I eat fast, so possess your souls in patience but a few moments, gentlemen, and then I'm your man."

Squire Trevor selected a churchwarden, opened a tobacco-jar and bade his guests make use of it. While pipes were being lit, Dick Conway played havoc with the victuals before him and finally tossed off a glass of port and pushed back his chair with an expression of contentment on his weathered features.

"First tell us where you have been all these years," said Tom Eyton. "You vanished with such amazing celerity that all men vowed that you had either eloped with an heiress or the devil had claimed his own."

"Neither yet, Tom, though I have hopes for the one and fears for the other," replied Conway coolly. "As for where I have been, it's a long story. Rome first, then to Paris when the Prince moved there, and I have had a trip or two to Scotland to keep me from putting on weight."

"You have seen His Majesty?" inquired Seth Morrice.

"His Majesty King James the Third of England; the Eighth of Scotland, is a familiar sight in the streets of Rome where he is more absorbed in the study of religion than in the regaining of his lawful crown."

"Let us drink the health of his Majesty," exclaimed the Squire, who never missed an opportunity of toasting anyone.

There was a quick response. As the men rose to their feet the Squire nodded to Dick Conway. "As you are the one who has so frequently seen his Majesty, I beg of you, sir, to honour us by proposing the loyal toast."

Conway smiled grimly and replied with one of the numerous doggerels which were then prevalent.

> "*Here's health to the king whom the crown doth belong to;*
> *Confusion to those whom the right king would wrong so;*
> *I do not here mention either old king or new king;*
> *But here is a health, boys—a health to the true king!*"

He spoke with fire and intensity. The health was drunk with a chorus of shouts followed by a shattering of glasses.

"Well, Captain Conway, that's how matters stand," observed Squire Trevor as seats were resumed. "The squires and gentry of Flintshire, and much of North Wales for that matter, are strong for the Stuart. Bring your young Prince down here to lead us and you'll find plenty of blades awaiting to be drawn in his cause."

"He'll be here, ere long, sir; never you fret," said Dick Conway, confidently. "I'm telling you in confidence, though, that it is Scotland where he will land. Once he gets the clans behind him he will cross the Border soon enough and come marching south through Lancashire. I'm here to bid you start your preparations. Look to your arms, see to your horses, it is but a matter of weeks before Charles Edward will march on London with such a force that the German impostor will flee to Hanover, and the two kingdoms shall again have a lawful monarch reigning over 'em."

"Ay, but is the Prince in earnest?" queried Lieutenant Peris.

"It was a poor showing he made last year when Roquefeuille was master of the Channel. Norris's timidity allowed him to escape. Had the Prince shown resolution Saxe's troops might well have been landed in Kent, and a Stuart once again would have sat on the throne of England."

"You are not fair to his Highness, sir. He ran the same risk as any other member of the fleet. It was no fault of his that the transports were scattered far and wide by the gale. Many were driven ashore and others so damaged that the expedition was an utter failure. It was fortunate that his Highness managed to escape to Gravelines where he remained incognito."

"Stuart luck!" interposed young Morrice.

"The Prince has been living in seclusion in France, yet he has written to his father in Rome telling the King that he has been invited by friends of the cause to go to Scotland carrying what arms he could conveniently get. He says that so miserable has been the life he has been compelled to live in France that he would rather fling himself into the arms of his friends and die with them than to continue, and as for returning to Rome, it would just be giving up all hopes. If a horse which was for sale would not, when spurred, skip or show some sign of life, no one would be disposed to have him even for nothing. 'Just so,' he added, 'my friends would care very little to have me, if after such usage all the world is sensible of, I should not show that I have life in me.' The Prince has sent to Rome for his jewels in order that he might pawn them. He has written to inform his friends in Scotland that he will be with them by the middle of June."

"Of June!" exclaimed the Squire. "Then there is not much time to waste."

"I am here to impress that upon you."

There was an impressive silence, then the messenger turned to Squire Trevor. "You will not fail His Highness, sir?"

"No," said the Squire ponderously. "I will not fail him. I grow over-heavy to ride, but such help as I can manage shall be given to the Prince. I believe, gentlemen, we are all of one mind in this matter?"

There was a chorus of approval.

"I was told specially to seek you out, Mr. Trevor. It is reported that you were out in the 'Fifteen."

"Thirty years ago; how time flies!" said the Squire. "Ay, I was. We met under the Rose, Captain Conway . . . *sub rosa,* you understand. You will find the coats of arms of those who declared for the Stuart hidden away in many a North Wales home."

He crossed to the wainscoting and touched a secret spring. A panel sprung back disclosing a circular shield on which were painted the coats of arms of many well-known families.

He turned to Sir Watkin and addressed him by the pseudonym under which the third baronet so frequently figured in the Jacobean correspondence of those days. "Well, *Brutus,* you have sat silent to-night; tell us what you know of this matter."

"I cannot go back so far," said Sir Watkin quietly. "It was in 1723 that I founded the 'Cycle of the White Rose' and from that time Wynnstay has been the centre of all Stuart activity in North Wales.

We still stand as the most powerful source of Legitimist propaganda in North Wales. But I cannot go back to the 'Fifteen, though as a ten-year-old lad I can recollect the disturbances in Wrexham."

"They were lively times, I'm told, Sir Watkin," observed Morrice.

"Lively enough," said Sir Watkin drily. "During the latter part of July that year the Whig inhabitants of Wrexham and the neighbouring district lived in continual fear of outrage and riot. Their chapel was wrecked and the colliers came into the town to assist the rioters. On August the first, the day of King George's accession to the throne, not a bonfire was lit and not a bell was tolled, while treasonable songs were openly sung in the streets."

"And yet it failed," observed Thomas Eyton.

"The defeat at Preston was our undoing, but we in North Wales were undismayed. On Oak Apple Day there was a great riot and a ringing of bells, and the bells were rung on White Rose Day from morn till late at night."

"The Prince expects something more substantial than the ringing of bells," said Captain Conway succinctly. "You were better employed in wringing Hanoverian necks."

"We shall not be backward when the time comes," said Sir Watkin, and amid a chorus of approval the party began to break up.

"Who wants to stay for the night?" cried the Squire. "I shall be glad to put you up."

"I shall relish the comfort of a bed," said Captain Conway.

"You shall have it, lad! Any others? No. You're all disgustingly sober, all of you, though young Morrice looks as if he might roll into a ditch. Well, good night to you all. I'll call on you, Sir Watkin, to go into the matter of the getting together of arms."

Noisily the crowd made their way to the front porch where the grooms held their horses. Richard Conway stood with his back to the fire, alone, thoughtful.

"I fear I have driven your daughter away, sir," he said when the Squire returned. "I take it that it was your daughter who was at the table when I entered?"

"Demme, yes, what's happened to the girl? Not like Ann to run away. She's as full of curiosity as a puppy as a rule. Must know all that's going on."

"Perhaps she felt it advisable not to be involved in the conspiracy."

"Ha! You don't know Ann. Gone to bed, like as not. Have to ask her in the morning. Give that bell a tug. Morgan will show you to your room. Glad to have you with us, sir. Glad to entertain a messenger from the Young Chevalier. Good repose to you."

And the Squire, seeking a candle, sang in a somewhat broken voice:

> "... *True loyalty is shown,*
> *Devising plans e'en now to seat*
> *Royal James upon the throne.*
> *And messengers from Bar-le-Duc*
> *In secret guise arrayed,*
> *Convey the Monarch's hope that Wales*
> *Will don the White Cockade.*"

CHAPTER SEVEN

THOUGH ANN WAS AN EARLY RISER, SHE WAS NOT THE ONLY ONE WHO was up betimes. When she entered the breakfast room she started to see the guest of the previous evening standing before the newly-lit fire. He turned and bowed as she paused in surprise. Ann appraised him deliberately with her large, childish eyes, eyes which were frankly interested in everything and everybody. She found him not unpleasing to look upon. He was clean-shaven now, and his face looked keen and strong and clean. Though he still wore his spurred boots, these had been diligently polished. His coat was of bottle green.

"So you are Richard Conway," she said slowly. "I suppose I should say Captain Conway."

"It is but a courtesy title," he said with a French-like shrug of his shoulders. "I have never commanded a company in action. But serving his Highness as I do, I have to have some status, so he has given me his commission. Lud, he's free with his commissions; belike it is all the young man has to be free with."

"And you've seen him? Really seen the Prince, and talked to him?" Ann was ardent and eager.

"My faith, yes. It's a dull life he has to lead in France. Friends worth having are so scarce that the Young Chevalier is glad of the company even of a rascal like me."

"He will have no lack of friends when he lands in this country. Assure his Highness of that."

The man's eyes sparkled in a roguish smile. "Ay, he'll find friends enough among the fair sex. Lud, he was specially designed by Nature to be a breaker of hearts. But, dear lady, he is coming here to conquer a kingdom, not women's affections."

"Tell me all about him," commanded Ann.

"He's a rare lad; tall and straight and slim; twenty-five years of age; eloquent dark brown eyes, and a winsome smile that wins the hearts of men as well as women. Women succumb to his charm, men to his manliness, for he will endure hardship without a murmur, and bids defiance to odds with a gay bravado which is as inspiring as a trumpet blast."

"How I should love to see him."

"So you shall, doubtless, one day soon. But tell me, fair lady, now that I have you to myself for a moment, why did you flee at my appearance last night? Am I so terrifying?"

"I felt shy," said Ann candidly. "Never before can I recollect feeling so bashful. I felt myself flushing to the roots of my hair and I had darted out of the room before I knew what I was doing. I was sorry afterwards that I had been so foolish because I did so want to know what was taking place."

"You should have returned."

"Oh, but I did. I tiptoed back to the door and listened for a long while and I heard you speak out so bravely on behalf of the Prince that I was strangely stirred, and I vowed that I would give my all to aid his Highness in his gallant enterprise."

"Ay, you shall aid him; you can aid him," said Captain Conway. "My task is to stir up the sluggards. Time was when Wales was red hot for the Stuarts."

"To think of it, it is just a hundred years ago that Charles the Martyr was in these parts. In those days our Cavaliers contested every lane and hedgerow. Their descendants will be just as loyal to the Stuart."

Richard Conway looked thoughtful. "I wonder," he mused. "So far as I can judge, there is a lukewarmness creeping in. I do not like it. There is some subtle change, some influence, some unseen power which is altering men's outlook so that they do not respond to the old rallying cries."

"They seemed all zeal for Prince Charlie last night."

"Ah, but you would expect them to be. Their very presence here showed them to be his ardent supporters. It is your squire who has learnt to live comfortably who is our anxiety. He does not want upset and disturbance. He wants to farm his lands and collect his rents and cares not who is on the throne so long as he is not interfered with. I do not like it, the call of adventure, the longing for the difficult hazard is dying out of the race. It is a bad sign; an ugly omen."

As he spoke, Ann thought that he looked the incarnation of a dare-devil adventurer. She stared at him with such obvious admiration that he had the grace to turn his head uneasily, for too much adulation can be embarrassing even to a Prince's messenger.

"We gossip here," he said with an awkward laugh, "but what about breakfast."

"Oh, I am sorry. A thousand pardons. I had quite forgot." Ann was all contrition as she ran to hasten the servants.

Ann sat herself down at the head of the table and endeavoured to look dignified. "It is no use waiting for Father. He is always late getting up and always comes down with a funny head and no appetite. He drinks too much, you know, but he's rather a dear. Do you take tea to drink?" she added, laying a tiny hand on an ornate silver tea-pot.

"My taste runs to coffee, if you have any. I have dwelt so long in France that I fear I have acquired many of their habits and tastes."

"Coffee by all means; please pull the bell. Morgan will get it for you instantly."

It was a typical British breakfast with eggs and bacon and crisp home-baked bread and butter from the Home Farm. As Richard Conway ate he was conscious of Ann's wondering eyes fixed on him in frank admiration. It made him suddenly realize that, at any rate in the eyes of this fresh and delightful girl, he was a figure of romance. Engrossed in his task of fanning to flame the dying fires of Stuart loyalty, Conway had not given a thought to his own personality. Now it occurred to him that as the Prince's harbinger he must carry with him a reflected glory. Before this disquieting idea occurred to him he had conducted himself naturally, but now he became self-conscious, feeling that he must live up to his part, yet not knowing what to do.

"Do you run much risk; is your life continually in danger?" inquired Ann, a trifle breathlessly.

"If my horse put his foot in a rabbit hole I might break my neck."

"Now you are being facetious. I know that your life is in danger. Would you be shot or hanged or imprisoned if the Government laid hands on you?"

"To be candid, I am not at all certain, and believe me, Miss Ann, I am not at all anxious to put the matter to practical test."

"What would you do if, say, the local constable and some of our Militia came marching up to the house this very minute?"

"Probably hide behind your skirt and feel in perfect security."

"Will you be serious! Where is your sword, and where are your pistols?"

"I left them in my room. Do you wish me to wear them?"

"It seems so much more in keeping with the part you play."

"But they look horribly conspicuous and are sure to invite attention."

"Ah, I had not thought of that. And where is your horse?"

"In the stables. Properly cared for this time. No need for further dissembling, Miss Ann."

"Let us go and see. I adore the stables. Have you had a good breakfast? Are you quite satisfied?"

"It is with great reluctance I confess I could eat no more. I have not fed so well for a long time. Whatever habits we acquire from Europe, may the Continental breakfast never interfere with the English custom."

"Let's go to the stables." Ann darted off so rapidly that Conway had to hasten to keep her in sight. He overtook her with her arms about the old mastiff. "Isn't he a pet?" she demanded. Conway looked down upon the ponderous, somnolent frame of the aged dog and thought that a bullet in the brain would be the kindest service to render it, but he discreetly refrained from voicing his thoughts. Ann implanted a kiss upon the smooth hair of the animal's broad forehead and danced off to the stables.

"Howells! Howells! Oh, good morning. Are the animals all well? This is Captain Conway, Howells, of whom I spoke."

Howells touched his forehead without speaking, and the stable-boy followed suit.

"Oh, and that's Hughie," added Ann. "Hughie, you must take particular care of Captain Conway's horse, because, er, because you must."

"Very good, Miss."

Captain Conway leaned against the half-door in the morning sunshine, well content to be a spectator. Ann was making her morning inspection of the stables with the critical eye of a cavalry officer. Richard Conway knew that he was forgotten. He was well content to stand back and watch. He saw her lay her smooth cheek against the broad neck of Black Prince, a massive hunter which could have trampled her dainty form to pulp, but who exhibited loving docility.

32

Ann walked to the passage behind the stalls and let her eyes run along the length of the stables. There was a little pucker on her brow. This meant that Ann was thinking of something really important.

"We must have their names painted over their stalls, Howells."

"Why, come now, why should that be, Mistress Ann?"

"Because I think that it would look nice."

"Beggin' pardon, but it do seem a bit unnecessary, Mistress Ann. There's me, now, as cannot write, and so far as I know, them horses cannot read."

"Howells, I'm ashamed of you. You are making fun of me and trying to evade the issue. But it must be done. Think how fine it will be to see BLACK PRINCE printed along that beam."

"Just so as we'll know which he is, us not knowing like?"

"You are in a very awkward mood this morning, Howells, and I'm not at all sure that I like you. I understand you perfectly; you want to get out of doing it and I am not going to let you have your own way. It is very bad to let people have their own way."

"Well, Mistress Ann, you should know."

Ann looked at him suspiciously but Howells's face was the picture of bland innocence. "If you cannot do it, we must find someone who can," she added.

"Ay, ay, but who?"

"Please, Mistress Ann, I could do it."

"Hold your tongue, boy. I'll clout your ear if you speak in front of your betters."

But Ann had turned eagerly towards the stable-boy who was staring up at her with respectful eagerness. "Why, Hughie, do you mean to say you can print the words?"

"Yes, Mistress Ann, if it please you. I have learnt to letter and to read, and figger a bit, too."

"Well, I am surprised!"

"I don't like it," growled Howells. "You see what comes of it, Mistress Ann, putting ideas into young rascals' heads. He'll be thinkin' he knows more than me soon, and then he'd better watch his steps. I won't have no boys givin' themselves airs in my presence."

"Where did you learn, Hughie? Have you been to school?"

"Not exactly school, Mistress Ann, there being none in these parts, but a kind gentleman has been good enough to teach me o' nights after work is over."

"But how interesting. And who might this good man be?"

"It's a Mister Yorke, Mistress Ann; him who's come to live at old Rectory."

"Oh," said Ann, and fell silent. She walked across to Starlight and commenced to stroke her sleek flank thoughtfully.

"Hughie?"

"Yes, Mistress Ann."

"Do you pay for this tuition?"

"Oh, no, Mistress Ann. I ain't got no money for the like of that. He don't want no pay. I mean, he does not want any pay."

33

"I see he is teaching you grammar, too. But why does he do this ?"

"It's just his kindness, Ma'am. He said something one day about the land being dark with ignorance and it was time somebody started to light the lamps."

"I hope no harm comes of it," muttered Howells. "Bit o' strap's the best eddication for a lad to my way of thinkin' !"

"What harm could come of it ?" asked Ann as she moved away, but there was no one to answer her. When she rejoined Captain Conway she was unusually silent and walked with head bent and her eyes fixed on the ground. Conway respected her silence and paced beside her, stealing now and then a surreptitious glance at the fair head so close beside him.

"Captain Conway ?"

"Yes ?"

"Do you believe in education ?"

"Education ? Haven't thought of it. All life is education of a sort, I suppose. We're always learning."

"Yes, but that is learning by personal experience; that is the right kind of learning. Is it good to put thoughts into people's heads ?"

"I suppose they have to have thoughts of some kind or another."

"Yes, but they should have the right kind of thoughts. Is it not better for these people simply to do as they are told and leave all thinking to their betters ?"

"I am inclined to agree with you. I have not done much soldiering, but I have done a little and my experience has been that the best soldier is the one who obeys orders without question. The man who is hard to handle is the man who thinks he knows as much as you do yourself."

"What if he does ?"

"My dear young lady, you have a disconcerting knack of putting awkward questions without warning. If he does I suppose that sooner or later there will be a clash of wills."

"Which means trouble, I suppose ?"

"To my way of thinking it is inevitable."

"I wonder if I ought to stop young Hughie from learning to read and write. In a way I am glad he is acquiring a little knowledge, but perhaps he would be happier if it were withheld from him. I seem to remember the parson reading, '*He that increaseth knowledge increaseth sorrow*'. Was it Solomon said it ?"

"I fear that my knowledge of the Scriptures is not what it ought to be. It sounds common sense. Let us accept it for what it is worth."

They walked briskly back to the house.

CHAPTER EIGHT

SQUIRE TREVOR WAS LEISURELY OF A MORNING. HE DESCENDED TO A belated breakfast like an oriental potentate. His morning robe was of scarlet embroidered with gold brocade and in place of his wig he wore a turban, usually of yellow silk spotted with red. It was

34

thus Ann found him, seated at the head of the table, endeavouring to work up an interest in food.

"You are late for breakfast," he admonished.

"You know perfectly well I had mine ages ago; I have been to the stables."

"You are always at the stables. Why don't you sleep in the stables?"

"May I?"

"No, certainly not. What put that ridiculous idea into your head?"

"You did."

"Absurd. Certainly not. Ah, Conway. 'Morning to you. How long are you staying with us? Mind you, you're welcome to stay as long as you like."

"I shall have to ride on soon, I fear. There is much to see to. You will have to get some arms together for the retainers if this uprising is going to assume the proportions I have every hope that it will reach."

"Ah, that reminds me. That sailor fellow, what's his name? Peris, that's right, said something as he was leaving about consulting me about running in a cargo of arms. These mariners must be for ever tinkering about with boats; can't think why he can't settle to dry land now he's ashore. Young Seth Morrice said he would come with him, though to my way of thinking the young spark is more interested in my daughter than in the Stuart cause."

"Well, sir, that is understandable."

"What? Rubbish. This chit is more trouble than an unbroken filly."

"All the same, sir, the idea is a sound one."

"What's that? To have this young blade coming to make sheep's eyes at Ann?"

"No, sir; I misled you; the fault was mine. My mind has gone to Lieutenant Peris's proposal. There are lonely places along the Caernarvonshire coast where a cargo of arms might well be run in without much risk if we can get past the watch ships off The Lizard."

"You think so, eh?"

"I do, sir."

"Then you'd better stay and talk it over with him. He will be here in, let me see, less than half an hour."

"Then we'll walk to meet him," decided Ann. "Come, Captain Conway. It is a glorious morning and Father is never at his best in the forenoon."

"I am at my best; that is, what's wrong with me?"

"You certainly look your best, darling. Like an emperor at least in that turban. You are very vain."

"Demme, girl, would you have me come to my meals in my nightcap? And vain! You dare to insinuate that I am vain!"

"Yes, you are vain, vain, vain. Come, Captain Conway, we must run for our lives. He is perfectly furious now."

She hurried into the garden while Richard Conway followed with greater decorum.

"Father really does fancy himself in that turban, you know. I—

I rather like it myself. I am sure that it would suit me far better than Father; his face is so red. Don't you think?"

"For heaven's sake don't involve me in a family dispute. I have sufficient cares as it is."

"I believe you are afraid of Father. He's not really fierce, though he can look amazingly so. I thought you were so valorous, too. Oh, look. Across the laurel bushes. Can you not see two riders moving along that road across the valley? It must be Lieutenant Peris and Seth."

She quickened her pace so that Captain Conway, more accustomed to the saddle than to walking, found it difficult to keep in step with her. Ann moved with a lissom grace and a smooth, springy stride, her shoes noiseless in the wayside grass. She chattered gaily as she walked until as they passed a roadside five-bar, she turned abruptly to gaze at a man standing there. He turned, looked into Ann's eyes, and swept off his three-cornered hat with a grave bow.

"Oh, how d'you do?" she cried without pausing. "What a glorious morning."

When they were out of earshot, Conway asked, "Who was that?"

"That was Mr. Yorke, Philip Yorke."

"And who might Philip Yorke be?"

"He, why I don't quite know, save that he has taken over the old Rectory. It was getting the worse for wear and when Father came here to live he had a new one built for the rector."

"That was kind of him."

"Oh, he is kind; very kind, when you know how to handle him. But he can be very stubborn. And the old dear does so like to have his own way."

"Perhaps he inherited that from his daughter."

"Inherited—don't be absurd. Besides I never have my own way, or not very often."

"Don't you?"

"Do I?"

"How can I tell?"

"This doesn't seem to be leading us anywhere; it's stupid. All questions and no answers. Now where were we? Oh, yes. About Mr. Yorke."

"What about Mr. Yorke?"

"That's just it. I don't know. He's queer. Folk call him the Mystery Man."

"What is mysterious about him?"

"He doesn't seem to do anything, ever."

"Is that mysterious?"

"Well, no. Not altogether. He's teaching young Hughie to read and write."

"So I heard."

"I forgot you were there at the stables. Well, that's queer surely! And he's very interested in things, but he's rather nice, you know."

"I don't know."

"Don't be silly. That's just a way of talking. And he always

36

looks very grave, yet all the while I somehow feel that he is laughing at me."

"Impossible."

"Now I believe you are laughing at me. Why is it? Oh, look. Here they come. Doesn't Seth sit a horse well; and how terrible the sailor looks. All bunched up and bumpy. He hangs on to the reins as if they were the tiller lines. The poor mouth of his horse!"

The riders drew up and hats were swept off ere they dismounted quickly and greeted Ann who looked as fresh as the morning.

Ann laid gentle fingers on the neck of Peris's mount which was foam-flecked. "You poor darling," she whispered. "Just bathed in sweat."

" 'Fraid I'm rather heavy," apologized the sailor awkwardly. "Bit out of practice, too."

"Let's tie the animals to the five-bar yonder and we will all sit on those warm rocks in the sun and talk!" suggested Ann brightly.

Ostensibly, then, the assembly was convened for the discussion of gun-running, though in its initial stages it appeared to resemble a manœuvring for the positions on either side of Ann. Richard Conway secured the place at her right hand; young Morrice on the left, and the sailor—who might have been more successful afloat—had to content himself with a place at her feet.

"You will find it damp there; the dew is still on the grass," remarked Ann solicitously. "Won't you sit on the rock beside Mr. Morrice?"

"I prefer to remain here."

"I understand that the morning dew is admirable for the complexion," observed Captain Conway gravely.

"See here," broke in Peris, "this matter of arms is urgent. I propose that we tackle the question and cut out this nonsense."

"What nonsense?" inquired Ann. "But you are right. How are we to get the boat?"

"I can see to that," said Peris. "I know a man in the port of Liverpool who is just the fellow for picking up useful small craft. Knows how to keep his mouth shut, too. Does a bit of smuggling, I'm told, and certainly he has got shares in several slavers plying from that port."

"Slavers!" said Ann. "How horrid. Do you think that we ought to have dealings with him?"

"The purchasing of the vessel is the first consideration," Conway assured her. "There is no time to be lost. It will not be long before His Highness sails from France, and then——"

"Oh," cried Ann. "And then, then all sorts of things will happen. We'll raise the gentry of the district and march to join the Prince, and King James will be on the throne in no time."

"I can get the ship, but what about the arms?" said Peris.

"That is easily arranged if the money is forthcoming. We have friends in Brittany. The Prince has one very loyal supporter there who has placed his château at his disposal. The cellars are already well-stocked, but that is as far as the matter goes. Since last year's fiasco,

the King of France frowns on the venture. What is to be done must
be done without his aid, though we may count on his connivance."

"Would a hundred pounds be of assistance?" interposed young
Morrice. "I have had a long talk with my revered parent and I think
he would be good for that much at least."

"Sir, we are your debtor," exclaimed Conway grandiloquently.
"This is good news. My friends in France will supply quite a present-
able showing of muskets and pistols for a hundred pounds in good
English gold."

"Don't forget cutlasses and boarding-pikes," interposed Peris.

"What the deuce d'y' want with boarding-pikes? Still, a few
common swords would not come amiss. I take it the gentry supply
their own weapons."

"This is positively delicious," exclaimed Ann with a wriggle of
delight. "Fancy a ship landing by stealth, muskets and pistols and
cutlasses and—what are boarding-pikes, Mr. Peris?"

"Never mind," interrupted Conway. "We are not having them
and you can ask Mr. Peris some other time. How soon can we see
this slaver acquaintance of yours, Peris?"

"Whenever you like. I know where to put hands on him."

"Good. I'm all for striking while the iron's hot. How can we
reach him?"

"There's a small craft at the quay at Mostyn which would take
us there. The wind is fair. If we ride down right away"—Lieutenant
Peris scrutinized the skies with a sailor's eye, "—we ought to just
reach the shore by the turn of the tide."

"Good," cried Conway, jumping up with an alacrity which gave
the others the confident feeling that great events were pending. "I'll
hurry back to the house for my horse."

"Take mine and save time," exclaimed Morrice. "And don't
let a guinea or two stand in your way. My respected sire has more
of this world's goods than is good for him and his heir would sooner
see some of it go to the Prince's cause than inherit wealth while better
men starve."

"You're a sportsman, sir, 'pon my oath," cried Conway, grasping
his hand.

They untied the horses and Peris and Conway were quickly in
the saddle. They swept off their hats, and Ann waved her hand until
they had galloped around a bend and out of her sight.

"I shall have the pleasure of escorting you home," said Seth
Morrice with a bow.

"Seth, you villain. I believe that was why you lent Captain Conway
your mare!"

"It was," confessed Seth unblushingly.

"And I thought you so generous."

"Test me, Ann. You will still find that I am."

"Then my test is that you shall declare for the Prince when he
lands."

"That I have already resolved upon. Have you no other means
of proving my devotion?"

38

"Oh, devotion. What a silly word. Look, who is that man? Oh, I see now. It is only Mr. Yorke."

"Heavens, I hope he did not hear what we were talking about."

"Of course not. He is not interested in anything but wild flowers. See, he is collecting them now. Seth, let's go by way of the stile. I'll race you home."

CHAPTER NINE

THE SQUIRE WAS FULLY DRESSED WHEN ANN AND HER ESCORT REACHED the hall. They found him, cane in hand, strutting about the terrace, criticizing the wallflowers to the obvious anxiety of one of the under-gardeners. Ann thought her father seemed a trifle paler than usual. He looked up quickly at their approach and turned his back on the gardener.

"Well, girl, so you've changed partners. Glad to see you, Morrice. You didn't take a toss into the ditch, after all?"

"Heaven forbid, sir. My head was as clear as a bell and the moon was kind."

"Great thing to be young, boy. I slept infernally badly; in fact, I doubt if I closed an eyelid all night."

"Darling, you were snoring like a grampus when I went to bed and when I got up," said Ann.

"You are infernally disrespectful, girl; no sense of veneration for your elders. Besides, your imagination runs away with you——" He paused and stared across the meadows to where a gleam of red showed above the distant hedgerows. The colour ebbed from his face. "Damnation!" he cried.

Ann and Seth followed the direction of his gaze. "Ah!" said Ann coolly, "I have a presentiment. Something tells me trouble is brewing."

"Dragoons," exclaimed Seth. "I wonder if they can be on the track of that messenger fellow."

"We must throw them off the scent," exclaimed the Squire, "but what the deuce are we to say?" He was plainly worried. Ann was serenely calm.

"This is going to be fun!" she exclaimed. "It has been so uneventful here and now at last we are going to have a little excitement."

"Fun! Excitement! Demme, child, what nonsense you talk. I wish I'd never tampered with this silly business. Burn my fingers, sure as fate."

"Not you, darling. Let's all walk to the house, slowly now, in case they can see us. Just saunter. Let me take your arm."

"But what shall we tell them? They're after that fellow, 'pon my oath. What can I say?"

"Say he's been here, of course."

"Never. I'll lie like Satan."

"I'm sure you are capable of it, darling, but there's really no occasion. The truth is ever so much more effective told discreetly."

"Then I shall leave you to do the talking."

39

"That's the most sensible remark you have made for a long, long time."

Once within the shadow of the porch, Ann's deliberation fell from her like a garment. "Now, Seth," she exclaimed, catching the young man by the arm. "You can save the situation. To the stables, quick, and get Captain Conway's horse saddled. I'll slip up to his room and collect his sword and pistols and anything else he may have left lying about in his room. Be quick. I'll join you at the back door in a couple of minutes."

Her little feet raced up stairs and Seth with less grace but equal celerity sped through the servants' quarters and made for the stables. The captain's mount, saddled and bridled, was at the back door with Seth in the saddle when Ann made her way out with her arms full. It took Seth but a moment to thrust the pistols into the saddle-holsters and to catch up the captain's valise and sword in his right hand.

"Where shall I go?"

"Not far or they may see you once you are free of the cover of the trees. I know. Ride to the old Rectory. Tell Mr. Yorke I sent you. I'll join you there as soon as we have got rid of our unwelcome guests."

"But——"

"It's all right. Don't stay here talking. Ride." Ann emphasized her final word by a slap on the horse's flank which made it move nervously. In another instant Seth, with the docility of a lover, had obeyed her command and was urging his steed down the lane which led to the rear road. Ann rejoined her father who was pacing restlessly about the front room.

"Father! Father! You will never make a conspirator. You look positively agitated. About what, pray? See how calm I am."

"Demme, girl," cried the Squire positively frowning, "I believe you are enjoying the whole affair."

"Of course I am, darling. I haven't had such a delicious thrill for ages and ages. But now, look unconcerned, but a little surprised. Here they come up the front drive. See, a couple of the troopers have been sent to search the back premises, or at any rate to keep watch. You're too late, lads, the bird has flown!"

"'Zounds, girl, it's the High Sheriff himself. We're caught like rats in a trap."

"Not a bit of it, Father. It just shows friendliness." Ann walked out of the front door and on to the gravel.

"Why, Mr. Sheriff, this is an unexpected honour," she exclaimed, her face bright with a welcome which would have gladdened a less susceptible man than the High Sheriff. He lowered his portly figure from the saddle and bowed low over Ann's extended fingers.

"Your humble and devoted admirer, Ma'am," he said with affected gallantry. "'Pon my honour, Ann, you grow lovelier every time I see you."

"Lud, Mr. Sheriff, would you turn a poor girl's head? But I vow you have not ridden here to pay me compliments, and with such an imposing escort, too. Are the roads dangerous these days?"

40

"Matter of duty, my dear, 'pon my honour. Nothing more."

"Will you not present me to this young lady?" interrupted a suave voice, and Ann, glancing over the Sheriff's shoulder, saw an officer standing regarding her intently. He wore a red jacket and at first glance she had assumed he was one of the dragoons. He had a hard mouth, intolerant eyes and a rounded head which suggested Teutonic ancestry.

"Major Manstein—Miss Trevor," observed the Sheriff formally. "I forgot; 'pon my soul. Can't think what came over me unless I was dazzled by your bright eyes, Ann. Bad form, 'pon my word."

"Not at all, Mr. Sheriff. In any case I had thought that Major Manstein was one of the soldiers, so there is no harm done."

"You are correct; I am a soldier, Miss Trevor," said the officer, flushing. "I am here in the capacity of a soldier to see that duty is carried out. Without further discussion I must ask leave to see your father. I presume Squire Trevor is your father?"

"He is, and he awaits you in the hall. I left him wondering about the reason for this visit."

"We shall enlighten him."

The Sheriff walked towards the house, the major at his heels and Ann, her head held high, a little apart.

"Ah, Trevor; glad to see you looking so fit. This is Major Manstein."

The High Sheriff was a trifle boisterous; it was apparent that he did not relish his task. Major Manstein clicked his spurred heels together and bowed from the waist. Though his English was impeccable there was a subtle suggestion of Prussia about him. There was also an implacable efficiency which was disconcerting.

"Ah!" said the Squire, glancing from one to the other. "This looks like a formal visit; something official, I suppose. Demme, if I have ever had red-coats riding to my door before."

"Not unless they wore hunting pink, eh, Trevor?" cried the Sheriff, slapping his boot with his riding-crop and laughing somewhat louder than he need.

"The object of my visit, sir, can be quickly explained," said the soldier sternly. "I am on the trail of a Jacobite emissary who is known to be in this district for the purpose of disturbing the peace of the realm. I call on you, in the King's name, to assist me in his apprehension."

"On me?" cried the Squire, looking choleric. " 'Zounds, why do you come to me? What have I to do with it that you should single me out?"

"Easy, easy, friend Trevor," interposed the Sheriff. "This is all a matter of routine. We are visiting all the principal houses in the district. We have not singled out your house more than any other."

"Ah!" exclaimed the Squire, endeavouring to look appeased and trusting that they would not notice that he looked relieved. His relief was short-lived.

"Why, Father," exclaimed Ann. "I wonder if it could be that stranger who called here last night?"

41

"Eh, what's that? what's that?" Her father was plainly disconcerted.

"Pray explain yourself, Miss Trevor," said Major Manstein, fixing his piercing eyes on her. "What you say may be of vital importance. A stranger called here last night?"

"Yes, as we were at dinner."

"Never saw the fellow before," burst in the Squire.

"What was he like? Tall, brown-faced man, wearing a sword and riding a light chestnut with a white off foreleg?"

"The same; the same!" exclaimed Ann ecstatically. "Oh, how exciting! Is he really a—a, what did you call him?—a Jacobite emissary? But how positively thrilling."

"And what was he doing here?" demanded the Major, turning his gaze to the Squire.

"Demme, how should I know?" burst out the Squire. "He came by mistake. Had been abroad for years and thought to find the Holts living here. I did not know the fellow was an enemy of the King. Couldn't turn him adrift at that hour of night. Had to offer hospitality. Demme, a man could not do less."

"That's so," interposed the Sheriff. "Most probable; most feasible. Trevor bought this place from the Holts a couple of years ago. Like as not the rogue did not know the place had changed hands."

"I am quite sure he didn't from the manner in which he spoke," added Ann.

"Where is he now?"

"I don't know. He went a walk over the fields with me after breakfast and as he met two men I left him and came home."

"And his horse? Did he leave that in your stables?"

"Of course."

"Good. Then we'll catch the bird. He is sure to return for his mount."

"And will you wait in ambush, Major? May I peep? And would you like to see the room in which he slept? He might have left his sword or something incriminating behind? How marvellous to be able to trap a Jacobite what-you-said. Is there a reward?"

"Stables first," said the Major, unperturbed by Ann's enthusiasm. He strode forward briskly, Ann close beside him, her tongue wagging freely. The Sheriff and Squire Trevor followed more leisurely.

"Sorry to let you in for this, Trevor; 'pon my honour. No option. The bird descended on me and I had to undertake responsibilities of my office. No offence, old friend. Thought that it would be better to come myself than to let him descend on you unaccompanied."

"Very friendly, Thelwall. Demmed embarrassing, all the same."

They came to the stables. Ann ran ahead and unlatched the door. "Now you can see his horse for yourself, Major!" she cried, flinging it wide. Then her hands flew to her mouth and an expression of utter consternation crossed her expressive features. "It's gone!" she exclaimed. "Oh, how annoying."

Black Prince was in a stall; so were Starlight and the other Trevor steeds, but the stall which had housed the stranger's horse stood empty, plainly but recently vacated.

"Hell and damnation!" snapped the major.

"Oh, Major Manstein!" exclaimed Ann, looking up in wide-eyed disapprobation at the irate officer.

"This is no time for courtesies," he snapped. "Fetch me the stable-man to interrogate. Here, fellow."

Howells came slowly forward, looking from one to the other seeking a clue. The old retainer knew one thing; he would not speak until he was spoken to. He touched his forehead.

"Where is the horse that was in that stall?" demanded Major Manstein.

"Gone."

"Of course it is gone, you dolt. But where?"

"Did a man come and take it, Howells?"

"Yes, Mistress Ann."

"Not very long ago?"

"I could not say just when."

"But it was after breakfast, Howells?"

"Oh yes, Mistress Ann; after breakfast it was for sure."

"There, you see, Major! I know what has happened. The stranger saw you coming and slipped back across the fields and stole his horse away when we were in the front of the house. Your red coats are very conspicuous, you know."

"And you let him take the horse, fellow?" exclaimed the soldier, frowning.

"Of course he let him take it," said Ann. "You are not to scold Howells. How was he to know what you know? The man was a guest—or so Howells thought—and it would have been out of place to interfere if the man wished to take away his horse."

"Which way did he go? No, never mind, you need not answer. I can find out for myself. I see I will get little assistance from you. But I have eyes in my head. Corporal, corporal: ask those two troopers on duty at the rear of the house if they have seen anything suspicious? No! I thought not. Then bring my charger round from the front."

With head bowed Major Manstein walked off without the formality of farewell. The troopers followed slowly behind in disciplined silence. The Sheriff shook the Squire warmly by the hand and renewed his apologies.

Major Manstein scrutinized the ground until he came across the hoof-prints of the stranger's horse. Then he paused and waited for his own mount to be brought to him.

"Howells," said Ann in a firm voice. "Saddle Starlight quickly. I'm going to see what Major Manstein is up to. We can't let him have things all his own way."

CHAPTER TEN

THE OLD RECTORY LAY LESS THAN HALF-A-MILE DISTANT FROM THE Plas. The road which led to it passed the entrance to the stables and wound between hedgerows, broken by occasional roadside trees. It would be hard to differentiate between it and a thousand other strips of country road, yet to Ann it suddenly seemed fraught with significance. Until a few moments ago she had been buoyant, elated at the success of her ruse. Now it was impressed upon her that this Major Manstein was a man to be reckoned with; one well used to pitting his wits against the cunning of adversaries. She felt less assured and began to be a trifle apprehensive. But it was only for a moment. She cast her doubts and fears from her and rode with chin held high and an expression of calm assurance which she was far from feeling. The road undulated and as they topped an incline the major drew rein. The escort obediently followed suit. Major Manstein rose in his stirrups and puckered his eyes as he took deliberate stock of the landscape.

"Corporal!"

"Sir." The non-commissioned officer pushed his horse forward a couple of paces.

"Cast your eyes over the countryside and see if you notice any clumps of Scots pines."

"Scots pines?"

"Yes. Jacobite sympathizers have a trick of planting some near their houses to let fugitives know where they can find shelter."

"Don't see any round abouts here, sir."

"Neither do I. We will push on. Keep your eyes on the roadside turf to make sure the horse we are following has not turned off."

Try as she would Ann could not prevent herself from flushing. She followed at the rear of the troopers so fortunately there was no one to notice. Her father had not accompanied them; neither, for that matter, had the High Sheriff. She could picture them sampling a bottle of port in the dining-room. Ann stared at the road. With a feeling akin to thankfulness, she found that the surface was dry now and that no tell-tale hoof-prints were noticeable, only here and there an indication that a horse had recently passed that way. The old Rectory lay in a hollow, surrounded by high-hedged meadows, an orchard and a stable-yard which also served as a farm-yard, for the rector had kept a few cows, a pig or two and sufficient poultry for his needs. Major Manstein had drawn rein again near the five-bar gate. An overhanging tree had shielded this patch of earth from the morning sun and on the damp ground a line of hoof-tracks led into the stable-yard. He dismounted and tossed his reins to a trooper. Ann did likewise. She walked towards him a trifle timidly, but he seemed oblivious of her presence. His brow was puckered and his gaze fixed on the ground. He appeared a slow-thinking, tenacious man, who took one thing at a time and favoured it with his full concentration. Save for the occasional stamp of a hoof the mounted troopers were motionless. Ann gave a quick look about her. The old Rectory, she noticed, presented a smarter appearance since it had been occupied afresh. The hedges and the lawns were well trimmed; flower beds which the rector had allowed to become weed-ridden were now bright with blooms; the woodwork had been painted a cheerful green. The creak of the opening gate brought her attention back to the officer. He was entering the yard, careful to avoid treading on the incriminating hoof-marks. He walked to the side door. On it there gleamed a large, brightly-polished brass knocker. He sent his peremptory summons resounding through the house. The door did not open. Instead there was a movement down the stable-yard and Ann saw, coming through a small wicket which led to a paddock, the tall figure of Mr. Philip Yorke. In place of stockings he wore spurred boots and his coat was looped back for riding. He swung a crop idly as he walked gravely forward.

"Do you wish to see me, sir ?" he inquired of the soldier.

"I do, sir," said Major Manstein curtly. He turned and took stock of Mr. Yorke. "Are you the owner of this place ?"

"I am."

"I wish to see the horse which made these tracks."

Ann tried to catch Mr. Yorke's eye but he seemed oblivious of her existence.

"Indeed ?" Mr. Yorke's expressive eyebrows were slightly elevated. "And why, pray ?"

"That is my business."

"I am not interested in your business. This is my private house and no business is transacted here. You come here uninvited and demand to see a horse ! I resent such cavalier conduct and am not minded to gratify your whims."

"Whims ! Damnation, sir, do you not see the colour of my coat ?"

"One could scarcely miss seeing it."

"Then let that suffice. I am here on the King's business, and in the name of His Majesty I order you to show me the horse."

"You have your authority ?"

"Certainly."

"Show it to me."

"Does not my word suffice ?"

Mr. Yorke slowly shook his head, and with a muttered curse the officer fumbled in his tunic pocket and produced a large official-looking document. "Here is my warrant !" he exclaimed.

Mr. Yorke took it leisurely, unfolded it, and began to read with calm deliberation. Once or twice Major Manstein took a deep breath or moved impatiently as if he found the restraint irksome. "Damnation, are you going to read every word ?"

"Every word," said Mr. Yorke, placidly, and continued to read. Major Manstein strode briskly across to the stables and rattled the door. It was fastened.

"Don't let him see the horse," entreated Ann hurriedly.

Philip Yorke raised his eyes a moment and looked gravely into her pleading face. Then he resumed his reading without speaking.

As Major Manstein came striding irritably towards them, Mr. Yorke folded the document and handed it back with a slight bow. "I am at your service, Major Manstein," he said civilly. "You hold the King's commission to search, and my premises are at your disposal. Permit me to comment, sir, that had you showed me your warrant in the first instance we might have been spared this little misunderstanding."

"The stable door is locked," said the soldier, ignoring Mr. Yorke's polished utterances.

"The key is here," said Mr. Yorke calmly, and walking across the cobbles he unlocked the door and flung it back. Major Manstein stepped briskly inside and paused. Ann, peering apprehensively over his shoulder, paused too. The horse in the stall was coal black.

"Whose horse is this?" snapped Major Manstein.

"Mine."

"How long has it been yours?"

"A matter of, let me think, fifteen months."

"Have you any other horse on the premises?"

"This is the only animal here. Pray search if you so desire."

Major Manstein frowned. Stooping, he ran his hand down the foreleg of the beast and lifted its foot. The traces of moist earth indicated that it had come in but a few moments before.

The major looked about him. There was no place for another horse to be concealed, but despite this he walked from building to building, scrutinizing. He came back scowling to face the imperturbable Philip Yorke.

"I trust you are satisfied with the result of your search," Mr. Yorke observed suavely.

"The horse I seek is not here."

"Sir, permit me to remark that I appear to detect a certain hostility in your tone. I fail to see in what manner I have given offence. I have, but a few moments since, ridden into my own premises on my own mount, after a perfectly innocuous ride; yet you leave me with the impression that I have done something which is contrary to the law of the realm. Pray enlighten me. In what way have I offended, Major Manstein?"

The officer bit his lip. "None, sir, none. I am chagrined that my plans have not materialized. If I appear discourteous, I beg of you to make allowance. There is no time to lose; I bid you good-day."

With a gesture of his gauntleted hand which might have been interpreted as a salute, the discomfited soldier strode to the gate and flung himself into the saddle. Ann ran forward to catch her horse, for the trooper who held it had dropped her rein at the word of command. She stood staring uncomprehendingly at the red backs of the dragoons as they receded down the road. Relief and bewilderment contended for supremacy. She started with surprise at the sound of a voice at her elbow.

"Now that you have honoured my unworthy abode with your presence, may I invite you inside—Ann?"

"Oh, Mr. Yorke, Mr. Yorke," she said impulsively as she held out both her hands. "I feel I ought to thank you, thank you tremendously, only, only——"

"Only what, Ann?"

"Only I don't understand. And I think that I will come in and sit down for my knees are trembling."

He slipped his hand under her arm; a strong, firm hand which seemed to exude confidence, and led her to the door.

"Go into the parlour and lie on the sofa," he ordered. "I will join you as soon as I have put your mare in the paddock."

It was a sparsely but neatly furnished room, Ann noticed. One corner was entirely taken up by a harpsichord of large dimensions, and there were many shelves of books. There was a large bowl of flowers on the polished oak table on which lay also some paper and a quill as though the owner had been interrupted in the midst of a task. There was a violoncello leaning against the wall and in the far corner stood a sheathed sword, all but hidden from sight. So much she noticed, but her eyes were closed when Mr. Yorke strode in from the hall.

"My dear girl, can I get you anything? Are you feeling faint?"

"Faint? How absurd." Ann was scornful.

"A little water, or some wine?"

"No," said Ann, sitting up and looking wide awake. "Let's talk. My knees have stopped shaking; it was only excitement, I think. And wasn't it exciting?"

"Was it?"

"Of course it was. I could have hated you for letting him see inside the stable, and all the while . . . all the while . . ."

"My horse was there waiting to be inspected. Do you know, Ann, I formed the impression that it was not what he was expecting?"

Ann caught him by the lapels of his coat and turned his face to the light. "You are laughing at me; you are always laughing at me. I have a mind to be cross with you, but I will overlook it if you tell me the truth."

"The truth, Ann? But of course."

"Now you knew the major did not expect to find your horse there! Am I not right?"

"Well, it did occur to me that he might be looking for a chestnut with a white foreleg which I happened to encounter in the lane a short while before."

"There, I was right. You see, you may deceive Major Manstein but you can't deceive me."

"I should feel easier if I were certain that I had deceived Major Manstein."

"Of course you have. Now tell me what happened."

"Why, I was idly pacing the road, communing with Nature as is my practice, when an excited and flustered young man on a chestnut stopped me to inquire whether I were Mr. Yorke, and on my assuring him that I was, he told me that you had sent him to hide the horse in my stable. He seemed a most admirable young fellow, but I would not call him discreet. He told me that the military were coming to your house to search for the animal which belonged to a Jacobite whom they were out to capture. He also told me that the emissary had ridden to Mostyn. Now it seemed apparent to me that, when they failed to find the horse at your house, they would start searching elsewhere, and as my house was nearest, I suggested to this admirable young man that he rode to Mostyn and exchanged the horse perilous for his own honest steed, and incidentally told the Jacobite of the state of affairs. So when we came to a gate I spread my coat for the horse to walk over so that it would leave no tracks, and off went your friend across country to what I trust will be a happy and satisfactory reunion. It occurred to me that these soldiers might try to follow the tracks of a horse, so I hurried home, changed into my riding clothes, saddled my own mount, took him through the paddock, jumped the hedge and was able to bring him through the gate just in time to leave the tracks which so interested your friend the major. All very simple, Ann, and a pleasant deviation from my matutinal rambles."

"Why should you do it?" asked Ann, wide-eyed. "Are you a supporter of King James?"

"No, my dear. I am in the service of Queen Ann."

CHAPTER ELEVEN

FOR A LONG TIME PHILIP YORKE STOOD LOOKING DOWN AT ANN. THE whimsical smile which had crossed his grave features when he uttered the last observation had passed. Ann stared back at him with the frank, slightly curious gaze of a child. Why was he looking at her thus? No one had ever looked at her so steadfastly before. She did not feel ill at ease; there was nothing in those steady eyes which could cause alarm. They seemed, thought Ann, to be a little pensive and curiously tender. Mr. Yorke drew a deep breath and turned on his heel with a rapidity which took Ann by surprise. No longer was she looking at those brown, arresting eyes, but at a broad back. He had drawn a stool to the harpsichord and the silence of the room was broken by harmony. The white hands moved over the keys. Ann watched them, fascinated more by their combined firmness and gentleness than by the melody they played. That, too, was fascinating, haunting. She had heard nothing like it before.

"What is it?" she inquired in a low voice when the last harp-like note had faded.

"Purcell. Do you not know it?"

"No. What is it called?"

"Some day I may tell you. Do you like Bach? He is so different. Yet there is a calm majesty about his works which tranquillizes like a soothing touch."

When the last chord was struck, his fingers remained on the keys as though reluctant to let go. They moved again, this time slowly, caressingly, stroking out a soft, sensuous air which made the girl's eyes feel moist. The hands fell from the keys and Philip Yorke walked to the window and stared over the garden. Ann could see his profile, curiously firm.

"What was that? It was exquisite. Who composed it?"

"It is not composed yet—Ann."

"You mean—it is your own?"

He did not deny it.

"Are you, then, a musician?"

"Alas! Have I not demonstrated that I am not? I only play sufficiently well to realize that I cannot play."

"A teacher, then? Hughie told me this morning that you instructed him in reading and writing. You are a teacher?"

"Who am I to teach? I am but a humble seeker after truth."

"But what is your task in life?"

"To fight."

The look of perplexity had been deepening on Ann's face, but at this she brightened. This was language she understood. Light-footed she tripped to the distant corner and picked up the sheathed sword.

"Ah!" he exclaimed. "So your quick eyes discerned that!"

"Is it yours?"

"I wore it—once."

"Only once?"

"Well, only once to any effect. It was at Dettingen."

"Oh!" Ann stared at him with something akin to awe. "I have heard Captain Berners speak of the battle. He was there with the Twenty-Third Foot. They lost fifteen killed and their colonel died of wounds. You see, I know all about the battle." She turned the weapon slowly in her hands, drew out the blade a few inches and clicked it back again. "So you are a soldier?"

"Say, rather, I was, for a short time. It pleased my honour to volunteer to serve under His Majesty. Despite all his detractors may say, King George bore himself right gallantly in the battle—and afoot at that. But when we came home I resigned my commission. There was something greater which demanded my allegiance; a more deadly foe than the French to fight."

"You mean you threw in your lot with the Stuarts?" asked Ann, her eyes glowing with excitement.

"On the contrary. I am a loyal adherent of the House of Hanover."

"Oh!" Ann was plainly crestfallen and nonplussed. "Then why, why did you deceive that officer this morning? You were serving King James then, of a surety."

"I imagined I was serving Queen Ann."

"Now you are just playing with my name. You are always laughing at me."

"Heaven forbid. Are you offended?"

"Offended? I think you have been remarkably kind. But, Mr. Yorke, I cannot make you out. You talk in riddles, and my poor brain cannot follow you. What is it you fight, then?"

"Ignorance."

Her face was puzzled. He took her gently by the arm and led her to a chair. "Sit down a moment, Ann. Do you like to see suffering?"

"Suffering? Oh, no. I cannot bear to see either mortals or animals suffer."

"I am sure of it. I can read your gentle nature in your face. Yet there is suffering throughout the length and breadth of the land. It should not be."

"But who can understand the mystery of suffering? Parson Price preached upon it not so long ago. He said that we must be resigned to the will of God."

"He would! It avoids a considerable amount of inconvenience and exertion. Now I, Ann, sinful though I be, believe that no mission in life is more blessed than the alleviation of human suffering. You dwell in comfort, even luxury, in your comfortable home. You are kind to those about you, but if you had seen the scenes that I have seen your gentle heart would be harrowed. Do you know that there are a hundred and sixty felonies punishable by instant death? If a starving man picks a pocket of a shilling and a farthing—death! Have you witnessed the degrading festival of a Tyburn hanging? Have you ever entered the precincts of a noisome gaol when debtors are herded with criminals, women and men, into filthy cells and lie on the flags without a rag to cover them? While your sporting parsons ride to hounds or attend cock-fighting mains, human beings are passing into eternity without benefit of religion. The common folk are illiterate. If they are callous, indifferent to human suffering, who can blame them? It is a hard school in which they have been educated. The press gang raids to secure sailors for the royal fleet about which we boast, forgetting that the men are ill-fed because of dishonest contractors. Who cares for them? Does the squire or the lord?"

"I am sure my father is not unkind to the tenants on his estate."

"But does he care for them? Does he care whether young Hughie possesses a brain? Does he care whether the thatch is off the cottage roof, or the slates leak, or the walls are damp? Does he care if the parson does his duty? Tell me, have you ever heard him speak of Jethro Tull?"

Ann shook her head. She was a little awed. The line of the man's mouth seemed to have hardened; the deep-set eyes were glowing now with a subdued fire.

"Of course he has not heard of Jethro Tull. Tull has invented a threshing-machine which will revolutionize agriculture, but the tenants can still go on flogging away with the flail in the old-fashioned way. Has your father studied the rotation of crops?"

"My father leaves such matters to his bailiff; he has other things to attend to," said Ann a trifle haughtily.

"Such as riding to hounds, or fowling, or sampling port."

"I will not have you criticize my father!"

Philip Yorke, at the tone of her voice, pulled up as if he had been struck.

"I crave your pardon," he said with a slight bow. "I have been inexcusably rude. Believe me, it was not my intention to be personal; I merely thought of the squire as a specimen of his class. If I have wounded your feelings, I beg you will give me credit for that."

"I give you credit for sincerity," said Ann, looking a little dignified. "And with being enthusiastic about your subject. I do not understand half you tell me, but I am sure that your intentions are of the best. I shall not object to Hughie coming to you for lessons."

"Your condescension touches me."

50

Ann looked up quickly, looked into his eyes to see whether the tantalizing light was dancing there. "You had better take back your sword," she said, placing it in his hands. "You have not yet shown me what you fight with."

"This," said he, holding up a quill. "An educated populace, an intelligent, thinking people will do more to bring peace and prosperity to our country than regiments of marching red-coats."

"Oh, look at the time!" cried Ann, as the grandfather clock gave an ominous whirr preparatory to striking the hour. She sprang to her feet and Philip Yorke held open the door. "Allow me to fetch your horse from the paddock," he said quietly. Ann toyed with the flowers until he returned.

"You will come to see me again one day?" he asked quietly. "Since you have entered the house it is impressed on me how deserted and colourless the place is."

"Colourless? The flowers on the table are a delightful shade."

"It would be enhanced, nonetheless, by more animated beauty."

"I will come again on the understanding that you play to me."

"Then that is a bargain."

Ann urged Starlight into a trot. As she entered the road which led to her home, she looked back and waved. Philip Yorke was standing, grave and motionless, on the cobbled yard. She noticed that he still held in his hand the sword she had returned to him; the sword he had worn at Dettingen.

* * * * *

"Demme, girl, where have you been all this time?" The Squire was inclined to be irascible as his errant daughter walked with composure into the room. "What the deuce must you go riding off with those confounded lobster-backs for? Couldn't make out what had become of you. Sheriff was asking about you."

"Where is he?" inquired Ann, ignoring her parent's interrogation.

"Gone, girl, this long time. We had a glass of port together, and then he went."

"Only one, darling?" asked Ann, lifting up the bottle.

"Put that down and don't shake it. You are insubordinate, girl. Demme, that's a good word; wish I'd thought of it before."

"But what happened to the Sheriff?"

"Went back home when that infernal Major What-is-it did not return. Glad to see the back of the whole interfering lot, I've no doubt. Don't like that fellow; the major I mean. Bit of the Prussian somewhere in his ancestry, or I'm a Dutchman. That's the worst of having a confounded German princeling on the throne; birds of a feather, eh? Good thing when we have a Stuart back again. No more of this silly nonsense. But what happened, girl? What happened? You stay there chattering and keep me in suspense."

"I'm not chattering, darling."

"Do you infer that I am? You are impudent, Miss. What was I saying? Ah, yes. About that Major What-d'y'-call-him."

"Major Manstein, Father. He followed the tracks of Captain Conway's horse."

"The devil he did."

"And when we reached Mr. Yorke's yard there were a horse's tracks leading right across the moist turf."

"Awkward that; plaguy awkward. Took some explaining, I'll be bound." The Squire shifted uneasily in his seat.

"Keep calm, dearest. All is not lost. Major Manstein insisted on having the stable door opened, and Mr. Yorke complied."

"Bah! Spirit of a louse. Never did like what you told me about the fellow. And there was the horse, of course?"

"There was a horse."

"A horse; what d'y' mean?"

"Mr. Yorke met Seth in the road and sent him across country while he brought his own animal in through the gate to throw them off the track."

"Neat, that, 'pon my oath. Much beholden to the fellow. Must have him in for a glass of wine, Ann. Remind me. He must be one of us."

"He isn't, Father. I asked him. He fought at Dettingen for King George and is all for the House of Hanover."

"More fool him. Well, steer clear of him, girl. He's not fit company for honest folk. What does the chap do for a living?"

"He seems to have a competency. He did try to explain but I couldn't follow him. He wants to educate people and make the world better."

"The man's mad."

"Says that there are far too many people suffering in our gaols——"

"Rubbish. Far too many rogues at large; place is infested with footpads. He's a crank, that's what he is. Why, demme!" The Squire paused, and a look of repugnance, akin to horror crossed his ruddy features. "Why, demme, girl, the man must be a reformer!"

CHAPTER TWELVE

IN THE GLOAMING, JUST WHEN A SLEEPY HUSH FELL ON THE WORLD and the thrushes were ending their singing, and yellow squares of light were beginning to appear in distant windows of cottage and farm, Ann stood by the tall windows looking forth on the drowsy world. Suddenly she said: "There is a horseman coming up the road from the coast; it will be Seth, I have no doubt."

The Squire, who had been dozing in his chair, waiting for the servants to light the lamps, stirred.

"Eh? Seth? Young Morrice? Ah, yes." He took off his wig and rubbed his head where the scalp irritated. "Yes," he repeated, "Yes," and Ann, glancing across at him, knew that he was addressing himself and not her. In the half-light the florid colour in his face which gave him such a look of ruddy health was no longer noticeable; and the glow of the embers made the shadows on his features appear more pronounced. She thought that he looked older; much older.

"I've been thinking, girl," he said ponderously. It was, Ann might have observed, an unusual occurrence, but levity seemed out of place so she said nothing, but just continued to look at her father, curiously and perhaps a little tenderly.

"I have been thinking," he reiterated, as though to stress the importance of the event. "This young Seth Morrice. The young spark's obviously fallen head over heels in love with you; follows you about and does your bidding like a well-trained hound."

"But Father, dear, I have given him no encouragement."

"Encouragement? The flowers don't have to encourage folk to admire 'em. The lad's not blind; how can he help but be conscious of your charm, eh, lass? And he's not dense, so he must be aware of your sweetness."

"But, darling, you are always impressing upon me that I am ungrateful and undutiful and I don't know what else."

"So you are; quite shameless. Don't treat your parent with respect. Interrupted me now. What was I saying? Oh, yes, about this Seth Morrice. Well, lass, I don't look unfavourably upon him and I may as well say so. He comes of a good family; he's an only son and his family are wealthy. You could make a worse match, girl."

"Oh, Father!" There was consternation in Ann's tone. She liked Seth as one would like an old playmate; a companion of sunny hours, but the making of a match! Her father was speaking again. "You might do worse, much worse. Ann, I'm beginning to feel my years. I'm not as young as I was and I'd like to see you provided for."

Ann stared out into the deepening shades of evening. The figure on horseback was drawing nearer, but she no longer saw Seth. For Ann had dreamed dreams. She had pictured a knight in shining armour; a gay troubadour who came beneath her chamber window to woo her when the jasmine scent was heavy on the night air. She wanted adventure and romance, and here was her father prosaically speaking of his desire to see her provided for. The dream castles of many languorous hours rocked to their foundations.

"Why are you silent, girl?"

"I wanted to marry for love."

"Stuff and nonsense, girl. Marrying for love is all moonshine. What a woman wants is a good house to live in, a man to protect her, and enough money to spend on her falderals."

"Did you tell my mother that when you loved her?"

Ann saw him start, open his mouth to reply and then fall silent. He sat staring into the fire and suddenly, to Ann's vivid imagination, the years slipped away and she saw her father as he was in the 'Fifteen Rebellion. Not portly and rubicund and florid, but a gay young cavalier, slim and agile, swinging into his saddle, sword at side, ready to ride for the Stuart. He had told her often how her mother had given him a bunch of white roses to wear in lieu of a cockade. Where were the roses now? Shrivelled and faded. Nothing but a memory. Alas that youth should pass! At the thought of Life containing nothing but the practical, prosaic things of everyday existence, Ann felt a desire to cry out and beat futile, puny hands against the walls of remorseless Fate. She felt rebellious. She would be happy while she could. Of what use waiting for a Future which might never come to pass?

"I want love," she said almost defiantly.

"And you don't want young Seth?" The Squire's voice was unnaturally gentle. "Well, girl, I won't press you. God forbid. I spoke in your own interests. My mind is not wholly at ease. I intend to plunge; to play for high stakes. I'm backing Prince Charlie to the hilt, and if the gamble fails to come off——" He broke off abruptly and shook his head. "I'm a ruined man, lass, and you will be turned out to beg for bread. That's why I'd like to see you provided for, but I'll not press you."

"You are a dear," said Ann and impetuously kissed the top of his bowed head. "But the Rising will not fail. It is bound to succeed, and darling, if you gamble, I will, too. And if I fail, if we fail, which is not likely, I'll pay the price and you'll not find me whining."

"You're a good girl, Ann; a right sound sporting lass. I'm proud to have bred you. They are almost the words your mother used when I rode out in the 'Fifteen.'" He sighed.

Ann looked up quickly "It is Seth," she said. "He is coming up the drive. And he is riding his own horse so he must have made the exchange safely."

"Ring the bell, Ann, and let's have a light on the subject."

Ann put a hand to a flushed cheek. "Not for a moment, dear. We don't know whether the house is watched and it would be as well if Seth came in with as little fuss as possible."

Instead of dismounting at the front door, the young man took his mount to the stable yard. Ann walked from the side door to meet him. Seth looked tired and travel-stained, but he greeted her with a bright smile.

"You have succeeded?" she whispered. He slipped an arm around her waist and gave her a quick squeeze ere they reached the door of the house.

"Yes, I came up with them. Just in time. I've left my mare with Howells. I've ridden her fairly hard coming back and she could do with attention."

"Come in and tell Father all about it. You must stay and have a meal with us. You must be famished."

"Now you mention it, I am. Until this moment all I could think about was getting back to you, Ann."

"With news of your success! I compliment you, Seth, on a useful piece of work. Father will be pleased—and relieved. Wait. I'll just tell Morgan to draw the curtains and bring in the candles, then we'll have a cosy meal. Like to wash off the dust of travel?"

Seth might be the bearer of news of consequence, but he was young enough to put food before facts, and the Squire was wise enough to humour him. Squire Trevor prided himself on keeping a good table. Seth ate with the zest of hungry youth, and conversation was desultory until the table had been cleared. Then the Squire himself poured out the port with the deliberate formality of one who observes a ritual. Ann placed the bowl of water in the centre of the table. Solemnly they toasted King James.

"So you made it ?" exclaimed the Squire, breaking the long silence

"I did, sir. The chestnut went well once he warmed to the job but I was only just in time. The tide was full and the vessel had actually left the quay when I hove in sight. Fortunately Conway spotted me, and Petis hove-to while he came ashore in the ship's boat. I'll say this of Conway; he took the news as calmly as any man could have done. He was thankful to secure his sword, pistols and valise. He sends you grateful thanks, Ann."

"What of the horse ?" asked the Squire. "What have you done with his horse ?"

"Left it stabled at the inn at Mostyn."

"Bad move, Seth; bad move."

"It was Conway's suggestion."

"But it will be recognized; that Major what-d'y'-call-it will find it, sure as fate."

"That is what Conway desires, sir."

"Desires ? The fellow's mad. Want 'em to take his horse ? Fine animal, too, egad."

"Well, sir; you see, he argues that if they get the horse which he has left behind they will take it as a sure proof that he has fled the country and will cease to search for him."

"Eh ? There's something in that, too. Still, it would be a pity to sacrifice the horse; well-bred beast with staying power, if I'm a judge." He rose with ponderous deliberation and selected a church-warden from the rack. "Pass me the tobacco-jar, girl. Now, young man, help yourself to a pipe."

"Not yet, sir, thanks."

"Other means of consolation, eh ? Well, when a man reaches my age, a pipe by his own fireside is a solace. Helps me to think."

"You are doing a lot of thinking these days, darling," suggested Ann, pressing the tobacco into the pipe bowl with dainty finger, and then holding a lighted spill while her parent sucked somewhat noisily until the pipe was drawing to his satisfaction. "Ah," said he, and gave the stem a sceptre-like wave in the direction of Seth. "Shall want you in the morning, lad, to do an errand for me. Is it asking too great a favour to ask you to ride to Wrexham ?"

"Not at all, sir."

"Better stay the night, then. Do they expect you home ?"

"I can stay, sir, thank you. We have an admirable arrangement, my parent and I. He gives me a free hand to act as I think fit, so I come and go as I choose."

"He is in this then, lad ? He's going to plunge, too ?"

"Not plunge, sir. You do not know my worthy sire. It is only a flutter with him. He has paid a sum over to my account which I am to use as I think fit, which means, of course, that I am to back the Prince. My father, on the other hand, stays quietly at home, a respected subject of King George. Should the Prince win, he will come in for the credit due for his support; should the Prince lose, I am the scapegoat and he will deplore the folly of hot-headed youth, and vow it was all done behind his back and without his consent.

It's as safe as tossing a two-headed penny. We are bound to come out on top, sir."

"So it would seem. Your father is an astute man. Yet, demme, I was ever a plunger. It's neck or nothing with me."

"I have followed you to hounds, sir!"

"Demme, very neatly turned, lad. You have a pretty trick of speech. Well, let's to business. The outcome of this talk is that I want you to ride to Wrexham in the forenoon and seek out Lawyer Hughes—you know him?"

"As well as I know the road to Chester."

"Hark 'ee, he's one of us, but cautious and judicious as you'd expect a lawyer to be. No plunging for him. But he has the Prince's interests at heart. Well, say to him that I want to raise a mortgage on this place, and could he come up with the necessary papers and see me about it."

"I will, sir."

"And if he could get some ready money to hand as soon as possible it would be as well. I have no doubt but what there will be some quick moves made when the Prince actually lands and, well, ready money is always useful."

"I agree, sir. It would be as well if we appointed a treasurer. I was saying so only a day or so ago to *Brutus*."

"*Brutus, Brutus,*—who the devil?"

"It's becoming too risky to name names now. That is the name under which Sir Watkin has been corresponding with the Prince."

"I recollect now! The baronet becomes Brutus. Well, Brutus was an honourable man if I remember my Shakespeare. I think you are right, boy. We must get a man of repute appointed to whom we can send in our respective contributions so that all will go well for the Prince's cause."

"I will bring you word the moment he is appointed."

"Do so, my boy. I'm heart and soul in this business but I am not so agile as I was and my gout gives me the devil at times."

"I will do the running about, sir; and moreover, I will enjoy the task. But bear in mind, sir, no names if you can help it."

"That is so; no names. Hell's furies, what's that?"

With unmistakable clearness four sharp raps resounded through the room. Conversation dropped and the three sat upright in their chairs, heads turned, listening.

"Someone is tapping on the window," said Ann.

"Look in that drawer, Morrice," said the Squire quickly. "There's a brace of pistols there, ready loaded. No, don't take 'em out yet. Just open the drawer and keep 'em within reach."

The tapping came again; it seemed insistent. Ann walked to the door.

"Let me go," cried Seth in an urgent, low voice, but Ann shook her head. She was quite calm.

"There may be danger," added Seth.

"If there is, the sight of a woman will disarm suspicion. Stay where you are, and for goodness sake, appear at your ease."

She walked into the hall. The two men sat listening, Seth with his fingers very near to the open drawer where lay the pistols. The Squire appeared calm; only the vigorous puffs of his pipe indicated his agitation. A low hum of voices sounded. Then the door swung open and they saw, framed against the dark of the hallway, the figure of a man.

It was Captain Conway, hat in hand, and a reckless smile on his sun-tanned features.

CHAPTER THIRTEEN

HE LOOKED THE PERFECT ADVENTURER, DID RICHARD CONWAY, AS HE stood with the candle-light beating on his keen, reckless face, and glinting on the polished steel hilt of his sword. Dare-devilry danced in his eyes; so Ann noticed as she stood aside gazing up at him with a blend of awe and admiration in her ingenuous eyes. This was the man with a price on his head! This was the man for whom the Hanoverian major with his posse of dragoons was searching. This was the man who was believed to have found security in flight, coolly and of deliberation returning to the scene of danger. Captain Conway seemed not unconscious of his own temerity for he gave a laugh which savoured of a mischievous boy as he greeted the amazed Squire.

"Like a bad penny I keep turning up, sir, as you see."

The Squire relieved his feelings by swearing roundly. "Is this safe, lad? Is this prudent? 'Zounds, don't think we are not glad to see you, but, egad, it seems to me you are cutting matters a bit close."

"You are taking a chance, Conway," added Seth soberly.

"Lud, man, I was never backward about taking chances. It adds zest to the game of life."

"You might bring misfortune to those who befriend you," said Seth meaningly.

"Nay, I am not that reckless—or ungrateful." Conway turned to Ann with a bow, held out his hand and escorted her into the room. He did it as formally as if he led her to a minuet, and Ann, to her surprise, suffered him to do so. Hitherto, she had always assumed herself capable of moving about her own house unaided, but this time she accepted the unexpected courtesy with gravity and walked into the room with the dignity of a queen. She felt herself blushing, but Captain Conway retained his perfect sangfroid. When Ann was seated, Conway stood with his back to the fire and faced the Squire. Ann saw that his boots were splashed, there was a smear of mud on the green broadcloth of his coat, and some tiny strands were showing where a brier had plucked at him as he passed by.

"I came on a borrowed horse, sir, which I have hid in the copse. I pride myself that not even a poacher saw me approach your house and, as you can testify, I came so stealthily that not a watch-dog barked."

"That is so," said the Squire. "That is so; but you must have a reason for returning."

57

"A variety of reasons. One is I am ever loath to run away. Were it not for my work I would remain and exchange thrusts with that blustering Hanoverian swine who forces his way into honest men's dwellings. Peris has gone on to Liverpool to arrange for the acquisition of the ship in which we are to run our cargo of arms from Brittany, but the wind dropped at the set of sun, and when darkness fell I had 'em put me ashore at a spot I know well on the Sands o' Dee, and so I came back by stealth. I do not think you need fear another visit from the soldiers, sir. That was why I left my horse behind; a goodly sacrifice for a goodly cause!"

"Maybe you are right; but I am still waiting for the reason for your return."

"One more reason. How many men can you raise in Flintshire; or for that matter, in North Wales?"

"Hum. All the retainers will follow where we lead just as they did when Charles appointed his Commissioners of Array and called for his levies. I could personally promise, let me see, a dozen men, and I'll pay for the arming of them if you will guarantee to fetch the arms."

"I'll see to that provided I get the ship."

"I thought that was all arranged."

"Why, no. Nothing but the preliminaries; only the suggestion, as it were. Once we were under way Peris and I fell to talking matters over with the skipper of the coasting craft, and it was impressed upon us that no man would loan a vessel or hire a vessel for so hazardous a mission. We must buy her outright, and that would cost money."

The Squire was having trouble with his pipe. He drew hard at it, shifted the stem, tapped the bowl. Ann noticed that his face was unusually flushed. "Why, now," said the Squire, clearing his throat, "there should be no difficulty about a little matter like that. All that one has to do is to make proper advances in the right quarter."

"So I thought," said the Prince's messenger. "The proper advances in the right quarter. You express yourself lucidly, Squire. And so I came——"

"To ask my advice. Quite right, sir, quite right. And I shall give it. Ann, girl, it is time you were abed."

"It is not late, Father. The night is young. I am used to staying up late."

"Yes, my girl, you are cultivating bad habits. Now, say good night to Captain Conway and off to your bed."

"But I am most interested in what Captain Conway is telling us. I am in this venture, don't forget. And, darling, it is not often that one gets real excitement like this. This is a charming spot to live in out but no one could call it exciting."

"We are going to talk business now. There will be no more excitement, will there, Conway?"

"I trust not, sir. No more excitement—unless something unforeseen occurs."

"I trust that nothing like that will transpire. Well, kiss me good night, girl. And be dutiful for once in your life."

"I am always dutiful. It is my outstanding characteristic." Ann

58

walked forward with becoming docility and placed a kiss on her parent's forehead. It was damp with perspiration.

"Good night, Captain Conway. Safe journeying should I fail to see you in the morning, and success to your mission."

The messenger bowed.

"Good night, Seth. Morgan will show you to your room." Merrice saw her to the door and closed it after her. He stood with his hand on the handle and looked across at the Squire.

"Would you like me to retire, sir, while you and Captain Conway discuss this business?"

"What's that? Retire? Good heavens, no. Remain here, Seth, by all means. Go back—go back to where you were sitting when we heard the rapping on the window. It is a comfortable seat. There is nothing Conway and I want to discuss which should be private from your ears."

Young Seth Morrice looked the Squire in the eyes and then walked quietly to the seat beside the table and lying back at ease let his arm stray as though casually along the table so that his fingers drooped near the partly-opened drawer. The Squire watched him narrowly then he tapped the ashes from his pipe and spoke more briskly. "Now, sir, what is your real message. I could sense that you could not tell me when that lass of mine was in the room."

"Quite right, sir. Delicacy shut my mouth."

"Delicacy? Ah! well, out with it."

"During our conversation with the skipper of the coasting craft he let fall an observation which was of particular interest to me. He mentioned, almost inadvertently it seemed, the name of the man who held the controlling interest in the firm of slavers who owned the vessel we thought of purchasing."

"Indeed." The Squire was non-committal. With some deliberation he leaned forward, and selecting a spill, held it to the flame and then essayed to light his pipe. He looked calm, but his fingers trembled. Seth was conscious of a tension in the atmosphere of the room. He moved slightly forward in his chair, alert. He was breathing faster but was not conscious of it.

"So you discovered the name of the man who held the controlling interest in the firm of slavers. Well, sir, what of it? Why have you come to tell me this?"

"It would make a considerable difference to the success of the Prince's venture if this man—who must, obviously, possess means—would save us the expense of the ship by, shall I say, loaning us the vessel?"

The Squire puffed a cloud of smoke and peered at the messenger through half-closed eyes. "Is this—blackmail?" he shot out.

Captain Conway's expression mingled surprise with indignation. "Sir," he cried affronted, "Sir, I must ask you to explain your—amazing words. Has anything I have said or done suggested the slightest impropriety? Out of deference to you I refrained from touching on a sordid subject in the presence of your charming daughter, and, if I may say so, even now my conversation has been free from the—er—bluntness which has characterized your own."

59

"Ah, well, let that pass. Speak more freely."

Conway cast a glance at Seth Morrice who sat, white of face, watching intently. "Have I your permission to speak freely in the presence of this young man?"

"Ay, you have. Let there be no beating about the bush. Seth, did you know I made my money from slaving ventures?"

Young Morrice stood up. "Sir," he stammered, "you have taken me by surprise. I—I have never given a thought to how you came by your money. Come to think of it, I presumed you had come by some small fortune or other when you moved to a bigger estate."

"You are right. I was tempted to put money into the venture four years ago, and mighty profitable it proved to be; so profitable that against my better judgment I remained in; in fact, I took out more shares. I have kept the matter dark for fear my dear girl should think less of me. But now you, sir, have tumbled upon the secret. What are you going to do about it?"

"My dear Squire Trevor," said Conway cautiously, "obviously I shall treat the matter as being of the greatest secrecy. No one is more anxious than I am that your daughter should be preserved from anything which would give her the slightest pain. From your attitude, from the tone of your conversation, I cannot help but draw the conclusion that you have misunderstood my motives. I have no thought but to serve the Prince. I merely ask—nay, not ask, suggest —that it would be a gracious gesture on your part if you would allow the vessel to be used for the carrying of these arms without any cost to the cause. Need I add that it is well known that at the moment our greatest handicap is lack of gold. Do this, sir, and I take it upon myself to promise you that his Highness will not prove ungrateful."

"Hum. Would I, do y' think, get a knighthood out of it?"

"A knighthood? My dear sir, you are too modest. You will find King James, or his Highness on behalf of his father, very lavish in rewards. They know how to recompense those loyal hearts who have stood by them in their hour of need. It is not for me to say, but I should imagine that the Prince would recognize such yeoman service by a peerage, at least."

"Which ship is it you want?"

"There is a snow there called the *Happy Chance*. She seems a likely craft, not too big, easy to handle, and I fancy her name."

"You shall have her; for this venture only. But you must see to the manning of her. I am not so well-off that I can afford to pay for a crew's wages into the bargain."

"Sir, this is magnificent; this is royal of you. We ask no more. She will have a crew of stout-hearted volunteers who will serve their sovereign without thought of pay, so set your mind at rest on that point."

"I will, sir. When do you rejoin Lieutenant Peris?"

"Without delay. By this time next month I hope to have the arms stored in a cave in the Ormeshead I know of. So the sooner I am off the better."

The Squire rose slowly and walked across to the sideboard. H
60

selected a bottle and glasses with care. Then he passed round the wine. "Success to the *Happy Chance!*" he cried.

Captain Conway tossed off his wine with a quick gesture and then strode to the door with a burst of energy which indicated that he was a man who did not let grass grow under his feet, He called a farewell to the Squire over his shoulder and clapped on his hat. Seth was at his side. "I will see you to the spinney," he said. They let themselves through the front door silently, skirted the gravel and crossed the meadow in the shadow of the hedge. When they came to the tethered horse, Conway mounted and, bending down, held out his hand. "Adieu—and thanks!" he said curtly.

"I would do a lot for the Prince," said Seth, looking up in the face which showed faintly above him.

"I am sure you would."

"I would do even more for Miss Ann. There is nothing I would not do to shield her from harm."

"Your sentiments do you credit, Morrice. I feel sure there are others who would be equally zealous in rendering her service and preserving her from harm."

With a jingle of bit-ring the horse moved into the night. As Seth let himself in at the front door he was conscious of a shadowy shape on the stairs. It was Ann in her dressing-wrap.

"He has gone?" she whispered. "Is all well?"

"All is well."

"Thank you, Seth. I felt something was amiss. Your assurance will bring me sleep. Good night, and thank you for your loyalty."

CHAPTER FOURTEEN

IT WAS ALL VERY WELL FOR ANN TO SAY GOOD NIGHT SO SWEETLY AND retire to rest. The night was not good; it was too disturbing; and Ann could not rest. She sat with her knees drawn up and her hands clasped behind them, staring at the casement where the lozenge-shaped panes traced their pattern against the moonlit sky. The house was still, but in the woods an owl hooted. Was it the moonlight which affected one's sleep, Ann wondered, or was it something more tangible? The whole air seemed charged with disturbing elements. Her father was perturbed; she knew him well enough to read his moods. Was it on account of the coming of Captain Conway? Seth had assured her that all was well and Seth was incapable of dissembling.

Captain Richard Conway, Prince Charles Edward's emissary, had departed; he had gone without a word of farewell. Ann was conscious of a pang of regret. She tried to tell herself that she did not care but she could not deceive herself. She did care. She wanted to bid him God's speed. She wanted to ask him to convey an assurance of her loyalty to the Young Chevalier. She wanted to ask him to accept a white cockade she had made him in lieu of that which he had left in her lap. Little things, trivial things, but Ann had set her heart on them and now they had come to naught.

She wondered where Captain Conway might be; pictured him riding cautiously through the night, his keen eyes searching every hedgerow, every shadow, alert for a possible ambuscade. His pistols would be loose in their holsters and their primings dry. His sword would be loose in its scabbard. His ears keyed for any suspicious rustle. How she wished she had been born a boy so that she could ride with him! How thrilling it must be to go stealing across hostile territory knowing that a false move might bring the troopers of King George slashing at his head. Ann tried to picture what her hero would do. She could catch his gay laugh as he drew his sword and rode blithely into the midst of his foes.

Something struck her window with the suddenness of a bullet and Ann's heart gave a furious bound. So perfectly did the noise synchronize with her thoughts that it might well have been the crack of a pistol. She put her hand against her night-robe as though to quell the pounding of her heart. Her breath was coming fast and her eyes were large, more with surprise than apprehension. Scarcely had she begun to think what the sound might be than it was repeated. This time she recognized it only too well. It was the sound of gravel flung against her pane. She slid to the edge of the bed and groped for her wrap. Her heart, now, appeared to have moved and seemed to be beating in her throbbing throat, intent on choking her. With difficulty she overcame her breathing and went tip-toeing to the casement. There, on the gravel, stood the dark silhouette she had expected. Save that there was no caped-riding coat this time, it was so like a repetition of the previous episode that it savoured of a dream; a product of her vivid, over-stimulated imagination. But when she opened the window the whispered voice was real enough.

"Ann. A word with you. I'm coming up." A ladder was reared softly against the creeper-covered wall and a booted foot was placed on the lowest rung. "No." Ann's lips shaped the word but it was never uttered. The tricorne hat was ascending; a strong hand gripped the sill; there was a flash of white teeth as Richard Conway laughed in her face.

"Where did you get that ladder?" she whispered. Later, she thought that it was a foolish and irrelevant thing to say. He answered quite sensibly, "Noticed it in the orchard."

"They must have forgotten it after gathering last year's apples," she explained, seriously. Captain Conway came back to earth. "I did not run the risk of returning to talk about ladders."

"Why did you come back?"

"Your worthy father extracted several reasons from me; he did not get the chiefest of all."

"What reasons did you give him?"

"Oh, about the vessel, but that's beside the point. My real reason was——"

"What?"

"To see you, Ann."

"How preposterous," protested Ann, all decorum, forgetting that only a few moments before she had deplored the unceremonious nature of his departure. "You were foolish; it was wrong of you."

"Why ?"

"Oh, I can't explain. It is—well, it is unusual."

"To be standing on a ladder talking to you at this hour of night ? Granted. But none the less pleasant on that account."

"I must close the window. I shall get cold."

"Put another wrap on; I cannot lose you yet, my beautiful white rose."

"You—you must not speak like that."

"Why not, Ann ? From the moment I set eyes on you I was bewitched. What a companion you would make for a soldier of fortune. I have ridden in a dream since I stole away in the early morning hours leaving you half asleep in the great armchair, weary from your self-imposed vigil. Shall I confess ?"

"It was stupid of me to fall asleep. I was annoyed with myself."

"I kissed the silken strands of your hair before I departed, and, quite shamelessly, I shore off a curl which even now reposes in the breast of my waistcoat."

"Oh," said Ann, a little dismayed, and clasped her hand to her hair.

"Nay, I could not have disfigured you for you have not been aware of your loss."

"But you ought not to have done it."

"I know. That's why I did it."

He looked so impudent that Ann burst into a laugh and then clapped her hand to her mouth. "Oh, I forgot. You really are—preposterous. Now go."

"Not yet."

"Why not ?"

"I have not had enough of you; not nearly enough. Also, I have not told you what I came back for."

"What was it ?"

"I have forgotten, unless it was to see you; to ask you to bid me God's luck on my mission."

"Just that ?"

"Just that."

"Then I'm glad you came. I was sitting up in bed grieving because you had gone without an adieu from me, and then, all of a sudden——"

"The gravel rattled on your window and you realized that the vagabond was still with you."

"But you really must go. I ought to be cross with you."

"Why ?"

"For your temerity in waking me—at least, disturbing me—at this unearthly hour."

"Much is forgiven to a Prince's messenger."

"Well, I forgive you—because you are a Prince's messenger. Tell me, is Prince Charlie as bonny as folks say ?"

"He's a great lad; gallant and debonair. You'll lose your heart to him if you see him."

"If he comes this way, will you present me to his Highness ?"

"Of course, Ann. And what will my reward be ?"

"We will discuss that after the presentation."

63

"But my devotion merits some recompense, surely?"

"You merit a box on the ears!"

She leaned forward and touched him gently with her open hand. He caught it in a firm grasp, raised it part way to his lips and then paused. "May I?" he asked.

"May you what?"

"Kiss your fingers?"

"Of course not."

"Then I will not. I would not so much as kiss your hand without your gracious leave."

"Oh! Then in that case you may. Now are you satisfied? But I must get me back to bed; I am nigh perished with cold. But first, I have something for you." She darted back into the room and returned with her white cockade.

"I made this for you," she said frankly.

"You are adorable. So you thought of me—Ann? After I had gone."

"Only as the Prince's messenger. Now go, and good luck be with you."

"We are landing the arms at Ormeshead. I shall see you in a month, queen of my heart."

"Hide the ladder in the laurels," said Ann, becoming practical. He nodded, and descended with agility. Ann had forgotten about feeling cold and leaned out of the casement as he cautiously inserted the ladder behind the bushes, taking care that no dead leaf rustled. He took off his hat, his hat on which the white cockade gleamed, and raised it on high in a last gay salute.

Conway's riding boots were lightly soled and he crossed the path jauntily. As Ann watched his straight back and springy step she was reminded of his description of the Prince—gallant and debonair. Ann felt that the words were apt, and applicable to one nearer than the young Chevalier. From the path at the side of the house, a broad ride, flanked by borders of turf which was picturesquely dotted with daffodils, stretched towards a meadow from which it was separated by a five-barred gate which showed white in the shadow of the trees. Half-way down this grassy ride Ann could now see Conway's horse tethered to a fence. He was walking towards the animal, walking across a patch of moonlight, when a shadow moved.

It seemed a shadow; it was as noiseless as one, but Ann clapped her hands to her mouth to stifle a cry of horror as she saw Conway leap aside as nimbly as a cat and the moonbeams made white fire as he swept out his blade.

Ann leaned out of her casement, wide-eyed with amazed surprise, petrified with horror. The Prince's messenger was trapped! He had walked into an ambush. She never thought to cry aloud for help, so fascinated was she. It was like looking at two marionettes to see these two black figures posture and leap. Their nimble feet made no sound on the grass; nothing was heard but the rasp of steel on steel. Conway had the moonlight full on him; she could even see the hue of his green coat. The stranger was nothing but a silhouette a sable form save for his sword which flickered as the moonlight danced along its narrow blade. They were hard at it; lunge and parry, feet wide apart, knees bent, bodies crouched low, right arms extended, left arms daintily behind. It seemed more like a formal dance. Only that ominous sound of steel told her that the dancers played with death. The first honour came to the stranger. Ann saw his sword dart in and Conway's hat—the hat with the white cockade—fell from his head. She could see his face now, white in the moonlight save for a dark stain which cut across the cheek. But Conway was undaunted. He leaped back with an agility which amazed Ann. The swords clashed again. This time Conway forced the pace. His blade slithered and the stranger sagged and stumbled to his knees, propping himself on one hand. Conway stopped to snatch his hat and then ran for his restive horse. A dog in the stable was barking uneasily. By the time Ann dragged her eyes from the figure which crouched like an animal on all fours, Conway was in the saddle, sword sheathed, reins in hand. There came a rush of hoofs. The dog barked loudly. The panting of a horse reached Ann's ears as the animal rose to the gate. Conway was over the five-bar like a bird; over and away. Ann stood up and realized she was all a-tremble !

CHAPTER FIFTEEN

SAVE FOR THE BARKING OF THE DOG IN THE STABLES, THE WORLD WAS still as though wrapped in sleep. Ann suddenly became conscious that she was shivering with cold and, with the impetuosity of a child, ran across the room, sprang into her feather bed, pulled the clothes high about her ears and wriggled her feet to warm the sheets. The glow of heat and comfort had scarcely begun to return when she thought of the man who had been wounded. To think was to act. Out of bed she slid and commenced to drag on her stockings and then her outer clothes. She peered through the window. There was no sign of the dark figure crouching painfully on the moonlit grass. Perhaps he had crawled into the bushes and was bleeding to death ! She picked up a pillow-slip which could be torn into bandages and walked to her bedchamber door. Even though he might be an enemy she could not allow him to die, or even to suffer, if her hands could minister comfort. She crept across the landing, noticing as she had done the previous night how the quarrel-pattern of the landing window showed in diamonds of light on the floor. The old, worn, broad boards were prone to creak, especially in dry weather, and she moved with caution. Just as she laid her hand on the banister-rail, a bedroom door swung open noiselessly. A white-shirted figure with a drawn sword stepped forth. She caught her breath in alarm but the gasp turned to one of relief.

"Seth !" she breathed.

"Ann ! Were you disturbed too ? What is it ?"

"Hush ! Come to the dining-room. I have something to tell you."

"Go on down. I will follow you once I have fetched my boots."

Seth joined Ann who stood where a patch of moonlight cut a white strip across the dark room. He still carried his unsheathed sword.

"Well?" he whispered.

"There were two men duelling in the moonlight."

"Ha! Something awakened me. Then the dog barked. You saw them?"

"Plainly."

"How could you? Were you disturbed, too?"

"Yes. I was."

"Could you recognize them?"

"Well, one seemed—I am sure one was Captain Conway."

"The devil. I saw him off the premises. What has he come sneaking back for?"

Ann did not look, but she felt that Seth was staring at her suspiciously. "Let's go and find out," she suggested. With practised hands she unbarred the front door and dropped the chain. Seth followed her as she walked a grassy border to deaden the sound of footfalls. The dog had stopped barking and the world was still. Down the ride which led to the field gate they went and Ann paused where the duel had been, and with Seth at her side looked down upon the trampled grass. There was no sign of the man who had fallen, but on stooping down to examine the place where he had lain, Ann touched the wet grass. On looking at her hand she saw that it was marked by a dark stain. Seth saw it, too, and wiped the blood carefully with his kerchief. Ann gave a little shudder. They walked to the bushes where Ann peered a trifle fearfully, but no body lay in the dew. Then they crossed to the gate and saw where Conway's horse had taken off. They stood beside the white gate and looked at one another.

"There is nothing more we can do," said Ann.

"Then let us go back before we are missed."

They retraced their steps and Ann bolted the door noiselessly.

"Seth!"

"Yes, Ann."

"I—I think we had better say nothing about this."

"I don't know; let's sleep on it."

"Very well. But don't say anything without telling me first. Promise."

"Very well, Ann. I promise."

They tip-toed upstairs.

* * * * *

Breakfast was a silent affair. Ann was pale, for she had slept badly. Seth was moody and heavy-eyed for he had slept not at all.

"Ann," he burst out when the meal was ended, "Ann, what made him come back? I have had it over and over in my brain all night. Ann, he came back to see you. I know it."

"How could you *know* it, Seth?"

She looked at him with something akin to maternal pity in her eyes. He was only a year older than she was, yet he seemed so young that Ann wanted to mother him; and he was so obviously distressed. She looked at him with large, tender eyes, and continued to look at him. He was such a dear boy; not handsome or dashing, but so wholesome, and she knew that he loved her. Ann could not bear to hurt anyone, least of all one whom she cared about, and so she said nothing, until he burst out: "Ann, Ann, you won't lose your precious heart to yon fly-by-night? Tell me, Ann!"

"Hush, Seth, you must not talk like that."

"I know that I have no right, but I love you. And, and he's not worthy of you, Ann."

"How could you say such a thing of the Prince's messenger; besides, how foolishly you talk of love. I regard him as a brave man who risks his life to serve the Prince whom we, too, are pledged to serve."

"Only that, Ann?" Seth's eyes were wistful.

"Come, you had best see Father. He wants you to ride to Wrexham," said Ann rising with a dignity which a queen might well have envied. Seth stood up meekly, miserably. The interview was at an end. The Squire was coming down the staircase when Seth went out into the hall, an imposing, ornate figure in red and gold. Seth waited dutifully until the descent was accomplished.

"Now, boy, ready for the road? Up in the morning early is the maxim. I was up with the lark when I was your age. Now, where did I put that letter for Hughes; let's see. Look in the top of that secretaire. Right first time. Demme, my memory is getting better, or else I didn't put away so much port last night. Now, lad, I've been guarded in what I have written. 'Zounds, need to be with this perishing Major What-is-it on the war-path, but you have my permission to unfold matters to Hughes; in private, mark you. I have told him in the letter that you act for me and know my wishes."

"I will do my best, sir."

"Sure you will; sure you will, and—see here. Where's that girl o' mine?"

"She went out to the stables."

"Might have known it. A word in your ear then. Say nothing to her about this slaving venture."

"Certainly not; not if you do not wish it, sir. Not that I think there is anything discreditable in it."

"Demme, no, I should think not. John Hawkins started it and you could not find a better old sea-dog than John Hawkins. Why, Queen Bess was so delighted that she knighted him for it."

"Well, sir, from what I have read it was hardly that reason. . . ."

"Tut, I don't know what rubbish you lads learn nowadays. Anyhow, keeping slaves was practised in the days of the Bible and you can't improve on that now, can you?"

"Certainly not, sir."

"Matter of fact, St. Paul had a slave; or didn't he?"

"Couldn't say, sir."

"Hum. Have to ask Parson Price. But what I'm coming to is— I don't want Ann to know. She has some queer ideas; all manner

67

of new-fangled notions such a girl should not bother her head about. And I would not like her to think less of her old Dad."

"She'd never do that, sir."

"We'll never give her the chance, lad. Well, off with you."

Seth lingered over the saddling of his mount, hoping for word of Ann, but she was not to be seen and disconsolately he took the road which led to Wrexham. He let his mare take her own pace and rode with loose rein, sombre-eyed.

When Ann left the stables, she felt curiously restless, and in need of someone in whom she could confide. If only she had someone to advise her; someone to whom she could turn! And then the thoughtful brown eyes of Philip Yorke came suddenly to her mind. He seemed so calm and kindly, so reasonable and reliable, and he had been kind over the matter of getting Seth away with the Captain's horse. She turned her steps, a little uncertainly, down the road which led to the old Rectory. Perhaps she would encounter the sombre figure idly strolling along, pausing to examine a hedgerow flower or watch the flight of a bird. But there was no one in sight. At the old Rectory gate she paused and looked about her. No smoke curled from the chimney into the morning air. Feeling as if she did a courageous thing, she walked up to the door and took the big brass knocker in her hand. Her rat-tat sounded loud; it seemed to echo as though through an empty house. She waited. There was no sign or sound from within. Again she knocked and again she waited in vain. Then she walked away with her head held high. She tried to look dignified though there was no one to watch her. The lack of response had hurt her; it seemed like an affront; as though she had asked for something and had met with a rebuff.

Of course it was silly, she told herself, because after all, if Mr. Philip Yorke was not at home, he was not at home, and that was all there was to it. She walked briskly hoping no one had noticed where she had been.

When she reached the drive Hughie told her that Mr. Morrice had ridden off for Wrexham and that the Squire had gone to the Home Farm. Ann felt aggrieved at being left alone. This, also, was silly, for really she desired to be alone.

"Oh, dear, what's come over me?" she said addressing a chaffinch who regarded her with a beady eye. "I don't seem a bit like me to-day." She picked up a fallen stick and began to swish the long grasses as she walked between the trees. Her eyes were attracted to the white gate which Captain Conway had leaped so neatly only a few hours before. The scene of the fight attracted her, drew her like a magnet draws steel, and she turned thither, still swishing the grasses. Once again she stared down at the trampled grass. She saw the blood stains because she knew where to look, but already they were becoming less conspicuous. Then a dark object attracted her attention. Ann walked quickly to where it lay and picked it up. It was a black crêpe mask.

The empty eye-holes seemed to gaze enigmatically at her as she held it in her hand wonderingly. Which of the fighters had dropped it ? Captain Conway had not worn one when he bade her adieu—but perhaps he chose to ride masked.

The sound of hoofs caused her to turn and she thrust the ominous black mask into the bosom of her dress. A woman on a high-stepping bay was trotting up the drive; a woman in a dark blue riding habit; a woman who rode with vigorous ease.

Ann remembered that her father was absent and walked to meet the newcomer. She found herself being examined coolly and critically by a pair of bold and haughty eyes. From her superior height the horsewoman talked down to Ann as if she were a child.

"Hello. You must be Ann Trevor. I have heard of you. Know me?"

"I'm afraid I don't."

"Must have heard of me. I'm Frances Holt. This was my home till the old fool who sired me lost too much at the tables and had to sell up to pay his debts. Demme, I've no patience with a gambler who can't win."

"I am sure we are pleased to have you return to your old home," said Ann politely.

"More than I am. No pleasure in being reminded of one's folly." She turned her head. "That used to be my room," she added, nodding upwards. "Lud, it seems an age since I dreamed dreams of innocence in my chaste bed."

"I sleep there now."

"Well, I didn't ride over to discuss our respective bedchambers. I heard Dicon was over. Is that so?"

"Dicon?" said Ann, looking plainly puzzled.

"Dicon Conway; Dick Conway. Don't say you haven't heard of him? One of my gossips swore she had seen him in these parts."

"Oh, you mean Captain Conway?"

"He's Captain Conway now, is he? Lud, he was ever ambitious. Has he taken to soldiering, or is the 'captain' merely assumed to cut a dash in your eyes."

"I don't know what you mean," said Ann flushing, but perhaps she did.

"Anyhow, where is the slippery blade? He's plaguy elusive. Taken me a long time to run him to earth but now I have, he'll not shake me off so easily. Is he inside?"

"He is not here."

"Come, come, no lies. He was seen coming to this very house last night."

"Lies!" Ann's head went back proudly. "I think you forget yourself."

"You give yourself airs, you little fool. Answer me, is Dicon Conway in this house?"

"I decline to answer."

"You shall answer. You shall tell me."

Ann turned haughtily on her heel and walked with regal dignity towards the porch where Hughie, who had been brushing the drive, stood with a besom in his hand.

"Damn you! Will you turn your back on me?" cried the horse-

69

woman furiously and wrenching at her horse's bit, she urged it towards the unsuspecting Ann. Miss Holt swung her whip over her head but it never fell on Ann. With a yell, partly of warning, partly of rage, Hughie sprang forward and intercepted the cut with his upstretched arms. At the cry of pain which was wrung from him by the keenness of the blow, Ann leaped, eyes agleam, furious as a mother protecting her young. Her angry hands wrenched the whip from Miss Holt and with a quick cut she sent the restive bay backing and plunging so that Miss Holt had her work cut out to bring it under control. Ann and Hughie hurried to the protection of the porch as the steel-shod hoofs flashed in the air.

"Curse you!" shouted the irate rider. A lock of hair had come loose in the struggle and floated, witch-like, behind her. "You shall be sorry for this day's work."

Without another glance at Ann, she wrenched her steed about and set its head for the white gate. Down the ride she galloped, the flying hoofs showering clods of earth as they swept over the turf. Then she, too, cleared the five-bar, her horse's hoofs all but placed in the very marks which Captain Conway made when he leaped in the moonlight.

Ann, flushed of face and with heaving breast, watched her vanish behind the grove of trees, and then she turned to Hughie who was nursing his weals and endeavouring to stifle tears.

"Oh, Hughie," said Ann, anger submerged in a rush of pity.

"I'd do more and welcome for you, Mistress Ann," he said shakily.

CHAPTER SIXTEEN

IT IS ONLY BECAUSE EXCITEMENT IS SPASMODIC THAT IT IS EXCITEMENT, but Ann's philosophy (which, it must be confessed, was governed by emotions, rather than reason) failed to carry her thus far, and so, having tasted excitement and found it infinitely to her liking, she eagerly awaited more. When none was forthcoming and the days began to drag through their monotonous round just as they did before the coming of the Prince's messenger, Ann found herself beset by a restlessness hitherto foreign to her nature. Before Captain Conway's arrival she had not found the days tedious or her life monotonous. There was always something to be done: the Home Farm to be visited where there were lambs and calves and chicks waiting to be exclaimed over; or there were the aged and infirm of the parish to be called upon; or, best of all, the stables to be lingered in, until her father's strident voice from the porch sent her hurrying back to her neglected household duties. Undoubtedly there had been plenty to occupy the time. And now, having tasted the heady wine of romance, she found these erstwhile pleasurable and innocuous occupations insipid in comparison. She went to her bed not drowsily but wakefully, and lay with eyes closed but ears alert and waiting, waiting (she would never have confessed it!), waiting for the rattle of gravel on the window pane. But none came, and as spring began to merge into summer, sadly and regretfully she relegated the exciting events of those few hectic days to the archives of memory and set about her accustomed round with something of her customary brightness.

Save for faithful Seth, all the actors of the drama had vanished. It was as though they had never been. She knew nothing, nothing at all. That was what troubled her. If only she could have obtained a little news, a mere fragment of gossip, it would have gratified, if not satisfied, her. She did not know whether Captain Conway had fled the country. She did not know whether Lieutenant Peris had been successful in obtaining the vessel in which the arms were to be fetched from Brittany. She did not know whether Bonnie Prince Charlie had sailed. She did not know what had happened to that objectionable woman who had caused a scene. She did not know what had become of Philip Yorke.

"I know nothing, nothing whatever," she complained in an aggrieved tone as she confided her troubles in Black Prince's sympathetic ear. "It's plaguy annoying, but I don't know what we can do about it. And I'm so disappointed, Princie. You see, my beauty, I was not intended for a stay-at-home. I want to ride behind Bonnie Prince Charlie's banner and,—Oh, you're not a bit interested. Your mind doesn't soar above oats, and I won't give you a handful more no, not if the house was full."

She patted his glossy neck more vigorously than was her wont as a means of relieving her repressed feelings. Then she set off along the road which led past the old Rectory. This, she frequently assured herself, was merely because it was a convenient place to walk. She neither expected nor wanted to encounter Mr. Yorke. All the same, it would be interesting to know—just casually—whether he had returned. She wondered where he had been, and then told herself she was not in the least interested.

As though to prove to herself that she really meant what she said—or, at any rate, thought—she turned about and walked home briskly.

"Where is my father, Morgan?" she inquired as she threw her hat on to a chair in the hall.

"In the library, Mistress Ann, with Lawyer Hughes."

"What, again? Oh, bother. That means he will not want to be disturbed. Having to think about business matters is always a strain on him."

A step on the gravel outside caused Ann to walk to the door. It might be Seth, she thought, and while she did not encourage Seth the lover, Seth the friend of her childhood was an ever-welcome means of whiling away tedious hours. But it was not Seth. The man was a stranger, neatly dressed in a royal blue coat with silver buttons, and though he wore no uniform his shoulders were square and his back as straight as though he had a board for a spine. He had a hard, weather-tanned, stern (almost brutal) face, but he saluted Ann with deference and spoke with respect.

"Your pardon, Ma'am, I take it I address Mistress Ann Trevor?"

"That is my name. May I ask yours and inquire why you seek me?"

71

"Your servant, Ma'am. Caradoc Keene at your service, Master-at-Arms attached to His Majesty's Twenty-Third Regiment of Foot. Newly come from the Low Countries."

"Indeed,—I do not know the correct way of addressing a Master-at-Arms of His Majesty's Twenty-Third Regiment of Foot!"

"Just plain Mr. Keene, Ma'am, I being off duty, as it were, and having discarded my rank with my uniform."

"And you wish to see me?"

"At the suggestion of Mr. Philip Yorke, Ma'am."

"Mr. Yorke? Has he . . . Has he returned?"

"This very morning, and me with him. By post-chaise from Shrewsbury. He sent me to acquaint you; but maybe the news has reached you of our reverse in the Low Countries? The Squire, maybe, has received a news-letter setting forth the details of the great battle?"

"Battle? Indeed, no; we have heard nothing. Did I hear you refer to a reverse?"

"A sad set-back to British arms, Ma'am. It was near the village of Fontenoy where on May the eleventh our troops, in company with the Dutch, some Austrian cavalry and other Continentals, set forth to attack a superior enemy in a position deemed unassailable. His Royal 'Ighness, the Duke o' Cumberland, officer commanding, though being exposed to a cross-fire from the French, resolved on a daring attack which he pressed home with such resolution that the French were panic-stricken and old Marshal Saxe gave orders for retreat. If the Dutch had moved to our aid, or the Austrian cavalry made but a single charge, the day was ours. It was the brigade of Irish who were our undoing."

"Irish?" reiterated Ann, puzzled.

"Catholic exiles in French pay. 'Why not bring cannon to bear on them?' suggested Lally, their commander, to Saxe, which he did and smote us so sorely that fearful breaches were made and the tide of battle turned. A charge by the Irish brigade beat us back, though the Duke brought us safely to the strong walls of Ath."

"So our army was defeated!" said Ann, a little awed. "It was kind of you, nevertheless, to come here to acquaint me with the news, sad though it is. Is—is that all you have to say?"

"Well, Ma'am, yes and no. I should prefer if you saw Mr. Yorke for any further news. In fact, he asked me to escort you to him if you would be so good."

Ann looked at her visitor keenly and a little of the colour left her face. "The Twenty-Third was engaged. Were—were any people from this district killed?"

"Ma'am, it was Mr. Yorke's request that you would come to see him."

"I will go alone," said Ann resolutely. "Remain here and give your tidings to Squire Trevor. Morgan, see that Mr. Keene receives refreshment."

Ann seized her bonnet and hurried to the road. When intent on accomplishing anything she gave no thought to decorum. She ran part of the way. The door of the old Rectory stood open and as she approached, a voice, now familiar, greeted her.

"Walk in, Ann."

She did so and beheld Philip Yorke seated in a comfortable chair. "Forgive my abominable discourtesy in not rising to greet you," he said with a quiet smile.

"You have been ill?" she said quickly. "You look pale."

"Not ill. A slight accident to my leg. It mends rapidly and before long I shall be hopping about as merry as a sparrow."

"I am sorry."

"Sorry I shall be hopping about again?"

"You deliberately choose to misunderstand me, Mr. Yorke. But you did not send for me to bandy pleasantries. Your messenger, Mr. Keene, brings word of a grievous defeat at Fontenoy. The Twenty-Third Foot were engaged. Tell me . . . have we lost anyone I know?"

"I cannot deny it, Ann. Your womanly intuition has saved me the difficult preliminaries. Your friend, Captain Berners, was killed."

Ann took a deep breath. She did not cry, though her fixed look seemed to indicate that tears were not far below the surface. She sat without speaking.

"He was a courageous and capable officer," added Yorke gently.

"He did not have to die for men to praise him," replied Ann. "I am thinking of his wife and two young daughters. How they will miss him. I can see his brown eyes, brave, eloquent and yet amazingly gentle. He was so kind and courteous. He called to bid us farewell before he left to join his regiment. What happened?"

"He was cut asunder by a cannon-ball."

"How terrible. The Master-at-Arms who called described how the cannon were turned on the massed British ranks when the battle seemed won."

"Turned at the suggestion of Irish Catholic exiles who followed it up with a charge which won the day for the French."

"There is bitterness in your tone!"

"They are the men who would place James the Third back on the throne of this country—if they could."

"Oh, I think not."

"If you said you did not think, it would be nearer the mark. I do not wish to hurt your feelings, Ann, but I cannot imagine that you have given profound thought to the cause you are so gaily espousing."

"Oh, but I have."

"Then you would like to see this a Catholic country?"

"Don't be absurd. I am a loyal member of the Church of England."

"James the Second was chased out of the country for trying to force us to accept Rome."

"Ah, but this is different."

"I fail to see it. His son, whom you call James the Third, lives in Rome and is frankly more interested in his religion than in politics."

"Anyhow, it would be preferable to have a good English king on the throne of England to a German."

"So you follow Bonnie Prince Charlie?"

"Yes, what a King he will make."

"I understand that he dances excellently."

73

Ann looked at him sharply. She thought she could discern the light flicking in those grave eyes, but she was not sure.

"At least he is a good Englishman."

"He has a good English name. Also a Polish mother."

"I wish you had not an answer to everything I say, Mr. Yorke. But no matter what you say I shall go on my own way. I'm for the gallant Stuarts. Hey! for the White Cockade! I believe you only talk as you do to try to reveal how little I know."

"Truly I wish you knew more. A little knowledge is a dangerous thing—in politics. I wish you would study more about the cause you espouse: or, better still, I wish you would leave it alone entirely."

"That I never shall. I was not cut out for books. I prefer a horse and a flashing blade. Do you know, I thought more highly of you, Mr. Yorke, when it came out that you had fought at Dettingen."

"Made a poor show of it, I fear. Anyhow, I've beaten my sword into a ploughshare—or nearly so."

"Now what do you mean by 'nearly so'?"

"I talk too much. Give me your arm, Ann, and help me to the harpsichord. It is time we let Purcell speak for us. To-day, we have nearly disagreed, which is unthinkable. Let Purcell restore—harmony."

He settled himself, a trifle stiffly, on the music stool and his firm white fingers ran over the keys. Ann stood with her hand on the top of the instrument, listening silently, watching intently the absorbed look on Philip Yorke's face. Politics had ceased to interest him. He was safe on neutral ground. "Play me the piece I love so well," she coaxed, "and tell me its name."

He shook his head.

"Have you a reason for withholding the name, Mr. Yorke?"

"It is better nameless. So listen, Ann, to one who is greater than Charles Edward who is but a Stuart Prince. Purcell is a Prince of Musicians!"

Never before had Ann succumbed so to the spell of music. It enraptured her. Hitherto, flowers had been her most beautiful, most appealing source of sensuous delight. Now music added its magic. Some of the chords stirred her emotions until she felt she could have wept from sheer happiness. Music was to her ears what flowers were to her eyes and nose. Perhaps Philip Yorke had discovered the association. There was always a bowl of flowers on the polished table near the harpsichord. Her eyes rested on these, a cluster of pinks, homely blooms from a country garden. For the rest of her life she associated the fragrance of clove-pinks with Purcell.

Philip Yorke stopped playing and sat with bowed head, his fingers resting motionless on the dumb keys. He sighed and rose slowly to his feet.

"I am in no mood for music to-day," he said, as though apologizing.

"Oh, but you played exquisitely. I could listen for ever."

He shook his head. "I sought consolation but did not find it. The mood communicates itself to the finger-tips. To-day my emotions clash. There is turmoil within me. Dear girl, truly I desire to help

74

you. I advise you for the best; for your good. You do believe me, Ann?" He took one of her small hands in his and looked at it. "Those little fingers are too tender to be burnt in the political flame. Keep them for your flowers and your horses, I beg."

Ann pulled away her hand. "If you talk like that I must leave you. Indeed, it is time for me to go."

"Leave it alone, Ann."

"If you are trying to turn me from my loyalty to the Stuarts, you waste your time."

"So you hold with the tenet of the divine right of kings?"

"I don't know what you mean, quite. England belongs to King James."

"I had no idea! You astound me, Ann. Do you know, in my ignorance I imagined it belonged to the people of England."

"The people? You mean the common people?"

"I mean all the people, the rich and the poor ; the strong and the weak; the good and the bad."

"But many of them are—oh, horrible. They are not—not fit to——"

"To live in palaces and wear fine raiment? But why not educate them and teach them to become so?"

"They—they could not understand. The land must be owned by the gentry. They know how to manage it."

"Do they? Some may do. Others take their comfort and look upon their servants as superior cattle."

"How hateful. I am sure we treat our servants most kindly."

"You treat your horses kindly."

"Our servants never complain."

"Dare they? You speak of treating them well. Where do they spend their time? Segregated from the rest of the house, big though it is. Their days are spent in underground basements, little better than cellars, and when they desire to sleep, they crawl up by way of back stairs to stuffy or draughty attics. It's good enough for them."

Ann was looking thoughtful. Then she shrugged her shoulders. "But what has this to do with Prince Charles Edward, I would like to know!"

"Think it out for yourself, Ann. *Noblesse oblige.* The king should be the true leader of his people, the father of a national family, desirous of their good, not regarding them as a means of providing him with luxury and pleasure, because he claims—save the mark !—that he holds his power direct from God. The first to promulgate this exalted doctrine was that erudite pantaloon, James the First. His father was a rake called Darnley, and I fail utterly to trace deification in such an ancestry."

"Nothing you say will change me, Mr. Yorke. I'm for the Stuarts."

"But why, Ann?"

"It means—Romance !"

"There is nothing in Romance. Romance is just—moonshine."

"I am but half your age, Mr. Yorke, and therefore we cannot be expected to see alike."

She saw his eyes intent on her. When he spoke his voice was curiously restrained. "I am twice your age. How true it is. Adieu, Ann. You will come to see me again one day, I trust. And we will try to avoid politics and talk of music and flowers. I spoke truer than I knew. Romance is—moonshine!"

CHAPTER SEVENTEEN

JUNE WAS NEARING ITS END; THE ROSES WERE ABLOOM AND THE RHYTHMIC sweep of the scythes told that hay-cutting had commenced. And yet there was no word of the cargo of arms which was to have been run to the cave in the Ormeshead. The vessel with Lieutenant Peris in charge had left Liverpool port long since; that much Squire Trevor had learnt from his agents. But that was all he knew. That was all anyone knew. Couriers were few, and frequently what information was received came fortuitously from passers-by. The Squire was restless, more irascible, more prone to turn to the port bottle. There seemed, he asserted, less enthusiasm for the Stuart cause than there was in the 'Fifteen. However, Lawyer Hughes had been able to arrange a mortgage and the money was available, in hard cash, ready for his Royal Highness when he chose to put in an appearance. Rumours from London were that the King of France was holding aloof, not so much from lack of sympathy as from a general disinclination to make closer acquaintance with the British Fleet which kept close watch in the Channel.

Now that Mr. Yorke had returned, the old Rectory took on more animation than had been noticeable before his mysterious departure. For one thing, Caradoc Keene, Master-at-Arms, remained as his guest for several weeks—an unusual visitor, people in the village remarked, for one of Mr. Philip Yorke's studious tastes. Mr. Yorke was about again now, with a suspicion of a limp, perhaps, but otherwise quite his usual self. Once, when Ann passed by his barn, she heard the Master-at-Arms' curt voice declaiming: "tierce" . . . "riposte", which made Ann wonder if Mr. Keene was a conscientious man who practised his strange craft even when he was on vacation. Curious as a child, she walked to the barn and opened the door. The creak of the hinge caused two men to turn. Both were in shirts and breeches and had foils in their hands. The Master-at-Arms frowned at the interruption, but Mr. Yorke dropped his point and bowed with an easy grace.

"Oh," said Ann, "I am intruding."

"Yes, Mistress, you interrupt a lesson," said Caradoc Keene bluntly. "There was a time when Mr. Yorke was one of the finest swordsmen in the Army. Why, Ma'am, such an adept was he that men found it a positive pleasure to be pinked by him. But he grows stale and his wrist stiffens. I fear that he is more partial to that jangling musical intrument than he is to the rare art of fence."

"But surely you cannot blame him? And what use now has Mr. Yorke for a sword? Personally I adore the harpsichord and . . .

76

and . . . but it is desirable that a man should wield a sword, too, in these uncertain days, so pray proceed."

"What is it you want of me, Ann?" asked Philip Yorke quietly.

"I did but look in in passing, but now I am here, do let me watch."

"No, Ann. 'Tis no pastime for young women."

"Please?"

But he shook his head. Caradoc Keene, Master-at-Arms, came to the rescue of his favourite pupil. "Well, Mistress, it is like this; he could not, at the moment, do himself justice. His left thigh is still somewhat stiff from his wound."

Philip Yorke tried to catch the eye of the Master-at-Arms but his warning glance went unnoticed. Ann's eyes grew large with surprise. She was conscious of an increase in her heart-beat as the duel in the moonlight leaped to her mind. She steadied her voice and remarked, "Wounded? Oh, were you wounded, Mr. Yorke? I am so sorry. You told me that you had been hurt."

"The description was not inaccurate."

"Yes, I am sure it must have hurt, hurt terribly."

"My body did not suffer so much as my pride."

"So you see, Mistress," interposed Mr. Keene, "Mr. Yorke, hearing I was come home from the Low Countries, invited me to holiday with him (for a consideration, of course, Ma'am, him being a gentleman of generous disposition) so that he will give a better account of himself when next they meet."

"When next—they—meet!" Ann repeated the words haltingly.

"Come, Master-at-Arms, you are disturbing Miss Trevor needlessly. I fear our conversation has drifted into an unpleasant channel. I pray you forget it, Ann. Shall we go to the music-room?"

"No, I must go. Another time. Please resume." She walked to the door, anxious to escape from a situation which had suddenly grown embarrassing. Philip Yorke held the door open, watching her gravely until she reached the gate. She turned and waved him adieu. Then he shut the door.

"Keene, you talk too much. You are not among your pupils in your fencing-school. I pay you to sharpen up my swordsmanship, not to embarrass my guests." Yorke spoke curtly, and the burly Master-at-Arms turned restlessly before his piercing eye.

"Come now, sir, there's no harm done by a few pleasantries."

"There is more harm done than you know. You have rendered me a disservice."

"Then, sir, all I can say is that I am sorry. You have been generous to me, treated me handsome, and far be it from me to render ill for good, though I'm quick enough to render ill for ill as you know. Still, I cannot see how a few words with a young lady can do harm. She will think the better of you for knowing you were one of the best blades in the Army; take my word for it."

"We will not discuss the matter further. What has been said has been said, and there is no gainsaying it. Put the foils away. I am in no mood for further practice."

Philip Yorke picked up his coat and walked across to the house with it over his arm. He stood for a while staring out of the window and then turned to the harpsichord. His fingers strayed casually over the keys, picking out chord after chord without sequence. He was agitated but like many highly-strung persons he disliked to reveal his emotions and fought inwardly to acquire an outward appearance of calm. He began to play and found solace in the soft and soothing sounds. So engrossed was he in his music that he failed to hear the arrival of a horse, until a shout from without brought him to his feet. It was a woman's voice. But the tones were strange and a trifle strident. A look of annoyance crossed his features but this vanished almost instantly, for Philip Yorke had trained himself with the assiduity of a diplomat to conceal his feelings. He crossed to the open door. A woman in a blue riding habit was dismounting from a foam-flecked bay. She tossed her reins to Caradoc Keene with a curt "Attend to this brute," and walked away before the amazed Master-at-Arms could find appropriate words in which to express his astonishment. Mr. Yorke bowed slightly as she approached.

"I'm Frances Holt," she said, slapping her riding-crop against her boot. "May I come in? I've come to see you."

"By all means; please enter." He led the way, not to the room where the harpsichord stood, but to a small parlour.

Miss Holt seated herself without invitation and tossed her hat on to a table. "It's as hot as the pit," she asserted.

"A cooling drink, perhaps?" suggested Mr. Yorke.

"Yes, I could do with one. But I've come to talk, not to drink. You've heard of me?"

"I have heard your name mentioned, Miss Holt."

"As a hoyden, I'll warrant; a shrew, a termagant."

"None of those names were mentioned in my hearing, Miss Holt."

"Lud, man, you're gallant—or discreet! Don't strive to spare my feelings. They're as hard as my horse's mouth."

"His mouth was not always hard; it's the way he's been ridden."

Miss Holt set down her glass and leaned forward in her chair. "By gad, you've hit the nail clean on the head." She stared at him shrewdly. "Was there a double meaning to your words? Eh? Do y' insinuate that I was not always hard? Can you read character so quickly, or is it but a random shot?"

"As you press me, I should say you were not averse to posing, Miss Holt. It was you, if you recollect, who used the words hoyden and termagant."

"Huh!" Miss Holt sipped her glass and regarded Philip Yorke dubiously. "You are too suave for me. I speak my mind. Don't you believe in people speaking their mind?"

"If they have a mind to speak."

"Demme, that's something else I could take two ways. Well, it will do me good to cross swords with you, for, egad, there are so many mutton-heads in these parts that what is left of my brain is nigh atrophied."

"You have not told me yet why you have honoured me with a

visit, Miss Holt. I presume you are the Miss Holt who formerly lived at the Plas?"

"You presume right. The whole estate was mine by right but my fool of a father gambled it away at Wills's Coffee House in a single night. Curse the dolt."

"You have my sympathy. And the reason for your visit is . . .?"

"Demme, you tie a body down to hard facts. Quite right, too. We must join forces."

"Join forces?"

"Work together. Help one another. Put it how you will."

"I am at your service, Miss Holt, but I cannot help feeling that I might be of greater use to you were you more explicit."

"It's Dicon. We must clip his wings. The cock crows too loud. Demme, he's become unbearable; intolerable."

"You distress me. And who might Dicon be?"

"Gad, you should know. I mean Dicon Conway; he who calls himself Captain, now; save the expression. You should know Dicon, God wot, seeing he ran you through the thigh."

"Indeed. You appear to have acquired certain interesting information, Miss Holt. You are well informed."

"I deserve to be. It is little money I get from that spendthrift parent of mine, but most of it goes to reimburse informers. I like to know what goes on, Mr. Yorke, and 'tis more than womanly curiosity. Tell me, is it true Dicon had a ladder to her window? My watcher could not see clearly by reason of the shadow, but such he surmised."

"Her window?"

"Come, come, you are not so dense as you pretend. You found him going by stealth to call on her and lay in wait. Hell's furies, could anything be more exasperating? For three years he has deserted me. Never so much as a scratch of a quill have I had. Then, when he comes back he goes to the old room and—finds it occupied by that pale-faced chit."

"Surely it is obvious that he was unaware that the house had changed hands?"

"On the occasion of his first visit, I grant you. Scarcely the second. He is absent-minded, is Dicon, but his aberration would scarce carry him so far."

"I am given to understand that Miss Trevor's interest in Captain Conway derives from her admiration of the Young Chevalier."

"Lud, man, your delicacy of thought does more justice to your chivalry than your intelligence."

"It is my fortune to know Miss Trevor."

"It is my misfortune to know Dicon Conway."

Miss Holt walked to the sideboard and helped herself to a glass of wine. "Come, this sort of talk gets us nowhere. It was not the desire to bandy words that brought me here. I tell you we must join forces."

"Must, Miss Holt?"

"Ay, must. See here. I am jealous of Dicon and would have my revenge. You're the lad to help me. He pays court to that young hussy and I'm jealous; you are jealous, too."

79

"My dear Miss Holt, jealousy is the most primitive and puerile of passions."

"If you don't feel jealous, your actions belie you. Why lie in wait for Dicon and attempt to take his life?"

"Merely as a warning that he must conduct himself with greater propriety when associating with that estimable if impetuous and impressionable young lady."

"Bah! It amounts to the same thing. Let's call it jealousy; I can't lay tongue to your fine phrases. You will admit that they see too much of each other?"

"Possibly, but permit me to observe, Miss Holt, that I fail to see why you should consult me. I am a man who is accustomed to plough a lone furrow. I find that temperamentally I am not suited to the company of my fellows. So I remain alone."

"So do I. Yet two heads are better than one. I'll be more frank with you. You insinuated that my mouth was not always hard. Time was when I was as tender a maid as—well, as this wench you profess to admire so disinterestedly. Then Dicon Conway played me false. Love to hatred turned! Don't preach to me about loving your enemies. My one desire in life is to get even with that devil. I'll clip his spurs. He's a rare lad, is Dicon, and he can win over most women with that gay devilry of his. He made this district too hot to hold him ere he fled to France. He's a trusted servant of Charles Edward now; full of nobility and loyalty I've no doubt, though I fancy there is either money or a knighthood in the background to tempt Dicon to risk his neck. Give the devil his due, he took a chance when he came back to his old haunts. It's the devil's luck which usually comes my way that I missed seeing him."

"So you still love him?" Mr. Yorke's tone was quiet.

"Love him? Hate him like hell."

"Then why be jealous."

"Egad, I am not jealous."

"But a moment since you assured me that you were."

"I'm a dog in the manger. If I cannot have Dicon, no other woman shall. So you'll find me a staunch ally. There's another reason, you are for the House of Hanover."

"Am I?"

"It is obvious. Well, I'm no Jacobite. I might be if there was anything to be had out of it. My father is apathetic, and I've no fondness for the beer-swilling little German you Whigs have imported, but I'd work in his interests right royally if it would put a spoke in Dicon's wheel."

"It is refreshing to meet one of your candour in these days of dissembling."

"Lud, I wish you were more candid. I don't know yet for sure whether you are Hanoverian."

"I am a loyal subject of His Majesty."

"Then you'd fight the Stuart?"

"If I am not too busy fighting a greater enemy."

"A greater? You mean, France?"

"No, I mean ignorance."

"Lud, man, you mystify me. I'm for fighting the Stuarts for by so doing I strike at that faithless rogue Dicon. If they invade, as rumour has it they are like to do, you will draw the sword against them?"

"I should prefer to fight them with a more deadly weapon."

"More deadly?" inquired Miss Holt in surprise and then burst into laughter as Philip Yorke held up a pen.

"Education," he said, balancing the quill in neat fingers, "is likely to settle their business. An enlightened man will not support the tenet of the divine right of kings. When they are enlightened they will learn something of the divine right of the people. Let us start by doing away with squalor, gin-drinking, footpadding. Give the people an incentive, an impetus, and they will redouble their efforts to provide a home for themselves and a future for their children. They will not run as fools to be mown down for a Stuart's vanity as were the Welsh pikemen at Edgehill. Already the people begin to think for themselves. Squire Trevor and his neighbours count on their tenantry marching forth with due docility at their bidding when Charles Edward comes over the border. But we shall see! I am sowing seed and I hope to be spared to see the garnering of the harvest."

"'Zounds, man, I never thought of it in this light. Demme, it tickles my fancy to think of you wrecking Dicon's plans with a dominie's slate. It will puzzle Dicon's rapier to get under that guard. You'll prove a queer and awkward partner."

"We are not going to be partners, Miss Holt."

"But I thought, I imagined . . . Demme, don't tell me you turn my offer down?"

"I prefer to hunt alone."

"But why?"

"You have been frank with me; I will be equally so with you. You have spoken disrespectfully of Miss Trevor. I tell you candidly that because of that there could be no question of our joining forces. You ask me if I serve the House of Hanover. I answer you by saying that I serve Miss Trevor, with my brain, my sword, my life."

"Man, you're mad. You are twice her age. She would never give you a passing thought. Well, they say there's no fool like an old one."

"I am indifferent to what they say, Miss Holt. I am accustomed to going my own way; I shall continue to do so. So there is no reason why you should pursue the matter further."

"You—you turn me down?" The hard look returned to her eyes. She rose and stood slapping her riding-boot nervously with her crop. Then she said almost plaintively, "You—you won't betray me?"

"Rest assured that your confidences will be respected, Miss Holt. Nay, more, let me assure you of a certain sympathy I feel for you in your distress. Should it rest in my power to aid you, provided it does not clash with the interests of the one I serve, it shall be my privilege to do so. But we cannot, as you suggest, join forces. I work alone."

81

"Damnation, I'm disappointed, plaguy disappointed. Well, you've been candid and there's no harm done."

"None whatever; I am sure I wish you well, Miss Holt."

"And I wish you luck, though the best thing I could wish you is to be free of Ann Trevor. There's nothing so heart-sickening in life as to love a person who does not return that love."

"On the contrary, Miss Holt, there is such a thing as a love which finds expression in service and asks no return."

"Huh!" said Miss Holt sceptically as she walked to the door. "I wonder! Well, I've drawn blank, but I admire the way you take your fences. I'll give you a word in due season. Dicon's expecting to land a shipload of arms off the Ormeshead when the moon is full. Profit by it, if you can. You'd have found me a useful ally, but go your own way. Good luck to you."

She strode into the yard and called for her horse.

CHAPTER EIGHTEEN

SQUIRE TREVOR WAS DOZING IN HIS CHAIR WHEN ANN WALKED RESO-lutely into the room and startled him wide awake.

"Father, I am going to ride to the Ormeshead."

"Eh, what's this? Why? What's the matter? Has the ship arrived with the arms?"

"No."

"Then what is the sense of your going?"

"Because I want to find out. I want to be there when she arrives. There's no sense in waiting here until the fun's all over, and then hearing about it. I want to be on the spot when the cargo is brought ashore."

"You're mad, girl. And demme, I can't see where the fun comes in."

"That's because you're getting so old and respectable, darling. If you were my age you'd be in this business right up to your neck, now, wouldn't you?"

"Don't talk nonsense. How'll y' go, anyway? Will you take young Seth along? Don't approve of young women riding abroad without protection."

"Hughie will be my escort. He's growing into a fine, sturdy youth."

"Too young. Better take Seth."

"He'd only want to make love to me and I've no time to be bothered with that. I want to see these arms safely housed. We'll bring them here by the old packhorse road."

"What's that? Bring 'em here? Why here, of all places? Demmed risky, that."

"If you're going to start getting cautious we'll never get anywhere. The Black Barn is hardly ever used and it would be just the place to conceal the muskets."

"Don't like it, girl. It needs careful thinking out."

"No it doesn't. It is all thought out. We can't leave the arms in a cove in the Orme. They'd be too far off to be any use. Here is the place. It's ideal. Close to the border so that we can be over into Shropshire if we find the Prince comes that way."

"Maybe you're right. Ann, girl, I haven't as much nerve as I used to have. I'm all for the Young Chevalier, but demme, when I think of the risks we run I'm uneasy in my mind."

"Then just leave everything to me and you stay quietly at home. Now I'll go and warn Hughie to get ready. I shall ride Black Prince. He's not getting enough exercise these days; he's as corpulent as an alderman. And I shall want some money, darling."

"Oh, yes, you want money," grumbled the Squire as he fumbled for his keys.

"Now you can't accuse me of extravagance! No man was ever blessed with a more economic daughter. And in any case, it is not for me, but for the Prince."

"Shut the door, Ann. There's a secret panel in the wainscoting here. I've never shown you how it works, but you may as well know now. Put your fingers under the end of the mantel. Feel that crevice? There's a spring concealed there. Press hard."

With a soft click one of the panels moved slightly and the Squire prised it open and lifted a small iron box from the cavity. This he stood on the table almost reverently, regarding it for a moment ere he inserted a key in the lock. When the lid was opened, Ann found it filled with golden coins. With deliberation the Squire counted out twenty guineas and handed them to his daughter. Ann kissed him with excitement aroused by the occasion and ran upstairs with her handful of gold, leaving her father to replace his treasure in its hiding place.

There was activity at the stables when she emerged to give her orders. Hughie was to ride Starlight, and a sturdy cob was harnessed to carry her valise. This seemed to the Squire unnecessary until Ann pointed out that there would almost certainly be a shortage of pack-horses and that the cob would be useful for bringing back a load of arms. Ann thrust pistols into her holsters and Hughie, to his delight, was equipped with pistols and a sword. Ann made a pretty picture as she rode the high black horse from the stable-yard, followed by her young retainer on Starlight, holding the rein of the led-horse. She waved a gay farewell to her father who stood watching her with a blend of anxiety and fondness in his eyes. This time Ann was careful to take a road which did not lead past the old Rectory.

Once clear of the park Ann stopped for a consultation as to the better road to take. Should it be by way of Mold or Ruthin? Hughie favoured Ruthin, so Ann resolved to ride to Mold. The weather was at its best and there was no hardship occasioned by the ride save what was due to heat and flies. These petty discomforts meant little to either rider. Thus they rode, gay of heart, eager for adventure, and when none came their way they felt a touch of disappointment. The land was quiet. There were haymakers in the meadows, and in the hamlet gardens men delved in the good soil, women spread newly-washed clothes to dry on the bushes, and children played in the roadway, pausing to gaze curiously as the riders passed by. Ann could not help but think that these homely persons appeared little interested in the aspirations of princes or the tenet of the divine right of kings.

At the Mold cross-roads they paused and Hughie looked down the road to Nerquis. "There's an old tower down there," he said slowly. "I've seen it once when I come this far with Master Howells, who was for buying a gelding at the fair. It's that old that there was fighting there in the Wars of the Roses. The folk captured the Mayor of Chester when he was at Mold Fair, and hanged him to a staple in the hall. I'd like to have that staple."

"What a cruel-minded wretch you are, Hughie. Have done with such thoughts. They ought to run on peace on a day like this."

"There'll be more murders and blood-lettings afore long, Mistress Ann, if they try to force a Popish prince on our country."

"Why, Hughie, what do you mean?"

"Ay, I've heard talk, Mistress Ann. And you do know that things be stirring, for all your innocent look. Where do we go with this led-horse, and for why, I'm wondering."

Ann sat in the hot sunlight while Black Prince fidgeted impatiently and her thoughts seemed far away.

"Who taught you to think thus?" she finally inquired.

"It's Mr. Yorke told me, Mistress Ann. He is afeared that harm may come to the people of this land."

"He had best not tamper with your allegiance. If he tries to turn you against me, Hughie, I shall hate him."

"'Taint likely he'll turn anyone against you, Mistress Ann."

"He shall not tamper with our servants; I'll not tolerate it."

"What he does is for the best. I've never seen a man so set on helping others and making the world better."

"Bah!" quoth Ann, quoting her father. "The man's a reformer."

"Not before it's time," added Hughie stoutly.

His young mistress turned and regarded him wonderingly. Here was a new Hughie; not the timid youth who dodged Howells' blows, but a sturdy, stubborn young fellow who appeared to be acquiring views of his own. He looked older, more thoughtful.

"If you are not prepared to follow me, Hughie, you had best return home," said Ann with dignity.

"Nay, I came to protect you and stay I must and shall. You speak hard, Mistress Ann, when you know I would give my life to serve you. It's only this Popish prince that I'm not anxious to serve."

"But suppose I am in his service? What then? No man can serve two masters, so what will you do about it?"

The lad looked puzzled. "Nay, I don't know. But I will complete this job first, and then we will face up to what may be going to happen."

"That sounds common sense. So let's move on."

They came to St. Asaph, that tiny city with its sturdy, square-towered cathedral topping the pleasant eminence near the confluence of the Elwy and the Clwyd. They looked down its sloping street to the bridge, but Ann thought less of the beauty of the scene than of the need for stabling for the horses and refreshment for herself.

It was a tiny enough city, yet ancient, for Christianity had flourished there since the sixth century and even the hill on which the city stood bore the name of Bryn Paulin, a reminder that the celebrated Roman General, Suetonius Paulinus, had once encamped there on his way to strike at the heart of Druidism in Mona.

Ann found the heat tiring and was more weary then she would have admitted. The hostelry was cool and the service good, so she put aside her impatience and resolved to stay the night. This suited young Hughie who, having attended to the horses, was eager, boy-like, to set forth exploring the little city about which he had heard so much but had never before been sufficiently far afield to visit. Left to her own devices, Ann walked to the shady banks of the river, and seating herself amid the lush grass, listened to the mellifluous rippling of the water over the stones. Few circumstances are more conducive to day-dreaming. As she sat there, in this new environment, with the venerable cathedral behind her and the sleepy, green-fringed river before, she suddenly realized her need for solitude. It was the most momentous, most sensational time of her young life and it was desirable to be alone with her thoughts to analy e the tumultuous and bewildering emotions which surged within her. Hitherto her life had been pleasant, peaceful, but uneventful. The issues which confronted her had been clear-cut and she could easily say yes or no. But now the river of her life had become turbulent, beset by cross-currents and unexpected danger spots. She found herself thinking less of Prince Charles Edward and his cause than the man who represented him, and she asked herself how much she was actually doing for her belief in the Stuarts and how much for the picturesque, dashing adventurer who represented the Young Pretender. Richard Conway's tall, lithe figure with its suggestion of swagger, his keen, tanned face with its reckless eyes, riveted her attention. As she closed her eyes she could see his form in the moon-light, his hand upraised in a gay salute. She found that she thought of Prince Charles Edward in terms of Richard Conway. He had stirred her as no other man had ever done. Love in its more tender sense was unknown to her; she did not meditate on kisses or caresses, rather did she crave to be at his side, sharing in his adventures and escapes, completely satisfied in the mere companionship of so fascinating a creature. It was not, she told herself, anxiety concerning the cargo of arms which had led her forth, but a desire to see him again. Ann was quite candid with herself. She also frankly admitted that it would not have done to have been equally candid with her father. How gallant was Dick Conway; how neatly his horse had cleared the five-bar after the duel in the moonlight. At that, her thoughts turned to his antagonist and a slight frown crossed her features. Why had Philip Yorke lain in wait for him? Why had he interfered? Supposing he had wounded Richard Conway; suppose, awful thought, he had killed him? Ann found herself perturbed at the mere contem-plation of such a possibility. It was intolerable of this Philip Yorke o interfere. Was he a Hanoverian spy? The thought gave her pause. Her heart beat faster. The man seemed to know so much about what vas going on. He was, for instance, tampering with the loyalty of young Hughie, putting new-fangled notions into his head? And then there came before her face a vision of those calm, grave eyes with just a suspicion of a twinkle lurking in them, and she felt that she could not think ill of him. She could not understand him; all she knew was that she was puzzled to account for the interest he took in her. He seemed so kind, so considerate, so solicitous of her well-being . . . and yet, it might merely be a pose while he watched for those who planted Charlie Trees near their lodge gates! No, decided Ann, shaking her head, Life was not all a matter of yes and no. It was involved and complicated, and the best decisions were made not by those who were warm of heart, but b, those who had trained themselves to think clearly.

And then Ann's thoughts came back to earth with a rush, for she heard the clatter of hoofs, slowly drawing nearer, and turning, she saw a gleam of red, and there were dragoons riding wearily down the hill, dragoons on sweat-caked chargers, men who perspired freely and whose faces were well-nigh as crimson as their tunics. And at their head, well in advance, staring straight ahead with hard, intolerant eyes, rode Major Manstein. Ann shrank back among the tall grasses. The major was not looking her way; had he done so, he would have seen nothing more than a pretty print frock and a chip hat—probably belonging to some village maiden. But Ann felt herself conspicuous. It seemed inevitable that she must be recognized. So, with fast-beating heart, she crouched low and watched from beneath the brim of her hat. Would they turn to the right along the road for Abergele, or would they go behind Kinmel Deer Park, along the old road which led to the crossing of the Conway? They took the road to Conway. The name seemed to assume a new significance. Conway! Somewhere over there Richard Conway would be arriving with his shipload of arms for the Young Pretender. Would he walk into a trap? Not, vowed Ann, if she could prevent it. Scrambling to her feet she commenced to climb hurriedly the grassy path which led back to the hostel and the horses.

CHAPTER NINETEEN

THE TINY CITY SEEMED SUBDUED AT THAT EVENING HOUR. THE DAY'S work was done. A haywain creaked as two weary horses hauled it homewards along the Holywell road. The sturdy, unpretentious cathedral raised its tutelary tower with paternal benevolence over the rows of houses which clustered close as though for comfort. Men gossiped beside the wall, relaxing after the toil of the day. The scene was peaceful enough but Ann found no consolation in it. The passing of the red-coated dragoons had filled her with unrest and she looked about her with apprehension. Something within her told her that the time had come when she must act if the Prince's cause was to be saved. Or was it the Prince's cause? She found herself blushing as she realized that she was chiefly actuated by a desire to prevent Captain Richard Conway from running into a trap. As she reached the street she took herself in hand. It would not do to go to the inn, hot and flustered. Ann walked with greater deliberation than she felt into the stable-yard and called for Hughie. A hostler told her that the boy had not returned. "Go seek him, and tell him to hasten," she said, slipping a silver coin into the man's hand. Then she sought her room and packed her valise. When she went downstairs there was no sign of Hughie. Ann pursed her lips. It was aggravating. Restlessly she paced the flagged hall. She was all impatience, eager to be up and away. Where had the lad got to? She turned to the window and gazed into the street. There was no sign of Hughie, but her eyes grew large, first with surprise, then with suspicion, as she beheld a familiar figure standing at the roadside, staring intently in the direction of the Denbighshire hills. It was Philip Yorke, his serious face and grey-flecked hair showing under his tricorne hat; his brown coat looped back for riding; his legs encased in dusty riding-boots. He slapped his leg mechanically with his riding-crop and he stood staring into the distance. Then he turned quickly away. A couple of minutes later, he reappeared, mounted on a well-groomed black horse. He rode at an easy pace down the hill to the river. Ann watched his receding back until it was out of sight. She sighed and bit her lip. What was Philip Yorke doing in St. Asaph?

She walked resolutely in search of the landlord. "Has that boy of mine returned?" she inquired brusquely.

"He's gone, Mistress."

"Gone? What do you mean? Has he left without seeking me when I sent word that I required him?"

"Nay, Mistress, he had departed before you came making inquiries. Came in hot and hurried, so Ben says, saddled his horse and off to go with never a word to no one."

Ann's eyes expressed her indignation but she kept her tongue in check. She called for her bill. "Have my horse saddled," she ordered. "I shall not stay the night as I intended. Have no fear, I shall pay for the room. And I wish you to take charge of my valise; oh, yes, and the led-horse. Let me know what I owe you."

The landlord demurred at her riding forth unaccompanied. The roads were unsafe. He offered to send a servant with her, but Ann had her own reasons for wishing to be alone. Black Prince was led forth, a trifle reluctantly, from his comfortable stable and Ann crossed to the mounting-block and clambered into the saddle. She looked smaller then usual perched high on this massive beast, but the hand which gripped the reins was insistent.

As she rode slowly down the hill which led to the bridge across the river her brow was puckered. Three events had occurred, any of which might have perturbed her. The dragoons had ridden towards the Conway; Philip Yorke had made an unexpected appearance; the boy Hughie had taken his horse and disappeared in a manner wholly unaccountable in one who had hitherto been her devoted servant. These three events had happened in close succession; Ann wondered whether they were connected with one another. She felt they might be! But how? One thing was apparent: she was left

to her own resources, and if a warning message was to be conveyed
to Captain Conway aboard the snow from France, she it was who
would have to contrive it. Once across the river she quickened her
pace, turning along the old road which led to Abergele. Once clear of
the village—Ann always found it difficult to remember to think of
the little place as a city—the broad fields with their clumps of woodland
stretched across the flat lands on either side. She rounded a wooded
bend where a lane forked seawards. A triangle of grass showed green
amid the dust of the highway. Ann had barely time to note this
indication of the branching of the road than a movement from the
mouth of the lane attracted her attention. A rough-looking man on
a ragged horse was pulling across her path. She saw that the fellow
had a black mask across his eyes and a heavy horse-pistol in his right
hand.

"Stand and deliver !" he croaked.

Ann acted instinctively. Black Prince, proceeding at a comfortable
trot, found a pair of spurs rammed home and firm insistent hands
urging him into a canter. She was conscious in a vague way of an
explosion, a flash of fire and a puff of smoke. Later, when she began
to sort out her thoughts, she realized that the highwayman had fired
at her. At the time her only reaction was to press her trigger. She
missed her mark, but Black Prince was more reliable. Snorting with
excitement and passion he swept into the fray with all the dash of
his illustrious namesake. His massive shoulder took the nondescript
nag on the flank sending it staggering and hurling its rider into the
ditch. On thundered Black Prince, full of the lust of battle and completely out of hand, while Ann, still clutching a smoking pistol, tugged
vainly at his mouth as he galloped wildly along the Abergele road.
Once she had got the great horse under control she essayed a backward
glance, but a bend in the road had taken her out of sight of the luckless
highwayman.

"Princie," gasped Ann, her eyes agleam, "you are a jewel. That's
the liveliest frolic we've had for a long time. I feel all happy and
excited about it. Now for the dragoons !"

As Black Prince's pace grew more sober, so did Ann's bellicose
mood. In fact, it was not long before she had no desire to pit her
strength against that of the dragoons ; her one desire was to give them
as wide a berth as circumstance would permit. She thrust her discharged
pistol back into its holster and rode with greater decorum. She was
amid the broad farm lands, flat as the great battle-renowned Morfa
Rhuddlan hard by, and before her stretched the sea, grey and placid
at the close of day. There had been a market at the old town of
Abergele, and a few farmers and shepherds, having lingered long in
the ale houses, were wending their way homeward with unsteady
deliberation. Ann paid them little heed. Her one thought was to
get to the Ormeshead before the dragoons could make their appearance.
She had no plan of campaign. The strangeness of the situation made
her conscious of her lack of experience. She wondered how Dicon
Conway would have conducted himself in the circumstances. Ann
felt that all she could do was to wait for something to happen. Some-

thing did happen. There were farm carts and waggons still in the main street at Abergele, and a cluster of men stood in the roadway staring up at the tower of St. Michael's Church, which rose with ponderous dignity above the roofs of the old town. The westering sun lit up the pale stones of the battlemented crest; it showed up, too, bright patches of scarlet, strangely incongruous in so pacific a setting. Ann's eyes dilated. Never before had that bright and war-like colour held such significance in her eyes. There were soldiers on the tower top scanning the sea! Ann could surmise what they were seeking. Her first impulse was to put spurs to Black Prince, but she restrained herself. Assuredly, there would be no surer way of attracting attention. So with self-restraint she walked her horse as unobtrusively as possible along the main street. A group of men were arguing outside the Bee Hotel. Could she but pass them unnoticed, she would be able to increase her pace shortly and get clear of the town. And then she became conscious of a horse's hoofs following close behind her own. An irresistible desire to turn took possession of her. She fought against it. looking ahead with expressionless countenance, but the impulse became too strong. She must know who followed so closely behind. As casually as possible she turned her head. The gleam of a red tunic set her heart pounding wildly. She heard a suave voice observe, "'Zounds, if I am not mistaken it is Miss Trevor?"

Ann found herself looking into the saturnine face of Major Manstein; Major Manstein whom she thought to be well on his road to Conway by way of Bettws-yn-Rhos. Ann forced a smile.

"Why, it is Major Manstein if I am not mistaken! How nice of you to remember me when we met but once."

"My dear young lady, you belittle yourself. I assure you that one encounter is quite sufficient to leave an impression even on a hardened veteran like myself."

"And such a brief encounter, too, Major Manstein."

"Brief, as you observe, Miss Trevor. Under unfortunate circumstances, too; engaged on a deucedly unpleasant task, you may recall. Soldier has to carry out his duties, you know."

"Of course, Major Manstein; we quite understood."

"But now I am happy to say that the duties of the day are over; one can relax. I have just ordered a humble evening meal. I should be honoured if my table were graced by the presence of the charming Miss Trevor."

"I thank you, but I fear it is impossible. I must push on."

"At so late an hour?" The Major raised his eyebrows. "It is surely a matter of some urgency when you ride so far from home. I trust nothing is wrong?"

"Oh, not at all, Major. Merely a—a visit to some friends."

"And you journey unaccompanied? My dear Miss Trevor, surely this is the height of indiscretion? There are, so I am told, footpads about. In fact, one of the Justices even went so far as to importune me to spare him a file of men to help round up one miscreant who is infecting the district about St. Asaph."

89

"Oh, but I am not alone; at least, I was not alone. I was accompanied by a servant, but the rascal disappeared at St. Asaph and I was left to my own devices."

"Plaguy annoying, egad. A taste of a horsewhip would doubtless do him good. Demme if I can tolerate an unreliable servant. However, you shall have an escort. I can spare a couple of troopers to keep you company."

"My dear Major Manstein, I would not dream of putting you to such inconvenience."

"No trouble at all, Miss Trevor. In fact, I could not look your worthy father in the face had I allowed his fair daughter to incur such a hazard. I feel my responsibility. Now, I pray you, join me at my lonely meal."

"I really could not accept your hospitality."

"And I really could not allow you to encounter the hazards of the highway unprotected. Come, Miss Trevor, I have a suggestion to make. Either you accept the escort of a couple of my men as far as—er—where you are bound for, or else join me at the inn, stay the night, and ride in our company in the morning. I promise you that no evil shall befall you."

Major Manstein spoke suavely, with a grave courtesy, but his penetrating eyes never left Ann's face. She felt that underneath his polished words lay the ominous suggestion that she was no longer free to do what she liked. Ann felt that she must have time to think. She forced a smile.

"How insistent you are, Major Manstein. I vow I must yield to your importunity. After all, there is no hurry and the road has been hot and dusty. A night at the inn will doubtless freshen me."

"I am charmed," said he bowing low, and laying his right hand quietly but firmly on Black Prince's bridle, he turned the animal's head towards the yard of the Bee Hotel. Ann held her head high and forced a smile, but her heart sank within her.

They handed their animals to a hostler and Ann was escorted with polished grace to the door of the inn. It would seem that they were not the only travellers. In the gloaming a tall, broad-shouldered man all but blocked the passage. He turned as they entered and uttered an exclamation.

"Why, Ann, what are you doing here?"

"Mr. Yorke! Why, I might observe the same of you."

"Ah, friend of yours?" inquired Major Manstein with uplifted eyebrow. "'Zounds, sir, your face is familiar. Have we not met before?"

"Lud, sir, I am not like to forget our encounter. You came raiding my house after some . . . let me see . . . missing horse or something. Yes, that was it; horse-thief if I mistake not. I trust you were successful in your mission."

"I usually succeed, sir, on any mission I undertake. Yes, I secured the horse I was after. The man, for the moment, eludes me. I have no doubt that the time is not far distant when I shall make the gentleman's closer acquaintance."

He spoke quietly with an indolent smile.

"I wish you success, sir," said Mr. Yorke.

"Thank you, sir. I have no doubt that the rascal's friends will endeavour to send him warning, and of course, it behoves me, in the pursuance of my duty, to see that no messenger gets through. However, the day's wearisome task is ended. I have persuaded Miss Trevor to sup with me. Perhaps you would care to join us. She has assured me that there is nothing urgent about her journey which would prevent her stopping the night in this agreeable hostelry."

"How fortunate. Assuredly I will join you, sir, and I thank you for your courtesy. Miss Trevor, as you recollect, is a neighbour of mine, and we usually find occasion for the exchange of ideas. As you say, there is no hurry; no hurry whatever."

His deep eyes turned to Ann. They were grave and penetrating and Ann found herself returning the gaze. Mr. Yorke raised his fingers to his lips and essayed to stifle a yawn. "How sultry hot it is," he said. "Not a breath of air. Not enough to stir the sails of a fishing-boat. I vow that every ship in St. George's Channel is becalmed. By all means let us sup. Come, Ann, take your ease and shake off the cares of the day. I have dined here before and I vow the cooking is excellent."

He bowed and held back the door for her to enter a room in which a waiter was just lighting the candles. Ann moved forward with fast-beating heart. Philip Yorke's words had given her fresh courage. There was still time. If the soldiers on the church tower top were watching for the vessel from France there could be no possibility of its arrival until a breeze sprang up. There was still time to scheme; perhaps time to escape. As Major Manstein placed a chair for Ann, that young lady favoured him with a smile so gracious, so charming that Philip Yorke might well have found room for envy had he not surmised that it was but the outward expression of a fresh hope which had sprung up within her heart.

CHAPTER TWENTY

IF ANN SLEPT BUT FITFULLY THAT NIGHT IT WAS NOT SURPRISING. The evening meal had not been a success. Philip Yorke had talked with customary calmness, yet Ann felt that the conversation was superficial and forced. It was clear that Major Manstein found his presence unwelcome and the soldier's observations, though few, left Ann with the impression that he was a master of cynicism and satire. She was not sorry to withdraw to her room.

Her bedchamber was at the rear of the inn, the small window overlooking the broad yard at the back. Instead of undressing, she sat on her bed and thought. It was intolerable, argued Ann, closing her teeth on her pretty lower lip, it was intolerable that this soldier should hold her in durance. She walked to the door with a firm step, opened it, paused, and closed it with greater deliberation. She slipped the bolt home. A red-coated dragoon was at the top of the stairs, a sinister figure in the dim light. Motionless she stood with the bolted door between her and the sentry and her little hands were clenched at the realization of her impotence. She crossed to the window and peered out into the moonlit yard. All was still; there was not a breath of air. Of a surety, Philip Yorke had been right; there was no chance of a vessel moving on such a night as this. Silent as a shadow a cat moved over the whitewashed stones of the wall's top. Ann's eyes followed its stealthy progress, envying the creature its freedom. The sound of a heavy step sounded. A soldier moved from the shade of the outhouse and crossed the yard. Freed from the vigilant eye of his superior officer, the man had tilted back his hat from his heated brow; his carbine was tucked comfortably under his arm. He was none the less on duty. With a sigh of chagrin, Ann returned to her seat on the edge of the bed and stared with hard, unseeing eyes at the wall opposite. How dare he place her under arrest like this? What effrontery! What right had this Major Manstein to interfere with her freedom? He had no legal right to detain her; she would complain to the justices! She bit her lip. He had not detained her; he was much too cunning for that. He had merely shown commendable solicitude because she rode unescorted. He had, with the greatest courtesy, invited her to a meal. As for the sentry, the man was merely carrying out part of his routine duties. She could picture Manstein's suave, plausible voice raised in explanatory protests. Ann decided that in the morning she would put the matter to the test. She would inform him that she intended to ride on her way alone. What then? The pucker appeared between Ann's eyes which was a sure sign that she was concentrating. Why, he would politely express regret at her decision and allow her to depart. His behaviour would be punctilious. Of that she was certain. She was also sure that he would detail one of his men to follow at a discreet distance to see where she went. For every move she could make he would have a counter-move. "Drat the man!" cried Ann, as she cast herself on the bed. This, for Ann, was strong language.

The room was stuffy and the night sultry. Ann tossed and turned, her brain in a turmoil. She pictured the vessel from France being boarded as soon as it made its appearance, Richard Conway and his fellow conspirators arrested, the arms confiscated. Perhaps their decapitated heads would be impaled on Temple Bar. Ann shuddered. And she could do nothing. Yet, after all Dicon Conway was not the man to be taken easily. Perhaps he would outwit them without her aid. With that consoling thought Ann fell asleep and slumbered deeply until the cocks were crowing in the morning sunlight.

At the breakfast table, Major Manstein, urbane as ever, inquired whether she had slept well. It was a polite platitude, but to Ann's sensitive ears it carried a suggestion of mockery.

"The night was sultry and I was somewhat slow in falling asleep. When I did, I slept most soundly. I think I should have gone off quicker had it not been for some noisy fellow who kept walking about in the yard outside."

"Ah. That would be the sentry. I have to keep one posted each night to keep guard over the horses."

"And was the one at the top of the stairs keeping guard over the horses also?"

For a second, Ann had the satisfaction of seeing the major a trifle nonplussed. He elevated his eyebrows slightly. "Was there a man there? There is always a second fellow on guard in case of emergency, you know. He is at liberty to move where he will—within reason. The rascal did not cause you annoyance, I trust?"

"Oh, not at all, Major Manstein. It is just that I am unfamiliar with military ways."

"I trust that you will long remain so."

Ann bent over her dish of tea. She wished that she could talk naturally. It all savoured of fencing. Still, she was holding her own.

"I presume you will be thinking of resuming your journey to your friends shortly, Miss Trevor. Do you still prefer to ride unescorted?"

Ann looked him boldly in the face. "I should feel so much safer if you would allow me to ride with you, Major Manstein."

"Ah, that would certainly simplify matters."

"That is, of course, if we happen to be going in the same direction. I could not trouble you otherwise. I am sure that, as a soldier, even in peace time, you have duties which must be performed."

"As you observe, Miss Trevor, they must be performed. And they are not always so agreeable as playing the cavalier to, permit me to observe, a singularly charming young lady. And where are you to visit these—these friends of yours?"

"I am very anxious to see Conway as soon as possible," said Ann, amazed at her own audacity. Did the major know the name? If so, he never gave an indication.

"What a happy coincidence, Miss Trevor. Conway is the object of my journey also. I have not been to the town before, and I vow that I am desirous of making Conway's closer acquaintance. Shall we prepare for our ride?"

He rose gravely to his feet and bowed Ann from the room.

At the front door two horses were being held. Ann looked about her.

"If it is Mr.—er—Yorke you seek, I fear he left early," said Major Manstein. "He did not acquaint me his destination."

Ann was conscious of a momentary feeling of panic. Hanoverian though he might be there was something substantial about Philip Yorke. He was a rock beneath which she could shelter. His departure savoured of desertion, yet, she asked herself, how was he to know of the quandary she was in? But she turned a face which admirably simulated surprise as she replied——

"Mr. Yorke? Forgive me, I fear last night's chance encounter had slipped from my memory. No, it was the soldiers I missed."

"I have sent them on ahead by devious routes, thinking that the presence of so many armed men might embarrass you, Miss Trevor. I am sufficiently conceited to assume that my own right arm is enough to protect you from any perils which we may encounter."

"I have as much confidence in your courage as in your chivalry, Major Manstein," said Ann smoothly as she urged Black Prince to a walk.

93

Major Manstein endeavoured to engage her in light conversation as they rode, but Ann, for the most part, was unusually silent. A handsome enough pair they must have looked, and yet, for all Major Manstein's courtesy, Ann could not shake off the impression that she was a captive. As they rode in single file around the narrow ledge which was cut in the face of the headland at Penmaenrhos, Ann gave a little shudder.

"I cannot abide this spot," said she as they reached the western side.

"It is certainly uncomfortable," agreed Major Manstein. "The rock face is precipitous and the drop to those sea-washed boulders is deucedly unpleasant to contemplate."

"It is not the danger of the passage which appals me," said Ann. "It is the tragedy which occurred here which fills me with sadness."

"What tragedy, Miss Trevor? Pardon my ignorance."

"Why, this is the very spot where the luckless monarch, Richard II, was betrayed into the hands of his enemies. Trusting the oath of the false Earl of Northumberland, he left the security of Conway Castle and rode into an ambush here. I pity the poor captive as much as I despise the treachery which led to his doom."

"A captive is to be commiserated with," returned the major coolly, "though there are times when protective custody is desirable to avert a greater evil."

"I do not follow you, Major Manstein."

"So long as you accompany me, Miss Trevor, that will suffice."

Ann rode awhile in silence and then as her eyes wandered over the broad expanse of placid sea, they came to rest on the topmasts of a vessel which rode motionless off the Anglesey coast.

"There appears to be a ship of sorts out there," she hazarded

"There is undoubtedly a ship—of sorts, Miss Trevor."

"I wonder what she can be, Major Manstein?"

"I have permitted myself the same speculation, Miss Trevor."

"It would seem that speculation is likely to be as much as we shall achieve!"

"For the present, presumably, Miss Trevor. It is possible that our pardonable curiosity may one day be gratified."

"Oh, I am not really curious, Major Manstein. It was just something to talk about."

"Ah, yes. Something to talk about. Indeed, you may be right."

Ann resumed her silence. Suddenly she thought of a favourite cat of hers, one whose paws were of velvety softness but whose claws were scarce below the surface of the smooth fur. She had tried so valiantly to converse in a natural and normal manner, but her effort invariably seemed to terminate in tension. They reached the hamlet of Colwyn, the pathway winding inland a while in order to cross the stream where the banks shelved sufficiently to permit fording. On they went, Ann instinctively glancing seawards whenever they passed a gap in the trees which were now commencing to cluster thickly on the verdant slopes. With swishing tails and drooping heads, their mounts climbed slowly the narrow road through the woods; the road which the Romans were said to have made when they came down the coast from Chester in search of pearls in the Conway and copper in the Ormeshead. From around a bend there came a horseman, riding downhill at a comfortable trot, and at the sight of him both raised their heads.

"Ah," observed Major Manstein coolly, "our acquaintance of the inn. Your friend, Mr. Yorke, it would appear, Miss Trevor. He seems to have shown commendable expedition this morning."

"I fear I am unacquainted with his movements, Major Manstien."

Mr. Yorke reined in and swept off his hat with easy grace. "Ann, I give you good morning. Sir, my compliments."

"Sir," replied Major Manstein, saluting formally, "your obedient servant." (No man looked less.) "Might I ask if you were seeking me?"

"Seeking is scarcely the word. I was on the look-out in case I might encounter you. I have been asked to convey a message."

"Pray deliver it, sir."

"It is this: Three ships' boats from his Majesty's frigate *Talisman* are at the quay at Conway."

"Indeed."

"Lieutenant Keith who is in command awaits your co-operation. He begs that you will assemble your men there with all possible dispatch as he proposes to set forth immediately you arrive."

"Indeed."

"His opinion is that this calm is like to last some days and that the move which is to be undertaken will call for a change in plans."

"If this matter is of a secret nature, perhaps you would like me to withdraw," said Ann, feeling uncomfortable.

"It is unnecessary, Miss Trevor," said Major Manstein suavely. "You have proved so agreeable a companion that I do not think I shall exceed discretionary powers if I take you into my confidence. The vessel which you noticed but a short while since is suspected of being in the pay of the Jacobites and is off this coast for the purpose of running a cargo of arms to be used by North Wales supporters of the Pretender. This, of course, will come as a great shock and surprise to you, Miss Trevor, but it is as well that you and your father should know that there are disloyal elements even in North Wales. It will also add to his assurance and give him a feeling of confidence if you acquaint him that loyal servants of His Majesty are alert in the national interests and intend to see to it that the machinations of these traitors and miscreants come to naught. So I beg that you will accompany me, Miss Trevor. Your journey to visit these friends of yours takes you to the pleasant town of Conway. Let us resume our way by all means. Perhaps while you are there you will be able to witness the landing of the frigate's boats when, after rowing out to the becalmed vessel, they bring ashore a load of confiscated muskets and probably a traitor or two. It should prove an unusual and possibly interesting experience, Miss Trevor."

"Certainly unusual, Major Manstein," said Ann, endeavouring to speak with composure.

"And there should be no danger," added Mr. Yorke, gravely.

"Oh, not in the slightest. In addition to the boats' crews, there will be my dragoons. More than sufficient to stifle any opposition, though I suspect that the rogues will have no fight in them when they see how matters lie. Now, Miss Trevor, shall we resume our journey in the hope that shortly we shall see what Conway looks like?"

What Conway looks like? Ann moistened her dry lips and forced a smile.

"I think I should take advantage of Major Manstein's offer," observed Mr. Yorke.

"Oh, how could you be so heartless?" burst out Ann, the colour flooding her cheeks. "You are completely callous. I believe that you positively relish the thought of seeing brave men brought to their doom."

"Miss Trevor, you surprise me," interposed Major Manstein as he gathered up his reins. "You do Mr. Yorke injustice in the tenderness of your heart. All that any loyal subject of His Majesty desires is not brave men brought to their doom, but traitors brought to justice. Mr. Yorke, I give you thanks for your message. Your servant, sir. Now, Miss Trevor, forward. Let us see how Conway looks on such a day as this."

CHAPTER TWENTY-ONE

ANN STOOD ON THE QUAY AT CONWAY AT THE TIME OF THE SETTING of the sun and gazed at as fair a scene as one could well look upon. The broad river was as calm as a mirror, the vessels at anchor seemed to float upon their own reflections. Beyond the curtain wall, the trees grew thick to the river's edge. Backed by the encircling hills stood the quaint, quiet, grey old town, its venerable walls with their defensive towers much as they were a century before, when intrepid Roundheads stormed the ramparts while valiant Cavaliers made a last desperate endeavour to hold out for King Charles. But Ann was not thinking of history, nor of the stately castle, nor of the green rounded humps of Deganwy on the eastern bank. She saw only a silent ship coming in from the sea—a vessel from whose bows three hawsers stretched taut as three ships' boats, pulled by sweating seamen, towed the unresisting vessel to port. Major Manstein, his tunic a vivid patch of colour on the old quay, stood beside her, booted legs apart, and watched the slow progress of the frigate's boats with grim satisfaction. The tide was full and the tars were bringing their capture right up the river to Conway's quay. A cluster of fishermen assembled to watch curiously the approach and to speculate as to why the naval men had made their capture. They did not draw too close, however (at least, not the younger men), for there was a war raging with France and thoughts of the press-gang were always present in the minds of any likely men who promised to make seamen for his Majesty's fleet. Dismounted dragoons stood motionless near the Lower Gate. Each man carried a carbine, and the swords which hung suspended from the broad pipe-clayed cross-belts bore a businesslike look. The men at the oars were stripped to the waist. Ann could see their short, tarry pigtails, and the tattooing on their arms as they bent their broad, sweating backs to the oars. In the leading boat Lieutenant Keith stood upright, hand on tiller, his eyes intent on the passage to the quay. He was wearing the new blue and white uniform which was gradually coming into fashion in the navy: a keen brown-faced man who seemed to know his job. "Steady now," she heard his voice call sharply as they drew alongside. "Bowman, heave a line ashore. That's right, my lads, haul in and make fast. Major Manstein, I will trouble you for half-a-dozen of your men to help warp the ship alongside? My lads have had a long row and a hot one and your fellows look as if they could do with a little exercise."

"Happy to oblige, Mr. Keith," replied the major, issuing a crisp order. "I hope your prize is to your liking."

"We'll discuss that all in good time, sir. Let's get her made fast before we ease off."

Once the hawsers from the ship were made fast to the bollards the boats' crews ran their craft on to the shingle nearby and went staggering stiffly towards the nearest alehouse. Ann noticed that each man had a cutlass at his side. As she looked silently down upon the deck of the snow, she felt sick with apprehension. Were there blood-stains on the none-too-clean decks? She could see no trace of strife. Neither could she see any prisoners in chains. Several men leaned against the bulwarks in surly silence. There was an armed bluejacket on the forecastle, and several more in the waist. There was a sense of unreality about it all. Had it not been for the name which she had clearly seen as the vessel came alongside, the whole affair might have been something of no concern to Ann. She saw Lieutenant Keith swing himself aboard by the main-chains. He walked aft and a moment later emerged with a seafaring man who carried himself like an officer. Ann's heart commenced to pound as she recognized him as Richard Conway's companion, Andrew Peris, formerly lieutenant of H.M.S. *Centurion*. His eyes passed Ann by without recognition. She looked again. There was no sign of Richard Conway. What had happened to him? Had he—Ann's courage ebbed at the thought—had he been killed? And his body thrown overboard? She believed that was the procedure after fights at sea. The silence, the uncertainty, was almost beyond endurance, yet she must appear nonchalant.

If Peris ignored Ann, he was quick to notice Major Manstein. "Well, sir," he cried sharply, "what is the meaning of this damned outrage? I ask you; are you concerned in it?"

"I am concerned in protecting his Majesty's interests, and I shall ask you to keep silent. I will do what questioning is necessary. Now, keep quiet!" His voice had a peremptory ring and Peris, who was about to speak, closed his mouth. Major Manstein leaped down to the ship's forecastle and made his way towards the two men.

"Well, Mr. Keith, what luck?"

"The devil's own luck."

97

The sailor spoke crisply. Ann, looking down from the quay, could hear every word.

"How d' mean? Drawn blank?" Major Manstein's face was set in a scowl.

"Never a trace of arms that I can find!" said the lieutenant crisply. "Demme, if you think you can search a ship better than I can, come, see for yourself." He called to two bluejackets and pointed to Peris. "That man is under arrest," he said curtly. "Cut him down if he attempts to escape."

He led the way down below, Major Manstein following hard on his heels. The minutes dragged by. Peris made no attempt to look up at Ann but stood in stoical silence, the seamen with drawn cutlasses at either side. As for Ann, she felt bewildered. 'Drawn blank' could only mean that the smuggled arms were not aboard. Neither for that matter was Richard Conway. Ann's bewilderment was tinged with thankfulness which was the less profound because the whole affair seemed so unreal. Had Dicon Conway really outwitted his enemies? A fierce satisfaction glowed within her. Why had she worried? She might have known that the daring adventurer would be equal to the occasion. If only she knew more! Curiosity took hold of her so that she could scarce control herself. Her imagination had full play until Lieutenant Keith emerged from the forecastle, followed by the soldier. Major Manstein looked more dishevelled and less urbane than Ann had ever seen him. There were streaks of dirt on his perspiring face and dust on his fine coat. He took off his hat, mopped his face and then confronted Peris, who was now, in every sense of the word, the cooler of the two.

"Well," said Major Manstein, taking his place before him with booted legs apart and thrusting forth his jaw pugnaciously, "what have you to say?"

"The devil of a lot. First I would ask by what right you board my ship and detain me."

"You are suspect."

"Suspect be damned. Where's your proof? I might suspect you of being an impostor. I say that I have a right to sail the high sea unmolested, and any man who boards me is a pirate. Nothing less."

Manstein's flushed face grew even more red. "Where are your papers?" he demanded.

"All in order."

"Is that so, Mr. Keith?"

"Hum! More or less. Cleared from Liverpool on the fourth of last month for Cork for a cargo of hides."

"You've been the devil of a time over the voyage," snapped Manstein.

"Any wonder with weather like this?" returned Peris coolly.

"Who are you, anyway?"

"Name of Peris, Andrew. Formerly lieutenant in H.M.S. *Centurion.*"

"What's that?" asked Keith smartly. "Are you a *Centurion* man? One of Anson's officers?"

"Yes. Not long back from a world cruise of which you may have heard mention."

Keith pointed a finger at this. "Name the vessels which set out with the *Centurion*. Quick!"

"*Gloucester*," said Peris calmly, "of fifty guns; *Severn*, another fifty; *Pearl*, forty; *Wager*, twenty-eight; *Trial*, eight, and the victuallers, *Anna* and *Industry*."

"Hum! Now the names of some of the company?"

"Keppel, Saumarez, Saunders, Brett, Hyde Parker, Denis, Campbell."

"What is Saumarez's christian name?"

"Philip."

Lieutenant Keith shrugged his shoulders. The promptness of Peris's replies had surprised him, for he had obviously hoped to trap his victim into confessing that he was an impostor.

"Then why the devil should you sink to this dirty coaster if you are one of Anson's men? Why aren't you in the Service? There's a war on."

"Because they treated me as they treated Brett. The Commodore applied for promotion for us and the Admiralty refused to confirm the grant. Brett stood for the insult. I had no occasion to, having a competency of my own. I have finished with a Navy which does not know how to serve out justice to the men who served it faithfully."

"Ha! Man with a grouch, are you?" snapped Keith. "Well, you haven't told me yet what you are doing as skipper of this queer craft."

Peris shrugged his shoulders. "Can't keep away from the sea. Bored before I was long ashore."

"So you chucked up his Majesty's commission to become skipper of a coaster? Plaguy strange notion. Anyway, where is your cargo of hides?"

"Couldn't get 'em." Peris was succinct.

"Why not?"

"Why not? Because there was the devil of a sea duel raging off the coast. We turned back after getting a stray round shot through our mains'l. You can examine it if you want."

"I intend to. Tell us more of the fight."

"There was a French sixty-gun ship accompanied by a fast brig. Looked to me like the *Dontelle* privateer. They were fell in with by the *Lion*, fifty-eight, and went at it hammer and tongs. By the way, I've heard say that the *Lion* is commanded by Brett. Is it right he was posted after all?"

But Keith did not hear him. He had turned to Major Manstein with a look of interrogation in his eyes.

Major Manstein nodded as though he had read his thoughts. "Yes, it looks as if it was the break out. The Young Chevalier is making a bid for the throne for his father by the look of things. Look here, what happened to the brig?"

"Last I saw of her she was heading north'rds. The *Lion* and the Frenchman fought till they could scarce swim."

The soldier paid little heed. He took an impatient turn or two up and down the deck. "Keith, I must leave the matter in your hands," he said crisply. "It is time I was stirring. Find the arms if you can; as for me, there's bigger game afoot."

99

"What shall we do with this bird?" asked Keith.

"Oh, detain him, and his ship. This isn't a time to stand on ceremony."

"I protest," began Peris. "I demand my freedom. You have no right to interfere with me on my lawful occasions——"

"Stow your talk, or I'll clap you in irons," snapped Keith.

"I'll take the matter to court——"

"Well, let the lawyers fight it out. Meanwhile get back to your cabin and stay there. Cox'n, see there is a guard at the door and watch the port-hole."

Major Manstein and Lieutenant Keith walked to the bulwarks and stood with heads close together talking eagerly in low voices. Then, with a brisk, "I leave it to you," Manstein scrambled hastily to the quay and called his corporal of horse towards him. "Get the men mounted instantly! Every jack man of them. And fetch our horses to the Lower Gate."

He walked slowly towards the town with his head bowed in thought. Ann, after a last look at the deck of the snow, turned to follow. She was still puzzled, but something told her more forcefully than ever that the great game had started: that after sixteen months of hesitating Prince Charles Edward was making a bid to restore the Stuart dynasty. The major assisted her to her saddle without speaking, and in silence they rode towards the ferry followed by the troopers. Once on the eastern bank, the major set a brisk pace. Ann rode with her thoughts, which were undisturbed save for the clatter of hoofs and the jingle of bit or chain or scabbard.

As they neared St. Asaph a courier, spurring a sweating and jaded horse, galloped towards them. He held a letter in his uplifted hand and Major Manstein halted his posse as he awaited the messenger. He broke the seal and read eagerly.

Ann, watching closely, saw the man's eyes gleam. He thrust the dispatch into his sabretache and turned to his men. Ere he spoke, his eye lit on Ann and he gave a start of surprise as if he had been oblivious of her presence and was surprised to find her in so military a setting.

"Egad, Miss Trevor," he said, "you have been eager and willing to ride alone and now fate decides that you must proceed without escort. My orders which permit of no delay, decree that I must leave you to your own resources."

"I can find my own way from here, Major Manstein," said Ann rimly.

"You relieve my mind of an intolerable burden, Miss Trevor. My chivalry rebelled at my desertion." Major Manstein gathered up his reins. Suddenly his white teeth gleamed in a sarcastic smile, which Ann found more galling than any words. "My dear Miss Trevor, both you and I are very absent-minded. It has just occurred to me: you rode to Conway to visit some friends and I, in my aberration, have brought you away without your gladdening their lives with your charming presence. Forgive me. But perhaps in the circumstances, much will be overlooked—or at any rate, understood."

He saluted with punctilious smartness and trotted away, followed by his clanking dragoons.

Ann sat watching until the gleam of red was lost amid the trees. Then she bent forward and patted Black Prince's familiar neck. "Come, lad," she said, "Home!" She spoke quietly. Reaction had set in. Ann was conscious of weariness, depression, and a desire not for adventure but for peace.

CHAPTER TWENTY-TWO

AT A SOBER PACE, ANN RODE HOME OVER THE SELFSAME ROAD WHICH she had traversed not long before, when she was buoyed up by the prospect of adventure. She had tasted adventure and she wondered why she was not more exhilarated. Dicon Conway had escaped. The arms had not been captured. There seemed a suggestion that the Prince had actually landed somewhere in the North. Why, then, she asked herself, was she not more elated? The reason, had she but known it, was not hard to find. She was physically weary and was suffering a reaction after the excitement and strain and uncertainty during her nominal captivity. All she knew was that her body ached, her eyes ached and what she most desired was a good meal, a cool room, a comfortable bed and no more red-coated dragoons for a long, long time. Black Prince, the reins loose on his broad neck, maintained a steady pace as though he understood his young mistress's aberration and was letting her know that she could safely leave the question of transportation to him. His steady trot was so regular that it acted almost as a soporofic and Ann was almost asleep in the saddle when the sound of hoofs ahead caused Black Prince to prick his ears and Ann to open wide her eyes. A smile of pleasure crossed her face as she recognized the approaching rider as Seth Morrice—Seth whom she had seen but a few days before but who now appeared as one whom she had not encountered for years, so long did it seem since she rode away from home.

Seth looked harassed. "Ann, my dear, where have you been? I only just learnt of this mad escapade of yours and set forth to come to you. Tell me, are you safe and well?" Without waiting for her to answer he pulled his mount alongside hers and caught up her right hand. "And where is the led-horse? And has the boy deserted you? And what happened to the arms?"

"Mercy, Seth, one question at a time!" she protested.

"You really ought not to have ventured out unprotected," he resumed. "It was your duty to have sent for me. Anything might have happened to you. Why, there's a fellow in the stocks at St. Asaph even now. They found him lying in a ditch with a black mask still over his ugly glib and a discharged pistol lying nearby."

Ann's eyes sparkled. "Ah!" she observed and held her peace.

Seth's company cheered her and the way became less tedious. As they rode she narrated her experiences. He promised to send a serving man for the valise and the led-horse.

101

"I'd main like to know what happened to the arms," he muttered. "You must go over all this in detail after you are rested. There's to be a meeting of the Cycle at your house this evening. Rumours of happenings in Scotland are filtering through, but no one knows quite what is going on. The report is that the Prince has actually landed."

When Squire Trevor saw Ann's tired face, questions and reprimands died on his lips. He kissed her with greater fervour than was his wont, gave her a paternal pat of approbation on the shoulder, and with a husky, "Bless you, my girl," he let her go to bed.

When the table was being set for the evening meal, Ann came down the stairs, pink of cheek, bright of eye, her usual fresh, fragrant self.

"You look a new woman," commented the Squire.

"Darling, I have had such a wonderful sleep. I don't know if the scent of sweet-peas is a soporific, but I slept beautifully with a bunch of them by my bed. It was the kind of sleep that I like—very light—like floating on waves. I felt I should wake if a petal fell."

"Rubbish," ejaculated the Squire. "I have been shouting for you half-a-dozen times this last hour. Sir Watkin is here, in the gun-room, and Eyton and the others, all curious to know what has befallen you."

Ann stood in the centre of an admiring throng of men who drank in every word. She told them everything; everything, that is, save the highwayman episode. She had a suspicion that if that story leaked out her parent would stop her riding abroad.

"You have no idea what has happened to the arms?" asked the baronet.

"No, Sir Watkin. Major Manstein seemed in a fine old rage about missing them."

"Well, they've got Peris," said the Squire heavily "and they've got my ship, damn 'em. A pretty penny that is going to cost me."

"King James will see you are not the loser once he is on his rightful throne," said Sir Watkin.

"Aye, but what are the chances of his getting there?"

"The chances, sir," said Sir Watkin sententiously, "are so rosy that the most cautious gambler would be tempted to try a throw. I have at last received an authentic dispatch from Scotland. It is true, gentlemen, Prince Charles Edward has landed at Eriskay."

He was interrupted by a sound. Several of the men grasped hands while the Squire bustled off to fetch the wine decanter and glasses. It was an obvious occasion for a toast.

"Here's to the brown-eyed lad with the bloom of a lass!" cried Eyton

"Success to Charles Stuart, Prince of Wales!" and "God save King James the Third" were other toasts offered. When the excitement abated, Sir Watkin resumed.

"He slipped out of Nantes in a small privateer, vowing to win or lose all. He had a sixty-gun ship for escort but they fell in with a British man-o'-war of about the same strength and the two fought to a standstill while the *Dontelle*, as the Prince's brig is named, showed a clean pair of heels and, though pursued by another warship, got through to the west coast of Scotland. He has now landed at Borrada in Moidart."

"How many men has he with him?" asked the practical Eyton.

"Ah, not many, I grant you. A mere handful of adventurers, but the Scottish chiefs are rallying to his banner. Once he has secured Scotland, as I feel sure that he will do, his Highness will march south and, having linked up with the forces which we shall raise in Wales, will move on London. They tell me that there is something approaching a panic in the city already."

"That's as it may be, Sir Watkin," observed the Squire. "The Scots will rise, of that I've no doubt, but unless the Duke of Beaufort and the Gentlemen of the Cycle are more enthusiastic in the south of Wales, I cannot picture the Principality being of much assistance to his Highness."

"Surely, surely there is enthusiasm in Wales. The Catholics round about Holywell are ardent for the Stuarts. There are old men still living who recollect the day when James the Second himself paid a visit to the holy well. I think you are misinformed."

"There are a few of the gentry interested, I grant you, but there seems a lukewarmness about. I get little or no response from any of my tenants. They say they have had enough of war, and they care not who reigns provided they get good homes and a living wage."

"It's that fellow Yorke," interposed Seth. "He is for ever tampering with them. Our tenantry are the same. He calls it education, but what he is doing is to make them discontented with their lot in life."

"Perhaps their lot is not such a lot after all," observed Ann, but no one paid her heed.

"I tell you," went on Seth vehemently, "the man is a traitor. He openly avers his Hanoverian principles."

"Well, it is safe for him to do so while German George is on the throne," remarked Eyton drily.

"I care not what you say. He is our greatest stumbling block. We shall make no progress here until he is removed."

Ann looked startled. "Do you mean—kill him?"

The men looked at one another. Eyton spoke first. "Kill him? Egad, no. Merely ship him abroad to the College in Paris where he can be kept out of further mischief."

"But are we sure that he is at the root of the trouble?" asked Ann dubiously.

"I, for one, am sure," said Seth emphatically, "and I, for one, am willing to search his house and see what incriminating correspondence we can find."

Sir Watkin demurred. "Lad, that's hardly the procedure for a gentleman. I'll have none of it."

"I have none of your scruples, Sir Watkin," retorted Seth. "The rogue's away and I'm for striking while the iron's hot. Who'll come with me?"

There was a silence and then Ann said in a subdued voice, "I will accompany you."

"Demme, Ann," burst out her father. "You don't know what you say. You shall not soil your little fingers with this sort of work."

"Quite right, Ann," interposed Seth hastily. "I shall go alone."

103

Squire Trevor expected a protest but Ann said nothing. Seth took his leave and as the remaining men conversed over their wine, Ann slipped out unobserved. She remained unnoticed until Seth, pausing at the gate of the old Rectory to look about him, started with surprise at a figure close behind.

"Go back, Ann," he said in a fierce whisper. "This is too much. Demme, I may have to break in."

"There is no need. I have seen where he hides the key." Ann was adamant, nor could she explain why it was that she had acted in this manner save that she experienced revulsion at the idea of anyone ransacking the rooms which held pleasant memories for her. The house was in utter darkness, the shutters all closed. No smoke came from the chimneys. No dog barked. Like two conspirators they crossed the lawn and Ann, slipping her fingers under a stone near the front doorstep, produced the key. Quietly, they let themselves in and locked the door behind them. Seth fumbled for a flint and steel. "It will be safe to have a light," he whispered. "Not a chink will show through those closed shutters." He lit a candle and then handed another to Ann. "See that the wax does not drop on the floor," he cautioned.

"I will see to this room," said Ann, pausing at the door of what she had come to call the music-room. "Do you see to the remainder of the house, Seth."

She heard him move softly away yet still she stood motionless, candle raised, at the entrance to the room. It savoured of desecration to enter on such a mission. The harpsichord stood open and seemed to look at her reproachfully. Almost she could picture Philip Yorke running his fingers over the keys in that beautiful melody of Purcell's which haunted her. She glanced into the corner. The sword which had won honour at Dettingen was not in its accustomed place. Ann looked about her. She had no desire to search. Still she could not account for the whim which had brought her to the place; it might have been that she felt it would be more respectable to have one friendly person on the premises. A rosebud, somewhat faded, lay on the table and beside it a sheet of paper and a quill-pen. Curiosity got the better of her. Shielding her candle she walked to the table. On one sheet of paper lines were scribbled at random, as though the writer had experimented. Were they, she wondered, some code? They seemed to be an attempt to apostrophize a rose. Not the White Rose of the Stuarts, she thought. Perhaps the rose on the table was the flower which had inspired the lines, and that rosebud was pink. She glanced at the second piece of paper where the completed verses appeared. As she read them, she experienced an emotional reaction which surprised her; the words, simple as they were, possessed poignancy.

> O, radiant rose,
>   So fair and fresh and fragrant,
>   You banish sleep; my closing eyes behold
> You in repose;
>   My restless thoughts are vagrant
>   Until enmeshed in your seductive fold .

> *O, lovely flower,*
>   *My lonely life enriching,*
>   *Rare is your scent, and smooth your velvet touch;*
> *Slave to your power,*
>   *So subtle and bewitching,*
>   *Fain would I pluck what I desire so much.*

"How beautiful," she whispered, and picked up the rosebud. "Poor, faded flower, how could you inspire such eloquence?" A faint footfall sounded in the passage. "Oh, Seth, we must not stay here. Let us go. I feel as though I had pried at that which no eyes were intended to see."

"That, at least, is correct, Ann," said a quiet voice which caused her to spring about with her hand pressed to her palpitating heart. The tall figure of Philip Yorke was framed in the doorway. In the light of the candle, Ann could see his eyes. They seemed darker, more penetrating. His face was as grave as ever.

"Seth, I fear, is locked in an upper room," explained Mr. Yorke. "Forgive the seeming discourtesy, but I mistook him for an intruder and not a neighbour bent on a friendly call."

"Oh, Mr. Yorke," stammered Ann.

"It is, indeed, friendly of you to come so informally," he resumed. "Will you not sit down? You have no objection to my remaining?"

"Mr. Yorke . . . I don't know what to say——"

"Then it is simple not to say it. Do sit down."

"I cannot. Really I cannot. I have no right to be here, I know."

"My dear, you have every right. Come when you will. Stay as long as you choose. The benefit of being master of one's own house is that one is in a position to confer favours on friends."

"You will never regard me as a friend again, Mr. Yorke. I can only apologize. I—am so sorry——"

"Dear little girl," he said gently as he dropped his hands on her shoulders. "Do not distress yourself. Indeed, I rejoice to see you under any conditions. Dear girl—for that is all you are—so full of dreams of romance and adventure! The dreams do not always take shape after our fashioning, do they? I will not ask why you are here, Ann, but let me take this opportunity of assuring you that you are ever welcome and that all that I have is yours to do with what you will." He held out a key. "See, here is the key of the door. I have another. Take it and use it when you wish."

Ann shook her head in dumb misery. The tears were not far from her eyes.

"You are too kind. You—almost kill me with your chivalry. But you do not know——"

"Perhaps I can guess! Better let me remain in ignorance. And if it is something which distresses you, I beg you to forget it also."

Ann turned pitiful eyes up to his steady ones. "I am so ashamed," she whispered. "I— I read your poem and I had no right. It—it is so beautiful."

"I lay no claim to being a poet," he said quietly. "I just tried to

105

write what I felt. The effort is humble but if it has pleased you it has justified its creation."

He picked up the paper, folded it and handed it to her. She took it almost reluctantly. "May I have the rosebud, too?" she asked. "Though I cannot understand how you could be inspired to write such exquisite lines by a humble flower."

"A rose can be an inspiration."

"Oh, I have it. You are in love. It is your poem to—her. And her name must be Rose. How beautiful."

He smiled gravely.

"I am so glad, Mr. Yorke. So glad you are in love. It must be lonely living without love. I hope you will be very happy. Is—is she lovely?"

"The loveliest thing about her is that she is utterly unconscious of her own loveliness."

"I—I will take the poem, if I may? Thank you. I shall not let it be desecrated by other eyes. Your secret is safe with me, Mr. Yorke."

"Is it, Ann? Well, I must entrust you with it, willynilly."

The tears were dried now. She gave him a shy smile. "Will you—will you release Mr. Morrice sometime, and forgive him, too?"

"He shall accompany you home."

"And you forgive me, Mr. Yorke?"

Philip Yorke regarded her intently. His face was serious, yet Ann thought she detected a subtle light dancing in his eyes. "No matter how often you call on me, Ann, I shall always forgive you!"

CHAPTER TWENTY-THREE

THE FOLLOWING MORNING ANN ACCOMPANIED SQUIRE TREVOR WHEN he rode to Wrexham, for he had business with his solicitor. He was quieter than usual, preoccupied, and as she glanced at him she noted the silver in his hair, and wondered whether she had been wise in encouraging him to venture for the Prince. The zest which had inspired him in the 'Fifteen was over and done with; futile, perhaps dangerous it was to fan the embers of a dying flame into a blaze when little that was combustible remained.

Ann never tired of going to Wrexham; to her it was the metropolis of North Wales. Its stately church was a thing of beauty. She took pride in its graceful pinnacle-crested tower and rich carvings, and frequently asked why this should not be a cathedral when it was so much more dignified than the square squat structure at St. Asaph. Ann wandered about the streets, looking at the shops while her father was shut in with the lawyer. There was unrest in the streets. Outside the 'Horse and Jockey' the footpath was blocked by miners who argued in loud voices. Rumours of the landing of the Prince in Scotland spread like wildfire. Some were palpably wild and exaggerated but all were sufficient to set men talking. Ann was alone. Seth had ridden off home in a fit of the sulks for Philip Yorke's magnanimity had left him under an obligation which he found irksome and obnoxious. The hothead would have infinitely preferred to have fought h

106

way out than to be liberated with a quiet courtesy which was galling to his wounded pride. His common sense told him that he was in the wrong and that Philip Yorke had acted with forbearance—which made him all the more bitter and unreasonable. Ann was a little disappointed in Seth. She felt that Philip Yorke had been particularly nice under the circumstances and she failed to see why Seth could not have thought so, too. She walked up the gentle incline which led to the old church. She never entered the great door without wondering whether she trod on the very stones which Charles the Martyr had walked upon when he visited Wrexham a century before. And she liked to stare up at the quaint faces and designs which long-dead craftsmen had carved on the corbels. There was one old fellow with a beard who looked particularly incongruous. Ann adored him. She could never quite determine whether he was supposed to be one of the Prophets or was merely a caricature of the stonemason. Her eyes took in the beauty of the stained glass windows, the monuments, and brasses setting forth in ponderous sentences the virtues of the departed, and then she fell to thinking about Philip Yorke again. The villagers were right when they dubbed him a Mystery Man; she could not sum him up. It did look as though he conspired to wreck the Jacobite cause in North Wales, and yet he was so kindly. Perhaps that was just a pose. Reason suggested that it was, but Ann was more guided by intuition, and something within her felt drawn to him, she knew not why. He was a paradox. But then, thought Ann, she was herself a paradox for while she doubted him, she liked him. She had counted on his friendship. What beautiful words he could write . . . perhaps being in love inspired one to do one's best. She rather envied this unknown Rose who was the object of his adoration. Ann felt—she might as well admit it—just a tiny, tiny bit jealous. "Oh, don't be such a fool," she said, and then glanced over her shoulder to see if anyone had heard her. The building was still empty; not even the verger was about. Feeling self-conscious, Ann walked briskly back into the main street. She encountered her father coming in search of her. He looked a better colour.

"Demme, girl, by what they say there's a sporting chance of young Charlie pulling off his *coup*. Perhaps I was wise to plunge after all. Well, lass, it's sink or swim. I've staked heavily. Either you'll be a lady of title and fortune or—or——"

"Your daughter. Darling, isn't there some place where we could have luncheon? I'm ravenous."

"Bless the girl. What a figure you will acquire if you don't control your appetite. There's the 'Lion,' they put on a good meal. Let's try our luck, Ann. I'm pretty peckish myself."

As the Squire ate, he talked in staccato sentences punctuated by periods of mastication. "He's put the cat among the pigeons, has young Charlie. . . . They say he landed with but seven men, would you believe it? . . . But the heads of the Clans are declaring for him. . . . He should have brought French troops with him, though . . . that was the stipulation. . . . Lord, how does he expect to accomplish anything without artillery against Cope? Eh, lass?"

107

"I am sure Prince Charles Edward is able to cope with him."

"Eh, what's that? You're laughing at me. Ann, call that fellow. I could do with another tankard of small ale . . . what was I saying? . . . It's a mad venture. . . . Folk in Wrexham favour the Stuart, so they say . . . they talk loud and half are soused from drinking his health, but demme if I see any sign of volunteering . . . and they are loath to part with their money."

The Squire sunk his worried countenance in a comforting tankard. The clatter of many hoofs and the clank of equipment made Ann hurry to a window. Crowds were surging to watch as a squadron of dragoons walked their weary chargers down the centre of the road, making a vivid patch of colour amid the more sober coats of the townsfolk. Several officers were in front. Foremost was Major Manstein, who rode with an expression of grim resolution on his remorseless face. He did not turn his head but stared fixedly in front as though despising the curious crowd. Ann, nevertheless, drew back behind the curtain, and she felt her gooseflesh creep as though she had encountered something of evil omen.

"What is it, girl? The red-jackets? I heard that they were mustering in the town. Which way do they go?"

"Towards the English border, Father."

"Ay, they say there's a fine how-d'y'-do. There are not enough troops to stop the Prince marching on London and our lads are being recalled from Flanders to stand between the capital and its foes."

"Say, rather, its rightful Prince," cried Ann, her face aglow with pleasure. "Father, Father, our chance has come at last."

"Maybe, girl, maybe. But don't forget. It's been all talking and no fighting so far. Our regiments who fought at Dettingen and Fontenoy are the picked troops of Europe and are not likely to run away from a crowd of bare-legged Highlanders."

When the Squire and his daughter reached home, Howells was awaiting them to take charge of the horses. As Squire Trevor walked, a little stiffly, to the house, the head groom made signs behind his back that he wished Ann to follow him. Ann's curiosity was roused and she required no second bidding. These were exciting days and anything was liable to happen. Once around the corner of the building she hurried to Howells' side.

"A note for you, Mistress Ann," said the man in a low voice as he slipped a small square of paper into her hand. "A drover brought it; said it was important and that you'd understand who sent it."

"Oh, thank you. I—I'll read it in the harness-room." Ann hurried to her favourite seat and was soon ensconced on the lid of the corn-bin. The outer cover was soiled from the messenger's hands; Ann's fingers trembled as she opened the note and read.

'GOLDEN EYES,

This, to tell you that the arms are safe, and for that matter that I am, too. I have heard of your effort to get to me and though it was unsuccessful I adore you for making the attempt. I shall not risk another visit to your window—it was a close call the last time.

If you would see me, come to the north end of the Black Barn to-night. Any time after 10 o'c. I shall carry arms, but the only ones I hope to make use of this time will be the ones which hunger for your embrace.

Your devoted
DICON.'

Ann's face flushed as she re-read the note. She had never had anything resembling a love-letter before. She concealed it in her bosom and walked back to the house with an assumption of indifference, but she knew that her cheeks were burning and that a corner of the note was sticking into her soft flesh. It was a pleasurable discomfort and seemed to be a spur to her thoughts. She felt curiously elated. Gone was the lassitude of the previous day. Her step had suddenly become springy and the sunshine seemed brighter. She was discovering, though she knew it not, that weariness was frequently a thing of the spirit. Dicon was safe ; Dicon was coming to see her ! The grandfather clock in the corner seemed to tick with irritating deliberation.

"You're looking more like your old self, Ann," observed her father. "Glad to be back home, that's what it is. Have done with this gallivanting. I'm plaguy glad to have you back, safe from harm. When next you go a-riding, you ride with your old father. Our little jaunt to-day has done you the world of good. You look positively blooming."

"Yes, Father," said Ann demurely, and made an excuse to get into the garden where the air would cool her burning cheeks. Dicon had said he meant to take her in his arms. Ought she to let him ? She decided that she ought not to—but she hoped he would all the same. She whistled for Rip and walked across the meadows and the way she took led to the Black Barn. It was set apart from the rest of the buildings on the home farm; an antiquated structure of overlapping slabs of wood, well-tarred to preserve them from the weather. It was not often visited and was utilized mainly for the storing of tumbrels or implements which were not in everyday use. She lifted the heavy wooden latch and peered into the dusty, musty gloom. The ground was coated with old hay and straw. A few sparrows flew protestingly to the roof at her intrusion. Ann stood and stared and the untidy structure with its cobwebs seemed an enchanted place. Dicon would be there at ten that very night. She closed the door almost reverently and looked about her to see whether she had been observed. There was, of course, no one to see her. There was, for that matter, no reason why she should not look in at the old barn, yet she felt like a conspirator. A copse straggled to the wall of loose stones which ran across the rear of the barn, and beyond this lay a broad stretch of woodland through which a ride had been cut long years before. Ann peered down the green alley and pictured Dicon's horse pacing its noiseless sward. Then she glanced at the sun. Would it never set ? With a sigh she returned home.

When at length dusk had fallen, Ann tip-toed from the hall,

slipped a hooded cloak over her shoulders, looked about her furtively, and made her way with caution to the edge of the wood. In the shade of the trees, she walked through the grass, noiseless as a moving shadow. The dew wet her stockings and the hem of her dress grew sodden, but she paid no heed. Her eyes, wide and bright, were concentrated on the old Black Barn. She saw a horse tethered beneath an oak and her heart gave a bound.

Then she saw Dicon, bare-headed, his keen brown face illuminated by a smile of welcome. He flung up his hand in a gay salute.

Ann broke into a run and before she knew it a pair of arms with muscles like steel were about her and her cheek was pressed against a button on his coat. She remembered afterwards that it was uncomfortable, but at the time she was conscious of nothing but his nearness and dearness; and that Dicon had come to her at last.

"Golden eyes!" he whispered as he tilted her face to his.

"Oh, Dicon," she whispered, and all the longing of interminable hours were in the words.

His cheek was against hers, he seemed to grow closer, seeking, demanding.

"Dicon, you—you mustn't kiss me."

"No, my sweet? Then I won't if you don't want me to."

"But I do!"

"Of course you do. Then why tell me not to?"

"I don't know what made me say it. It was silly."

"Very silly, my dear."

She sighed and closed her eyes. Presently she said in a drowsy voice, "Dicon, I don't . . . ever . . . want . . . to talk . . . again!"

He gave a low laugh.

"Save your breath for kisses, sweet. Rest content."

"Content," she whispered.

Presently Dicon straightened up and appeared to be listening. At the alertness and tenseness of his body Ann looked up, his mood communicating itself to her. "What is it?" she asked.

"The packhorses," he said, "I am sure I heard them. They ought to be here shortly. Then—an end to kisses, beloved."

"Packhorses?" repeated Ann.

"We are bringing the arms here for concealment."

"Here?"

"Yes. To the Black Barn. I could not think of a safer place."

"Does Father know?"

"Not a thing. I had no time to notify him. Also, if he knows he will fidget and worry."

"Yes," said Ann. "He will worry."

Dicon's arm was about her waist and her head was against his shoulder. "Tell me, Dicon, I forgot to ask you—how did you escape the frigate's boats? I thought you were doomed. You have no idea what I went through."

Conway gave her a slight squeeze. "We owe our escape to you."

"To me?"

"Well, to that stable lad of yours. It was just before dawn when

110

our look-out sighted him. He had rowed out in a small boat from Llanddulas and was about exhausted. We helped him aboard and he told us about the dragoons who had joined the riding officers and were patrolling the coast, having (God knows how) received word of our coming. He told us, too, that three boats from a man-o'-war were lying concealed at the mouth of the Conway ready to board us and that, the wind having dropped, they meant to row out and capture both ship and arms. It was almost dawn and we had to act quickly. Our lads worked like fiends getting the cases of arms out of the hold. We rowed 'em to Puffin Island—and the devil of a time we had finding a suitable landing spot with that tiderace to fight against. Anyhow, by the time the sun was up the cases were stored in the tower of that little ruined church which crowns the island, and Hughie and I lay among the bracken and watched the three ship's boats pulling towards their mare's nest. Peris had got his tale ready and thought he could bluff them, though I don't think he felt too happy. I wasn't too happy either when I saw them take the old craft in tow and make for the Conway."

"I was there when they brought her in," said Ann. "They have detained the ship and Mr. Peris."

"Ay. They would! Well, it's the luck of the game. Anyhow, we have the arms safe and that is half the battle. Thanks to you."

"But Dicon, I did nothing. I did set out to warn you but that abominable Major Manstein found me and would not let me go."

"Damn him. But who sent Hughie, then? I understood he came from you?"

"He did accompany me but I do not know how he obtained his information. He must have overheard something when we stayed in St. Asaph. He's an intelligent lad and would do much to serve me."

"Well, he certainly served us and saved the cause in these parts."

"I must thank him. Where is he, Dicon? With the packhorses?"

"No. Just before we started I wanted to have a word with him but he was not to be found. Hark! The pack train is approaching through the wood. Let us get the barn door open so that they can go straight inside."

Ann helped him to pull the wide door open and then said, "And what then, Dicon? What is your next move?"

"Scotland, my dear, without a moment's delay. I must report to the Prince and see what is taking place up there."

"Dicon! You are not going to leave me?"

"I must, my sweet. The Prince depends on me."

"I will come with you."

"Not this time. The next, perhaps. Listen. I will not stay. Give me three weeks. Perhaps a month, for I do not know where the Prince is to be found. Then I shall be back with you again and we will make our plans for the future."

"A month. Oh, Dicon. And every hour seems an age."

"I shall come back to you, Golden Eyes. Never fear."

"Dicon?"

"Yes?"

111

"Did you love Frances Holt?"

Richard Conway swore softly. "Now what on earth put that into your pretty head?"

"But did you?"

"I—liked her. I thought I did. It seems long ago. But that was before I set eyes on you. I did not know the meaning of real love. I have discovered since."

"When?"

"The morning I woke up on the hearth-rug and saw you asleep in the chair trying to keep guard over me. Bless you."

"Oh, Dicon, I did so mean to keep awake but I was so sleepy. Did you really fall in love with me? I must have looked ridiculous."

"Adorable. I loved you then and I love you now, and I shall always love you."

"Oh, Dicon, I love you, too. Kiss me."

Dicon looked up with a sigh. "Confound the packhorses!" he said, almost viciously.

CHAPTER TWENTY-FOUR

WHEN RICHARD CONWAY TURNED HIS BACK ON HAPPINESS AND RODE northward, his first thought was to conserve his horse. He had a long ride before him and though the distance in no wise daunted him, he felt concerned about the staying powers of his mount. He could, of course, have obtained remounts on the way, but he was averse to this, because of the probability of his own good steed being commandeered before he could return for it. He resolved to sacrifice time rather than his animal and so rode easily, pausing periodically to rest his mount and, incidentally, himself. Beyond looking to his primings and seeing that his sword hilt was unencumbered, he took no precautions against the perils of the way. Footpads and highwaymen he scorned; his chief danger was a chance encounter with some Hanoverian dragoons who were, in all probability, patrolling the main roads which led to the Scottish border. Fortune, however, favoured him, and as General Wade had resolved to concentrate on Newcastle, the majority of the horse were on the eastern side of England. This, it was surmised, would be the route chosen by the Prince should he decide to invade England.

Richard Conway was a paradox. There were people who said that he was too reckless to be trusted, yet here he was, tearing himself away from the lovelight in Ann's eyes at the very moment when her virginal love was awakened. He did so in order to take his place beside a royal adventurer who had embarked on as mad-brained a scheme as that favoured by his mother when she ran away from the Polish court to wed England's disinherited monarch. How was one to place confidence in a young man who set out with but seven followers to conquer a kingdom? Richard Conway's traducers would find it hard to substantiate their charge of inconstancy in the face of such blind devotion. Dicon himself often wondered what charm there was about the Stuarts which could exact such fealty from subjects who usually had all to lose and nothing to gain but royal thanks—if remembered. Dicon confessed that he had succumbed to the manly charm of this twenty-five-year-old prince; this son of a Pretender king and a run-away princess; this lad with a slim figure and lustrous brown eyes which could melt ladies' hearts or glance down a gun sight with unerring precision.

Conway soon had proof that he was by no means alone; there were others greater than he who had struck their colours to the Stuart magnetism. Lochiel, the grizzled veteran who wielded probably the greatest influence of any chief in Scotland, had proved vulnerable. Men were discussing the matter when Conway rode his weary horse into the camp beside the loch. The Prince tarried at Borradale and it was here Dicon found him when he arrived after a week's riding. Lochiel, he heard, had urged Prince Charles to return to France. The clans had only agreed to support him on the understanding that a substantial French force with artillery landed in Scotland. Here was the Prince arriving without arms and a following of seven men. It was madness. How could he succeed? Prince Charles replied with simple dignity—"In a few days, with the few friends I have, I will erect the Royal Standard, and proclaim to the people of Britain that Charles Stuart is come to claim the crown of his ancestors, to win it, or to perish in the attempt. Lochiel, who, my father has often told me, was our firmest friend, may stay at home and learn from the newspapers the fate of his Prince." The world heard the answer. "I'll share the fate of my Prince, and so shall every man over whom nature or fortune has given me any power."

On that reply hung the issue of the rebellion. Had Lochiel refused, there would have been no 'Forty-Five. But Lochiel could not resist the appeal of Charles Edward, he declared for the Prince, the clans began to rally, and the 'Forty-Five came to pass. When Dicon Conway saw Charles Edward standing for the first time on Scottish soil he scarcely recognized his leader. The Prince was wearing a plain black coat, a plain shirt (not very clean), a cambric stock fixed with a silver buckle, a fair round wig, and a plain hat fastened by a canvas string to one of his coat buckles. He was endeavouring to pass as an English clergyman who was anxious to see and converse with Highlanders. The garb did not become him. After Lochiel's resolve the Prince forsook his sable attire and appeared in the Highland garb which was ever after to be associated with the name of Bonnie Prince Charlie. It fitted him as though he had been born a true son of the heather; as much a Highlander as any of the chieftains who rallied to do his bidding.

These were stirring times and Richard Conway had little opportunity of dreaming of the girl he had left behind. Wales seemed a far country to him as he rode amid the heather and listened to the skirling of the pipes. On August the nineteenth the Standard of the White Rose was unfurled at Glenfinnan at the head of Loch Shiel.

The Prince rode along the front rank of the assembled clansmen. With a significant gesture he drew his sword crying, "I have flung away the scabbard."

At his magnetic voice the blue bonnets were flung into the air and a bristle of claymores and Lochaber-axes testified that the Highlanders were ready to fight for their Stuart leader. The moment was opportune. Three days before two companies of the First Regiment of Foot (now the Royal Scots), marching from Fort Augustus to the relief of Fort William, were surrounded in the lonely hills by Highlanders and forced to surrender after two of their number had been slain by marksmen amid the heather, and their commanding officer wounded. Thus it was that when the Macdonalds and the Stuarts were lined up at Glenfinnan wondering whether they would be joined by the Camerons, they heard the sound of pipes, saw the long lines of Camerons advancing over the crest of a hill, and in their midst walked the two companies of captured redcoats.

With this augury the Royal Standard was unfurled. King James's commission appointing his son as Prince Regent was read with becoming circumstance, the golden cross of Saint Andrew on a blue field (the clan colour of the Stuarts) took its place beside the Standard. The rebellion was officially launched.

The men were eager for the fight; eager to come to grips with Sir John Cope, commander-in-chief of the Royal forces in Scotland. It was reported that he had assembled eighteen hundred foot and six hundred dragoons at Stirling. It was tempting, but first Charles had to go recruiting. Early in September the Prince was in Perth, where he was proclaimed Regent for King James the Eighth of Scotland and the Third of England. Richard Conway marched with the clansmen. He suffered their hardships, shared their privations, subsisted on oatmeal and scraps of beef roasted on roadside fires. Word came through that Sir John Cope intended to bring his army from Inverness to Aberdeen where transports were awaiting them. The men were to be shipped to Edinburgh. It was his intention to occupy Scotland's capital before the rebels could get there. Prince Charles Edward resolved to forestall him and the southward march began. With colours flying and bagpipes playing the Highlanders moved resolutely towards the capital. When the army reached the upper waters of the Forth, the Prince, who had a natural flair for doing the right thing, leaped from his saddle and was the first to put foot in the water. He led the first detachment across the ford. At Stirling they drank wine offered them by enthusiastic townspeople while the English garrison in the castle fired indignant but innocuous grape-shot in their direction. Having encircled the castle at a safe distance, the Prince's army resumed its march on Edinburgh.

Richard Conway was there when it made its triumphal entry. He saw the King's dragoons gallop off in ignominious flight after a brief exchange of pistol shots with Charles's handful of cavaliers. The Jacobite women of Edinburgh—and there were many—had their kerchiefs fluttering as the advance guard of the Highlanders drew near to the city walls. The garrison shut itself in the castle high on its precipitous rock. As Charles Edward possessed no artillery, they remained immune, but within and without the walls of the city there was enthusiasm for the invader. Lochiel and his Camerons had

114

captured the Netherbow and had thrown wide the gate. With uplifted broadswords and fierce yells the Camerons swept through the city streets. Alarmed citizens peered down from upper windows on the moving mass of blue bonnets and white cockades. Edinburgh had been captured. In the wynds and closes there was ample opportunity for resistance but none was forthcoming. There might have been hand-to-hand fighting; there was none.

Sir John Cope's transports were anchored off Dunbar and his men were landed ready to march on Edinburgh. Though he had arrived too late, Cope had no intention of allowing the rebel prince to remain in the capital unmolested.

The Prince was proclaimed Regent at the Cross. The populace looked in amused amazement at the motley crew of clansmen; men in ragged plaids of differing patterns, men with long muskets, men with rusty claymores and leathern targets, men with old Lochaber axes bound to handles with twine, men with the light of triumph in their wild eyes. And the Prince ? Everyone was staring at his handsome face. He was wearing a short tartan coat without a plaid, a blue bonnet with the white cockade, and on his breast there glittered the star of Saint Andrew. He good-humouredly let the people gaze their fill. Then, mounting his charger, he rode down the royal mile to Holyrood Castle. Its grim doors received him and the debonair prince disappeared from sight. The venerable palace again had a Stuart beneath its roof.

CHAPTER TWENTY-FIVE

IT WAS SOME TIME BEFORE ANN LEARNED OF THE STIRRING EVENTS IN Scotland and then the news reached her in fragmentary fashion as messengers rode south to visit the Jacobites in North Wales. She would have preferred to have heard the reports from the lips of Dicon Conway, but it was not to be. When the arms had been safely concealed in the Black Barn and the string of unladen packhorses had vanished into the dark silence of the woods, Ann went home in a daze, her face still burning from the ardour of Dicon's parting kisses. She felt strangely stirred. It was, to her, a new experience and a new emotion: heady wine for a young girl. Restlessly she tossed in her bed, a prey to her desires, until the cocks crowed in the stackyard of the Home Farm and the grey light of dawn filtered into her bed-chamber. For the first time in her life she was late in going downstairs, and her heavy eyes attracted the notice of her father who, for once, was at the breakfast table before her. Ann attributed her pallor to a headache and, being a lover of truth, persuaded herself that her heaviness was almost a headache, though heartache might have been nearer the truth. She sought solace out of doors. Across the meadows she could see the significant outline of the Black Barn, the place where the arms were concealed, the spot where she had surrendered lips and heart to Dicon Conway. Almost she wished that she had taken Black Prince from the stables and had gone riding with Dicon up the north road, the road which led to the great adventure.

Without premeditation, Ann turned along the road which ran past the old Rectory. So full was her mind of Dicon that she gave no thought to its occupant. The sound of her name caused her to start with surprise. Philip Yorke was in the garden, and as she looked up he swung open a wicket-gate and begged her to enter.

"But I could not, Mr. Yorke," cried Ann in confusion.

"Why not, Ann?"

"Have you forgotten my last visit and the nature of it?"

"I never forget your visits, Ann. They are not sufficiently frequent to impose undue strain on the memory."

"Have you really forgiven me, Mr. Yorke?"

"I shall find it harder to forgive you if you do not enter in now."

"But I have no excuse for entering."

"Let me devise one. We could, you know, resume the search which my unexpected appearance inconsiderately interrupted."

His face was grave but his eyes twinkled. Ann, however, blushed and Yorke apologized hastily. "That was ungenerous of me, Ann. Forgive my levity. But seriously, my dear, if you require an excuse I can let you have one. There is something of importance which I have to say to you; something which affects the welfare of those who are dear to you."

"What is it, Mr. Yorke?"

"Come inside and I will tell you. I dare not whisper it here lest the birds of the air should hear my words."

He led the way to the house. Ann followed meekly, without protest. She felt uneasy, a little annoyed for capitulating so easily, for experiencing this interruption when all she asked for was to be alone with her thoughts of Dicon and his fascinating impetuosity. There was a quiet magnetism about Philip Yorke which was compelling. He flung wide the door and stood back as she entered. Instinctively she walked towards the music-room. Yorke placed a chair for her but did not speak. He crossed to the music-stool and his expressive fingers began to move softly over the keys of the harpsichord. He played the melody of Purcell which had so charmed her.

"When will you tell me the name of that piece?" she demanded.

"Ann," exclaimed Philip Yorke as he wheeled quickly. "Ann, might I suggest that you give orders to one of your farmhands to drive a herd of cows down the ride which is cut through your woods?"

"I do not understand, Mr. Yorke!" Ann's surprise was not simulated. She met the keen gaze without wavering. "We never send our cows that way; why should we?"

"I passed that way this morning, Ann, on my rambles. The turf was marked by horses' hoofs coming and going. They ended at the Black Barn; plain enough for a blind man to read; laden horses going to the barn, unladen animals departing. It made me think of packhorses from the coast."

"Mr. Yorke, you know . . ."

"I know nothing, my dear, and I do not wish to know. Let me rather say that I surmise."

"I may as well speak. If you have seen so much——"

116

"Others may see and surmise. They may not be as disinterested as I am. For instance as I came away I passed a lady whom we both know slightly. I refer to Miss Frances Holt."

"Had she seen the tracks?" asked Ann quickly.

"I could not say. She was not in the wood when I saw her. I do suggest that you get the incriminating tracks obliterated as speedily as possible. The next passer-by might not be friendly disposed. There is our friend Major Manstein, for example."

"He has ridden towards England. I saw him pass through Wrexham at the head of his men."

"He has probably left his spies behind him. Is there any guarantee that he will not unexpectedly return?"

"You make me quite nervous, Mr. Yorke."

"It is the last thing I wish to do. I would, if I could, make you cautious. I do not want you to run into danger."

"But why, Mr. Yorke, should you be so solicitous? That is what I fail to understand. Truly you are rightly termed the Mystery Man."

Yorke began to pick out the Purcell melody softly. "There is no mystery, Ann. I am as transparent as the day. It is because you seek for mysteries that you find them where none exist. I am suspected of being a spy, it seems. But, my dear girl, I am a loyal adherent of the reigning House, how, then, could I be a spy? I support the Whig ministry because it labours for the stability of the country. That is what we need above all else, stability. How can the reforms which cry aloud for adoption ever come to pass? How can the crimes be stamped out, the injustices remedied? I will be frank with you. I care not greatly for the reigning dynasty. Princes may fall out among themselves if they choose but why should they drag other men into their quarrels? Many a man who has laid down his life for a cause did not desire martial glory. All he asked of life was a home of his own and a wife to work for and to love. I repeat, I care little for one House or another. But I am concerned, greatly concerned, at the possibility of one whom I regard as a dear friend incurring risks which are far greater than she realizes."

"You mean me, Mr. Yorke?"

"I mean you, Ann. It is so obvious that you have been swept off your feet by those frothy words, Romance and Adventure. The latter merely means privation and the former is a bubble: mere moonshine."

"You do not believe that really, Mr. Yorke? Did you not go adventuring when you wore that sword at Dettingen? Did you condemn romance when you were my age? I tell you I had as soon not live at all as to live a life untouched by romance. Tell me, has romance never touched your life: your orderly, self-contained, self-controlled existence? I seem to recollect once seeing some verses addressed to—a rose."

Philip Yorke gazed down into the eloquent eyes upturned to his. The corners of his mouth twitched. The light which danced in his eyes was unmistakable now. "You have me there, Ann! A shrewd hit: harder than you know. You got clean through my guard. I see

117

I must qualify my words, though I will not withdraw them. As for moonshine: why not? There is some subtle witchery in the light of the moon."

"So you will leave me my romance, Mr. Yorke?"

"On the condition that you leave me mine."

"That is a bargain then. No, not a bargain. What a hard, mercenary word that is! Let us say 'understanding'. A better word, is it not?"

"A much better word. Nothing surpasses understanding."

"I think that you are the most understanding man I have ever met; you whom many have misunderstood."

"It is easy for you to understand me, Ann. My desire is to serve you, to protect you from harm, to make you happy. I have little else to think about so I am able to devote considerable time and thought to the delectable subject."

"That is what I cannot understand; why should you want to do this?"

"Shall we say for friendship's sake?"

"For friendship's sake?"

"I would like you to regard me as a friend. You do count me as one?"

"I will do if you wish, though it seems strange that one of your age and outlook should desire it."

"Why strange?"

"You are learned, you have seen the world, you have high ideals while I——"

"Yes, what of you, Ann?"

"I am just a scatterbrain. I do not want to be serious; I do not want to concern myself about educating the poor. I like a horse, and the open road, and—and—romance."

"Have your romance, Ann, but do not, I implore you, mistake the shadow for the substance: the glamour for the glory. Disguise your political sentiments when you ride abroad; there is no need for it when you are with me. It is so apparent where your sympathies lie. You have succumbed to the lure of the white cockade. You see in the Young Pretender a picturesque figure; I see in him a menace to prosperity and progress. You are carried away by stories of his large brown eyes and slim figure; I see in him a foolhardy adventurer who is prepared to squander the lives of hundreds of men to satisfy his vanity. Who but a fool would embark on such a venture with the support of only seven men? It is folly; utter folly. I am sorry that your father has been persuaded into risking his home and your future by backing a venture which is doomed before it is begun."

"I wish you would not talk thus. You discourage me. I am filled with forebodings."

"I wish that I could not merely discourage but dissuade you, but already I understand you so well that I know you will go your wilful way. You remind me of a moth that flutters about a candle flame. May you not burn your wings. I find it ironical that so frequently in life we require to be saved less from our enemies than from ourselves." He gave a short laugh, and rising to his feet, began to pace the room

118

hands clasped behind his back. He appeared momentarily to have forgotten Ann's presence; his conversation savoured of soliloquy. "What's at the back of this thing we call Life? Is every happening fortuitous, or is there some profound scheme in the making? It would be so much easier to determine our conduct if we knew why we were here and what was expected of us. Why should people of high principles strive against one another because they differ over some detail? So far as I can see the Power which created us gave us reason so that we might acquire wisdom to guide our faltering steps through the fog of perplexity that so often settles on human life. That is why I want to see the minds of people developed. Surely life must attain a higher standard if men are taught to use their reason?"

Ann looked perplexed and remarked, "I don't know, Mr. Yorke." Instantly the laughter returned to his eyes. "Of course you don't, my dear. I have committed the unpardonable sin of becoming serious in the presence of a lady. Was I asking you to solve the riddle of the universe? What were we talking about when I digressed?"

"I think you were persuading me to give up taking risks for the Stuart cause. Let me tell you, Mr. Yorke, that much as I appreciate your generous motives in trying to protect me from the results of my folly, I intend to go my own way. I am for Bonnie Prince Charlie. For him I'll scheme, and I'll fight (if necessary); I want to see his father returned to his rightful throne. Nothing you say can alter me."

"Go your own way then, you headstrong, adorable child. Let me ask this favour, Ann. When you are in difficulties—as you are bound to be—always feel that I am in the background. Nothing will be too great or too small for me to attempt on your behalf. I have no wife, no one to care about me, so I can say without hesitation that my life is at your service."

"I thank you, Mr. Yorke. What you say is hard to believe. I mean about your not having anybody to care for you. What of your Rose Girl? And do you think that she would approve of your wishing to be so friendly with me?"

"A difficult question that to answer, Ann."

"She might possibly be jealous. They tell me I am not unattractive."

"Scarcely jealous, Ann. Possibly surprised."

"You are laughing at me. I can see the light dancing in your eyes."

"Do you object to my laughing at you?"

"It would make no difference. I vow you would persist."

"Not if it hurt you. Let me have my secret mirth, Ann. It will help me along life's lonely path."

"You must be lonely. Cannot I persuade you to get married?"

"What inveterate match makers most women are! No, Ann, I prefer to remain as I am; at any rate for the present."

"You have a reason?"

"I have a reason. Ann, when I was a young man my father was counted well to do. I lived much in London. I became enamoured of a woman, a society beauty, a reigning toast, but it was not long before I saw through the sham of her life. She cared for naught save to have a man dancing attendance on her. She took all and gave nothing.

119

I learnt my lesson so thoroughly that I have shunned the society of women ever since. I vowed that unless I could meet a woman I could reverence and cherish I would have none of them. I am not sorry for that early experience. It sickened me of the so-called pleasures of Vanity Fair. I have forsaken the town for the country which, I find, is vastly more wholesome. Amid the trees and hills and hedgerows I find myself closer to the Creator. I still experience awe when I contemplate the mystery at the back of the life in a humble seed. I have not desired company for years, but since our encounter, Ann, you have brought a fresh interest into my life. You are so gentle, wholesome, sincere, I tell you frankly that friendship with you means more to me than another woman's love."

"You amaze me, Mr. Yorke. But you understand that I have little to offer in return?"

"I ask nothing, Ann. The privilege of serving is its own recompense."

The girl sat silent. There was something touching about such devotion. A sudden tenderness amounting almost to compassion took hold of her.

"Mr. Yorke," she asked unexpectedly. "Do you believe that marriages are made in heaven?"

"I think that marriages are a legal necessity; no more. From what I have read the denizens of heaven neither marry nor are given in marriage."

"But you believe in love?"

"It is the greatest power in the world. I can only think of God in terms of love."

"Are not marriage and love the same thing?"

"If you think so, my dear, let nothing I say disillusion you."

Ann shook her head. "Your thoughts go too deep for me. I wish that you were married. You would be happier, less lonely, I know."

"Let me have your friendship, Ann, and I shall be well content. In this let me do my own choosing; in all else, command me and I am your obedient servant. I shall stand your loyal friend, Ann, when the storm breaks."

"Already I begin to look upon you as such. There is no one to whom I would more readily turn. You are a rock, a tree, a sanctuary."

"I ask no more."

"I must go," said Ann with a sigh as she rose to her feet. "I must really go. It has been a strange conversation, hasn't it?"

"But not, I trust, unprofitable."

"No, Mr. Yorke, not unprofitable."

"It has convinced you that I am your friend; that I ask nothing better than to serve you?"

"I am convinced utterly, Mr. Yorke."

"Isn't Mr. Yorke a somewhat formal manner of addressing a friend?"

"I think it is. So good night—Philip."

"Good night, Ann." He swung wide the door. "One word before you depart." She looked at him quickly, wondering.

"Do not forget my warning. Have the packhorse tracks obliterated. If the arms are discovered in your father's barn, he is doomed. I wish they were not there."

She nodded and walked towards the gate. Her head was bowed in thought. Ann did not realize it but she had forgotten to dream about Dicon Conway who had ridden to join the Prince.

CHAPTER TWENTY-SIX

AS PHILIP YORKE STOOD GAZING AFTER THE RETREATING FORM OF ANN a rush of emotion swept over him all but unnerving him. How indescribably sweet she was. Her walk was lithe and graceful, like the effortless glide of a wild creature for ever in close contact with nature. Her very nearness filled him with wild longings. Merely to look on her was happiness; to serve her was Life's highest ambition. The casual meeting with her had altered the whole tenor of his life. Until the moment of that meeting he had imagined himself immune from a woman's spell. He felt secure in his isolation; content with the fellowship of the mind. But now all was different. His carefully acquired philosophy had crumpled like the walls of Jericho, not at the brazen blare of war-trumpets, but to the mellifluous voice of a girl; a voice which persisted in echoing in his mind long after the one who uttered the words had departed from sight. He wondered what he could do about it because he could no more stem its irresistible course than feeble man could dam a torrent in flood. He knew, too, that his was a nature which must have a great love or none at all.

He leaned his arms along the top bar of a gate and stood gazing across the meadows to a hillside which lifted its hedge-patterned slopes until they merged with a bracken-crested ridge which stood out sharply against the heavens in all the glory of the sunlight. He scarcely saw the view consciously but ever after that particular landscape was indelibly associated with her. Often in the days to come, when the yearning grew so great that it could hardly be borne, he would rest his hungry eyes upon that lovely landscape, which reminded him of her presence, and he found much solace therein.

It filled him, moreover, with a rugged resolve not to give in to despair. It was as though her spirit hovered about that delectable scene. At times the words of the Psalmist ran through his brain—

"I will lift up mine eyes unto the hills, from whence cometh my help."

He was to have full occasion to require help before many days were ended.

Though not given to sombre introspection, Philip Yorke spent much time in meditation, believing that most of Life's problems were possible of solution if man's intellect were properly applied. But here was a problem not of the intellect: it was a product of the emotions. He had not asked for it to happen, but it had happened. He rejoiced in it and yet wisdom warned him that the road he was treading was thorny and beset by pitfalls. It was impossible for a girl in the first flush and ardour of youth to spare more than a passing thought for a man twice her age (literally twice her age) and to whom constant study had given a gravity in excess of his years. He had been brought up to believe that a benevolent Deity so arranged the lives of mankind that all things worked together for good to those who were upright in heart. Now he was inclined to detect the mockery of some mischievous influence which aimed at making Life's already complicated pattern even more involved by deliberately provoking a wealth of unnecessary suffering. Why, he asked himself, should he have come under the spell of this fascinating girl if he were doomed to failure from the very outset? It was a discouraging thought!

He took himself to task. He must cease asking 'why?' about a condition of affairs for which no one could give an answer. It had happened; there was no gainsaying it. Very well, then, instead of railing against Fate, the only thing a wise man could do was to accept conditions as they were and see to it that the greatest possible good was extracted. Not avoidance but acceptance was the solution—or at least in part. His eye rested casually on the roadside stream. A large stone almost blocked the channel in a narrow part, but the water, swirling and bubbling, coursed around it and resumed its onward way. That, he meditated, was the way to treat the impediments of life; if they were too formidable to be removed, the only thing that remained was to go round them and continue as one had started: the obstacle might ruffle the surface but it could not impede the flow. He would accept gratefully the fact that Ann had come into his life and instead of mourning that he could not have her for himself, he would sublimate his desires into a life devoted to her wellbeing. It was a quiet resolve but it was steadfast. Philip Yorke was not a demonstrative man; he was none the less sincere. He confessed to himself that he loved Ann. He could give no reason. He loved her because he could not help it.

After the bewildering turmoil in his brain, this simple resolve was as soothing as an opiate. He looked again across to the distant bracken-crested ridge and bowed slightly as though calling upon it to bear witness to the vow that he had taken; to note the high resolve which was in his heart. With a sigh on his lips but a smile in his eyes, Philip Yorke turned and walked back to his lonely house which he now knew was likely to remain lonely for evermore.

The place seemed strangely quiet and deserted. He looked fondly at the chair in which she sat. The ghost of her presence hovered near at hand. The more he was alone the more she seemed to be with him. The image of her face was continually before his eyes. If only he might claim her. Depression swept over him in huge engulfing waves. Of what use was the making of vows? What good came of trying to be noble, self-effacing? In his inmost heart he knew that he wanted to take her in his arms and press his lips to hers.

There could be no other satisfactory way of communicating to her the passionate tenderness which she aroused in him. A shrewd blow was struck at his carefully formulated philosophy. Life would be much simpler if one could only be sure: sure of heaven, sure of hell, sure that sin was punished, sure that virtue was rewarded, sure that self-sacrifice was worth while, sure that one had an immortal soul. He would deny himself everything that life held dear if only he could be sure that they would meet in some future state and hold sweet counsel together. But he was not sure: he could only hope. He was sure of nothing save that he loved her and must go on loving her because he could not help himself. His brain was charged with teeming thoughts which raced feverishly, forming themselves into rhyme almost of their own volition. He snatched a pencil.

> *'Is there a purpose in each transient meeting?*
> *Does Destiny control each ardent breath?*
> *Can Permanence exist in joy so fleeting?*
> *Do we create what does not die at Death?*
>
> *Of what avail the praying and the fasting,*
> *The yearning for a bliss not to be bought?*
> *The precious moment speeds. . . .'*

Philip Yorke flung the pencil from him with a gesture of despair. He could ask questions, but who could answer them?

The day passed slowly. Why had this trial come to him? He had not asked great things of life. Ever since his first youthful disillusionment he had shunned women, expending his energies on works which aimed at the amelioration of the conditions of his less fortunate fellow men. Surely this was meritorious? If so, might not one count on some reasonable recompense? Was not the labourer worthy of his hire? It would appear that the bestowal of favours could not be induced by merit. He was not like the gamblers, the libertines, the drunkards with which Society was saturated. He did not ask for much: only a quiet home and a woman to love. But perhaps that was asking much, for the love of such a woman was to him more to be desired than riches. If it was not good for a man to be alone, why was he denied the helpmeet he wished to have beside him as they journeyed along Life's highway? He was back at his old trick—asking questions which no one could answer. He wondered whether the unseen Power which governed the destinies of mortals really did take a personal interest in the sufferings and strivings of each individual man and woman. Or was it left to man to work out his own destiny? At least he could do the best which lay in his power. He vowed that Ann's life should never be the worse for any act or deed of his. He would give her his best: that was his homage.

It was growing dusk. He had forgotten about eating. Indeed his mind had been in such a turmoil that bodily needs had been forgotten. A sudden stealthy tapping on the window-pane brought his soaring fancy back to earth. He was alert now. With a noiseless stride he crossed to the corner and picked up the Dettingen sword. Then he walked to the door, dropped the chain and stepped back. A figure crouched in the gloaming; a figure which tried to creep stealthily inside and only paused in affright when a cold point touched its breast.

"No, no, Mr. Yorke. It's me!" whispered an apprehensive voice.

123

"Hughie? How did you get here?" Philip Yorke lowered the sword and closed the door carefully. He led the youth inside. Not until the shutters were fastened and the windows secure did Philip Yorke light the candles. He then saw that the lad was unkempt, pallid, ragged. Hugh seemed to have grown taller in a short time but perhaps it was because he was thinner. He had obviously suffered. Yorke ceased to be a dreamer and became a man of action.

"Where have you been all this time?" he demanded. "Miss Trevor has been concerned about you. You followed out my instructions?"

"I did, Mr. Yorke. I rowed out to the ship as you told me to, and I was in time to carry them warning. It was a long pull all the way from Llanddulas and I was nigh played out when I got to the vessel. But I was in time. The arms were all safely landed on Puffin Island. That man and me laid among the bracken and watched the man-o'-war's boats pulling out over the calm sea. We saw them board the snow. But they didn't get nothing."

"Good. I am pleased with you. You shall be rewarded."

"I did it for Mistress Ann, sir; I don't want no reward."

"Any reward, Hughie."

"I know, Mr. Yorke. I haven't forgotten your teaching but I'm all upset now, and tired, and I drift back into my old ways of speaking like."

"But why haven't you come home before, my boy? And where have you been? I instructed you to land on the Anglesey coast and make your way back home with all possible dispatch."

"I did so, Mr. Yorke. On my honour. But a parish constable got his hands on me and I was hauled before the magistrates at Beaumaris court-house because I could not give an account of myself. I was clapped in gaol as a rogue and vagabond and I've been there till yesterday when I escaped."

"Ah. There's no need to ask whether you suffered. I would not wish my worst enemy to see the inside of one of the gaols in this Christian country. I am sorry you were caught, my boy."

"I would go through more than that to serve Mistress Ann."

"I am sure that you would. So would many of us."

"You feel like that, too, Mr. Yorke, sir?"

"Could anyone come in contact with her and not desire to serve her?"

Hughie did not answer. He was staring hard before him, his brow wrinkled, his fingers were nervously plucking at his jacket. It was obvious that he was agitated. "There's something I must tell you, and I don't know what to say nor how to say it."

"If it is something I ought to know, tell me: never mind how you say it. Is it about Mistress Ann?"

"It is, sir. I wouldn't do her no harm; not for nothing on earth."

"I am certain of it, my boy."

"Well, I don't know whether I am doing her a wrong by telling what I know, or by keeping my mouth shut and saying nothing about it."

"Why not leave that for me to decide? I have more experience in life than you."

"You would never do her no harm, Mr. Yorke?"

"You ask *me* that question?"

"No, Mr. Yorke, I take it back. I will tell you everything. When I come back through the woods, I did not want to go to the house till it was dark, so I crept into the Black Barn and hid. I must have fallen asleep. There were two men talking and I never saw them come in. One was the man who serves the Prince; the one who hid with me on Puffin Island, Captain Conway, I think he's called. I don't know the other. They were looking at some cases which were hid in the straw and from their talk I could tell that the boxes was full of swords and muskets; same as those in the ship you sent me to."

"Very likely, go on."

"Well, this man, Captain Conway, he sent the other man away, and then he keeps pacing up and down, restless like, as though he were waiting for somebody. I heard a step and the door opened and there was . . . who should come in, but . . ."

"Yes, go on."

"I can't say no more, Mr. Yorke."

"It was Mistress Ann, wasn't it?"

The boy nodded. "I didn't look, sir. I turned my head away lest she should think I spied on her, but I couldn't help hearing things what they said. I didn't want to, honest."

"You have the makings of a gentleman in you. You must forget what you heard. Put it from your mind."

"I will try. But there was something I can't forget; something I must tell you now I've gone so far."

"Well, as briefly as possible. Give the purport, not the actual words."

"It was this. Captain Conway is to ride again to Scotland to the Prince. There's been a big victory up there over the King's troops who all ran away and the Prince has captured Edinburgh."

"That's not pleasant hearing. Is that all?"

"I have not got to the thing that troubles me, Mr. Yorke."

"Out with it then. It's no use beating about the bush."

"Captain Conway rides north to-night, and—and—he's persuaded Mistress Ann to go with him—to run away from home."

The boy looked fearfully at Philip Yorke's face as he spoke. He saw the muscles twitch a moment. The colour rushed into the man's cheeks and then swept back leaving them deadly white. The eyes, usually so kindly, grew tense. But he kept his self-control.

"You did wisely, my boy, to tell me," he said evenly.

"There is to be a big meeting at the Plas this evening. The Captain is to make his report there and while the gentlemen are engaged in discussing it, Mistress Ann is to slip away unobserved. Black Prince is to be ready waiting for her to ride off. Then Captain Conway is to make his excuses and get away and join her."

"Ah!" Philip Yorke's fingers fidgeted with the hilt of the Dettingen sword. "He is to join her, you say. What a pity, my boy, that you did not hear where they are to meet."

"But I did hear, sir. They are to breakfast at a little inn called the Cross Foxes."

CHAPTER TWENTY-SEVEN

ANN FOUND IT DIFFICULT TO SHAKE OFF THE REFLECTIVE MOOD IN
which she found herself. It was unusual for her. Hitherto she had
gone blithely through life with as little thought as it was possible for
a girl to have. Now problems, which appeared to her to be profound,
began shaping themselves in her brain. She was more conscious of
her mind than her body, and she found, somewhat to her surprise,
that her mind and her emotions were curiously intermingled. She had
walked out that morning with her thoughts full of Dicon Conway,
her heart beating faster at the recollection of his kisses. She went
soberly home along the self-same road and this time her mind was
equally intent on Philip Yorke. If her emotions entered into this
phase they were undoubtedly of a less stimulating character. She
felt towards Philip Yorke a tenderness, a warmth of appreciation
which surprised her. To be with him gave her a sense of security
which she had never before known. She knew that she could rely on
him; that he was always to be counted on. Though he meant nothing
to her—not in the sense Dicon Conway did!—she was persuaded
that in an emergency, or at any crises in her life, she could turn to him
for wise counsel or for protection. She was glad, too, that he was
there for her to turn to. To herself she confessed that she was fond
of him, and the next instant she reproached herself for being disloyal
to Dicon, even in her thoughts. What a complex creature she was!
She asked herself whether it was an absolute necessity to care for one
person only. In any case, how could you help yourself, for if you
cared, you cared, and that was all there was to it. She wondered if
it might be possible to care for several persons just as a mother could
give to each of her children different qualities of her love. Of course
she loved Dicon. She loved no one but Dicon, she would never love
anyone but Dicon, and yet indubitably she was fond of Philip Yorke,
too. She sighed and shrugged her shoulders. A few months ago
she was lamenting that her life contained no romance; that she had
never known the meaning of love. Now both had come suddenly and
in abundance, pressed down and running over, for Ann was woman
enough to sense in Philip Yorke's tender devotion a wealth of love,
different, possibly, from Dicon's gay impetuosity, but just as intense.
It was not long since she grieved that she had no love; now, as though
some unseen power had heard her prayer, she was given love; too
much love if such a state were possible. She gave an embarrassed
laugh; it seemed as though the Fates were overdoing it. All she
asked was for the love of one man, the security of one home. She had
never desired life to become so complex. Was life always like that?
Nothing straightforward and plain and easy to understand?

As though to escape from her thoughts Ann broke into a run.
The year was beginning to slip away. The leaves rustled underfoot
and the hips and haws brightened the hedges with their contrasting
hues of red. They looked, thought Ann, like drops of blood and
then she shuddered as though it were an omen. If the Prince came
marching south, as indeed he was bound to do, blood would

assuredly flow. Ann sighed. She would have liked adventure without suffering.

When she reached the house she found her father gone to the Home Farm. She was glad for she was in no mood for talking. There was a cold luncheon on the table so she toyed with some food, and then hurried off to the woods before her parent could return. She wanted to be by herself. Ann had but recently discovered the meaning of thought. It pleased her mightily. It was as though she had come upon a new world within herself and was amazed at its possibilities. She wondered where Dicon could be. She endeavoured to visualize what the Highlanders looked like; probably akin to savages. She sauntered along the wood's edge absorbed in her reflections when a distant shout caused her to look up in time to see Seth putting his roan mare to a gap in the hedge. He cleared it beautifully and crossed the meadow at an easy canter. He slipped from the saddle almost before the mare was at a standstill and caught Ann's hands in an eager grasp. "News, Ann, great news !" he almost shouted.

"Of the Prince?"

"Of the Prince, of course. He is a wizard ! A magician ! He has conjured up an army out of nothing. He has marched on Edinburgh and has slept in the royal palace at Holyrood——"

"Oh, Seth, how glorious. And it's really true?"

"Then he marched out to meet the regular army which General Cope had landed from transports at Dunbar——"

"And there was a battle? Quick, tell me !"

"A battle? Say, rather, a rout. The redcoats turned at the sight of the claymores and ran away. They are running yet."

"Seth. It sounds too good to be true. Where was it?"

"At a village called Preston something——Yes, Prestonpans. Queer names the Scotch folk choose."

"How did you come to hear all this? You are sure it is right?"

The ardour left Seth's face.

"A messenger brought the news."

"A messenger?"

"Ay. That fellow who has been here before. Conway by name."

"Dicon ! He's here? He's returned? And you never told me !"

"Thought you'd find out soon enough. There's to be a meeting at your place to-night. Council of war. Your father has summoned the folk round about to discuss the new development. I'm just rounding them up."

"Then I must not keep you. Hurry. Time is precious."

"But, Ann, a word with you first. It is ages since we were together——"

"No, Seth, no. There is too much to be done. And I am in no mood for your company. I am much too excited."

"You will see me again, Ann?"

"Oh, perhaps. Now go. Hasten or you will never get those messages delivered."

With a shrug of his shoulders Seth turned away, groped for a stirrup, climbed into his saddle with a bad grace and galloped off with never a backward glance. Ann scarcely heeded him. Her cheeks were flushed. She was right when she said she was excited. But was it the Prince's victory which had caused it? Instinctively she turned towards the Black Barn. She could not have told why. She acted intuitively. Perhaps the mere mention of Dicon's name brought to mind their last glad meeting. Her heart bounded when she saw a horse tied to a fence rail. She commenced to run. The next instant the barn door was open. Dicon's hand swept high in a gay salute as he heard her step; the gay salute she knew so well. She was in his arms.

"Golden eyes," he whispered as he kissed her.

"Oh, you are back; you are back at last."

"Back at last. Tell me, how long is twenty-four hours when every hour's an age?"

"It has been an age without you."

"You have missed me?"

"Terribly. More than words can tell. When I see you I behold not only the desire of my eyes but the desire of my heart."

"No one has the gift of words like you. Tell me, why have you missed me?"

"You know."

"Of course I know. I want to hear you speak the words."

"I love you. Is that what you wanted?"

"How clever of you to guess right first time. But suppose such a thought had never entered my head?"

"Dicon, you can be ridiculous. But tell me, is it true that there has been a great victory for the Prince's forces?"

"Quite true. But his victory is as nothing compared to mine."

"Your victory, Dicon?"

"He gained a kingdom. I have won the heart of the dearest woman in the world."

*   *   *   *   *

It was all very exciting. Ann never forgot the scene in the dining-room of her home that evening. The shutters were closed. A fire burned brightly for there was an autumnal touch in the air, accentuated rather than relieved by the pale rays of a full moon. Extra candelabra had been brought out for the occasion and their points of light danced on the silver and the cut glass decanters as the gentlemen stood about the table, gay in coats of many hues, drinking to the King across the water or pledging Bonnie Prince Charlie the victor of Prestonpans.

"Tell us more about the fight, Dicon," demanded the Squire as he refilled his glass. "And seat yourselves, gentlemen, please."

Dicon, standing with his back to the fire, feet apart, and a look of grim pleasure on his tanned features, was not slow to comply. "Not a great deal to tell, gentlemen. It was no sooner started than it was over. The mere sight of the claymores made the dragoons turn tail."

"They have no stomach for Highland steel," observed Sir Watkin.

"Say, rather, they have no love for the House of Hanover," added Mr. Eyton. "I'll warrant our English lads could fight if so minded."

128

"And was there no fighting at all?" demanded Mr. Pryce.

"Little enough." Dicon smiled grimly and lifted his left hand. Ann noticed for the first time that there was a bandage about the wrist. She gave an ejaculation but Dicon resumed carelessly, "The dragoons loosed off their carbines and pistols as they rode from the field. I managed to take a bullet in my bridle-arm; a mere scratch but I bled like a stuck pig."

"Oh, Dicon," Ann was distressed. "I am sorry."

"Sorry? Nothing has given me greater pleasure. The scar will be a happy reminder of my first engagement. There was so little firing that I might easily have missed so interesting a souvenir. I feel more entitled to my rank now that I have been blooded."

"Never mind that. Get on with the story. Why must that girl of mine be for ever interrupting?" grumbled the Squire. "Another word from you, you baggage, and I'll have you turned out of the room."

"Then, as I refuse to be muzzled, I will go now," said Ann with unexpected eagerness. "This is no place for a lady. I leave you to your narrative, Dicon!"

Their eyes met and lingered a moment before Ann slipped from the room, after dropping a somewhat mocking curtsy to the men, who rose to their feet.

"Let's have the facts, Conway," interposed Eyton. "There's too much at stake for frivolity. What are His Highness's chances of success? How big an army has he mustered?"

"It must be fifteen hundred strong and more are coming in now that news of the victory has spread abroad. From the raising of the standard last August everything has gone in favour of the Prince. I attribute much of his success to his personality and his impatience to push on. He has adopted Highland garb, and faith, gentlemen, he wears it to the manner born. When first he drew his sword he exclaimed, 'I have thrown away the scabbard.' His whole outlook confirms this. There is no drawing back for him. He will take every risk. I tell you, he is a leader of men."

"But the battle, man, the battle."

"I'll come to it in due course, though there's little to say. It took us longer to get to the field than to fight the battle. Their dragoons galloped off when we advanced on Edinburgh. We expected a hot fight, instead we got a warm welcome. I vow every woman in the place is a Jacobite. We rushed one of the gates and were inside the walls before the garrison knew what had happened. Those narrow streets and closes are specially adapted for resistance yet we met with none. When the Prince rode into his new capital on a coal black steed he was wearing a tartan coat, a blue bonnet with the white cockade and the star of Saint Andrew on his breast. He cut a gallant figure."

"Never mind that, Dicon, get to Prestonpans."

"Well, on the day Cope marched his army out of Dunbar to assault Edinburgh, the Prince led his men to meet the English. When the mist lifted the two armies were within close range. We had but fifty horse, but the Highlanders were as good as cavalry to us. The sight of so many redcoats roused them to a blind fury. Before the

129

English guns could open up on us we had driven off the gunners by musketry. Then the Highlanders threw away their muskets, drew their claymores and charged with wild yells. Off rode the dragoons without drawing their sabres. The infantry might have checked us but they loosed off a few shots and ran after the cavalry. I'll give you a song, gentlemen, which everyone is singing in Scotland." And Dicon struck up—"*Hey, Johnnie Cope, are ye waukin' yet?*"

It afforded an excuse for the Squire to call for another toast to the victors of Prestonpans. Richard Conway was plied with questions. How many were killed? What was to be the Prince's next move? How had he conducted himself in the battle? Would the army move south now or wait until the spring?

"The Prince will move south," said Dicon emphatically. "He cannot afford to wait. He must strike hard and strike quick. The rumour is that he is to advance down by way of Yorkshire, and Wade is at Newcastle to bar his way. In confidence, gentlemen, I may tell you that his Highness's real intention is to come through Lancashire, the better"—Dicon looked from face to face as he paused impressively, —"the better to link up with his loyal adherents in North Wales."

There were cries of approval. "You have told him about the arms which we have concealed?" asked Eyton.

"I have. His Highness sends his thanks and asks me to express his gratitude. Your loyalty will not be forgotten when the King comes to his own again."

"The question is, when shall we distribute them? We must guard against being premature."

"Possess yourselves in patience a while longer. I should say that within a month the Prince will be on the Welsh borders on his way to London."

"Then we had better discuss our plans for giving out the arms," remarked the Squire.

"As that is a matter in which I can be of little assistance," said Dicon as he formally bowed to the Squire, "I will ask leave to depart. My mission is completed; my horse is rested; I must get back to his Highness who anxiously awaits news from Wales. God keep you, gentlemen, and success to the venture!"

Cool and urbane, Dicon Conway sauntered from the room and made his unhurried way to the stables. He mounted the horse which Howells held for him and rode quietly down the lane. Once free of the hall, the walk turned to a trot; the trot to a gallop. At the edge of a wood he drew rein and sat peering over his horse's ears into the darkness ahead. He gave a low whistle. It was answered. In another instant he was urging his horse alongside Black Prince. His arm was about Ann's waist.

"You managed it? Dear heart, is there nothing you would not do for me?"

"Nothing, Dicon. There is nothing I would not attempt."

"You are game to take the north road with me? All the way to Scotland?"

"Farther if need be."

130

"We may have to fly to France?"

"Who cares!"

"There'll be the devil to pay when the Squire finds out."

"I shall have you so what does it matter? You are sure you love me, Dicon?"

"I was never more sure of anything in my life. Ann, you were specially made to love and be loved."

"I know it, Dicon."

They rode awhile in silence, happy in each other's nearness. Presently Dicon laid a firm hand on Ann's rein and drew both animals to a halt while he bent forward listening.

"There are horses ahead," he said in a low voice.

"Is there danger?"

"Who knows? On a job like this one must always be on the alert. I will open the gate of yonder field and we will take cover in the copse until the riders have passed."

He left Ann holding the animals while he crept down a hedgerow to reconnoitre. Presently she heard the swish of the long dewy grass as he came running back to her. He caught the horses by their noses. "Soldiers," he whispered. "Three of them. We are lost if the animals whinny."

They stood side by side in the moonlight at their horses' heads while the sound of hoofs grew nearer and nearer. Ann could see the roadway distinctly. There were three of them—three horsemen and the moonlight showed up their red coats and burnished steel. The leader was well in advance. He was an officer; the two who followed were troopers. When they had passed on their way Dicon smiled grimly. "A fortunate evasion," he said lightly, preparing to lead the horses back to the road. "Why, Ann, what is the matter? Are you cold? You are trembling."

"Did you see who it was, Dicon?"

"Who? The man in front? No, I did not recognize him."

"It was Major Manstein. That man haunts me, Dicon. I am sure he will be my undoing. I wish we had not seen him. It is like an evil omen. His face is like a curse to me. It augurs ill. Let us turn back, Dicon. Let us turn back."

"Turn back? Ann, you do not know me. I will ride to join the Prince nor shall fifty Mansteins stop us."

CHAPTER TWENTY-EIGHT

THEY RODE THROUGH THE NIGHT WHILE THE MOONBEAMS CAST DARK shadows athwart the highway. They rode for the most part in silence; Ann because she was getting sleepy and found the rhythmic clatter of the hoofs a soporific; Dicon Conway because his mind was full of confused thoughts. Would his loyalty to his Prince be affected by this new loyalty which it was incumbent on him to honour? The odds were not in favour of his Highness yet Dicon could see no reason why the two loyalties should not be blended to their mutual advantage.

He stole a covert glance at Ann. Her face, usually so high in colour, looked pale in the moonlight; her long-lashed eyes were partly closed. She had made no further reference to the passing of Major Manstein but Dicon could tell that the encounter had perturbed her. Dicon, himself, was uneasy though he would not have had Ann aware of it. At a time when it was generally supposed that the Duke of Cumberland (who had been summoned home from the Continent by his royal father to take charge of the defence of the realm) was flinging a barrier of troops across England between Scotland and the capital, it was difficult to account for the journey into Wales of so experienced an officer as Major Manstein. His reverie was interrupted.

"Oh, Dicon, I am so sleepy. I could doze in the saddle."

"Why not do so?"

"I might fall off."

"My arm about you would prevent that."

"Dicon, be sensible. I do not feel the least romantic. Have we far to go?"

"Not far, my sweet. Dawn is at hand and before the sun is well above the horizon we ought to come to the inn. It is somewhat off the beaten track for I have no mind to be followed by your irate parent, or, say, that young hot-head Seth Morrice who has the temerity to imagine himself in love with you."

"Poor Seth."

"I parted with some hardly-won gold to induce the landlord of the Cross Foxes to be up betimes and to have a fire going at dawn. Soon you shall smell rashers of bacon."

"Hush, Dicon, you make me ravenous. How was it that you were so confident that I should be with you?"

"If I told you, you would deem me conceited."

"And so you are."

"Small wonder if I can captivate the dearest woman in the world."

"Oh, Dicon, I do love you; my love is yours, so yours."

"I know it, queen of my heart."

"Dicon, how inconsistent we are."

"How so?"

"We talk of love when all I crave for is breakfast and a soft pillow."

"You shall have both shortly. You shall eat and sleep your fill. See the east is already brightening. Dawn is upon us."

"You never seem to get tired, Dicon. Do you often ride by night?"

"Quite often. I find it safer. Apart from that I like to be out when the world is still."

"I have never ridden by night before. Will I have to do it often when we join the Prince?"

"I doubt it; not unless there should be a retreat."

"Retreat? How preposterous. The Prince will carry all before him."

"I believe that he will though the odds are all against him. Anyhow, I am backing him for all I am worth. I shall be a great man if he succeeds, my sweet."

"To me you are great now, Dicon."

"Then nothing else matters. See, we turn left at the fork. It is but half a league to the Cross Foxes. Did I not say that we should be there by dawn?"

"You did, Dicon. It is getting light. My father has put all into the hazard. He told me only yesterday that if the Prince failed we were ruined. I should not worry now that I have you. It is a great game. With you beside me I do not trouble about consequences."

"What a woman you are, Ann. I shall never find another like you."

"Do you want to?"

"Never, Ann, never. That is one thing you have done—made all other women appear insipid."

A dog barked. As they rounded a bend Ann saw close ahead a hamlet which clustered about a cross-roads. Conspicuous on one corner was a low rambling inn with a swinging sign. To her satisfaction there was smoke arising from a tall chimney, and the glow of a fire showed through the kitchen casement. Dicon's gold had produced results. Ann allowed Dicon to help her from her saddle and she walked stiffly to the door as the horses were led to the stables. Could anything be more appetizing than the smell of bacon on a crisp autumn morning? Ann thought not. She hurried over her ablutions and joined Dicon in the parlour where a round table was set for a meal; a homely meal, but a substantial one. It was what they both needed.

Dicon pushed back his chair with a sigh of satisfaction. "There is a bed prepared for you in the best bedchamber upstairs, Ann. Sleep as long as you like, my dear. The horses will benefit by the rest."

"I don't want to go just yet, Dicon. I feel rested now, and so satisfied. I just want to sit here and look at you from drowsy eyes. I could never tire of looking at you. Nothing seems as important as watching your eyes crinkle before your lips smile."

"You make me feel self-conscious, Ann. Dearest, would you mind very much if I told you that I loved you?"

"I don't think I should really mind."

"That is a relief because I intend to say it so frequently that you will weary of its repetition."

"Try me and test me."

"I mean to. What a woman you are, Ann; my woman of all women. Tell me, have you considered the difficulties ahead?"

"No. They do not interest me. If you are with me they will not appear as difficulties."

"Suppose we separated?"

"I should wait until we were united. I don't think that I could ever be separated from you utterly, Dicon. Our spirits would remain in touch. All the words of endearment you have spoken to me seem to have recorded themselves in my mind and I can recall them at will."

"You do not regret the step you have taken?"

"Regret it? I burnt my boats with the first kiss."

"And you will follow me to Scotland."

"I am this minute on my way with you."

Dicon, as he stretched forth his hand to lay hold on hers, paused, staring so intently with an almost startled expression that Ann turned

133

her head. She heard a door hinge creak and a level voice said—"I think you are both mistaken."

"Damnation!" cried Dicon but he did not move. Ann saw that a brace of pistols were directed at Dicon's head; pistols held in the steady hands of Philip Yorke. His eyes were stern. Look as she might Ann could see no sign of any dancing light twinkling in them. She caught her breath. Dicon flashed a glance towards the chair where lay his sword and pistols.

"There is no occasion for you to show any interest in your weapons, Captain Conway," remarked Philip Yorke suavely. "I have looked carefully to my primings and I assure you that there is little chance of a misfire. Remain perfectly still."

Dicon leant back in his chair. "I see," he drawled insolently, "that as you were worsted in our last encounter you prefer not to trust to your sword. You play safe, sir. You take no chances."

"What you say is entirely correct. I play safe. I do not take chances. On the occasion of our previous meeting there was nothing at stake of more consequence than my life. Now the stake is nothing less than a lady's honour."

"Damnation! What right have you to interfere?"

"No right whatever! I am just—interfering. It does not concern me whether it meets with your approval or not."

"I always suspected you of being in Hanoverian pay."

"Not pay, Captain Conway. You do me an injustice. I have been left with a competency so that there is no need for me to enter politics from mercenary motives. I am no needy adventurer who makes a reckless throw in the hope of bettering his impoverished estate."

"So you try to insult me?"

"Lud, no, Captain Conway. If I chose to insult you I should be far more explicit. I can be, should the occasion arise."

"Come outside with the swords and I will give you what satisfaction honour requires."

"The only satisfaction honour requires is that this lady returns instantly to her home."

"I shall not go back." Ann spoke for the first time. Her voice was low but resolute; her tone emphatic.

"It is my duty to escort you to your father, Ann."

"I refuse to go. What will you do now? Use force?"

"I would endeavour to persuade you."

"You would waste your breath."

"Let me point out the folly of the step which you are taking. No one flies in the face of convention without paying a price."

"I ride to join the Prince."

"That merely makes matters worse. The Prince has had temporary success. It will prove ephemeral. His ragged army of Highlanders cannot stand up to the onslaught of the trained veterans of Dettingen and Fontenoy. Our own Welch Fusiliers are coming back from Flanders; they alone could give a good account of themselves. The Prince has no artillery. He is doomed to failure. But all that is beside the point; it is your reputation I am concerned about."

134

"It is in safe hands."

"I should like to think so."

"Mr. Yorke, what right, I repeat, what right have you to interfere in my affairs thus ? There was a time when I held you in high regard; when I looked upon you as a loyal friend. It seems I was mistaken."

"I never stood your friend more truly than I do this instant, Ann. I would, if I could, protect you from yourself. If I cannot persuade you, let me entreat you. Have done with this folly. Turn back while there is yet time."

"Turn back ? Never. Where Dicon goes, I go."

"You are resolved ?"

"I am. You shall never move me."

Philip Yorke sighed. "Very well," he said quietly. "If you must ride farther with this man, you shall ride as his wife. There is a vicarage across the way and I have had word with the parson. We will step across there and see that things are done decently and in proper order."

"We mean to be married at Gretna Green," said Ann in a low voice.

"You shall be married here and now. There is little more service that I can render you, Ann, but I shall endeavour to see that what I do I do thoroughly. Come, sir, to the vicarage."

"Never, damn you !" cried Conway leaping to his feet.

"Ah ! So you balk at matrimony ? I thought as much. My visit was opportune after all." There was a cynical sneer on the face of Philip Yorke.

"Balk at matrimony?" cried Dicon Conway furiously. "Put down those pistols and I'll strike you across your lying mouth. Not want to marry Ann ? There's nothing on earth I more desire. But by heaven I'll marry her because I choose and I'll marry her in the way she wishes and not because a rogue holds a pistol at my head and tells me that I must. Demme if I'll be driven into matrimony at a pistol point. Never ! Shoot and be damned to you !"

He stood there, fists clenched, eyes flashing, panting with fury.

"No, no," cried Ann as she ran in front of the threatening pistols. "No, Mr. Yorke, if you shoot him, you must shoot me, too. I shall never leave him."

"Ann," said Yorke in a low voice which he endeavoured unsuccessfully to control, "Ann, do you love him so much ?"

"I do love him. There is no one on earth to compare with Dicon. I want to marry him, but married or not I care for him so greatly that I will follow him to the ends of the earth."

"And you, sir, prefer to be shot rather than be driven into marriage at the point of a pistol ?"

Dicon nodded sullenly.

Yorke took a step forward and the menacing pistol was but a couple of feet from Conway's head. "No, no," cried Ann, pale of face. "You cannot, Philip. It would be murder. I should hate you; I should kill you."

Dicon's eyes never wavered as they stared at the round dark barrel.

135

"I admire your principles, sir," said Philip Yorke. "I am prepared to compromise. If I leave it to your honour, will you give me your word to marry Ann before you leave this place?"

"I will," said Richard Conway.

Philip Yorke lowered his pistols. "My felicitations," he said with a formal bow. "Ann, I pray that no ill comes of it. I desire your happiness, your abiding happiness, before all else in life. Nothing is more precious to me than your happiness, Girl. I leave you to—your husband. Should disaster overtake you—and God knows the way you have chosen is likely to prove a rough one—I beg of you to remember that I am ever at your service."

Dicon's arms tightened about Ann's almost fainting form. Though her eyes were closed she was conscious of the latch clicking as Philip Yorke shut himself out.

CHAPTER TWENTY-NINE

WHEN PHILIP YORKE RODE BACK TO HIS LONELY HOME HE WAS IN A sombre mood but whatever his feelings he gave no outward manifestation of the emotions which surged within. His face was grave and his steady eyes stared forward thoughtfully. He allowed his horse to pick its own way along the morning road, and although the sun was shining it afforded him scant solace for there was no warmth in his heart. He seemed apathetic; indeed, he had reached that stage of mental and emotional suffering which approximates shock, and kindly nature administered an opiate which numbed his lacerated feelings so that he was not fully aware of how much pain he felt. All he knew was that Ann had gone out of his life. He wondered how it had come to pass. He wondered why she had ever been brought into it. Before her appearance he had been quite resigned to his loneliness. As he had ridden out to bring her safely home he had pictured her gratitude to him for having rescued her from such a scheming scoundrel. But women, he meditated, are capricious creatures, and the outcome had been vastly different from what he had foreseen. Had he acted wisely? Certainly it had been against his inclinations if not his judgment. Still, the matter was settled. It was futile to open a door in life which had been closed. He hoped that she would be happy. There was consolation of a sort in the knowledge of her happiness. He could be happy if she were happy; or at any rate he could not be happy if she were unhappy. After all, that was what he most desired in life, her happiness. Would that it had been his right to give her the happiness she merited; if he could not do so, at least he must not begrudge a luckier man his privilege. Then he fell to wondering why he had ever met her. It had not been of deliberate intent on his part. She had burst unexpectedly in upon his drab and desolate life as a ray of sunshine will penetrate a room after the drawing back of a curtain. Did he regret having met her? No! a thousand times no! Whatever the suffering it was well worth while; the joy of knowing her was full recompense. He blamed himself for being so deluded as to cherish even a faint hope that life might have accorded him the bliss which he desired above all else, but now this was denied him he must be content with the recollection that his life was richer, more glorious, for having known her. And he could serve her still. He liked to picture himself as being always in the background ready to help should misfortune come her way. Perhaps from his wider experience of life he might prove of value in the troublous days which lay ahead; days which, if he read the signs of the times aright, would prove both brutal and bloody. He would have felt more contented could he have ridden at her side when she set forth up the long road to the Scottish border, but another possessed the right. He consoled himself that Dicon Conway was not the type of man to allow harm to befall the precious jewel entrusted to him; the more so if he had become its proud possessor.

So Philip Yorke came home again and walked into a deserted house. Standing in the music-room he was oppressed by an over-whelming sense of loneliness. He wondered how he was going to face the interminable years ahead. Life without her seemed so pointless. The studies which once absorbed his attention no longer held any appeal. His mind persisted in drifting from the printed page; he saw no words but an image of a slim, graceful, curving form, and eyes of a rich amber tint which changed with the changing light; eyes which could be animated or eloquent or tender as occasion called forth. Had his encounter with her been but the sport of chance? Something within him rebelled at the mere thought. He felt that he had been sent into her life for a purpose: to serve her. Perhaps the time was yet to come. He asked for nothing better than to express his unspoken devotion in service.

Grimly he unbuckled the Dettingen sword and laid it with delibera-tion against the wall in the corner. It had not been required after all. He was glad. His mind turned from edged tools and crossing to the harpsichord he commenced to play. Intuitively his fingers touched the familiar chords which he had grown to associate with Ann. Purcell, he mused, must have known such another when he wrote that piece. Though Philip Yorke knew every chord by heart he searched for the music and opened it on the rest in front of him. Perhaps it was because it suited his fancy to see the title in print. It stood out plain enough. The daylight was beginning to fade but even in the gloaming he could read—'WHAT SHALL I DO TO SHOW HOW MUCH I LOVE HER?' He was glad that Ann had never noticed the title; he felt that he possessed a secret which was now too precious to share. He kept on playing long after it was too dark for him to see, his fingers finding the notes almost by instinct. It was as though the deprivation of the sense of sight had sharpened his other senses. He played with rare feeling. A step on the gravel, a hurrying, urgent step disturbed him. There came a rapping on the door, the sound of heavy, laboured breathing, and a voice—"Mr. Yorke, Mr. Yorke, are you at home?" It was Hughie. Yorke flung open the door and the youth hurried in. "Thank God you're here, sir. There's awful happenings up at the Plas. I've come to you for help."

F*

"What happenings?" Philip Yorke's voice was calm.

"First and foremost there's Mistress Ann really run off; gone clean away on Black Prince, same as I said, with never a word left behind. I told you she planned to run off with that captain. Now it's really happened I feel all queer. I dare'n't say what I know. I've just got to pretend as I know nothing. Squire's nigh demented. He's had us all searching high and low but with no success. I came to you first thing this morning but you'd gone and no one knew where. Then to-night someone said they'd heard music in the darkness and I knew you were back home. You remember? I warned you!"

"Yes, you did warn me. Is that all you have to tell me?"

"Not all, sir. There's plenty more. This is but the start of troubles."

"Which come, not singly, but in battalions."

"I was over ten-acre field watching the road when I heard hoofs and who should ride by but that Major with a German name who was here some months back. He had two redcoats on horseback with him. Their animals was blown as though they'd come a long way. It seemed to me that they might be heading for the Plas, so I takes a short cut through the woods and comes to you for help."

"I have no help to offer."

"Then tell me what to do, Mr. Yorke."

"Keep out of it. If I were you I should keep out of the way."

"No you wouldn't neither. You know what's in the Black Barn. That's why the soldiers is here, you mark my words. The arms is hidden there and someone has split. If they finds the arms it is a hanging matter. I heard Howells say so. He was telling how they stuck traitors' heads on Temple Bar wherever that may be. I've no notion to see Squire's head on a spike. I run all the way through the woods in the dark because I thought you'd know what best to do."

"Why come to me? It is no concern of mine. If these people choose to take risks they must abide by the consequences."

"But you must do something—for Mistress Ann's sake."

"Mistress Ann is no longer here. I fear that you will find me unsympathetic if not completely callous."

"But Mr. Yorke, sir, this is not like you; if anything happens to Squire what will Mistress Ann do? Where will she live? If they stick Squire's head on a spike it will fair break Mistress Ann's heart."

"And that must be avoided if possible, my boy. You are right. I will come with you though I have no notion how I can assist. Stay! Run across to the hall and give the alarm; then come back to meet me."

Hughie darted off into the night. Philip Yorke with greater deliberation buckled on his sword again. He paused at the door and smiled a little grimly. It began to look as if the process of beating it into a ploughshare was more difficult than he had imagined. He was half-way to the hall when Hughie rejoined him. The boy was pale with excitement or apprehension and he walked beside Philip Yorke without speaking as that resolute person made his way with long strides to his neighbour's stately home.

There were lights in many windows and light streamed from the

138

wide open door. It fell on the hanging heads of three weary horses and illuminated the red jacket of the trooper who stood with the reins in his hand.

"Too late!" whispered Hughie. "Well, most of the gentlemen must have gotten away. There was a rare how-d'-y'-do when I shouted the news."

"They've only just arrived; see the animals are still panting and steaming with sweat. But keep in the background, boy. There is no point in your getting mixed up in this. I'll do what I can."

"For Mistress Ann's sake," reminded Hughie as he slipped behind some laurels.

"Ay!" said Yorke to himself as he strode towards the hall, "for Ann's sake."

He paused in the hallway to peer into the half-open door of the dining-room. The table still bore the remains of a meal. From the number of glasses there had been a substantial party present. Yorke could see only the Squire, young Seth Morrice and Major Manstein. The soldier was dusty from travel but his demeanour was as casual and unhurried as though he paid a social call.

"You have entertained lavishly, I perceive?" he was remarking.

"Why not? Cannot a man receive a few friends?"

"As you say, why not? You are so hospitably inclined, Mr. Trevor. I regret the precipitate departure of your guests should deny me the pleasure of their acquaintance. I notice that you do not offer me a glass of wine, Mr. Trevor."

"By gad, no man has ever had to ask before! Allow me, sir. I ask pardon for an unforgivable breach of hospitality." With a hand that trembled the Squire seized a decanter and poured out the wine. He handed a glass to his unwelcome visitor and filling another for himself he raised it a little unsteadily. The major did the same. With deliberation he exclaimed "The King."

"The King," echoed the Squire, and both drank.

"A plaguy convenient toast," observed Major Manstein, setting down his glass. "You observe, sir, that I am tactful; I do not ask to which King you drink."

"I drink to our lawful monarch," said the Squire.

" 'Zounds, I am convinced that you do. But to depart from the controversial question of royalty, where is that charming daughter of yours? A most bewitching baggage, sir. Demme, I had the pleasure of an unexpected encounter with her at, let me see? Abergele if my memory does not play me false. Abergele it was. I shall not forget it for I was led on a wild-goose chase on that occasion. Would you believe it? Someone warned me that a vessel carrying arms for the rebels—those damned Jacobites who are the aversion of every loyal subject of King George—was expected to land her contraband at the Ormeshead. You look shocked, sir! Scandalized! As every true Briton should naturally be! Yes, sir, those rascals had a plot to arm the Jacobites in North Wales, and to fetch hither the arms they chartered a vessel. Formerly a Liverpool slaver, though how she came to be in these parts I have no notion unless she was owned by some person in

North Wales. Ah, well, when we boarded her there were no arms to be found. Evidently I was misinformed—unless someone had given warning of my approach. That was the day I had the pleasure of encountering your charming daughter, sir. She honoured me by sharing my repast. I flatter myself that I proved such entertaining company that she quite forgot to call on the people she had ridden so far, unaccompanied, to visit. Does she frequently ride far from home, sir?"

"No, demme, never; that is, not often. Roads are too dangerous these days, sir. Too many scoundrels about."

"I agree, sir. Far too many. Never mind, we shall be hanging a few before the year is out. And your pretty daughter is out, I believe you said?"

"Yes, sir, out! So I understand."

"Gad, sir, I might observe that there is much you do not understand. Now I, sir, am well informed. Let me advise you, sir, if you want reliable information, employ a woman who is bitter; one who has gall in her heart. Spite is a sharp spur. I assure you there is much that you do not understand."

"I do not follow you," mumbled the Squire.

"Any more than you followed your daughter, eh? Your runaway daughter who has eloped with that graceless rogue, Dicon Conway."

"What's that? Ann run away? Ann eloped with Conway? Demme, sir, you joke. A poor, pitiful joke. My daughter, sir, has no interest in the fellow apart from his being the—er—that is he was acting——"

"Go on. Apart from his being the emissary of the Young Pretender! It must trouble your loyal conscience to think that such a villain was ever under your roof. Then let us say that he was acting for he acted a good part. He pulled the wool over your eyes."

"Demme, sir, you appear to know a lot about him."

"Enough, sir, to hang him. It is my duty to ferret out information about troublesome Jacobites. I take it your girl's fondness for the rascal comes as a surprise to you?"

There could be no possible doubt about that. The Squire had fallen back in his chair and his hands clutched the carved arms with twitching fingers. His lower jaw had fallen. The colour had ebbed from his face leaving it an unnatural pallor. It came back with a rush, dyeing his cheeks an ominous crimson. The sight would have been pitiful to one less hardened than the soldier.

"Ann!" whispered the Squire and moistened his lips with a thick tongue. "Ann! My little Ann. You've run away . . . without a word to your old Dad. And with that man . . . that devil . . . I'll . . . I'll . . ."

He struggled to his feet, panting with anger and emotion.

"Set your mind at rest, Mr. Trevor. Your daughter was at least respectably married."

The voice from the doorway caused the Squire to drop back into his chair. It brought a rush of profanity from the major.

"Who the devil are you?"

"Philip Yorke, at your service. We have met before; even dined together but you choose to have a short memory. I fear my face made less impression on you than that of our charming companion."

"I remember you. And what the deuce are you doing here?"

"An interloper. A curious sightseer. A neighbour who calls with pardonable curiosity to learn why soldiers arrive so late at night."

"Your curiosity may cost you dear. I am rounding up Jacobites, if you desire information. Perhaps you can account for your presence in Abergele coinciding with the warning sent to the Jacobite ship? You don't answer, eh?"

The Squire who had been breathing heavily in his chair interposed. "Is what you say true, Yorke?"

"What is that, sir? I fear this officer distracted my attention."

"Is it true that my girl, sir, is wed? Nothing else matters."

"I followed her, sir, with the intention of bringing her back."

"God bless you for that."

"But she vowed that she loved Conway and would never leave him. That being so I insisted that they should be married without loss of time."

"Married. Married! And to Dicon Conway! Ha! Well, perhaps it is as well."

"I should like to agree with you," interrupted Major Manstein suavely. "It would be well to have her provided for seeing that she will so soon be an orphan. Still, I confess it pains me deeply to think that she will shortly be a widow, too."

"Bereft of her father, sir?" The Squire's eyes were staring.

"A hanging matter, I understand. Treason has an ugly smack about it, Mr. Trevor; treason to the reigning House of Hanover is punishable by death. You may, of course, be innocent, but I must put the matter to the test. My informant tells me that arms for the Jacobite rebellion are concealed in the Black Barn on your estate. The moon has now risen. May I trouble you to walk there with me while I investigate?"

The Squire attempted to rise to his feet but fell back in his chair, panting hard.

"You do not accept my invitation, Mr. Trevor?"

"I cannot. I—I'm done for." Indeed, it was obvious that the Squire was in a sorry plight.

"Let me, sir, be your deputy," said Seth, speaking for the first time.

"No, no, my boy. You must not be drawn into this."

"Sir, my loyalty to the House of Hanover may be suspect; no one shall doubt my loyalty to the House of Trevor."

"No one ever shall, lad. I wish it had been you that was married to my girl, but there—my choice was not hers."

"Major Manstein," said Seth, "allow me to accompany you to the Black Barn. Squire Trevor is in no fit state."

"And you'll take the consequences, eh? It is all one to me. Forgive me if I have a doubting nature but there is just a possibility that you think that you may be able to pistol me while we are there, so I shall have one of my troopers accompany me. Bankes, look to

141

your priming and follow six paces behind. Shoot this man if he makes a suspicious gesture. Now, sir. Your humble servant!"

As Major Manstein and Seth Morrice walked from the room, the Squire sighed heavily and essayed to rise. His breath was coming in laboured gasps. Philip Yorke thought that he might have an apoplexy. Picking up a carafe he poured a glass of water which he held to the Squire's lips. The Squire drank gratefully, the tumbler clinking against his teeth. Some of the water slopped over his coat and it disturbed him. He tried to mop it up with his handkerchief, concentrating on the task as if nothing else mattered. Then he turned bloodshot eyes to Yorke.

"I'm finished, Yorke," he said huskily, "ruined; doomed. What a fool I was—nay, I'll not whine. I took a chance and lost, but I'll die game. She would wish it. A few minutes ago, Yorke, I nigh broke my heart when you told me she was married to that fly-by-night fellow. Now I see it is all for the best."

"Good often comes out of evil, sir, if we have sufficient faith; if one can discern in our daily happenings some connection with an ordained scheme of things."

"For the best! Can there be any best in this? I have not the faith to see it. He knew all along, that devil Manstein. He has played with us like a cat with a mouse. He'll get me, Yorke, or thinks he will. Yorke, promise me, man to man. You are a good fellow, Whig though you be. A true man if ever I saw one. Keep an eye on my girl. Care for my little girl. My one dread is leaving her unprotected."

"Ann? I would give my life to serve her, sir."

"She will be ruined. They'll sequester the estate; it's mortgaged anyway. And the money has all gone to the Prince. Well, I'm glad of that. Good luck to the bonny laddie. Give him my homage, sir."

"If I see him."

"Ah, I forgot you were not one of us. But you will see to Ann? You will see she doesn't starve?"

"I have money and no one to leave it to. Ann shall have every assistance."

"That's noble, sir, noble. I am grateful. Ah, Ann, my little girl, I love you so." The Squire drew a hand across his eyes. Then he composed his features. "They're coming; they're coming back. I hear steps on the gravel. Now for it. Yorke, push that table a little closer, there's a good fellow. Now stand across the room. You must not be drawn into this. Keep clear for Ann's sake. You must look after Ann. My little Ann. Demme, that devil must not have the satisfaction of seeing me broken. A glass of wine, quick, Yorke. Good pick-up. Ah, that's better!"

Seth Morrice, pale of face but of a quiet courage, walked into the room and stood rigidly with his back to the wall as if under arrest. Major Manstein's smile was satisfied and cynical as he stood regarding the Squire. The trooper behind him had his arms full of smuggled muskets.

"Strange agricultural implements to find in a barn, are they not, sir? Demme, you can imagine my amazement at such a discovery. You have, of course, a feasible explanation?"

142

"Why, no, sir. Let me say frankly that they were intended to be used in the service of Prince Charles Edward, Regent for His Majesty King James the Third, and our lawful Prince of Wales. I rode out in the 'Fifteen, sir, and I would have ridden out in the 'Forty-five if I could have stuck to my saddle. You've worsted me, damn you, but —God save King James and to hell with Hanover !"

The Squire's hand fell heavily on the table. The drawer was open and as his fingers slid inside Major Manstein yelled "Stop him !" He sprang forward, startled for once out of his taciturnity. The Squire had a pistol in his hand, the muzzle pointing to his flushed forehead. There was a crash as the trooper dropped his armful of muskets. There was a crash as Philip Yorke overturned a chair. There was an even louder crash as the pistol exploded. All Major Manstein achieved was to catch the dead man's body as it crashed to the bloodstained rug.

CHAPTER THIRTY

IN DRAB, DAMP NOVEMBER PRINCE CHARLES EDWARD CROSSED THE Border marching south by way of Carlisle, to the consternation of General Wade who waited at Newcastle for an attack which never materialized. It was a strange medley, this army of invasion—several thousand clansmen (the bulk of the force), some hundred mounted men, mostly Scottish, and the Irish volunteers. The like of it had never before been seen : a small force indeed with which to aspire to a kingdom.

So thought Richard Conway as he sat his horse at the top of a hilly Cumberland road and watched the ragged line of ragged men tramping stolidly along the valley towards him. There were horsemen, of course, but the Young Chevalier was pitifully deficient in cavalry and the general impression was that of an army of foot. Ann stared with fascinated eyes. She had never before seen an armed force of any magnitude and to her eyes it was imposing.

"How many there are !" she exclaimed, turning excited eyes to her husband.

"How few ! How confoundedly few. There were desertions after Prestonpans. The clansmen could not resist the temptation to return home with their booty."

"There seem to be a lot of soldiers to me, though of course they do not look so gay as the English troops with their scarlet jackets."

"We are hopelessly outnumbered, my dear," said Conway seriously. "Unless we recruit as we advance it will go hard with us. Speed and daring must do the trick. The Prince is depending on the gentry of Lancashire and Cheshire—and, of course, North Wales—to rally at his approach. Would that I were as certain of their loyalty as his Highness is. There was a lukewarmness in Flintshire, Ann, which chilled my ardour."

"I thought that our people seemed very enthusiastic."

"Those that met at your house, perhaps. But what a handful ! And some of those had their loyalty tempered by discretion. It is, it seems to me, chiefly the adventurers—like myself, my dear—who have nothing at stake who are hot for the Prince. But the men of fashion who have to risk their all, hang back. It is not for me to blame them, but to put it bluntly their influence counts for more than our swords. They hesitate. As we rode north I have called at house after house and met with the same reception invariably: fair words, good wishes, evasive answers."

"Oh, but the Prince will succeed. He must."

"It will not be his fault if he fails. His intrepidity may carry him through. No man was ever better fitted to lead a forlorn hope. Come, my dear, I will present you to His Highness."

Ann thought that she detected a touch of pride in his voice; it was as though her husband were proud of her. She felt gratified. Since the day of their wedding she had noticed a change come over Dicon; he seemed less boisterous, more considerate. It was as though he had become conscious of the new responsibility he had assumed. She missed his gay assurance, it had been so fascinating, but she liked him all the better for his tender possessiveness.

Slowly they rode to meet the marching column which wound its variegated length amid the green and grey of the rocky pass. The few mounted men were mostly well-dressed cavaliers, well-horsed and obviously men of quality. There were companies of horse farther down the line and a carriage drawn by a pair of horses—probably belonging to the Prince. For the most part the advancing army was composed of Highland footmen, squat, blue-bonneted fellows, many of them bearded, clad in kilts and plaids. They came onward at a dogged pace, kilts swirling with the effortless swing of men well used to tramping many miles through the heather. Ann was impressed by the rapidity with which they covered the ground. The mounted men were outpaced so that they had to touch their horses into a brief trot to keep their position on the flanks of the column. Ann wondered which of the cavaliers might be the Prince. She saw one particularly well-dressed horseman and pointed him out to her husband. "No," said Dicon and laughed. "That is Lord Elcho who joined us at Edinburgh. I have no doubt it would please him if he knew he had been mistaken for the Prince."

"Where is the Prince? Can you see him?"

"I can see him," observed Dicon, and said no more. As the column drew nearer he pulled the horses to the roadside and dismounted. The Macdonalds were leading, so he informed Ann, who stared at the sturdy clansmen with something akin to dread, so much like savages did they appear to her. In front of them walked a young officer. He wore the customary blue-bonnet with a white cockade which supported a feather. He had a tartan jacket and plaid, but in place of a kilt he wore breeches and a horseman's high boots. His figure was as slender as a girl's, his large brown eyes were of almost feminine beauty. There was nothing effeminate about the vigorous stride with which he led the column over the muddy roadway. Dicon stepped forward, swept off his tricorne hat and bowed low. The officer held up his hand and the column came to a halt.

"Ah, Conway, I am glad to have you back with us again. You see, we were so desirous of your presence that we have come all this way to meet you."

"I rejoice to see you so far penetrated into your illustrious father's kingdom, sir," said Dicon quietly. "Your Highness, since last we met I have had the temerity to add yet another recruit to your Highness's forces; may I be allowed to present my wife?"

"Your wife?" Prince Charles bowed to the blushing Ann. "Madam, we accept our new recruit joyfully. You are indeed welcome, Mrs. Conway, though I fear that our war preparations have not included the entertainment of ladies."

"Your Highness," cried Ann eagerly, "I have long looked forward to this day. I pray that the time is not far distant when King James is once more back in his kingdom. As for the roughness of the life, sir, with you to lead us and inspire us, we shall not notice the rigours of the way."

There was a growl of assent from those of the Macdonalds who understood her words.

"If we are inspired it is because so many of you gallant ladies have faith in us. Dicon, I used to regard you as my envoy *par excellence*; it seems you are also our leading connoisseur of beauty. But we hold up the march. Every moment is precious; our one hope is to strike at the capital before the Government can recall the veteran troops from Flanders. Ride at my side, Madam, and we will converse as we advance. You must forgive me if I do not ride beside you. I feel that my men realize so much better that I am one of them if I share on foot the hardships which they so generously undertake on my behalf."

The Prince gave the signal to advance. He strode well ahead of the marching column being able from the excellence of his condition, his perfect health and lissom frame to walk with surprising speed. Ann had frequently to urge her horse in order to keep level with him. He talked easily as they advanced, naturally and unaffectedly. There was no semblance of gallantry; he spoke as one comrade to another; and his talk was all of the chances of the invasion. A child could have told where his heart lay. Ann succumbed to his charm as most women did though the Prince seemed as indifferent to women as they were attracted to him. His mind ran solely on the prospects of the expedition. His converse was entirely of military matters, or else he speculated on the likelihood of the landed gentry of the district flocking to his banner.

"Dicon!"

"Your Highness?"

"You have never been backward in my service."

"Nor shall you ever find me so, sir."

"Would you, to serve me, even desert your bride? Nay, do not look so taken aback; it will not be for more than a couple of days. I am most anxious that Lord Barrymore should exert himself to rally the Cheshire sympathizers. Will you bear him a message saying that at long last we are on our way, and that I look to him to raise Cheshire

145

for my father? Say to him that it is now or never. We succeed now or we fail for all time. There can be no half-measures."

"As your Highness commands," said Dicon bowing.

"Not commands, Dicon, requests! Indeed, it grieves me to tear you from the side of your charming wife, but I have no one else on my staff who knows this district as you do and time is so precious a factor."

"Go, Dicon," said Ann quietly. "We came to serve his Highness, this is no time for the slightest hesitancy. I will ride with his Highness and await your safe return."

Dicon Conway took the letter which the Prince handed to him, bowed, and bent over his wife's hand. "Her lips, man, her lips," commanded the Prince, and with Ann's kiss on his mouth, Dicon turned his horse about and spurred out of sight.

"My coach is at your disposal, Madam," said the Prince, but Ann shook her head. "I prefer to share the march," she said. "I am young and used to outdoor exercise. It will do me no harm." So the invaders pressed onward, striking like a sword deep into the vitals of England. Ann noticed that horsemen were continually coming and going. As they passed on their way officers rode from the ranks to canter up the drives of the houses of the gentry. They usually returned with glum looks and moody mien. Small bodies of horse rode in advance and on either flank, scouting, foraging, or seeking shelter for the night. The Prince was courteous and entertaining. He explained to Ann the various tartans of the clans. There were the Macdonalds in the van, then the Camerons, the Stuarts and the Gordons. There followed the Macgregors, Mackinnons, Grants, Robertsons, Maclaughlins, Macphersons. There were also men of a Lowlands regiment commanded by Lord George Murray.

That night at the Prince's headquarters Ann met the leaders—the men who had risked their all for the Stuart cause: the Duke of Perth, Lord Nairn, Lord Ogilvie, Cluny, chief of the Macphersons, and that exquisite Lord Elcho about whom the Prince held mixed views. It was all strangely bewildering to Ann; some treated her with grave courtesy, some with exaggerated gallantry; some with the indifference of men whose minds were fully engrossed by the project on hand; others with the appraising eye which lingered appreciatively on her fresh face and slender figure. All accorded her the utmost deference and respect. It was one point on which his Highness was adamant. There was to be no looseness of living where he was concerned. Never had an army marched with so few camp followers. He appeared insensible to the charms of women. It was noticed that during his brief stay at Edinburgh he never danced. Night after night the orchestra had played, but though the Prince was renowned as a dancer he invariably wore his spurred riding-boots as though to intimate that he had no leisure for frivolity so long as there was serious business on hand.

It was on November the twentieth that he left Carlisle. By the twenty-second the Highland army was at Penrith; the next day they had reached Kendal. The advance cavalry rode through Lancaster

146

and by November the twenty-fifth they were at Preston. This was the farthest point south attained in the 'Fifteen rebellion. It seemed a town of ill omen and they pressed on to Wigan with as little delay as possible. Ann's admiration for the Prince grew with each passing day. He was always the first up in the mornings; he roused the officers and saw that the men were on the march before dawn which was slow enough in coming those drab, misty, November days. Those early marches left an indelible mark on Ann's impressionable mind. She watched through the first incipient gleam the Prince making his way amid the marshalled lines of the ragged Highlanders, the sturdy men with target and claymore who, wrapped in their plaids against the drizzle, jabbered in Gaelic as they formed their ranks.

Sometimes at nights when the toils of the day were over, Ann listened to the leaders wrangling amongst themselves. There was Lord George Murray, who was considered to be their best strategist, jealous of the Duke of Perth who also held lieutenant-general's rank though not so able a soldier. There were some, the Irish adventurers chiefly, who never argued but followed their Prince with a blind devotion which questioned nothing. Ann's sympathies were much with them. There were Scottish chiefs who favoured caution; who were for holding back until reinforcements came or until the King of France invaded England. There were some who still contended that the invasion should have been by way of Yorkshire, not Lancashire. This dissension disturbed Ann. She imagined that on so desperate an adventure all would have been of one mind. The Prince listened courteously but his ultimate decision was ever the same. There was no time to be lost. It was now or never. So the next day's march was as usual, southward, ever southward, farther and farther from the Scottish border, deeper and deeper into England, nearer and nearer the capital where King George made preparations for possible flight, and volunteers hurriedly drilled to impose their bodies as a living bulwark against the audacious and intrepid royal adventurer.

They marched and marched, these Highlanders. The Prince would never eat at midday. There was no time to be lost. It was now or never. A hurried supper when the night's billets were reached sufficed. Then, once the conference with his officers was over, he would throw himself fully-dressed on a bed and after a few hours' sleep he would be ready for the road again. The wine bills, which have been preserved, show how abstemious was the Prince at his meals.

On and on tramped the invaders, through hamlets where the villagers came to cottage doorways to stare with curious eyes as these ragged, armed men with their quaint plaids and bagpipes, the bearded, mud-splashed, hardy warriors who marched resolutely with their weather-tanned faces to the south. English rustics heard the unfamiliar drone of the pipes, strange discords of Celtic songs fell on their amazed ears. They admired the handsome young Prince, of course—but no one enlisted! There was curiosity, no enthusiasm. Something seemed to have killed the doctrine of the divine right of kings. It might yet flourish amid the patriarchal clans of the Highlands; in rural and industrial England the people had better things to think about.

147

It was different in Manchester which was reached on November 29th. By that time Dicon had rejoined the Prince and Ann felt happier if not more secure to have her husband riding once more at her side. It was evident that Manchester was more generously disposed towards 'the Pretender's Boy.' There was enthusiasm: real enthusiasm, no mere shouting and drinking but a rush to enlist. So many came forward that it was possible to form a Manchester Regiment composed entirely of Englishmen, incongruously out of place amid the thousands of Scottish clansmen and Irish volunteers.

"This is good," exclaimed Dicon with a sigh of satisfaction. "At long last the English are coming forward to declare for the Yellow-haired Laddie."

Ann, too, was enthusiastic, but when the new regiment paraded it was found that it did not exceed three hundred men. With such valiant but inadequate numbers did Prince Charles essay to conquer his father's kingdom. Soon it was apparent that the Manchester fervency was but short-lived. Dicon came dejectedly into his wife's bedchamber one night as Ann was settling herself for repose and sitting heavily on the bedside he stared moodily at the floor.

"What is it, Dicon? You are upset. I can read your moods."

"Matters are not going right for us."

"I thought that recruitment went on apace."

"It was but a flash in the pan. The people are holding back now. The men of position remain lukewarm. They will not risk their all for an uncertainty."

"Cowards! My father did."

"Yes, your father did! I wonder what the outcome will be. I wish there was word of him."

"Perhaps I ought to have written. But I am so bad at letter-writing. I often wonder what goes on at home. My conscience troubles me at times, Dicon. Father always pretended to be gruff but underneath he was tender. He loved me dearly, Dicon, and I fear I have treated him contemptibly. I have had disquieting dreams of late."

"I will get word through as soon as possible, Ann, but at the moment there are weightier things to think about."

"What matters, Dicon?"

"Well, Lord Elcho heads a party who disagree profoundly with the Prince's strategy. They are holding back."

"Traitors!"

"Nay, hardly that, Ann. It is a matter of difference of opinion. They vow that it is impossible to put a new king upon the throne of England without the consent of the people of England."

"Oh, Dicon!"

"And I confess, my dear, that there is something in what they say. We counted on the people of England rallying to the Prince once the invasion started. The handful we recruited in Manchester could not be construed to represent the country's consent."

"What, Dicon? Are you, too, going to abandon His Highness?"

"I? Perish the thought. I am but facing facts. As for deserting the Prince, I will stay by him come wind come weather; die with him if need be." Dicon began to pace the room. "Darling, I must leave you for a while."

"What, again, Dicon? So soon?"

"It is for his Highness, my sweet."

"Then it is settled; you must go."

"I will explain, Ann. Move over, I want to sit beside you. What the devil . . . I wish I were not so restless. No, I can't remain seated. There's unrest in the very air. Are you not conscious of it, Ann? Or am I susceptible to atmosphere? I will sit down beside you: I may not be able to do so for a while. Give me your hand. What was I telling you? Demme if I remember: oh, yes. The Duke of Cumberland has thrown his army between us and London. He is quartered at Newcastle-under-Lyme and at Stafford and Lichfield. Now, as you know, the Prince intends to drive straight at London and wants the Duke out of his way, so it is proposed that a body of us under Lord George Murray should make a feint as though we were marching across Cheshire with Wales as our objective. If we can draw the Duke's forces into Wales, or even to the Welsh border, we shall leave the way open for the Prince to strike. He counts on slipping round the back of the Duke's forces. At any rate the Prince marches for Derby in the morning. And I, my dear, ride with Murray. Give me your lips, my sweet, and wish me luck. If we bring this off there's a throne for King James and a knighthood for me, my Lady Ann: if not——"

"If not, Dicon?"

He shook off her embrace and walked from the room without answering.

CHAPTER THIRTY-ONE

NEVER BEFORE HAD ANN FELT SO DEJECTED. HITHERTO HER LIFE HAD been for the most part joyous. Certainly trial and tribulation had not come her way. She had not yet learned that character is fashioned out of disappointment and denial. Dicon had not returned. The raiders under Lord George Murray were back, elated at the success of their Cheshire thrust. They had encountered the royal dragoons near Congleton and had driven them from the field in headlong flight. The Prince's troopers were bragging in the streets, and drinking blackjacks of ale whenever that luxury could be got. But Dicon was not amongst them. No one had word of him. Ann passed from group to group plying the men with questions. They had seen him ride into the fray; that was all. No man could say more. Each had been busy attending to his own affairs. Ann wondered whether Dicon had been cut down. Possibly not, he was such a magnificent swordsman! But he might have been shot. She pictured him lying wounded in some Cheshire ditch that drab, damp December day. And she could do nothing about it. Ann shivered. There was no fire in her billet. The people of the house had fled when word of the Prince's approach reached them. They had taken with them every

149

scrap of food and fuel. Ann had gone to bed supperless the night before. She had had no breakfast. She was so cold that she had gone out to the shops to buy a thicker coat. It was then, and only then, that she realized that Dicon had carried the purse with him. She had no money. Not that it mattered because all the shops were shut and the shutters were up as a precaution against the predatory instincts of the invaders.

She looked out upon the street from the grime-streaked window of her little room. Two of the invaders were seated on the doorstep of the house opposite industriously searching for lice in the folds of their plaids. A quaint pair, thought Ann; stocky and undersized; one, a bearded man; the other a youth with a fresh but not too clean face. He bore a rusty sword and a musket which seemed too long for his meagre stature. The elder man had his basket-hilted broad-sword and leather target. Despite their weapons they appeared peaceable enough, a little lost, bewildered perhaps by their foreign environment, but ready to follow wherever their chief might lead.

Ann went out into the streets, streets which were strangely deserted for Derby. Church bells were ringing what was intended to be a peal of welcome to the Prince Regent. Actually it sounded to Ann's ears like a dirge. She wished the tolling would stop. The Mayor and other civic officials (having sent their chains and robes of office to a place of security) were waiting to accord a formal welcome to the Prince. This courtesy was prompted by discretion not inclination. The Prince's advance guard had ridden the day before into the town, demanding billets for nine thousand men! Of course the total was exaggerated; mere bluff; nevertheless the army of Prince Charles Edward was of sufficient magnitude to make the good folk of Derby a trifle apprehensive. Ann reached the Market Square and here she saw thirty horsemen sitting their chargers—a trifle wearily—in the hope of impressing the populace. They wore blue uniforms faced with red and their scarlet waistcoats were trimmed with gold lace. They looked imposing, but Ann's mind recalled the ragged Highlanders who formed the bulk of the Prince's force. She was soon to see them again, rank after rank of them, trudging with swinging kilts down the centre of the roadway. Then came Lord Elcho at the head of his life-guards. These, too, wore smart blue uniforms, faced with gold. The grenadier company passed with a defiant swagger. Each hat bore the legend—"A grave or a throne."

More clansmen followed. They came in tolerable order, six abreast, and over their heads flew the standards, chiefly the blue flag of St. Andrew with its white diagonal cross. And all the while, above the tramp of marching feet, there sounded the weird, stirring drone of the bagpipes. It was as though they lifted up their voices in protest against the clangour of the bells.

It was dusk when the Prince arrived. He walked, as was his custom, at the head of a body of Highlanders. Though not weary (the day's march never tired him, he was so fit) his Highness was in no mood for ceremony and he curtly dismissed the bodyguard drawn up in the Square to do him honour, and then walked moodily across to the house of the Earl of Exeter. It had been arranged that he should sleep there that night.

Ann watched him enter. She drew nearer with some trepidation, wondering if she possessed the courage to ask whether any word had been received of her husband's fate. There were so many officers coming and going, so many town officials about, so many soldiers on guard, that her courage failed her and she returned disconsolately to her chilly room. The Highlanders on the doorstep of the house opposite had been joined by comrades, newly arrived. They were making their supper of bread and cheese.

One of the men had taken the footwear from off some Derby citizen and he was endeavouring, not too successfully, to persuade the shoes to accommodate his broad and muddy feet. Ann no longer felt any apprehension about walking among these savages. Never were savages so well behaved. Occasional pilfering was the only charge ever directed against these men from the distant north. They were quiet enough, almost subdued. After their long march all they asked was a bite of food and some straw on which to stretch their limbs. And it was December, wet, cold, bleak December.

Ann felt as sombre as the day. Dicon had said that people were susceptible to atmosphere and he was right. Ann sensed a cloud of depression settling over the entire force. What could she do? Ought she to go in search of Dicon? Should she remain with the army in the hope of his returning? She did not know where to seek him; he at least would know where she was to be found. She decided to remain. It was not an easy decision for she felt restless. Yet it seemed wise. Night fell. Ann lit a candle. She endeavoured to coax a fire in the cold hearth by breaking up some small shelves. It took her some time to despoil the cupboard in which she found them. It seemed all wrong thus to shatter another person's property but she was getting colder and colder. As she drew comfort from the flames she decided that she would never again criticize soldiers who pilfered on a campaign; necessity knew no law. She wrapped a counterpane about her shoulders, shivered, sat with clasped hands staring at the feeble flickering of the flames, and wondered what had happened to Dicon.

The front door opened and closed. A step sounded on the stair. It was a man's tread. The step had a familiar sound. She sprang up and flung wide the door with a joyous cry. "Dicon! Oh Dicon!"

But it was not Dicon. She drew back in amazement.

"You! What are you doing here? How came you here?"

Ann stared incredulously at Philip Yorke. He removed his hat and bowed slightly. His face was pale and graver than usual. No longer could she see a mischievous light dancing in the eyes; she did not look for it. "Mr. Yorke . . . you have . . . I feel you have bad news!"

"Does my presence indeed suggest that I bear bad tidings, Ann?"

She nodded, mute with misery. "Dicon," she whispered. "Is . . . is . . .?" The dread words would not fashion on her lips.

"Dicon? I know nothing about Dicon, Ann. I come direct from your home."

"My home. Ah, Philip, what a familiar sound that has. How is—but what are your sad tidings? Do you mean something terrible has happened?"

"Sit down, Ann. I would give much to spare you but I fear that I must hurt you, you whom I would guard from all hurt."

"I think I know what you are trying to tell me, Philip, though I do not in the least understand. Something has happened to Father?"

"Yes, Ann. You will not see him again."

"He has been arrested? They have found out, and he is sent to the Tower?"

"They have found out; so much is right. The night you left, so unexpectedly, young Hughie came to my house saying that he had seen Major Manstein making for your home."

"That man! That devil! I might have known. He passed us on the way."

"I hastened over. He was there when I arrived; two troopers with him. Someone (I believe I know who it is) had told him about the arms stored in the Black Barn."

"Philip, you warned me that it was unwise to leave them there; how right you were. But go on."

"He invited your father to accompany him to the barn. Your father could not accept the invitation. He—he was not well."

"His heart has been giving him trouble of late."

"Yes, his heart was troubling him, Ann. I am glad that you realize that. He was very upset. I could tell by the colour of his face and his stertorous breathing. Seth Morrice went in place of him."

"That was good of Seth; it was so like him."

"The arms were discovered, of course. Manstein put Morrice under arrest; he has been sent to London for trial."

"Poor Seth."

"Then he turned to arrest your father, but—" Philip Yorke paused, staring at the white set face in front of him. How could he tell her the manner of her father's end? Better to leave her in ignorance. "Ann," he said gently, "your father became very excited, and you can imagine that this was most injurious. He defied Manstein. Then he fell forward. When we picked him up he was dead."

"Dead."

"Quite dead, Ann. I am sorry."

She gave a hysterical laugh. "Father dead; Dicon possibly dead. What am I to do?"

"I will take care of you, Ann."

She did not appear to hear him. She had taken out a handkerchief, a mere wisp of a thing, but instead of using it she sat dry-eyed, twisting it nervously in her fingers.

"What has happened to the house?"

"It is sequestered."

"Then I have no home. And I have no money and Dicon is gone."

Philip Yorke slipped a hand into his pocket. "While Manstein was out of the room, Ann, your father spoke about you to me. Let me say, first, that I was able to tell him that you were married and it

152

afforded him satisfaction—under the circumstances. Then he begged me to keep an eye on you, to care for you. Never was a promise given more readily, more gladly. I could have been entrusted with no more sacred task. Here, Ann, is money for your immediate needs."

He placed a purse on the table. It was heavy with gold. Ann lifted it abstractedly but her eyes were dreamy. "I am glad Father spoke of me, at the end, and with fondness; with forgiveness. I shall find it harder to forgive myself for deserting him. Be candid, Philip. Father did not send me this money. I know your ways."

"Well, he did indirectly, Ann."

"It is a gift from you. I cannot accept it."

"That is foolish. Call it your wedding present."

"But Philip: if Dicon were here what would he say?"

"He would vow it was a most timely and opportune means of relieving his straitened circumstances."

Ann gave a slight laugh. "I believe he would, Philip. Poor Dicon—and he is always poor, in truth—poor Dicon would be practical, so I must be, I suppose. Father was so set on my marrying Seth so that I should be well provided for. It was his chief concern."

"Let me make it mine."

"Oh, but I could not. Why, what claim have I on you?"

"Why should the question of claim enter in? May not a man do what he likes with his own? I have no kith or kin ; no one to whom I can leave my money. Allow me to care for you, Ann. It would afford me such intense pleasure. I take no joy in providing for my own needs, simple though they be."

Ann shook her head. "You have the most generous heart in the world, Philip. You never think about yourself."

"I have no time; I devote all my leisure to thinking of you."

"You must not talk like that, now. Tell me—do you think me hard-hearted? I have not shed a tear at my father's death. Yet I miss him. I think it is because nothing seems real. It sounds like a story you tell me. Either that or else it is because I am so worried about Dicon not returning from the skirmish . . . can one grieve over two things at the same time?"

"What of your husband?"

"He rode to Cheshire a few days ago with a raiding party and he has not returned. No one knows what has happened to him."

"He may come back. Do not despair. Ann, you must return with me until, well, until matters are straightened out. I cannot leave you here unprotected."

"No, I shall abide by the Prince. Dicon will come back to the army expecting to find me here. If I were not with the Prince he would be distracted. I shall follow his Highness on his march to London. When Dicon returns to Derby he will ride and overtake me."

Yorke shook his head gravely. "The Prince will not march to London."

"Oh, you always talk like that!" Ann exclaimed almost petulantly. "I tell you that the Prince is carrying all before him. He will be in the capital before the week is out."

"Dear, disillusioned child," said Yorke almost tenderly. "I have tried to prevent you from burning your fingers in the flame of this royal fool's folly, but you would not heed me. You were set on going your own way. You wanted adventure and romance. Wel Ann, you have it. Romance—a man with a price on his head: a penniless adventurer: a man, moreover, who has disappeared. What of your adventure? You sit in a cheerless room in a strange town. You lack supper. The prospects are black indeed."

"The prospects are bright indeed. In a few days the Prince Regent will be in London. King James will be restored. We shall all be rich and famous."

"To-morrow, Ann, the Prince will be in full retreat."

She stared incredulously. "Retreat! You said retreat? You are mad. His Highness is elated. He is resolute in his determination to capture London."

"But his staff are not. Every general; every chief in the party is now united in resolving to get back to Scotland while there is yet time. They do but await the opportunity of telling the Prince. Indeed everyone seems to know of the decision save the Prince himself. And the opportunity to tell him is here: in Derby."

"You only say this to discourage me."

"I think of nothing but your welfare, Ann." He came nearer and took one of her cold hands in his, gazing at the fingers as though they fascinated him. Ann made no effort to withdraw her hand. Her eyes were fixed on the wall; her thoughts were far away.

"Come back with me, Ann. You shall be safe, protected, cared for. If—if—your husband is still alive he will find you and come to claim you. Indeed, he is far more likely to come across you in your native place than he would if you go wandering across the country with an army of vagabonds. Already I have purchased some of the furniture from your old home for your use. My home is yours. I will move out to another place if propriety demands."

"I could not dream of putting you to such trouble."

"Ann, can you not perceive that my whole desire in life is to serve you; to make you happy? So long as you are happy, nothing else matters."

"But why should you feel like this?"

"That is a question which I shall not attempt to answer. Accept my statement for what it is worth. I plead with you, in your own interests, to return with me."

"No, Mr. Yorke—Philip. I stay by the Prince until Dicon comes to me."

"The Prince will be in retreat."

"He will never retreat; he is not made that way."

"I implore you to reconsider your decision. I cannot go away and leave you here unprotected. I should be distracted."

"I wish it. I shall not change my mind no matter how you plead, Philip. Why should I return? My father is dead. Our home is lost to us. There is nothing to take me back to the place where I was born. Rather will I follow the fortunes of my Prince. If he becomes a wanderer then I will too. If misfortune comes to him, I will share it. I can sympathize for already I have known the taste of it. I thank you for your offer, for all your kindness, Philip, but I do not accept. My mind is made up."

Philip Yorke sighed and rose to his feet. He lifted her fingers to his lips. "Never forget," he said softly, "whatever happens, wherever you are, whatever the circumstances, just as you are, I am yours to command. The dearest wish of my life is to serve you. I put your happiness before all else. God keep you."

He moved quietly from the room. The door closed. Ann was alone with her thoughts.

The next day the retreat from Derby began.

CHAPTER THIRTY-TWO

CERTAIN DATES STAND OUT IN THE MEMORY, ETCHED WITH INDELIBLE clarity. The fifth of December was one of these. Ann slept as one does in a strange house—in fits and starts. When settling for sleep a sense of awful, overwhelming desolation swept over her. It was not long since she was safe, protected, loved, cared for, satisfied, secure. Now she lay in a deserted dwelling alone with her thoughts; beset by conflicting emotions which stirred and strained her. She thought of her father—dead; of her home—lost; of her husband—missing; of the Prince's cause (if Philip Yorke proved to be correct)—doomed. If that were so, thought Ann as she rose from her disordered bed, if that were so she would stay by the Prince, suffering his misfortunes with him, dying, if need be, in a lost cause. When all that makes life worth living is taken away one becomes indifferent, reckless. So thought Ann. And she had nothing left to live for. In the midst of her thinking her eyes noticed the purse of gold which Philip Yorke had left her. There was always Philip in the background, steadfast, unchangeable as a rock. Perhaps the future was not entirely black. She took fresh courage. She would carry on with her life fortified by the realization that he was always present, a rock, a sanctuary, a hiding place in a tempest. And, in very truth, the tempest seemed like to break at any moment. There were sounds in the street beneath her window, shuffling feet, voices which came up to her in an unintelligible babble, the click of steel, hoarse orders. It was getting near dawn. She completed her dressing—there was little to do for she had lain down in most of her clothes—and then descended the stairs. She was hungry, no longer ravenous but experiencing a sinking, sickly feeling. There was no point in visiting the larder. Long ago she had searched every cupboard and shelf without finding a crumb. She took a sip of water from an earthenware jug; it tasted flat and insipid. She went out to the stables in search of Black Prince. Always she was haunted by the dread possibility of his being stolen. The Highlanders were thronging the streets. They appeared in good spirits after their night's rest and their boisterous good humour cheered Ann not a little. A burly, bearded fellow in a Cameron tartan was seated on a low wall eating bread and cheese. There must have been something in Ann's look which aroused a rough chivalry in this clansman who had himself known the pangs of hunger. He stood up, took off his bonnet respectfully and proffered his food. Ann coloured; her eyes brimmed with tears. Though she was so eager she could have devoured the lot she broke off but a fragment as though to indicate that she appreciated the thoughtfulness of the giver. "I thank you for your kindness to me," she said. The man mumbled something in Gaelic. Ann passed on her way cheered as much by the act as by the food. There were soldiers thronging the yard of the inn where Black Prince was stabled. For an agonizing moment she wondered whether the horse had gone. A familiar whinny reassured her. She noticed that her charger's curves were already less pronounced and that his coat had lost its ebony gloss. Like his mistress, Black Prince was tasting hardship for the first time in his sheltered life. He thrust his velvet muzzle into her hand as though to indicate that he comprehended that they were companions in misfortune and that he intended to stand by her as a good comrade should. A man who had recently enlisted in the Manchester Regiment assisted with the saddling.

"Did them Scots keep you awake last night, lady?" he inquired as he tightened the girth. "It's excited they are; they talk of getting to London within the week and they say it's ten times as big as the largest of their cities and will yield champion booty."

"They are to march on London then?"

"Why, yes, isn't that what we have all joined up for? The Prince holds a council of war this morning. All the leading officers are shut up with him."

Council of war! The expression carried with it an ominous ring to Ann's ears which had so recently hearkened to Philip Yorke's forebodings. Why was he always right? Had he greater vision than she, or was it merely his wider experience? Or the way he had of letting his reason and not his emotion guide his judgment? Ann felt that she must have word with Prince Charles without delay. She rode her horse to his headquarters and waited. The time passed slowly. A fine rain began to fall. She took Black Prince under cover and she sought shelter in the hall of the house. From behind a closed door there came the murmur of voices, sometimes low and indistinct, sometimes clear and angry. An armed sentry from the life-guards stood at the entrance. He looked curiously at Ann but having seen her riding beside the Prince he made no attempt to prevent her from standing inside the doorway. She tried not to listen but there were snatches of talk which could not fail to reach her ears.

"How do you expect forty-five hundred men to take and hold London?" demanded a voice which Ann thought might have belonged to Lord George Murray.

"I tell you," exclaimed the Prince, and for once his usually soft, courteous voice was raised in angry vehemence. "I tell you that another Prestonpans at the gates of London would put my father back on the throne. It is now or never. Every day lost gives more power to our foes. Do not forget, gentlemen, that the regulars have but

156

recently come from Europe in crowded transports. They are weary from sea-travel and forced marches. They will not stand up to a claymore charge. Why are you faint-hearted? When I drew the sword I threw away the scabbard. If you cannot face London let us turn aside into Wales; amid those mountains we could defy the pick of Cumberland's troops. Have I not a price on my head? There are many persons who are eager to claim the thirty thousand pounds which Hanoverian George is pleased to consider my monetary value. Do I not run a greater risk than any of you? And I counsel, press on; press on! I repeat, it is now or never. If we go back we are undone."

"My conclusion is that we should go back to Scotland without delay, join our friends there and live and die with them," said Lord George Murray.

"You are more likely to die with them than live with them. Why, once we retreat we confess defeat. Cumberland's forces will swell daily. When they attack they will outnumber us five to one, ten to one, nay, twenty to one. We shall have no chance. Now is the time. Now! Strike at the heart of England. Strike now! Once lost this chance will never occur again. I believe that the soldiers of the regulars will never fight against their true prince. There will be defection in the enemy's army, mark my words, if we press on. If we once turn our backs we are doomed. Now or never, gentlemen, now or never."

"I agree wi' his Highness," came the Duke of Perth's broad tones, but an angry tumult of sound drowned further conversation.

So, thought Ann, Philip Yorke was right. The leaders had combined against their Prince. They would shatter by their caution his cherished dream; they would ruin his only chance of success. Ann felt numb. It might have been her own throne which was toppling.

The door of the room was flung open. Ann could see a group of fashionably dressed men, all girt with swords, standing before their chairs as the Prince, white of face, his usually mild eyes blazing, stalked haughtily to the open door. "What!" he taunted, "a Macdonald turn his back? A Cameron run away from the enemy? For shame, Lochiel! Go forward and I will lead you to victory."

There was an ominous silence. The Prince walked out of the room and proceeded up the stairs, passing Ann without recognition. He strode with set, unseeing eyes.

They said that he was never the same again. Charles Edward, gallant adventurer, the man who footed it with his Highland clansmen into the heart of England, had been robbed of his victory. He had been defeated not by his foes but by his friends. To Ann the suffering in his face was a mute appeal. More than ever she was resolved to follow her Prince in his hour of trial.

* * * * *

The clansmen tramped silently through the mud those drear December days. No pipes sounded now. There were no banners flying, just rain-soaked men with rusty claymores, grim-faced, plodding sullenly northward with their backs to the foe. Ann never forgot the sound of their feet monotonously squelching along the mud-rutted roads.

The terror which beset London on Black Friday when success seemed on the point of the Young Pretender's sword, vanished like snow at the coming of a thaw. Those who had prepared for ignominious flight forgot that they had concealed their valuables in panic and began to talk vaingloriously. They jeered, they taunted, they boasted. They made mock of the Little Knave, they sneered at the jabbering, screaming wild monkeys who followed him. But the closeness of the escape had given a shock to the national pride and the national security. It found outlet in the vicious and brutal treatment meted out to the stragglers captured by the advancing regulars who, once word came through that Charles Edward was in retreat, took fresh heart and eagerly set forth in pursuit.

The Prince no longer walked. The day he left Derby he mounted his horse and thereafter the trudging footmen no longer saw his lithe figure walking before them. At times they caught glimpses of a white-faced man who rode as though in a dream, rarely speaking. All the fire and the ardour and the daring had gone out of him.

To Ann his Highness was pleased to be gracious. Two days after the retreat began he encountered her on the line of march. He drew his charger alongside the mud-spattered flanks of Black Prince.

"Madam, I am surprised to find you here."

"I am sharing the fortunes of my Prince, sir."

"I have no fortunes now—only misfortunes. All is lost. I am undone. Save yourself, my dear lady. Those traitors have encompassed my downfall."

"All the more reason why one loyal supporter should remain with your Highness."

"Your devotion touches me, Madam. Where is your husband?"

"I have lost my husband, sir. He never returned from the Congleton raid."

"You have lost a husband. I have lost a kingdom. We are well met, Madam. They say misery likes company." He rode a while sombrely, then he burst forth, "Why was I not told before that Dicon Conway was missing? No man ever served his Prince with greater devotion. I have too much on my mind or I should have missed his cheery presence. Ah, Dicon! It is hard to lose one's friends, God knows, and there will be tragedies enough and to spare before this wretched business is ended. I will bear you in mind, Mrs. Conway. The minute the time is opportune I will have you conducted to a place of security."

Through towns and villages they passed, over flat Lancashire lands, up green hills. They saw the tranquil lakes of Westmorland.

"I will find a lodging in Carlisle for you, Mrs. Conway," the Prince assured her. He made a point of speaking to her each day. "We shall garrison the castle at Carlisle. We must hold the border town to the last. It will check Cumberland's advance, I trust."

Ann thought that he added the last two words a trifle dubiously. One of the light field-pieces was stuck in the mud. A few snowflakes

158

came floating down and settled on the cloaks of the riders. The snowflakes were soft and delicate and chaste. Could anything so fragile menace the safety of an army?

"It will be hard going over Shap!" The Prince's voice sounded hard, anxious. "My poor lads. They have paid dearly for their loyalty. If the leaders had but a tithe of the faith and courage of their men I should have been in London ere this."

His chin sunk on his breast. Charles Edward rode in moody silence.

It was a sad journey, a tragic, pitiful affair. Ann, already burdened by sadness, shared her Prince's wretchedness to the full. Time and again the sense of awful, overwhelming desolation swept over her. There seemed nothing to cling to; nothing left in life but a fierce resolve not to give in, not to be beaten. All about her were men in like state. The footmen, muddy and footsore, hungry and heartsick, drew their saturated plaids about their lean forms and plodded stolidly on and on, up hill, down dale, heading back for the Scottish border where, for some inexplicable reason, all felt that security awaited them. There were stragglers, of course. The Prince, who seemed to have acquired a deep affection for his Highlanders whose devotion touched him, watched over them, sharing their hardships, sympathizing with them in their suffering, cheering them along their footsore way. Once, at the crossing of a river in spate, two of the men were swept off their feet. It was only the promptitude with which the Prince urged his horse into the flood that prevented them from being swept away to their death.

The crossing of Shap was a nightmare. It was accomplished. To Ann the whole thing seemed unreal.

The only thing about which she was really certain was that she was still alive. Her cold, aching, hungry body persisted in reminding her of this fact. Frequently she rode in a dream world. At such times her mind seemed to detach itself from her body and take its ease. She travelled to happier scenes. Was it only a few months ago that she sat on the corn-bin and talked to Howells? looked with rapt attention into Philip Yorke's serious but kindly eyes? tasted the rapture of Dicon's first passionate kisses? They seemed like scenes from another world. She must surely have been a spectator and not a participant. Such things could not possibly have happened to her.

For a short while each day the Prince rode at her side, either out of his fine courtesy or because he wished silently to assure her that he recognized her loyalty and devotion. He rarely spoke. Ann was glad. She was in no mood for conversation, not even with a Prince.

On one of these occasions as they were resting their jaded mounts at the top of a steep incline, the Prince suddenly beckoned to a mounted orderly who carried a telescope. The Prince directed the glass at the road over which his little army had recently passed. There was little fear of the regular foot overtaking them; the Highlanders marched too fast for that; but there was always the horse to be reckoned with. Prince Charles Edward's quick eye had caught the glimmer of distant steel. He was watching intently the summit of a distant pass. Ann, puckering her eyes, stared also. She detected a spot of colour, a red gleam amid the grey stones, then another and another. Two by two

159

a line of horsemen were riding over the crest. They, too, waited to breathe their winded chargers. The Prince straightened in his saddle with a grim laugh.

"The bloodhounds are close on our tracks," he said. "Would you care to look, Madam?"

He handed the glass to Ann. It took her a little time to focus. The spots of red were in her line of vision but they were blurred. Presently she had the glass adjusted to her satisfaction. The distant horsemen obligingly remained motionless in their ranks. She could count them all, every trooper. She could see the white cross-belts from which their sabres were suspended. They were dragoons of the regular army. Probably a scouting party sent in advance.

Ann gave an excited gasp and the glass began to tremble so that she had to readjust it. She looked again. There was no mistaking the sinister figure in the lead. The officer in charge of the dragoons was known to her. Major Manstein was again crossing her path.

CHAPTER THIRTY-THREE

ANN FREQUENTLY LOOKED BACK OVER HER SHOULDER AS THE RETREAT resumed its wearisome way. The enemy were hard on their heels now. Not infrequently the regular light horse could be seen riding two by two along the sky-line. If the wind blew towards Scotland it carried with it the sound of a prodigious number of trumpets and kettledrums. So far the invaders had to withstand nothing more drastic than this outburst of martial music, but this good fortune was not to last indefinitely. The Macdonalds who covered the retreat found themselves charged by two thousand of Cumberland's cavalry. There was fierce fighting among the hedgerows. In this confined space the men with the claymores had the advantage.

When the skirmishing grew more frequent Ann, by orders of the Prince, was hurried forward to be out of danger, or at any rate, to be as far from danger as possible. The precaution proved her undoing. Several officers had been assiduous in their care of her. Removed from their tutelage she grew careless, indifferent. She felt the cold more now, and was conscious of her lack of food and loss of sleep. Her beautiful eyes were ringed with weariness. She sat her horse as in a daze. Periodical fits of shivering took hold of her. These alternated with sudden bursts of heat which set her head throbbing. Hour after hour she pressed on mechanically, Black Prince walking at the rear of a body of footmen who, herded together like sheep, made their silent, stolid way along a deserted road which wound through a pass in the hills. A brook, looking brown amid its emerald banks cascaded over smooth stones beside the roadway. Ann dismounted to cup some water in her hands to cool her parched throat. A soldier paused in his marching to hold her bridle. It was an unnecessary courtesy; Black Prince had long since lost any inclination to bolt. He looked as weary and worn as his mistress. Ann felt ill; she could not recollect ever having felt so wretched.

"When do we reach Glasgow?" she asked and the roughness of her voice surprised her. She dried her hands on a soiled handkerchief. "I must see a physician. I am going to be ill; I am ill. I cannot afford to be ill."

"Glesca'?" The man glanced at her in surprise. "Ye'll no'be seein' Glesca'."

"But the Prince is making for Glasgow. I heard it from his own lips."

"Maybe the Prince is, but we're no'."

"What do you mean?"

"We're gaun hame. Nae ma'r fechtin' fur us."

"You mean!" Ann was incredulous. "You mean you are deserting his Highness?"

"A hard worrd, leddy, fur men wha hae suffered o'er much. We belang tae the Lowlands Regiment. It's time we disbanded."

"Then I must go back alone." But as Ann looked back along the deserted pass, grey with December mist, her heart misgave her.

"Ye'll dae nae sic' thing," said the man with rough kindness. "It's a warrm bed ye'll be needin' mair than the road to Glesca'."

The man was right. Ann had no strength to argue. Slowly she mounted and the two set off at a trot to overtake the other members of the party who were already rounding a distant bend.

Ann's head throbbed. She was feverish. If proof of this were needed it came about as they were entering a village which had somehow intruded into the lonely district. She saw a horse tethered to a rail outside a small farmstead, a horse which whinnied so eagerly at their approach that Black Prince pricked up his ears and answered.

"It's Starlight," cried Ann. "What is Starlight doing so far from home? I must find out."

"Nae. Ye mauna dae that!" interrupted her escort callously. "Ye're nigh tumblin' fra' the saddle as it is. Bide where ye be." Ann was too far gone to argue. She obeyed with the docility of an ailing child. "I am sure that it was Starlight," she whispered. "Prince knew, didn't you, Prince?"

A mean inn was found and here the soldier of the Lowlands Regiment left her to the mercies of the innkeeper who grudgingly gave her a room. He also undertook to attend to Black Prince's needs. The man was surly and appeared to resent having an ailing woman left on his hands. Perhaps he doubted her ability to pay. Ann took out her purse of gold. Should she give him some? Was it wise to let the man know she had so much wealth? It was a lonely place. Suppose she should be robbed? In a moment of panic she decided to hide her gold. She commenced ripping up the lining of her coat, the hem of her skirt, the inside of her bodice, and secreting coins here and there. Some, at least, would be preserved for future need. The effort exhausted her. She climbed into the bed and laid her burning cheek against the pillow. For a while she tossed restlessly and then fell asleep. At dawn she aroused, wet with sweat, weak, but feeling better. It called for an effort to dress. She made her way shakily down the stairs. She felt too restless to remain in her room.

161

She gave the landlord a single gold coin and he seemed relieved. She thought he appeared a trifle more civil. Something drew her towards the stables. Her worst fears were realized. Black Prince was not there. In her anguish she called aloud. It was not merely the loss of her horse —though that was bad enough—it was the loss of a tried companion, a friend of her youth, a link with her home. She was sobbing when a stableman came in and endeavoured to console her. Soldiers, he asserted, had come in the night and taken the animal away. Redcoats, curse them. Ann stared at the man uncomprehendingly. Then she fainted. She had no remembrance of being carried to her bedchamber. Her first recollection was of a hard, bony arm of a withered woman pressing her into an upright position so that she could sip some hot gruel from a horn spoon. The food revived Ann somewhat though she still felt weak. The alternating fits of shivering and burning returned. As she lay back on her pillow she felt curiously carefree. She had lost everything now and perhaps she was going to die so what did anything matter? Who cared who was king of England? Who cared who won battles? Who wanted a home or a horse or a husband or anything? All she knew was that the bed afforded comfort to her aching body, it was far, far preferable to the saddle. And it was good to lie warm instead of listening to the wet tramp, tramp, tramp of clansmen in the muddy upland passes. There would be no more weary, dejected, tartan-clad warriors to drain her sympathy; no disillusioned Prince to wring her heart. Nothing but rest and slumber. It was good to be in bed. Ann snuggled into the pillow and slept. A rap on the door aroused her. Instinctively she called "Come in !"

"I trust so ready an invitation will be followed by a cordial welcome," said a suave voice. The dim light from a small window fell on a scarlet tunic; the low ceiling seemed almost to brush the neat wig of Major Manstein as he removed his hat. With elaborate formality he bowed to Ann, drew off first one glove and then the other, folded them and dropped them on a round table which stood against the wall.

"One of the delights of campaigning," he said with attempted pleasantry, "is the opportunity it affords for unexpected encounters. I could hardly believe my eyes—or my good luck—when some of my men brought in a fine black horse I had no difficulty in recognizing. A magnificent brute, though he appears to have been overworked and underfed. And now, might I ask, how it is that the charming Miss Ann Trevor takes her rest in such a forsaken hole as this ?"

Ann was staring at him as though hypnotized. His words rang in her ears but they signified nothing. Of course it was not real. She smiled. People who were very ill got delirious. That was it; she was delirious. All the same she wished she could have imagined something a little more pleasant than Major Manstein. She did not want to have anything to do with him, not even in delirium. It did not matter really as it was all hallucination. Yet her visitant seemed real enough. She felt the bed give slightly as he seated himself on the side of it.

"You are a prodigious way from home," he said. Resting on one

162

hand he stared boldly at her flushed face and dishevelled hair. "Lud, much water has flown under the bridge, as the saying is, since you shook from your pretty feet the dust of Denbighshire. Or is it Flintshire? Demme if I can remember which is which of these little Welsh counties. And so you will not see your fond but bibulous parent again."

"You have no occasion to taunt me. I have heard of his death. I know you to be the cause." Ann spoke defiantly, almost fiercely.

"You misjudge me. I was but a spectator. It was not as I planned, I assure you. How was I to imagine that he would do the hangman out of a job by blowing out his brains?"

"Blowing out his brains?" Ann was incredulous. Philip had led her to suppose that her father died of heart failure. Was this but another of his chivalrous efforts to spare her feelings? Major Manstein was speaking. His metallic voice cut in on her musing.

"I presume it was his brains he scattered. A mere figure of speech, you understand. I did not examine too closely. He did the job properly, though. You can't imagine a sorrier mess."

"You beast. You brute. You inhuman devil."

"I am given to understand that all devils are inhuman; or at least not human. But why this outburst? I do but impart information. You should be grateful to me, Miss Trevor. Apparently you have been under some misapprehension."

Ann dried her eyes and looked haughty. "I am Mrs. Conway," she said with dignity. "I would have you remember it."

"Lud, yes. So you are. Word did reach my ears that you had bolted with some Jacobite rascal. Between ourselves, my dear lady, we did surmise that, in the heat of the moment, you might have overlooked the tedious formality of marriage. So you really were legally wed? You interest me vastly."

"I am married. Remember it and conduct yourself accordingly lest my husband thrash you."

"I will remember it if it please you, but what matter. Wife or widow? I scarce know which! By any chance, do you?"

Ann made no reply. The man chuckled. "I see you are in complete ignorance of your legally married husband's whereabouts? What an embarrassing position for a bride. It affords me amusement to think that I am better informed than you."

"You know! Is Dicon alive?"

"Ah, come, this is an improvement. We grow positively friendly. Dicon, too. Such delightful informality. Such animation. A kiss for my information."

"Tell me! Is Dicon alive?"

"Dear Dicon is alive if limping. He was wounded and taken prisoner in the Congleton affair. He will, of course, be hanged when he is sufficiently recovered. I am out of touch with affairs in Cheshire; therefore I speculate, wife or widow, you understand my perplexity?"

Ann made no reply to the taunt. She regarded him with a fixed gaze. It did not disconcert him. "Give our Dicon credit, he has a way with women. Just before I rode away there was another woman

163

pleading with me to spare his life. Offered me information, valuable assistance, and much else, to barter for his head. Or should I say his heart? I see a growing interest in your eyes. It is true, your dear Dicon is being nursed back to health by a woman, an old flame, I think the expression is. One Frances Holt. You know the name, I perceive. A bold woman. A woman with spleen. And not unattractive in a brazen way. I half fancied her myself (I was suffering from *ennui* at the time) but decided she was rather too masculine for my taste which runs to daintiness and charm such as yours, my dear Miss Trevor. Pardon, Mrs. Conway. So I left 'em to their billing and cooing, and I have no doubt that ere this Dicon Conway has been nursed back to health sufficiently to be drawn and quartered for his complicity in this dastardly rebellion."

Ann lay back on her pillow, eyes closed. The veins in her throat were throbbing until they threatened to burst.

"You naturally expected that your husband would be drawn and quartered? No! My dear young lady, permit me to observe that you do not appear to have given the matter profound thought before you embraced the glorious cause of romance and adventure. Be of good cheer, on your husband's demise I will console you."

He lifted Ann's hot hand to his lips and kissed the unresisting fingers. His own strong brown fingers slid suspiciously around the wrist, testing the pulsating heartbeats recorded there.

"Damnation, you are in a pretty fever! What a lost opportunity. Bah! I have no time to waste on an ailing wench. Hasten your recovery. I shall return in a few days, if this damned weather permits, and then 'Zounds, I shall expect you to entertain me."

He spoke lightly. Rising to his feet he began to draw on his gauntlets. Ann neither spoke nor stirred. She lay as one dead, save for the throbbing of the veins in her neck. With a shrug of his shoulders and a sneer of disappointment about his mouth, Major Manstein picked up his tricorne hat, dusted the braid at the brim, and left the room with never a backward glance.

Ann heard him depart as in a dream. She was conscious of the closing of the bedchamber door; of his heavy tread descending the board stairs. She heard the clatter of hoofs in the yard as he rode away. Still she did not stir. Her eyes remained closed. She had reached the stage of misery and exhaustion when nothing mattered any more. She was worrying, not about the appearance of Major Manstein, not about Dicon's captivity, nor the death of her father, but the losing of Black Prince. With his loss the last link was snapped. If Black Prince had been in the stables, she might have been able to creep downstairs and mount him and ride—anywhere. Over the passes, the hills and the moors, anywhere to get far away from that cynical devil in a red coat. Why had Manstein come into her life? She hated him. Ann who had never before known any emotion but kindness for a human being hated him. She execrated Major Manstein. She conceded that he was an efficient soldier. He was right in doing his duty but what need was there for him to take so fiendish a delight in the anguish he inflicted on others? She loathed him for gloating over

164

the sufferings of his victims for Ann was so tender of heart that she would not let a moth suffer needlessly.

Still, hating him would not put matters right. She had to devise a way of escape. She must escape. Nothing else mattered. Desperately she sat up in bed, threw back the blankets and lowered her white feet to the floor. She essayed to rise but her trembling knees would not support her and she collapsed on the bed. After a second unsuccessful attempt she abandoned the task, drew the clothes over her again and lay back, eyes closed, numb with disappointment. She was beaten. She was at the mercy of that beast who knew no mercy. Rather than succumb to him she would kill herself. Wildly she looked about the room. She had no knife, no dagger, no weapon of any description. Her pistols were in the holsters which had vanished with Black Prince. She must get a weapon somehow. He would come back when it suited his pleasure. Of that she was certain.

The downstairs door opened and closed. Ann sat very still, wide-eyed with fright, listening. There came a low hum of voices. Then a step on the stairs. The heavy step of a man who ascended with deliberation. At Ann's door the steps paused. She tried to scream but no sound came from her parted lips. Her staring eyes saw the door latch move. There came a low knock. The door was opening slowly. Ann clutched at her throat where the pulse throbbed more furiously than ever. She saw a coat sleeve. Not red but brown. As in a trance she found herself looking into eyes which she knew, deep, grave, tender eyes. As in a dream she heard a voice; a voice which seemed to fall from heaven bidding all fears depart. "Ann, my dear, thank God at last I have found you."

And then she had her tear-stained cheek against his coat, his strong right arm was round about her, she was repeating—"Philip! Philip! Philip! You have come to me in my hour of trial. I might have known that you would come when I needed you most. Oh, Philip!" And then her tired aching head settled against the curve of his shoulder, it fitted as though made to rest there, and an infinite peace came upon her as she found the security her soul desired.

CHAPTER THIRTY-FOUR

WEAK AND ILL THOUGH SHE WAS ANN ALWAYS REGARDED THE DAYS which followed as the happiest of her life. A sense of utter surety settled upon her; even in the midst of war's alarms she felt safe, protected, cared for. But for the coming of Philip Yorke she might have died for she had lost the will to live. Now all was different. She sank into a calm repose and allowed Nature to do her healing work unimpeded. The menace of Manstein had faded like an angry dream. She vaguely wondered more than once whether he would return; the realization that Philip was there to receive him afforded her instant reassurance. It was wonderful, she meditated, to have someone in whom one could place complete confidence, upon whom one could utterly rely, in whom one could confide and never fear misunderstanding. The presence of Philip Yorke not only buoyed her up, it worked other miracles. The innkeeper and his wife lost their surliness. The bedroom was brightened and polished, indifferent food was transformed to delicacies, even a few late flowers were discovered to add a touch of colour to the room. Nothing now seemed a trouble to these good folk. Ann marvelled at the metamorphosis, not realizing the transforming power of gold. Indeed, in fairness to the innkeeper and his wife, much of their sourness had its roots in the penury which persistently beset them. The hardness of the struggle to wrest a mere livelihood from life had, perhaps inevitably, produced a corresponding hardness in a disposition which had grown coarse from privation and disappointment.

Sometimes the innkeeper's wife sat beside Ann but mostly it was Philip who stayed on guard. Her closing eyes rested drowsily on his kindly face as she slid into slumber. Her opening eyes found him at his post, watching her tenderly, anxiously. Sometimes she felt herself slipping out of life and then her frail fingers would creep towards his and the firm comforting grasp of his strong capable hand renewed her strength. She had, literally and figuratively, something to hold on to now. A physician had been fetched in a post-chaise from Glasgow (only Philip knew the cost) and he pronounced Ann out of danger but suffering from the results of shock and exposure. She would recover, he was certain of that, but only if she had attention, rest and freedom from anxiety.

After a meal, and some excellent wine which was miraculously produced from a secret corner of the cellar, the doctor grew more genial and less professional. Instead of taking instant leave of his fair patient he seated himself in the most comfortable chair and began to outline for her benefit the march of events in Glasgow. The Prince was in better spirits, so were the troops. The Highlanders who were with him, that is. Most of the Lowlands men had turned aside to follow Lord George Murray who was making a feint on Edinburgh. The Whigs—and there were many in Glasgow—were hard-visaged and the clansmen met with scowling glances on all sides. They were undeterred by the scowls. Despite their long forced march they were in excellent fettle. Would nothing quench their ardour? Though the Prince had secured a thousand pounds by fining Dumfries for cutting off his baggage train in November, the army was short of money. The soldiers were beginning to plunder—'just a little.'

The doctor seemed to entertain a secret regard for the Stuart adventurer though he was too canny to express his opinions openly. The Prince himself was putting down plundering with a strong hand so his men, on the whole, were behaving pretty civilly. The Prince had been off shooting in Hamilton Park and amazed everyone by the unerring accuracy with which he brought down every bird he aimed at. "The best marksman in the army," the doctor assured Ann who lay with eyes closed. The situation in Glasgow was awkward. Here was the most Whiggish town in Scotland with a population of thirty thousand—and scarce a Jacobite among them—at the mercy of the invaders. The Prince had ordered six thousand pairs of shoes and an equal number of blue bonnets and tartan hose for his men, a galling price for Glasgow to pay. The Prince had entered the city on foot, just as he used to march into England. The crowds lined the streets six deep but gave never a cheer. There had been a review of troops—thirty-six hundred foot and five hundred horse. People wondered whether the Prince was wise thus to reveal his paucity of numbers. Some attributed it to the report that a French force had landed up north and that he was sure of doubling his army shortly. "He rode in French dress," said the doctor, "and of a truth he had a princely aspect, but this was deepened by the dejection that appeared in his pale countenance and his downcast eye."

But Ann was not listening. In her weak state martial affairs had lost their appeal. She wanted the doctor to depart so that Philip could sit beside her and hold her hand. He did her more good than a garrulous physician. The doctor might well have read her thoughts. Perhaps he merely noted her flushed cheeks and closed eyes. He stopped his narrative abruptly, bade her keep up her spirits and swallow a draught thrice daily, and with that took his departure. What the doctor did not tell Ann was that the Duke of Cumberland had captured Carlisle and the garrison which the Prince had left there "to protect his gateway into England" for a future invasion, were in the hands of a man who knew not the meaning of mercy.

With the going of the doctor a barrier descended between Ann and the outside world. Actually it was a fall of snow which blocked the passes and kept folk indoors until the sun shone again. Philip saw to it that there was a fire in Ann's room and that she suffered no setbacks. The days passed uneventfully. To Ann they brought returning health and a great peace. She never mentioned Dicon; neither did Philip. It was implied that the topic was better left alone. Finally, Ann broke the silence. "I do not know what has happened to Dicon," she said, and stared abstractedly at the white hands clasped on the coverlet. "I have had no word since he rode on the raid into Cheshire. No one saw him fall. He just disappeared."

"He may have escaped."

"Major Manstein said that he was wounded and a prisoner, and that he would be hanged, drawn and quartered."

"Do not fret unnecessarily. The man may have lied to torment you. But how did Manstein come to tell you this? Have you seen him?"

"On the very day you arrived. He was here just ahead of you." She laughed a little bitterly. "I was in such a fever that he did not find me sufficiently entertaining to make it worth while his tarrying. However, he honoured me by saying that he would return."

Yorke looked grave. "Ann, you did wrong to withhold this from me. Why did you not tell me before, girl?"

"I was too happy to talk about him. He is unpleasant. Let us put him out of our minds, Philip."

"Out of our conversation if you will. He shall not go out of my mind, Ann; not until I have you in a place of safety. Well, he is not likely to return until the snow vanishes."

"He commandeered Black Prince. I hate him."

"I am sorry he has your horse. Never mind; you shall have Starlight to ride once you are strong enough. Not so fine a mount, perhaps, but an old favourite. A link with the past."

"Starlight! Then it was Starlight I saw. I wasn't dreaming."

"Hughie has been riding her."

"Hughie! Is Hughie here, then?"

"He is downstairs. You shall see him as soon as you are strong enough. Since your father's death I have taken the lad under my wing. He has been invaluable. When I came in search of you—for on hearing of the retreat from Derby I feared the worst—he begged to be allowed to accompany me. It was he who found you. We had gone our divers ways: I followed the Prince; Hughie went in the wake of Lord George Murray's force. He learned that you were here, and ill, so he raced back post haste with the intelligence."

"Bless him. I will reward him amply."

"There is no need. The lad and I are in perfect accord on one issue—serving Mistress Ann is its own reward."

"Philip, you are so good to me. Why are you so good to me?"

"Am I good to you?" For the first time Ann saw the light of subdued laughter dance in those grave eyes. It was the first time since her marriage. To Ann it was a hopeful sign. It meant that she was getting better. There was a load off his mind.

"You know that you are good to me," she scolded. "No one ever before showed me such care and attention. No one ever showered such kindness on me as you have done. You seem to be continually thinking of me."

"It would be futile to deny it. If it affords you pleasure I am glad but I tell you frankly I get more than I give. You see, Ann, I was a lonely man when you came into my life. I thought that the study of nature, the reading of books, the delight of music, the labouring for political reform were enough to engross a man for a lifetime. I had not allowed for the human element. To get the best out of life, to be inspired, to receive full stimulus, it is necessary to labour for somebody one——"

He dropped her hand abruptly and stood up with the appearance of a man who was about to say more than he intended.

"Loves," said Ann calmly and deliberately. "You may as well speak the words, Philip. Your eyes and your actions said so long ago. I know that you love me."

He looked down upon her and shook his head with a sad smile. "Best leave it unsaid, Ann."

"But you do love me, Philip. You have shown it in a thousand ways. Tell me—am I the Rose Girl you wrote about?"

He shrugged his shoulders and smiled a trifle deprecatingly. "My attempts at poetry do not soar above mediocrity."

"I have never read sweeter verses, Philip. They moved me to tears. I have the poem still. I cherish it. And tell me, Philip, what was the title of the Purcell song I took so great a delight in hearing?"

"You cannot draw me, Ann. I shall not tell you."

"There is no need. The last time I was at your house I peeped. I know."

"Then why do you ask?"

"So that I can hear you say the words."

"Oh, Ann girl, where is this leading us to?"

"How can I tell? One cannot help love."

"No," he said slowly, "one cannot help love but one can help giving expression to it. I love you because I cannot help loving you, but I can help talking about it."

"Love is the greatest thing in the world. Can it be wrong?"

"Love itself can never be wrong. It is the use to which it is put which makes it right or wrong. The first qualification of love is that one forgets self. One must be ready to sacrifice selfish desires in order to serve."

"And you are prepared to sacrifice me?"

"Yes, Ann."

"But suppose I am not prepared to sacrifice you, what then?"

"You must, Ann."

"Sit down, Philip. I do not like you standing there, you look austere. I want to feel your hand on mine. It is strong. It gives me strength."

Instead he crossed to the window. "It is clearing up somewhat, I think," he remarked casually. There was no reply. Just a stifled sob. He saw Ann with her head thrown back and a slim white arm across her eyes. "I could weep I want you so," she whispered.

Philip Yorke was beside her. His arm was about her, tenderly. Her cheek was against his coat, wetting it with her tears. "That is all I ask," she murmured. "Just to put my tired head against the curve of your shoulder; to feel you near me; to be safe and wanted and protected. Can that be wrong, Philip?"

He did not reply but sat staring at the window. His fingers stroked her hair. It was a soothing touch. When finally he looked down upon the tear-stained face against his shoulder he saw that Ann had fallen asleep.

CHAPTER THIRTY-FIVE

BY THE TIME FEBRUARY WAS WELL ADVANCED THE WEATHER HAD improved and so had Ann. She was able to come downstairs and, during bursts of sunshine, to sit in a sheltered nook for a brief while or take short walks along the stone flags which paved the paths. Gradually she felt her strength return and her spirits revive. Hughie had been allowed to visit her as soon as she had sufficient strength to receive him. Thereafter he sat with her a while each day, proud to be allowed to deputize for his master. On the occasion of Ann's first appearance downstairs, Hughie brought Starlight to the door of the inn and watched with unconcealed delight as his young mistress stroked the shapely head thrust eagerly forward for her caress. Ann loved horses and the sight of Starlight did much to console her for the loss

F*

of Black Prince. Philip Yorke purchased another mount for Hughie, whose daily duty it was to groom the three horses and keep them well fed and ready to take the road at short notice. Then the boy disappeared for ten days. He came back proud and tired. Philip Yorke would not tell Ann where Hughie had been. Ann cheated. As soon as she had the boy to herself—and Philip had acquired a habit of absenting himself for several hours a day now—she unblushingly pressed Hughie to tell her where he had been. Her blandishments were too much for the boy's loyalty. He had ridden back to North Wales, he said, to procure some more money. He had felt concerned having to ride so far with a belt of gold with so many footpads about but he had his pistols with him and would have used them, too ! The other reason (Mistress Ann must promise never to tell or Mr. Yorke would not forgive him), the other reason was to make inquiries about the fate of Captain Conway.

"And did you find out, Hughie ?"

"He's alive, Mistress Ann." (She would never be Mrs. Conway to him.) "He was wounded and captured in some fight near a place just over the Cheshire border. I forget the name."

"Congleton ?"

"Maybe. His wound is healed and he has been put in prison awaiting trial. He's in Conway Castle, they say, along with tha Lieutenant Peris who sailed the *Happy Chance* and the fellows of the crew who were taken by the boats of the *Talisman*. You remembe the time I rowed across to the Anglesey coast to warn them ?"

"I am not likely to forget, Hughie."

"Neither am I, Mistress Ann. I can feel the blisters on my hand yet. Well, the *Happy Chance* is still anchored in the Conway River No one seems to know what to do with her until the Rebellion ha been put down. Then maybe she will be sold, but I don't know Anyhow, Mr. Yorke has got a mad scheme in his mind. No, I daren' tell you. He would flay me alive if he found out I'd told."

"You can trust me, Hughie. I will not let him touch you. No that he would. He is the kindest man in the world."

"Well, then, he is sending me back to Conway. I am to get a jo with the pastrycook who supplies food to the prisoners in Conwa Castle. The place is so ruinous now that it is only used as a lock-up and the prisoners get all their food from the town shops. When th time is ripe, that is when the weather clears up, I am to smuggle rope to Lieutenant Peris and the others and help 'em to escape."

"Hughie, how wonderful !" exclaimed Ann ecstatically. "How daring !"

"Daring ? You haven't heard half yet. To look at Mr. York with his quiet manner you would never think how daring he could be When I've got the seamen out of the castle I am to lead them to boat which I shall have concealed by the mouth of the Gyffin Strean which runs beside the south walls of the castle. Each boat will hav plenty of pistols, muskets, cutlasses and food hidden under th thwarts."

"Oh ! And they will all escape out to sea ? I understand."

170

"You do nothing of the kind, Mistress Ann. When they are armed they will pull out in the dark to midstream where the snow is moored and—" Hughie paused dramatically. "And they are to cut out the *Happy Chance!*"

"Cut out?" Ann looked puzzled.

"That's sailor's talk, Mistress Ann. I've picked it up. They are to board the snow and capture her out of hand and drift out to sea on the ebb tide."

"But suppose they are caught!"

"Not likely. There's no one to capture them, no one in all Conway with any arms to speak of save a few militia men and they would be outnumbered by the crew. No, once they can get clear of the castle, the *Happy Chance* is as good as captured. And I'm to be there sharing in all the fun."

"It seems too good to be true, Hughie."

"All that troubles Mr. Yorke is that he cannot join in, but he will not leave you. In fact, that's the object of it all. I thought he was doing it to rescue the crew and the ship, but he thinks farther ahead than that, does Mr. Yorke."

"I don't understand, Hughie."

"Well, what does Mr. Yorke really want the snow for? Tell me that, Mistress Ann."

"I am sure I don't know. I did not realize that he wanted the vessel and I am sure that I don't know what he wants her for."

"Where are you going when you leave here?"

"Why, home—ah! I have no home. I am a rebel. I have marched with the Prince. I—I do not know where I shall go, Hughie."

"That's just it. Mr. Yorke says that the Prince is doomed and there will be no going back to Wales for you, never! The Duke of Cumberland's army is stretching right across England until it links up with General Wade's army. And then there is General Ogilthorpe's army and I don't know how many more. Thousands of 'em, all dead set on wiping off old scores for they feel the invasion was a shocking disgrace. They are all savage. There will be no mercy shown. That is why Mr. Yorke wants the ship. It is to get you safe out of the country."

"Oh, Hughie!" Ann sat motionless, stunned into silence by the awful possibilities which lay ahead. Where would she have been but for Philip Yorke? "Oh, Hughie," she repeated. "How shall I ever repay him?"

"Mistress Ann!" Hughie was reproachful. "You have forgotten already. You know nothing about all this. I should not have told you. And you promised me not to say a word."

"And I will keep my promise. Help me upstairs to my room, Hughie. I feel shaken and I want to rest."

Ann lay quiet for an hour at least, her eyes closed, her mind teeming with bewildering thoughts. Never before had she realized how utterly alone she was in the world. Her home was gone. She had no money. She had, moreover, by her impetuous folly, sacrificed her right to the protection of citizenship. And all for the glamour of excitement, adventure, romance. "I don't care," she exclaimed aloud. "I think that Prince Charles Edward is a fine gentleman, a gallant adventurer. I would do it all again for his sake." Yet she was forced to admit that Prince Charles Edward did not appear to be much nearer the throne as the result of her sacrifices. She seemed to have helped no one—not even herself. All she had done was to injure herself and harm or at least worry those who were near and dear to her. She must have cost Philip Yorke a pretty penny already! Not that he was ever likely to remind her of the fact. How good he had been. How she depended on him for everything. His foot on the stairs brought her out of her reverie.

"Tired, Ann ?"

"Not tired, Philip ; just thinking."

"Of what, if I am permitted to ask ?"

"You are permitted to ask anything, my deliverer. I was thinking how amazingly good you were to me; wondering how I could ever repay you."

"Waste no more time thinking of that. I have my repayment in the privilege of serving you. Forget what I have done."

"Forget ? Never. Not while mortal memory endures."

"Ann, how soon will you be well enough to travel ? Travel by easy stages ? I have scoured the country trying to procure a coach. They are not to be had for money. They are not even to be stolen. They simply do not exist in this part of the country. I will be frank with you. Now that the weather is opening up the troops will be on the move. I should like to see you in a place of greater safety."

"Where, Philip ?"

"I want to get you to the western coast. It might be possible to get a ship of sorts. Ann, would you much mind living abroad ? I fear that it will have to be that. This country is no longer safe for you. I have transferred most of my money to a banker in Paris. I will give you his address in case—well, in case we are parted. He has been instructed to let you draw on the account as though it were your own."

He handed her a card. It bore the banker's address. Ann barely glanced at it but stood turning it nervously in her fingers. "Parted ? I cannot bear the mere mention of being parted from you : you who are half my life."

"It is inevitable, my dear. Happiness such as ours was never meant to endure. If happiness like this were permanent, heaven would lose its attraction. Already I feel the shadow of parting."

"No, no, Philip."

"Therefore I wish to make what provision I can for your welfare while there is yet time."

"Is it true, Philip, that I can never return to Wales ?"

"Quite true. You are proscribed. Nor do I think that you would ever be safe in this country. That Major Manstein is an evil beast and your fresh, fragrant beauty has roused him. He would take delight in hunting you down."

"But why? I have not been particularly unkind to him, even if I do detest him."

"My dear, you fail to realize how desirable you are—even to a beast like Manstein."

He turned away quickly as though to escape from his own thoughts. With a change in his voice he said hurriedly: "I fear that you must accustom yourself to managing without Hughie. I find it necessary that I should send him away on an errand."

"Might I ask where?"

"I would rather that you did not."

"Very well," said Ann with unnatural meekness.

"Could you start getting your things together, Ann. I feel that we ought to start with as little delay as possible."

"Get my things together? I have nothing in the world but what I stand in—and a heart which overflows with gratitude to you for all that you have done."

"Ah. I had forgotten that you had lost all. I will do what I can to replenish your wardrobe. But not now. We must travel light."

She sat down suddenly on the bed. "Philip, tell me, why must these things be?"

"What things?"

"All this suffering and plotting and hatred. There are so many people who do not ask much of life. Only a home and a loved one. It does not seem much to ask of God."

"Those two simple things might be much indeed."

"But it all sounds so simple, so reasonable, so natural. Why should it be so utterly unattainable? Why should we be denied that which means so much to us?"

"I cannot tell. I suppose it is all part of the Scheme of Things."

"You always fall back on that. You always hold that there is a Scheme at the back of life. I cannot see it. It all seems chaos. Do you still hold to your Scheme, in face of all this?"

"Why, yes," he said simply. "I believe that each person has an immortal soul; that the chief object of life is its fashioning, and that according to the manner of our shaping will we reap the harvest in an after life. I believe that we reward ourselves and we punish ourselves."

"What happens, then, when others punish us? Why should I be persecuted by Major Manstein? I have sufficient punishment in the rewards of my own folly."

"There must be overlapping. There is much I do not understand. All I know is that I believe that from the bottom of my heart I was sent into your life to help you through a difficult time, to sustain you, uplift you, perhaps to guide you."

"You have done all that, Philip. And what is your reward? To have your most tender feelings tortured and lacerated needlessly. Is that the reward of virtue?"

"But virtue is its own reward."

"It is about the only one it ever receives. I cannot see the Guiding Hand at the back of all this. To me it is hopeless confusion and unnecessary suffering."

173

"I suppose one has to walk by faith. At present we see through a glass darkly. But I shall never believe that our meeting was fortuitous."

"I think that everything is just the result of what happens: cause and effect."

"But what origin has the Cause?"

"I do not know. Do you?"

"No, I do not know, and yet I hold that there is some great Scheme. I cannot believe that we were set in life by chance; that we were given our emotions, our desires, our talents, our powers of reasoning without there being some purpose at the back of it all."

"What happiness has your Scheme brought to us? We, who are denied something before we even ask for it?"

"It has at least brought us together. That, in itself, is happiness to me. I shall always thank God for the privilege of just knowing you."

"I am rebellious. I ask greater happiness than that, Philip. Tell me, why are we permitted to make mistakes?"

"We do make mistakes and have to abide by them. I do not know that the question of our being 'permitted' to make them enters in."

"I made a mistake, Philip. What am I to do about it?"

"What mistake, Ann?"

"You know perfectly well. I married the wrong man. I did not know then that I was making a mistake. If this supernatural power guides our lives why did not some omen occur to warn me; why was I not frustrated? Why should one who acts in sincerity and innocence be permitted to make a mistake for which there is no remedy? Is it fair? Is this part of your Scheme of Things?"

"It would appear so, Ann, though why it should be I do not know. In accepting the existence of the Scheme it does not necessarily mean that it will fit in with our own plans and desires. Rather must we be permitted to subordinate our desires to the Scheme."

"I have neither your faith nor your philosophy, Philip. I married Dicon because he was gay and debonair, and I craved for romance. I had never tasted a passionate kiss before and it intoxicated me. I knew nothing then of that deep, abiding wealth of affection which expresses itself in constant devotion and consideration. How could I know? I had not come under your spell then. Now I know: now that it is too late. Never have I been so cherished. And all the good I can see that it does is to be a continual irritating reminder of what I have been deprived of."

"Perhaps Dicon will cherish you—when he has had an opportunity of learning your true worth."

"Dicon? Half his heart is with Frances Holt; of that I am certain. In any case it will be too late then. My heart is yours. My love is yours. You never asked me for it but you have won it."

"I cannot accept it, now, Ann. It is too late. All I live for is that I shall be able to claim you in some future state where, so we are told, there is no marriage or being given in marriage."

"I would rather not wait, Philip. There are times when I feel that I would gladly risk my chances of immortality for the joy of feeling your strong arms about me and your dear lips pressed on mine."

174

A clatter of hoofs in the courtyard cut short their talk. "That ill be Hughie leaving for the south," said Philip Yorke abstractedly. He did not move but stood staring straight before him. He was breathing deeply as though under the stress of deep emotion. Ann walked restlessly to the window and looked forth. Her hands flew to her lips to stifle a cry. There was a cavalry charger in the yard below. The saddle was empty. "Philip," she cried and for Ann the tone was bitter. "Philip, is this your Scheme of Things? Major Manstein is here."

Yorke did not answer. He walked to the corner and picked up the Dettingen sword.

CHAPTER THIRTY-SIX

THERE WAS STILLNESS IN THE ROOM. ONLY THE FLAMES IN THE HEARTH gave an occasional flicker. There was no other sound though Ann thought that the beating of her heart must have been audible so wildly did it pulsate. Philip Yorke was grave and quite unperturbed. His eyes, fixed on the door, never wavered. He seemed to have forgotten Ann. She noticed an eager, expectant look in his eyes. It was as though a smile of excitement was on the point of breaking through. She counted every step on the stairs. The door was flung open. This time there was no rap. Then Major Manstein brought his spurred heels together as though he stood at attention when he saw that Philip Yorke was in the room. His lip curled. He was the first to speak.

"I have dallied over-long. I beg of you to blame the weather for my neglect of you. It seems that you have been solaced in my absence." Neither Ann nor Philip Yorke vouchsafed any reply. The silence was chilly but Manstein was in no wise disconcerted.

"My felicitations, Madam, on your return to normal health—and might I add, habits? Beauty such as yours is wasted in a sick bed."

Philip Yorke continued to regard the intruder with grave eyes; he appeared to be assessing him. The intruder could not help but be aware of this steadfast gaze. His eyes narrowed as he returned it with a haughty stare. "We have met before, sir," he said sharply.

Yorke gravely inclined his head.

"I take it, sir, that you are interesting yourself in this desirable baggage? Demme, it would appear we are of a similar mind. Egad, let us give each other credit for discriminating taste."

"I am, as you observe, interesting myself in this young lady." Philip Yorke spoke for the first time. "Was it to ascertain that fact that you walked unannounced into her bedchamber?"

"Where, by gad, I find you had preceded me! Lud, sir, I must compliment you on your enterprise as much as your good taste."

"I have taken upon myself the responsibility of seeing that she escapes molestation. My presence indicates that she will not be pestered by undesirable persons."

"I am sure Captain Conway will be touched to think that his wife's honour is in the hands of so conscientious a guardian."

175

"Now that I have explained the reason for my presence, sir, perhaps you will explain yours. That is, if it can be explained."

"Easily. This young woman is a traitor. I am here to place her under arrest."

"I scarcely think so."

"Who would dare to prevent me?"

"I am here to prevent you."

"You exceed your rights, sir. If you intervene I have no option but to assume that you endorse her political sentiments, in which case I shall place you also under arrest."

"And have you troopers to enforce your orders?"

"It is unnecessary. I carry at my side sufficient enforcement." The major tapped his sword hilt.

"That argument is not conclusive."

"Have a care, sir, what you say. Others have found it so conclusive an argument that they have never disputed anything again in this world."

"I would remind you that I, too, carry a sword."

"I can only hope that you use it as well as you do your tongue. But there are too many demmed civilians carrying swords these days. You may be called upon to make use of it."

"I should welcome the opportunity. It will be, however, unnecessary."

"How so?" Major Manstein was toying with his hilt impatiently.

"Though a demmed civilian I once was privileged to fight at Dettingen."

"What of it?"

"A mere statement of fact. I thought that it might interest you."

"It does not."

"On one occasion in the Low Countries it was my fortune to render a signal service to the Duke of Cumberland."

"I compliment you on your luck, sir, but what the devil does it mean to me?"

"His Highness was graciously pleased to remember my service when I applied for permission to pass through his lines in search of a friend. I carry with me his royal approval and consent. You may recognize his signature."

Philip Yorke calmly drew from a breast pocket a folded paper from which a seal dangled on a green riband. The soldier took it with slight reluctance, unfolded it and read with deliberation.

"You are satisfied, I trust?" asked Yorke quietly.

"I am satisfied that it is genuine. But his Highness mentions no person by name, nor, demme, does he know that the woman you befriend is a Jacobite and the wife of one of the damnedest rogues and spies in the Young Pretender's pay. If you think that a document like this will save you, you are a fool. This is how I deal with traitors."

He ripped the paper angrily in half, crumpled it in a forceful hand and flung it to the flames. Ann gave a cry of anguish. She expected Yorke to snatch the precious document from the blaze but instead he stood unmoved and watched it turn to black ashes.

"That is unfortunate," he said calmly. "I had hopes that we might have settled the matter amicably. Being a man of peace I trusted that my passport would suffice. I do not deplore its loss so much as the manner of it, which was so deliberately insulting that I am left without option but to demand satisfaction. That is the worst of having dealings with a creature who is as destitute of breeding as he is of honour. We will adjourn to the yard. Ann, my dear, remain in your room. I will rejoin you in a few minutes."

"If your skill confirms your optimism!" With this parting thrust Manstein stalked to the door. Ann, with a cry of anguish, ran to Philip and caught him by the arm. "No, no. Let me entreat you."

"There is no other way. I tried and I failed."

"He may kill you."

"It is extremely improbable. These bullies are all bluster and brag. Do not forget, my dear, that I am not unaccustomed to the use of a small-sword."

"Oh, Philip, I love you so."

It was to a broad back which vanished through the doorway that Ann whispered the words. If Yorke heard them he gave no indication. When Ann had mustered sufficient courage she peeped through the casement. Both men were on the cobbles; Manstein in a yellow waistcoat, Yorke in a white cambric shirt. Their swords were in their hands. Manstein's face was set and hard. Yorke was smiling. Ann thought that she had never seen his eyes so bright. There was a light of boyish laughter dancing in them as though some unexpected joy had come his way.

There came to Ann's mind the duel which she had watched from a window. She recalled the dark figures which leaped and postured in silhouette like marionettes in the moonlight. Dicon had come off victorious that time. This time?

She caught her breath. There was a swish of steel. The fight had begun. What strength and suppleness there was in Philip Yorke! How light of foot he was, like a dancer! What power there was behind his thrust when he stiffened his right arm for a lunge! Ann had not watched a minute before all fear left her. So fascinated was she at the display of Yorke's swordsmanship that she forgot the deadliness of the game in her admiration of the skill and grace displayed. The swish of swords came not unmusically through the air. There was a slight sound of panting; it came from Major Manstein. He was perspiring. The smile curled about Yorke's mouth. His blade slithered forward and a long red gash showed on Manstein's forearm. The red blood trickled to his sword-hand and dripped to the ground. Yorke leaped back and saluted punctiliously. He counted without his adversary. With a curse of rage Manstein straightened his wounded arm and gave a vicious lunge. Yorke, taken by surprise, avoided it with difficulty. The smile vanished from his eyes. His mouth set hard. He pressed home his attack now with a fierceness and vigour which caused the soldier to give ground. Out went Yorke's right foot as he crouched to a lunge which drove his point out behind Manstein's shoulder. The soldier dropped his blade with a clatter on the cobbles and sank on one knee.

"Why not learn to fight like a gentleman?" asked Yorke coolly as he walked towards his coat. "It might not be too late to be taught."

"Damn you; you shall pay for this. You and your trull."

"I could, with equal ease, have run you through the heart. Do not make me regret my clemency. Here, landlord, bandage this fellow and hoist him on his horse."

Yorke turned his back and walked into the inn. Ann's first impulse was to run to him and sob her relief, but something restrained her. Philip Yorke always had his emotions under control. She would emulate him. It called for an effort.

"Let me compliment the victor," she said with assumed gaiety as he walked into the room and leaned his sheathed sword against the wall.

"I am loath to take human life," said Yorke seriously. "No man knows who puts the breath of life into us. What is man that he should take it away? Yet I fear that I have done you an ill service in sparing him. That wretch is without principles, my dear. Ann, get ready for the road. He will send soldiers after us with all expedition for he is seething with rage at his humiliation. We must escape while we can."

"I shall be ready in two minutes, Philip. Get the horses." It was a wild scramble. The landlord was paid. He watched Philip Yorke and Ann ride down the road with mixed feelings; good wishes for their safety conflicting with regret at the loss of the best paying guests he had ever been privileged to serve. Hughie remained behind. He had a role to play which was dear to his heart. In a woman's gown and bonnet he was waiting near the approach to the village so that he could set off across country to the east as soon as the redcoats appeared in sight. He would lead them on a wild-goose chase over the moors until the fugitives were out of reach. In the darkness he hoped to be able to break through the cordon of soldiers and set off on his risky ride to Wales. In after years Ann often thought with gratitude of the selfless devotion of this serving lad whose loyalty she had taken so much for granted.

In this time of testing Ann grew to know the meaning and beauty of loyalty; that unwavering and unswerving homage which gave all and asked nothing in return. As she rode she was conscious of a feeling of elation. The joy of life which, during her illness, seemed to have gone from her for ever, came back with a rush. There was a thrill in adventure after all; it was good to be riding through the Scottish passes, past lochs and cloud-topped mountains, with the knowledge that there were irate redcoats in pursuit, while somewhere ahead was the Prince, the intrepid adventurous Charles Edward with his army about him waiting to make one more bid for his father's throne. She had not felt thus during the retreat. Perhaps it was the presence of Philip Yorke at her side which made all the difference. Of course, added Ann to herself as she looked about her and saw the fresh green of young life covering the rain-soaked earth, of course, it might merely be the coming of spring which brought her new life. But she rather suspected that it was Philip Yorke. Was it barely a year since she first met him ? He seemed part of her life now. Was it barely a year since she set off in pursuit of that mischievous dog which had stolen her patten and so had collided with Mr. Yorke in the lane behind her home ? She would never see that home again but Philip Yorke was steadfast still. Ann felt more than a year older. "Why, Philip," she exclaimed, turning a flushed face towards him, "I am twenty-one. I have just remembered. I am a woman !"

"Are you—girl ?"

*　　*　　*　　*　　*

Though spring was on its way the weather was still cold. The farther north they rode the more they felt it. The snow from the mountains seemed to be in the very air. Ann was glad to make use of a plaid which Philip purchased for her. Secretly she was rather pleased to be wearing tartan, though she could not recognize what clan it belonged to. Someone told her it was Macpherson but she was not sure. They went to villages and towns with names she had never heard. They talked to people whose views differed. Some were sour, dour Whigs who welcomed Philip on hearing his views. Others were ardent Jacobites and Ann won their hearts partly by her charm but more because she had shared the retreat from Derby with Prince Charlie. Yet all these places seemed cut off from the world. There were no newspapers. Once they came across a news-letter but it was two months old. Information which came to them was by word of mouth; sometimes the Scottish accent was so pronounced that Ann after listening politely and smiling assent went away little the wiser. They heard that there had been another battle. This time it was at Falkirk in January, fought in blinding rain. The royal dragoons had an unpleasant time, the clansmen lying low and stabbing their dirks into the cavalry horses' bellies. It was the Prince again, men said, who turned what might have been a defeat into a victory. The Prince again ! Despite the retreat there was still fight left in him.

Philip Yorke wished to make for the western coast, the rocky seaboard where he had arranged for the *Happy Chance* to appear. There was, of course, an element of doubt. Hughie might not have got through the royal lines. There was no means of ascertaining. They just had to take the chance.

The Jacobite army lay at Stirling where the siege of the castle went on but slowly. Ann pleaded to cross that way to join the Prince. Somewhat against his better judgment Philip consented. He was to regret his weakness. When they got there the army had left for the north. Their route through the muddy, rutted road was easy to follow. It led to the Highlands. The two travellers turned their weary steeds northwards once again, and rode on and on until Crieff was reached. They were nearly at their destination. The Prince was staying at Menzie Castle a few miles away, they were told. To Menzie they rode and at last saw the royal banner in the breeze. At the castle doorway a strong guard of Highlanders was on duty for there was a rumour that an attempt was to be made to kidnap the Prince.

The officer in charge of the guard was Dicon Conway.

179

IT WAS THE MOST DESOLATE FARMSTEAD ANN HAD EVER SEEN. A LONELY, stone-built affair with a low, thatched roof and a broad open hearth in which a peat fire smouldered, filling the room with acrid fumes. Yet Ann had to remain indoors for rain was falling and the wind swept keenly across the open moorlands. Even the stunted hawthorns and heather seemed to bow before its unrelenting blast. It was April, but different from any April she had ever seen before. There were no daffodils to rustle at her touch, there was no apple blossom, there were no primroses. It was as though Nature had combined with the House of Hanover to stage a grim epilogue to the luckless 'Forty-five. Somewhere over the moors a few miles to the east the Prince was waiting at the head of his now diminished clans to give final battle. Dicon, of course, was with his Prince. Ann was all alone save for the worthy housewife, bent with age and anxiety, who moved about her daily tasks with a dreary method born of monotony. Philip had departed. Once Ann was united to her husband he had bidden her farewell formally and had ridden away to the west with the resolute air of one whose mission was accomplished, whose task was fulfilled. She missed him, missed him more than mere words or thoughts could express. Never had she needed him more. Dicon was near at hand, but Dicon seemed more interested in the Prince than in his wife. So thought Ann bitterly, and then took herself to task. Of course Dicon must be at the Prince's side, especially now that the final struggle was at hand. She would have reproached him had he been disloyal, yet somehow, she did feel a slight resentment at his being so much absent from her. Then, too, there was the suggestion that Dicon had been nursed back to health by Frances Holt. Dicon would talk little about that, which made her suspicious. Nor would he say how it came about that he had escaped while the members of the crew of the *Happy Chance* had been less fortunate. Ann suspected that Frances Holt had had a hand in it. She was jealous of Dicon being nursed by Frances Holt. The fact that Philip Yorke had saved her life under somewhat similar circumstances did not occur to her, all of which served to show that Ann was neither reasonable nor logical. The truth was that she was lonely, desperately lonely, but Dicon, his head full of military plans, failed to observe the fact.

Ann could not help but contrast his indifference with the devoted attendance of Philip Yorke. How she wished he could have remained near at hand. She would have felt so much more secure. What would be the outcome of the battle? Redcoats seemed to be everywhere. One had only to stand upon a nearby knoll to see in the distance ominous splashes of scarlet scattered about the moorlands. More than once a scouting party of light horse had made their way along the tiny rutted track which served as a road. When they appeared in sight Ann took cover. As a precaution her horse was concealed in a tiny stone pen out on the moors, a low structure so like the surrounding crags that it escaped the attention of all but the most observant passer-by. Dicon had seen to this precaution. He had rolled Ann's cloak

on the cantle and strapped on a bag of provisions. The animal stood
saddled and bridled, ready for instant use. Loaded pistols were in the
holsters. Evidently Dicon feared the worst. Starlight had never
before been so cavalierly treated and expressed resentment but Dicon
was in no mood for vagaries, horse or human. His temper seemed a
little frayed. Small wonder. After months of retreat and disappointment the final issue was at hand. And the odds were all with the
House of Hanover. When Ann put in her unexpected appearance at
the castle near Crieff, a touch of Dicon's former self asserted itself.
He caught her in his arms and, oblivious of the soldiers and Philip
Yorke, covered her face with kisses. Momentarily it warmed Ann
who liked to be loved. She was glad to be with her husband again,
yet all the while she was conscious of a curious unrest. She was also
aware, though it was a long time before she confessed it even to herself,
of a twinge of disappointment. Dicon explained that he had been
wounded in the Congleton affair and had been forced to lay up until
the wound was healed. When he recovered the retreat from Derby
had begun and the army of the Duke of Cumberland lay between him
and the Scottish border. He had been arrested and thrown into
Denbigh Castle—not Conway. He had escaped thanks to the kind
offices of a friend. Ann tactfully did not ask the name of the friend
and she was never told. Dicon set off to join the Prince but it was
not until he had reached the coast and found a brig bound for Glasgow
that he had been able to circumvent his enemies. He assured her
that he had been desolate when he discovered that she was not with
the Prince. He did not know where to seek her so he had remained
at his post, deeming this the only thing feasible. It sounded
logical, Ann was forced to admit. Of course it was Dicon's duty
to remain with the Prince. And how could he look for his wife
when he did not know where to look ? It was all perfectly logical.
Suddenly Ann became unreasonably illogical. What would Philip
Yorke have done under like circumstances ? She knew quite well.
His duty to her would have come before even his duty to his leader.
This might be unmoral but Ann would have cared for him all the more
for putting her first. She also knew that even if he had not known
where to look he would have searched and searched, consumed by a
restlessness which would give him no peace until he found her. With
Ann in danger he would never have tamely accepted the conditions
prescribed by fate. And something told Ann that sooner or later he
would have found her.

The fact remained that she was reunited to her husband so she
endeavoured to put Philip Yorke from her mind; not with entire
success. Dicon had been very specially nice; tender and sweet and
reasonable. She asked herself what more she had any right to expect.
She could not answer her own question. She confessed that she felt
wanted, necessary. But mind and body could not be disciplined in a
few days and she had become accustomed to depending on Philip
Yorke. He was so steadfast. And now Philip Yorke had gone out
of her life. Or had he ? Somehow she felt that a contact so deep, so
vital, was designed to abide for all time. Even though she could not

see his calm, steady eyes, or hear his modulated voice, his influence and his spirit would be with her always.

Ann's reverie was interrupted by the sound of hoofs. Not without trepidation she peered out of the tiny window. Fears were dispelled. It was Dicon, riding a weary horse. He came striding in and his serious expression vanished in a smile of welcome as he saw her. His arm went about her and he drew her close. "Golden Eyes!" he called.

"News, Dicon?"

"No fighting yet. By to-morrow there will be news enough, God knows. The Prince is resolved to give battle. It is inevitable." He paced the room restlessly. "There are regulars everywhere. They have even brought over Hanoverian troops to fight us." His lip curled. "There are English warships off the coast. They have fired on some of our parties of light horse who were scouting along the cliffs."

"Where is the Prince, Dicon?"

"He is sleeping in Culloden House. The clansmen are lined up on Culloden Plain. They are confident they will beat off the enemy."

"Are you confident, Dicon?"

"Oh, yes, we shall beat them," Dicon spoke casually but not, it seemed, with conviction.

"Ann," he said, "Ann."

"What is it?"

"It is not the battle which troubles me. I may be struck down and then what will happen to you? Nothing seems to matter to me provided you are safe and happy and cared for. I should never have persuaded you into this. God forgive me. I had not foreseen disaster such as this."

"Disaster?"

"Oh, we may as well face it. We are outnumbered. Even though our claymores cut their way through the regulars to-morrow, they will hound us down. You must be got out of the country somehow, sweet."

She crossed to him, put up her arms and kissed him. It touched her to find him solicitous on her behalf. He cared for her, not, perhaps, with the fervency of Philip Yorke, but she knew then that Dicon really cared. Why, oh why was life so involved? Why had she to choose not between good and evil but between two good things of different values? It was asking much. Which should she have? Had she been a child she might have replied—"both!" She gave a little laugh. "What is it?" Dicon looked surprised. He had seen nothing to laugh at in the situation.

"It was a thought which came to me," said Ann, blushing.

"Glad your thoughts are so pleasant," replied Dicon sombrely and fell to fidgeting with his sword hilt. "I must get back to the Prince, Ann. He could ill spare me. We tried a surprise attack last night. It might well have succeeded, but some fool's nerve failed at the last moment and we came back without striking a blow. They will attack us this morning. Your horse is still safe, Ann? My dear, if—if you see men fleeing in this direction, clansmen, that is, and you think that the battle has gone against us, never mind me. I can shift for myself. Get to your horse and ride for the west coast. Ride as if the devil was at your heels. It is your only chance. And then, get ship to France. Make for Paris and inquire for the Prince's headquarters. He has a place, of sorts. All of us who escape will make for it and then—well, we shall just have to plan a new future. I wish I could be more explicit. I must go. God bless you."

"God keep you safe, Dicon." They lingered over the kiss. It might be the last. Ann watched him ride down the track; watched him until he turned and waved her a semblance of his old gay salute before he turned past some crags and vanished from her sight. The moors seemed more lonely than ever.

Ann sat alone with her thoughts, staring out of the window. The rain had stopped but the world seemed sodden.

She tried to picture them, the hungry, forlorn, resolute adventurers; the tartan-clad clansmen loyal to their Stuart prince, huddling for the night under rocks and stunted trees, their muddy plaids wrapped close around them, muskets and claymores to hand. Then her thoughts turned to Dicon, her husband. He was less reckless, less blithe, less debonair than when he had first come to her house, but he was more considerate, more thoughtful. His face, when he left the farmstead, was set with a stern resolve. He would be plying his deadly sword soon . . .

Her ears caught the sound of steps, cautious steps. She was keyed-up, alert. Instantly she was on her feet, listening, peering. A figure was creeping along the farmyard wall, a dark form, not, thank God, a redcoat. Ann breathed more freely. She was still curious.

"Oh, Mistress Ann. Thank God I have found you !" A youth was on his knees kissing her hand, her skirt, sobbing with relief.

"Hughie ! My dear boy, you have got back ! But what are you doing here ? How did you get here ? How glad I am to see you, but what does it mean ?"

Ann was excited. She put her questions so fast that the lad could not answer if he had been so minded. Before he replied he had to control his voice, so shaken with relief and emotion was he. Presently he ceased kissing her skirt, stood up and took a deep breath.

"I thought I should never find you, Mistress Ann. I never knew that Scotland was so big a place."

"But how did you get here ? I am puzzled."

"I came with him."

"With whom ?"

"Mr. Yorke."

"He is here ! Where ? Quick, tell me."

"He's out in a hollow of the moors holding the horses. We have ridden from the coast, and a terrible job it has been dodging them confounded dragoons. The vessel's there, Mistress Ann. I got the ropes to Mr. Peris and they're all free. And we cut out the *Happy Chance*, as I said, and she's anchored in a cove waiting to sail to France with you. Mr. Yorke says you are to come at once. There's no time to be lost. He gave me this note for you."

183

He held a soiled slip of paper in his hand. It had evidently been torn from a notebook in which Mr. Yorke practised his verses. Some lines of poetry were on one side; on the other Ann read :

'DEAR ANN,

 I did not think to see you again but I can still serve you. The vessel has arrived and awaits you. Do not delay. Your cause is doomed. The Duke of C. outnumbers your army and has artillery which will mow down the clansmen before they can charge. There will be bloodshed and butchery. Escape while you can.

Your devoted servant,

P. YORKE.'

Ann sighed. "I cannot come, Hughie. Thank him but say I cannot come."

"He says I must make you."

"Why—why did he not come for me himself?"

"I dunno, Mistress Ann. He just wouldn't. He would not see you . . . and yet if you go to the horses he must see you unless he shuts his eyes."

"You must return without me, Hughie, I must stay with my husband."

"Where is he?"

"With the Prince."

"Then how can you stay with him if he isn't here?"

"Don't be stupid, Hughie. I mean that I cannot leave him, I will not desert him at a time like this."

"There is to be a big battle."

"I know. That is why I must stay."

"Mr. Yorke says that it is the reason why you must go. The Prince will be defeated."

"It is by no means sure. In any case I shall not run away."

"The Duke is bound to win. He has more men."

"There were more men at Prestonpans but the Highland claymores swept them away. They will do so again."

"Mr. Yorke says the Duke has plenty of cannon. He will thin their ranks before they charge."

"That will not check them."

"If they do charge they will be taken by surprise. The regulars have learnt a new drill."

"What might that be?"

"They used to lunge at the man who attacked them and the Highlander took their bayonet on his target. Now the British troops have been taught to lunge not at the man in front but at the man on his left so that each Highlander will be stabbed in his unprotected side."

Ann bit her lip. "I cannot help it. I will not go with you. Tell Mr. Yorke I thank him. My heartfelt wishes go out to him. But I will not desert my husband."

"He says the English are savage. They will butcher everyone. No woman will be safe. The wounded are to be stabbed to death."

"Then I will die beside my husband."

The boy looked at her sadly. "Then I've done all this for—nothing ! Got 'em out of Conway Castle, captured the ship, sailed her here, dodged the English frigates, rode across Scotland . . . all for nothing !" There was a wealth of feeling in his tones. Ann flung her arms about him. "Oh, no, no, my brave cavalier ! You have worked wonders. I shall always be grateful."

"Then come with me. Come to where Mr. Yorke is waiting with the horses. I was so sure that you would come that I have taken Starlight to join him. I found her in the little hut where the woman told me you had hidden her."

"Then fetch Starlight back ! I command you ! How dare you touch my horse without orders !"

The boy looked crestfallen. He turned sulkily without a word and walked from the room. When he had gone Ann's firm demeanour left her. She dropped in a chair and sobbed. Why, why, must her feelings be torn like this ? She was still there when Hughie burst into the room.

"Mistress Ann, Mistress Ann. There's redcoats coming this way, coming up the lane and there's a woman with them. I could not get to Mr. Yorke without being seen. Quick. They are heading for this farm. Come and hide in the heather. It is your only chance."

Ann snatched up hat and shawl. She followed Hughie down under cover of the farm wall, along a gully and then crouched behind some rocks. The boy peered anxiously forth. He kept her informed.

"There are six dragoons and the officer. He's got a woman with him. They're in the farmyard. They are talking to the old wife. Now they're going into the house, searching. They are pointing to the shed where Starlight was hidden. It's a good thing I took her away. They're all going that way. The woman's waiting in the yard. Phew !"

He broke off in a whistle of surprise. Ann looked up. "What is it, Hughie ?"

"That woman, Mistress Ann. It's the same as lashed me at Plas Mawr !"

"What ! Frances Holt ?" Ann in her amazement lifted herself on her hands to obtain a clearer view. Either the sound of her voice or her movement attracted attention for the woman on the horse turned her head and stared in their direction.

"Down !" whispered Hughie, dragging his mistress behind the boulder without ceremony. "Keep your head down."

Presently he peered out again. "It's all safe," he whispered. "The redcoats are going. They're mounting. Here comes the officer. Mistress Ann, it's that major who come to the Plas; you know the man who caused all the bother. Ssh !"

Once again Ann wriggled to the edge of the rock and was staring with white face at the group before the farm. Major Manstein climbed into the saddle. Ann noticed he held his right arm somewhat stiffly. He looked about him. The two flattened themselves in the heather. When they peeped forth again the soldiers were riding down the road.

Frances Holt was at Major Manstein's side. Ann stared at the broad red back of the officer and heaved a sigh.

"Thank God they're gone, Mistress Ann." Hughie grew impatient. "Let's be going, too."

Ann did not reply. She was so silent that the boy, turned to look at her. She lay with eyes closed, so still that he thought that she had fainted. But she had not fainted. It was just that she had reached the end of her tether. Manstein again! Was there no escaping that ominous man? Ever since he had crossed her path he had proved the fore-runner of disaster. He was on her trail again. Remorseless as Nemesis. Of what use struggling any longer. She might as well abandon the fight. Give in. Take the consequences. What matter? There was nothing to live for. Dicon would surely be killed. There was no one to whom she could turn.

Suddenly there came to her mind the vision of a man holding three horses in the hollow of the moor; a patient man . . . waiting . . . The way of escape was open. There was still Philip! Philip who had never failed her yet! Who never would fail her! She rose to her feet, a fresh light of hope in her eyes.

"Hughie. Where is Mr. Yorke? I have changed my mind. I will come with you. It is time I escaped."

CHAPTER THIRTY-EIGHT

IT WAS NOT UNTIL LONG AFTERWARDS THAT ANN LEARNT THE DETAILS of the fatal fight at Culloden. She heard then how the clansmen had slept foodless in the open and had given battle on an unprotected plain where the English gunners had them in full view. Dicon was through it all. He was close beside the Prince when a cannon-ball struck the gravel almost beneath the royal charger. Dicon had several abrasions caused by the flying stones.

Ann knew nothing of all this. All she knew was that Major Manstein was close at hand. To her there was something sinister in his presence. She might have given in from sheer despair, yielding like a rabbit with a stoat on its trail, had not the nearness of Philip Yorke renewed her strength. He was standing in the hollow when they arrived, the reins of three horses in his hands. The animals were muddy and rough of coat. Philip looked paler, older, thinner. His gentle courtesy was unchanged.

He assisted Ann into the saddle of Starlight. "I am sorry to have been so slow in coming," she said as they moved off. "We had to hide. That horrible man, Manstein, came over to search the farm."

"It is high time you left the district."

"After Manstein rode off with his soldiers, I had Hughie run back to the farm and chalk on the wall the place where we are to join the *Happy Chance*."

"Why?"

"Why? Because if Dicon escapes and comes seeking me and I am missing he will be distracted. He will not know where to search. He is sure to see the name of the ship and the rendezvous and will know where to follow me. Was it not clever of me to think of it?"

Philip Yorke made no reply and Ann repeated her question.

"Well, it is there for him to read. That was certainly considerate of you."

"Then why are you so silent? You look as if you did not approve. Do you not want Dicon to follow?"

"It is not that."

"What then?"

"It is also there for Manstein to read should he return instead of your husband. We may take it that he is equally astute."

Ann gave a gasp of consternation. "I will go back and rub it out."

"No. Let it stand. The chances are even. We must accept them. Listen!"

Far behind them, from the shores of Moray Firth, came a low, ominous rumble, like distant thunder only more angry.

"The guns have started," said Philip Yorke. "We shall be unmolested until the battle ends. Then they will scour the countryside like bloodhounds. Let us make the most of our start."

Ann never forgot that ride across the breadth of Scotland: the distant peep of Inverness, the attenuated length of Loch Ness. Yorke crossed the river to follow the northern bank; it seemed safer. It meant that they had to skirt Fort Augustus with caution. When the horses were showing signs of exhaustion they stopped at a farmhouse. The farmer agreed to let them stay for the night—for a consideration. His demeanour did not impress them. Yorke and Hughie took it in turns to stay on guard with loaded pistols. Ann slept more soundly than she had done for many a day. They were up and away at dawn. Thus the time passed. It was, for Ann, a period of endurance. There was no excitement of the chase; only continual apprehension and unrelaxed vigilance. Once the distant sight of marching redcoats drove them to cover for the better part of a day. Ann began to lose track of time. They knew nothing about what had taken place at Culloden. Yorke shunned all villages. He was a man of one purpose. He must get Ann to the coast where the snow was awaiting them. Nothing else mattered. Then one day, framed between two rocky promontories, they had their first glimpse of the sea stretching open and grey before them; a sea without a sail. The English frigates appeared to have been sent to the eastern sea-coast of Scotland, for which Philip Yorke thanked God and took courage. He kept glancing at Ann to see how she was standing up to the strain. She was paler and more mature, otherwise she seemed little the worse. She was quieter, more thoughtful. So, for that matter, was he. Philip Yorke was a believer in the Scheme of Things and at the moment he seemed quite definitely and actively to be playing an important role. But he looked ahead. What was to be the final outcome? Would Dicon be killed in action? If so, it would obviously be his privilege to care for this radiant girl who was so dear to him. It seemed a probable, and to him desirable, consequence. But he must wait and see. If one believed in the Scheme it was no use trying to precipitate its workings. A man must do his best, and have patience.

"Is this the place, Philip?"

"Here or hereabouts."

"Then where is the vessel?"

"She may have had to stand off. She may have dropped anchor just around the headland."

"Shall I see if she is there, Mr. Yorke?" It was Hughie, impatient as a boy would be. At Yorke's nod of consent he went scrambling over the rocks, glad to stretch his legs after so long in the saddle.

A path or sheep-track ran across the short-cropped grass until it wound its way between two steep walls of cliff which formed a defile beyond which lay the ocean. The place was strewn with boulders. Ann was talking excitedly but Philip for once paid no heed. He walked to the narrowest place and commenced to roll boulders to form a low wall. "It is an admirable spot to defend," he said quietly.

"To defend? Will it be necessary?"

"I hope not. I am a little anxious about the ship. She may have been seen by a cruiser and had to stand off. If we have to remain here for any length of time we may as well make ourselves as secure as possible. Seat yourself on that broad rock, Ann, and talk to me while I work."

"What shall I talk about?"

"Anything, so long as I hear your voice. I may not hear it much longer."

"But why, Philip?"

"Well, much depends on what happens in the next few hours. If your husband escapes and joins you here, you will sail for France together. I shall no longer be needed. My service will be ended."

"But our friendship never, Philip. We have been such good comrades. I cannot picture life without you. You must remain near me always."

He smiled a little sadly. "Life does not always work out as we plan. It has a queer trick of doing the unexpected. We assume that it will be logical and at times it becomes very illogical. I wonder what is at the back of it all. Sometimes I think that what happens does not matter at all: only our reaction to it."

The wall of stones was breast-high now. He dusted his hands, crossed to the horses, unsaddled and tethered them to a rowan tree which lifted its delicate but sturdy trunk from a fertile hollow amid the crags. He carried the saddles to the barricade and spread the pistols neatly on a flat rock.

"You look positively warlike, Philip."

"Let us hope the preparations are entirely unnecessary. Perhaps I am over-cautious but I feel my responsibility, Ann. You are a very precious jewel for a man to have in his keeping."

"You always contrive to make me feel that I am nicer than I really am. You are very good to me." She laid a hand upon his arm. "How can I thank you?"

"Why thank me? I please myself. What I do gives me happiness. Never in my life have I been so happy. Believe me, I am utterly selfish."

"You are the most selfless man I ever met. I find myself turning

188

to you in every difficulty. No one in my life has given me this sense of perfect security."

"I am glad that I have been able to serve you, Ann. At a time when there was nothing left in my life but work, you came and glorified it."

"How could I glorify it ?"

"By just being yourself."

He stood up and dropped both his hands on her slim shoulders. "Ann !" he whispered. "Ann."

"Yes, dear ?"

He turned away quickly. "Not yet !" he muttered, almost hardly.

"You may kiss me if you wish, Philip," she said, but he shook his head.

"Why not ?" she demanded. "Life is not easy or fair or merciful, and perhaps a little joy is not to be scorned."

"I must exercise patience. Time settles all things. I do not know yet."

She did not ask him. She knew that he was thinking of the battle, and its outcome. Would Dicon escape ? Would he find the message at the farm ? Would he come riding recklessly to join her ? She hoped that he would, yet if he did—she glanced up at Philip Yorke. He was standing statue-like, staring with penetrating eyes at the inland road over which they had ridden.

"Ann, your eyes are younger than mine. There is a horseman riding rapidly down the road. He is behind those rocks at present. Watch over there where he will emerge."

"I see him."

"I thought that it might be——"

Ann stared hard. "It is," she breathed. "It is Dicon. Oh, Philip !"

"Then your husband has escaped. I am glad, Ann."

"Philip. I am so sorry . . . so terribly sorry !"

"Sorry Dicon has escaped?" She caught the whimsical light in his eyes. His smile was mischievous.

"You know I did not mean that. I mean . . . I don't know what I mean, save that I know I must be making you suffer. I only know that I do not want you to be hurt, dearest and best of friends. Philip, you must be hurt. You do not show it but you must be wounded, you, who are so noble. And I—I feel that I would do anything for you, but my hands are tied and my lips are sealed. Brave, chivalrous, unselfish, I cannot bear to think of you suffering. Love has no right to wound where it cannot heal."

"To serve you is to salve the hurt."

"But Philip, why should it be necessary ? When you deserve so much why should this be ?"

"You mean this parting ? I do not know, Ann. Perhaps it is too soon to know what the purpose is. We may learn later. Ann, there is one line in the marriage service which I abhor."

"Philip !"

"It is 'Until death us do part.' When people love they should not love until death but through all eternity. Perhaps in some other part

189

of this wide universe we shall encounter again under more propitious circumstances."

"But Philip, we shall be friends always. Our friendship will have many, many years to run."

"I should like to think so, Ann. But I have a feeling that I shall not see you again—in this life. The parting this time is final. If in years to come you spare me a thought recollect that I regret nothing, and that serving you has been its own reward."

She nodded.

"Ann; would you mind going down the path behind us to see if there is any sign of that boy or the vessel? From the pace your husband sets there must be some urgency. He is probably pursued. My premonition was sound. I am glad that I spent the time building this barricade."

With quiet deliberation he looked to the priming of the pistols. Then he laid the Dettingen sword across the rocks. Ann returned to say that Hughie was climbing the cliff path which led to a sheltered bay. There was no sign of the snow but a ship's boat was hauled upon the shingle.

"A hopeful sign," commented Philip. "Ann, wave your handkerchief to let your husband know our whereabouts. He will find it a stimulating ending to an eventful ride."

Ann obeyed with docility. She saw her husband wave in reply. Dropping from the saddle he waited only to drag the pistols from the holsters before he abandoned his gasping horse and came running along the path to join them.

"Ann, thank God you are safe! Is the ship here? Quick, then! There's not a moment to lose. Manstein and a score of troopers are on my heels. He's put a ball through my hat already. Quick, girl."

Hughie was over the cliff brow now and behind him came Lieutenant Peris and a couple of seamen.

An ejaculation from Philip Yorke caused them all to turn. Along the road from the east, strung out in an irregular line, came galloping redcoats. The leader was known to them all. Philip Yorke picked up the Dettingen sword and tested the blade in his firm fingers.

"A pretty spot for a fight," cried Peris as he, too, drew his sword. "Miss Trevor, glad to see you, Ma'am. No, demme, it's Mrs. Conway now, but as charming as ever, egad."

"The best compliment you can pay Mrs. Conway is to carry her aboard the snow without delay." Philip Yorke spoke coolly.

"We can hold this pass against those red devils," cried Peris. "After six months in Conway clink I'm spoiling for a fight."

"And you would jeopardize the safety of Mrs. Conway to gratify your feelings? Oh, no, Mr. Peris, your chivalry cries out at such behaviour. I presume the snow is there?"

"Just around the headland."

"Here they come," cried Hughie. Several of the leading dragoons had reined in their panting chargers and were taking up their carbines. A shot rang out. It was fired by an unsteady hand and went high.

"Good-bye, Ann. *Bon voyage*," said Yorke.

"I shall not leave you, Philip."

"What? The *Happy Chance* awaits you! Make the most of it. When happy chances occur in life it is well not to miss the tide! No, don't delay, my dear. They may aim truer next time. Off you go. We shall meet again. Never forget that."

"Shall we, Philip?" A sudden fear beset her. 'Life is taking away something from us—the joy of being together!"

She ran towards him and held up her lips but he only lightly patted her cheek with his hand. "God bless you," said Yorke. "Conway, take your wife away, man. Do you want her hit? They will open fire in earnest any moment."

Major Manstein's voice sounded from up the pass demanding their surrender in the name of King George. Yorke replied with a pistol shot which, with characteristic courtesy, he aimed high. It was sufficient to cause Lieutenant Peris to catch Ann about the waist and hurry her to the path which led to the waiting boat. She was almost fainting and the two seamen went before lest she should slide down the cliff. Hughie scrambled after them with reluctant glances back to where Philip Yorke was arranging the pistols along the top of the barricade.

"This is my final warning." It was Manstein's voice. "Surrender or we open fire."

"Go!" said Philip Yorke, turning to Conway who was still beside him. "I can hold the pass with luck until you have got the ship out of range. But hasten. The odds are twenty to one, and I do not want your wife hit by a random shot just when you have liberty within your grasp."

"I stay here," said Conway stubbornly. "I have scores to settle with that Manstein swine."

"You have a duty to your wife. I will see to the settling of all scores."

"I will not leave you. Damnation, I will not run away from Manstein or any other of Cumberland's hired butchers."

"You must go."

"I will not leave you. Man, it is certain death for you."

"You love Ann?"

"You know I do."

"Enough to die for her?"

"Enough to die for her."

"May not I, then, have that privilege?"

Richard Conway stared hard at the steadfast eyes turned to him. Then he stepped back, clicked his heels together and raised his sword-hilt to his lips in the royal salute.

* * * * *

All was bustle and confusion aboard the *Happy Chance*. The crew were mostly volunteers and Lieutenant Peris's language was not intended for Ann's ears. Dicon was hauling on a rope. There seemed to be ropes everywhere. Ann skipped out of the way of the hurrying, hauling seamen and walked to the taffrail. She could feel the vessel move beneath her feet. From where she stood she could see puffs of smoke curling like cotton-wool among the grass and the crags above her. The sound of the firing came to her ears. It was an irregular fusillade, the sharp bark of Yorke's armoury of pistols contrasting with the heavier shots from the carbines of the dragoons. The soldiers seemed to be hemming him in. Now and again Ann could catch a glimpse of scarlet showing bright amid the rocks. The vessel was moving away from the land. She could see more clearly now : dragoons crouching behind boulders and taking shots at the place where Philip Yorke must be standing behind his lonely barricade. She could not see him but she could picture him. And he was doing all this for her ! The redcoats were closing in; drawing nearer and nearer. Ann thought they looked like drops of blood flowing over the grey rocks. Then the firing stopped. She listened. There was never a sound. The firing had frightened her ; she was terrified by the silence !

Nervously her fingers turned over a paper in her pocket. It was the paper which Philip Yorke had sent to her at the lonely farmhouse imploring her to flee while there was yet time. It was the last message she had received from him. She drew it out and scanned it sadly. But was it his last message ? The verse on the back caught her eyes. She read it slowly. This, of a truth, was the last message of Philip Yorke. It might almost be his epitaph.

> *Of what avail the praying and the fasting,*
> *The yearning for a bliss not to be bought ?*
> *The precious moment speeds. There is no lasting*
> *Save in the tender archives of our thought.*

* * * * *

A breeze touched the sails making the snow heel slightly. There came a clatter of blocks and stentorian orders from Lieutenant Peris. The vessel caught the breeze. There sounded the musical slapping of waves against her sides as her forefoot cut the grey waters of the bay. The sails were bellying now; every rope was taut.

Dicon came hurrying aft, wiping his heated brow.

"Golden Eyes !" he called as he gave his gay salute. "We have done it, by the skin of our teeth. We are safe, lass, we are free. Safe and free with the open sea before us."

But Ann did not heed him or did not hear him. The pass amid the rocks was strangely still and silent now. She could barely see it through the mist of her tears.

She was conscious of Dicon's strong arm about her and she laid her tear-stained face against his shoulder. She still had Dicon—and the tender archives of her thought.

THE END

NOTE.—For many of the facts about the invasion I am indebted to Mr. Clennell Wilkinson's Life of Bonnie Prince Charlie.

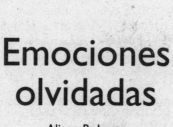

Emociones
olvidadas

Alison Roberts

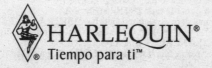

HARLEQUIN®
Tiempo para ti™

NOVELAS CON CORAZÓN

Editado por HARLEQUIN IBÉRICA, S.A.
Hermosilla, 21
28001 Madrid

I.S.B.N.: 84-396-9343-5
Depósito legal: B-47248-2001
Editor responsable: M. T. Villar
Diseño cubierta: María J. Velasco Juez
Fotomecánica: PREIMPRESIÓN 2000
C/. Matilde Hernández, 34. 28019 Madrid
Impresión y encuadernación: LITOGRAFÍA ROSÉS, S.A.
C/. Energía, 11. 08850 Gavá (Barcelona)
Fecha impresión Argentina:11.5.02
Distribuidor exclusivo para España: LOGISTA
Distribuidor para México: INTERMEX, S.A.
Distribuidores para Argentina: interior, BERTRAN, S.A.C. Vélez
Sársfield, 1950. Cap. Fed./ Buenos Aires y Gran Buenos Aires,
VACCARO SÁNCHEZ y Cía, S.A.
Distribuidor para Chile: DISTRIBUIDORA ALFA, S.A.

Capítulo 1

JAMÁS se había sentido tan bien. Hannah Duncan tomaba los últimos rayos de sol de aquel atardecer de verano. El calor acumulado por los guijarros de la playa donde estaba sentada contrarrestaba el frío del bañador mojado. Los ojos cerrados, el rostro levantado saboreando la caricia del sol. No había brisa.

Hannah abrió los ojos. El sol poniente bañaba de luz las montañas distantes y el lago con un resplandor rosado. Por fin se habían alejado los bulliciosos niños de la orilla del lago, y el agua permanecía inmóvil, reflejando los árboles a su alrededor. Bajo aquellos árboles, una pareja joven tumbada, absorta en sí misma. Hannah sonrió. Sabía cómo se sentían.

Inconscientemente se llevó una mano al vientre. Solo Ben y ella sabían qué se ocultaba bajo ese vientre plano. Habían decidido mantenerlo en secreto al menos hasta el final de ese verano. Hannah buscó a Ben con la mirada. Él desafiaba al frío, seguía bañándose, pero hasta a él le había alcanzado aquella paz. Ya no nadaba, flotaba sobre la espalda con los brazos extendidos. Su cuerpo estaba tan inmóvil que no producía siquiera ondas en el agua. Hannah estuvo tentada de llamarlo, pero no quiso perturbar aquella paz. Hasta los pájaros habían callado. De pronto se quedó helada. No podía gritar, sentía un nudo en la garganta. Ben no flotaba de espaldas, estaba boca abajo. ¡Se estaba ahogando!

¿Había gritado, o lo que oía era el eco en su cabeza? Algo alertó a la pareja. El hombre corrió a ayudar a Ben, buceando en el lago, y la mujer al camping. Una multitud se fue agrupando. ¿Cómo era posible que, entre tanta gente, nadie supiera qué hacer?

—Ya llega la ambulancia —dijo alguien.

—¡No creo que respire! —exclamó otro aterrorizado.

Hannah se arrodilló junto a Ben y tomó su rostro entre las manos. No respiraba. ¿Cuánto tiempo había estado boca abajo, sin respirar, mientras ella se tostaba al sol y disfrutaba de la indecible calma?

—Hazle el boca a boca —sugirió una voz masculina—. Yo le presionaré el pecho, lo he visto en televisión.

Los labios de Ben estaban fríos. Hannah sintió el calor de su propio aliento entrando en la boca de él. Y lo sintió escapando de nuevo, expelido por la entusiasta opresión del hombre que la ayudaba. ¿Por qué no tenía agua en los pulmones? Hannah también había visto la televisión. Al presionar el pecho, el agua debía salir. Entonces entraba aire y la víctima tosía, volviendo a respirar. Tenía que estar haciendo algo mal. Hannah tapó la nariz de Ben. El pánico fue adueñándose de ella.

La sirena de la ambulancia supuso un alivio. Hannah se aferró a la esperanza. Por fin alguien sabría qué hacer.

Pero ni los conocimientos ni la habilidad fueron suficientes en esa ocasión. Demasiado tarde. Ben no alcanzaría a oír el llanto de ningún corazón dolido, ni siquiera el de Hannah. Aquel grito trataba de salir de sus labios helados, pero quedó atrapado. Estaba atrapada. Luchó. ¿Quién la agarraba de la espalda? Tenía que librarse... soltar aquel grito de dolor que invadía su interior... ni siquiera podía respirar.

Aquel grito logró salir al fin. Los brazos que la sujetaban resultaron ser las sábanas revueltas. Hannah contuvo la respiración y volvió la cabeza en la almohada gritando una vez más. Se sentó y se aferró a la almohada húmeda por las lágrimas.

Tenía aquella pesadilla cada vez con menos frecuencia, pero el horror no era menor, y después seguía sintiéndose igual de mal. Sentía un enorme vacío en su interior, una tremenda pérdida. En cada ocasión, sin embargo, la sensación duraba menos. Hannah apartó las sábanas y se levantó. La oscuridad del pasillo no la detuvo, sabía a dónde iba. Y sabía que la pérdida no había sido total. Un vistazo a la cuna era suficiente para recordarle el júbilo de dar a luz a la hija de Ben, un júbilo que crecía con el paso del tiempo. Hannah contempló los rizos rubios de su hija. Su diminuto rostro parecía sonreír incluso dormida. Estaba a punto de besarla cuando notó un movimiento detrás de ella. Giró la cabeza y sonrió.

–Buenos días, mamá.

–Te has levantado pronto, cariño –contestó su madre preocupada–. ¿Va todo bien?

–Todo perfecto –aseguró Hannah señalando a su hija–. Creo que ya es hora de que la traslademos a una cama. Después de todo, tiene dos años y medio.

–Adora su cunita –comentó Norma Duncan–, y es tan pequeñita. No ha tratado de salir ni una sola vez.

–No –contestó Hannah bostezando–. Será mejor que tome una ducha.

–Debes estar agotada –añadió Norma siguiendo a su hija hasta el baño–. Anoche volviste a quedarte despierta hasta muy tarde, con la nariz enterrada en esos libros.

–Es que esta mañana tengo un test de revisión de conocimientos, y pasado una revisión práctica por la mañana y un examen escrito por la tarde. No quiero suspender.

–No suspenderás –sonrió Norma confiada–. Jamás te he visto fallar, cuando te pones todo tu empeño.

–No estoy tan segura, mamá –comentó Hannah parándose delante de la puerta del baño–. Somos diez en el curso, y solo seis pasarán y conseguirán el empleo.

–Y tú serás una de ellos –afirmó Norma–. Dúchate, te prepararé el desayuno.

Hannah dejó que el agua caliente borrara todo rastro de la pesadilla y trató de serenarse. Siempre se ponía nerviosa cuando tenía que hacer un test. Desde la muerte de Ben, el nacimiento de Heidi no había sido el único cambio importante en su vida. En buena medida, su capacidad para superar la muerte de Ben se debía al hecho de haber descubierto qué quería hacer con su vida.

Jamás podría haber salvado a Ben. Nadie habría podido. La autopsia había revelado una afección cardíaca congénita, causa de la muerte instantánea. Ben no se había ahogado. A pesar de ello, Hannah no había podido olvidar la sensación de impotencia y frustración por no poder ayudarlo, ni la esperanza que supuso la llegada de la ambulancia.

Pronto formaría parte de un equipo similar. Quizá no hubiera podido salvar a Ben, pero tendría la oportunidad de salvar a otras personas. Estaba lista para ponerse a prueba. Si tenía éxito, entonces había merecido la pena.

Capítulo 2

POR QUÉ demonios había escogido ese preciso momento para guiñarle un ojo? El resultado había sido desastroso. Hannah Duncan se ruborizó, incómoda, y volvió la vista hacia la hoja de papel sobre su mesa. El pulso le latía acelerado, comprendiendo lo frágil de su concentración. Unos segundos antes, la pregunta le había parecido de lo más fácil. Era capaz de enumerar los síntomas de una fractura incluso dormida. Con su técnica memorística a base de palabras clave, había aprendido grandes cantidades de información.

Hannah respiró hondo. En cuanto recordara la palabra clave, tendría la solución. De pronto lo consiguió. Sí, la palabra era DOPMOHS, las iniciales de dolor, pérdida de la función, movimientos poco naturales, hinchazón y shock. Hannah volvió a respirar. Le faltaba contestar a una sola pregunta, y la sabía.

No estaba dispuesta a volver a perder la concentración. ¿Quiénes, de los allí reunidos, fallarían el examen y no lograrían convertirse en oficial de ambulancia? Hannah no estaba dispuesta a ser una de ellas, y menos aún por culpa de una simple muestra de interés, como ese guiño.

Adam Lewis miró el reloj de pared. Les concedería cinco minutos más, y luego, hasta la hora de la comida, discutirían las respuestas. Esperaba con ansiedad ese descanso. Disfrutaba dando clases a los nuevos candidatos a oficial de ambulancia, pero tantas horas encerrados le producían dolor de cabeza.

Adam se inclinó en el respaldo de la silla y se relajó. En una semana volvería a la carretera, a ejercer como oficial de ambulancia, en lugar de como profesor. Los exámenes que quedaban no eran más que una formalidad. Sabía muy bien quién pasaría.

Derek era el mayor del grupo, tenía treinta y ocho años. Había sido policía, y era un hombre inteligente y callado. Su porte físico, más que imponente, resultaba reconfortante. Era el candidato ideal al puesto. Eddie tenía veintitrés años y era excesivamente tímido, pero la carretera lo curaría. Además, su timidez se debía al deseo de ocultar la atracción que sentía por Hannah. Adam sonrió comprensivo.

Michael escribía con seguridad, probablemente estuviera explicando más de lo que se le exigía. Sería interesante conocer sus respuestas durante la discusión posterior. Adam desvió la vista hacia Phil, el taxista, que miraba al techo y daba golpecitos con la pluma sobre la mesa. Phil no lo conseguiría. Solo le interesaban las situaciones dramáticas, y el trabajo en una ambulancia, en su mayor parte, no consistía en eso. Además, había faltado mucho a clase.

Anne era demasiado nerviosa para ese trabajo, y Jackie estaba más interesada en los hombres que en los estudios. En ese momento miraba a John, el fanático de los deportes, en lugar de hacer el test. Adam dirigió la vista hacia Christine. Tenía treinta y cuatro años, y era mucho más madura que Jackie, pero no estaba preparada para ser oficial de ambulancia. Y no es que lo creyera porque tuviera prejuicios contra ella, debido a su situación familiar. Adam Lewis sabía lo que hacía.

Adam observó a la mejor de todo el grupo: Hannah Duncan. Su rubor había cedido. Adam no sabía por qué le había guiñado el ojo, pero el efecto había sido sorprendente: había perdido la concentración. ¿Estaría molesta, o sencillamente se sentía violenta por el hecho de que él mostrara interés hacia ella?

—Se acabó el tiempo —anunció Adam—. Discutiremos las respuestas y luego haremos un descanso para comer.

Como era de esperar, Michael estaba ansioso por enumerar las causas de las fracturas. Adam le permitió explayarse mientras su mente divagaba sobre otro tema. Quizá Hannah Duncan no se diera cuenta de lo interesante que resultaba como persona. Desde luego ni alentaba ni respondía a ninguna de las insinuaciones de nadie, parecía no darse cuenta de que Eddie se desvivía por hacer las prácticas con ella.

Días antes, Adam había estado refrescándose la memoria, leyendo una vez más los formularios de solicitud rellenados por los asistentes al curso. Hannah tenía veintiocho años y, era de suponer, estaba soltera, porque a la pregunta de cuál era su pariente más cercano había respondido que su madre. Sus empleos anteriores incluían trabajos en el extranjero. Además, había trabajado como monitora de salvamento en una piscina de niños.

—Y luego están las causas patológicas —terminó Michael—, que se producen a causa de otras enfermedades de los huesos, como por ejemplo el cáncer o la osteoporosis.

—Gracias, Michael —dijo Adam—. ¿Qué significa que la causa de una fractura sea indirecta?

–Que el punto de impacto no es el punto en el que se produce la fractura –contestó Ross.

–¿Por ejemplo? –preguntó Adam.

–Caer sobre una mano y romperse el cuello –afirmó Christine–. A todos mis hijos les ha pasado eso.

–¿Y? –se apresuró Adam a preguntar, deseoso de evitar otra conversación más acerca de los accidentes de los hijos de Christine–. ¿Hannah?

–Caer sobre un pie desde cierta altura, provocando una fractura pélvica o de la columna vertebral –contestó Hannah sin vacilar.

–Excelente –contestó Adam–. Derek... cuéntanos algo sobre los dos grandes sistemas del cuerpo humano.

Hannah observó a Derek leer su respuesta. Hablaba tanto del sistema nervioso como del circulatorio, y lo hacía con calma, con seguridad. Adam asentía con aprobación.

–¿Cuándo deben medirse las constantes de esos dos sistemas?

Adam siempre hacía preguntas sobre las cuales la discusión podía extenderse infinitamente. Sin embargo aquella mañana Hannah estaba cansada, se distrajo. A esas alturas toda la clase conocía a su profesor lo suficiente como para apreciar su sentido del humor. Probablemente le guiñara el ojo a mucha gente. O quizá tuviera un tic del que no se hubiera dado cuenta. Pero no, Hannah sabía perfectamente que ni tenía tics ni tenía la costumbre de guiñar el ojo. De pronto comprendió que Adam le dirigía la pregunta a ella.

–Hipovolemia –se apresuró a responder, esperando haber entendido la pregunta.

–¿Por qué?

–Porque algunas fracturas producen una importante hemorragia interna.

–¿Cuáles, en particular? –volvió a preguntar Adam con la mirada fija en Hannah.

–La de la pelvis y las de los huesos largos.

Adam volvió la vista hacia Jackie y preguntó:

–¿Qué pérdida de sangre puede esperarse de una fractura de una pelvis?

Jackie giró los ojos en sus órbitas sin responder.

–Unos tres litros –contestó Michael sin poder resistirse, rompiendo el silencio.

–¿Y cuánto volumen de sangre tiene un adulto por término medio? –volvió a preguntar el profesor.

–Cinco litros –contestó de nuevo Michael–. Así que tres litros representa un sesenta por ciento del volumen de sangre, lo cual significa...

–Que se queda con el depósito vacío –lo interrumpió Ross.

–Exacto –convino Adam–. Shock por hipovolemia. ¿Qué otras complicaciones puede producir una fractura?

Hannah observó a Adam. Trataba de animar a Eddie para que participara en la discusión. Su mirada vagó contemplativa por aquel semblante. ¿Habría notado alguien la cicatriz que tenía en el puente de la nariz? ¿Y la de la ceja izquierda?

–Bien, Eddie. Un movimiento inadecuado puede producir daños tanto en el sistema nervioso como en el circulatorio –explicaba Adam sonriendo y mostrando sus hoyuelos.

¿Notaba alguien la forma en que Adam se quedaba completamente inmóvil cuando escuchaba?, ¿y la forma en que sus cejas parecían recalcar esa atención? A Anne, desde luego, la ponía nerviosa. La pobre chica tartamudeaba.

La discusión se alargaba. Hannah miró el reloj. Unos minutos más y llegaría la hora del descanso. El aire fresco la ayudaría a concentrarse. Después de aquel estúpido guiño, nada había vuelto a ser igual. Hannah se irritó al ver que Adam se apartaba los rizos de la frente. Era un gesto inconfundible: significaba que tenía que reflexionar sobre la respuesta. Sí, Hannah Duncan conocía perfectamente los gestos de Adam Lewis. Y guiñar un ojo, definitivamente, no era habitual en él.

Quizá él se hubiera dado cuenta de la forma en que lo observaba. Hannah rechazó la idea de inmediato. No lo hacía a menudo, ni deliberadamente. Durante el curso, comenzado un mes atrás, Adam había sido simplemente su profesor. Por eso le prestaba atención. Adam era oficial de ambulancia, el puesto más alto de la escala.

A principios de curso, durante la primera semana, la cantidad de información a asimilar había sido tremenda. Luego, paulatinamente, el entrenamiento intensivo había reducido las clases a una a la semana. Los candidatos tenían que acumular sesenta horas de carretera en un equipo de salvamento que se había organizado durante el último mes. Hannah había trabajado mucho. Y sabía que la valoración de sus oficiales pesaría considerablemente en la nota. Un informe desfavorable podía echar por tierra el resultado de los exámenes.

Hannah había alcanzado una cierta confianza en sí misma con el tiempo, había llegado incluso a relajarse. Hasta el punto de llegar a prestar tanta atención a Adam, como persona, como a sus clases. Solo había alcanzado a comprender la medida exacta de ese interés personal al descubrir cuánto se distraía en casa, durante las horas nocturnas de estudio, pensando en él. O después, al echarse en la cama y comprender que era incapaz de dormir. Las imágenes de Adam Lewis invadían su mente, su vida personal, pero la intrusión no le resultaba desagradable.

Aquella era la primera vez, desde la muerte de Ben, en que se interesaba por un hombre. ¿Y por qué no?, se preguntaba. Quizá estuviera preparada. La vida seguía, tenía que seguir. Hannah jamás había esperado que su hija colmara por entero sus necesidades.

—Pareces pensativa, Hannah —comentó Adam en voz alta, atrayendo la atención de toda la clase hacia ella.

—Es que tengo hambre —contestó Hannah.

Hubo carcajadas. Adam anunció que había llegado la hora del descanso y todos recogieron sus libros. Eddie se presentó delante de la mesa de Hannah.

—Voy a la tienda a comprar algo de comer, ¿quieres que te traiga algo?

—No, gracias —sonrió Hannah tratando de rechazarlo suavemente, para no herir sus sentimientos—. Me he traído el almuerzo de casa.

Adam recogió los papeles y libros de su mesa evitando mirar a Eddie y dejó las transparencias y el proyector para utilizarlos después del descanso. La sencillez de la respuesta de Hannah había incrementado la curiosidad que sentía por ella. ¿Cómo sería su casa?, ¿sería una lujosa casa de las afueras, o el típico apartamento en el centro de la ciudad, de chica soltera? Adam la observó una vez más, alejándose con Derek y Christine.

Llevaba vaqueros gastados, botas, una camisa de

algodón remangada y un chaleco de forro polar desabrochado. Ropa cómoda, pero con estilo. No, no le pegaba ni la casa de las afueras ni el apartamento de ciudad. Hannah tenía estilo, sobresalía de lo normal. Y sin hacer el menor esfuerzo. Adam sonrió. Hannah tendría estilo incluso con un saco. O sin nada... Adam suspiró. La clase estaba vacía. Quizá solo tuviera claustrofobia.

Jackie se acercó a Derek, Christine y Hannah, sentados en un banco fuera de clase.

–¡Dios, ese test ha sido horrible! Apenas he acertado una pregunta. Mañana voy a suspender –afirmó abriendo una chocolatina–. ¡Detesto estudiar!

–Y entonces, ¿por qué quieres ser oficial de ambulancia? –preguntó Derek divertido.

–Me encanta el uniforme. Además... –giró la cabeza mirando a John, que pasaba por delante en su bicicleta–... conoces a gente interesante.

–¿Qué harás si no apruebas? –preguntó Hannah, preocupada.

–Volver a intentarlo, supongo –contestó Jackie encogiéndose de hombros.

–Y tú, Hannah, ¿por qué quieres ser oficial de ambulancia?

–Una vez me encontré en una situación en la que una persona necesitaba ayuda desesperadamente –explicó Hannah–. Cuando llegó la ambulancia, no pude evitar envidiar sus conocimientos, el hecho de que supieran qué hacer. Por desgracia, en ese caso, no pudieron hacer nada.

–Tú eras monitora de salvamento para niños pequeños, ¿no? –intervino Christine–. Ese accidente que dices, ¿fue en el agua?

–En cierto sentido –contestó Hannah, deseosa de cambiar de tema–. Y tú, ¿qué te decidió a estudiar para oficial de ambulancia?

–Mis hijos llevan toda la vida sufriendo accidentes y poniéndose enfermos –contestó Christine riendo–. He pasado tanto tiempo en urgencias que se me ocurrió que quizá pudiera comenzar a cobrar por ello.

–Tienes cuatro hijos, ¿no? –preguntó Jackie desenvolviendo una segunda chocolatina–. ¿No crees que el horario de trabajo será un inconveniente, con tanta familia?

–Eso piensa Adam Lewis –suspiró Christine–. Lleva todo el mes metiéndose conmigo porque tengo hijos.

–¿En serio? –preguntó Hannah sorprendida–. ¿Por qué?

–Cree que mis responsabilidades en casa no me permiten trabajar, y menos en una ambulancia. Tengo la sensación de que no aprueba a las madres trabajadoras.

En la primera clase introductoria, cuando todos se presentaron y hablaron de sí mismos, Hannah omitió que tenía una hija. Quería sencillamente salvaguardar su intimidad. Era un alivio que Adam no conociera la existencia de Heidi.

–Aunque no es asunto suyo –continuó Christine de mal humor–. El tema del cuidado de los niños lo tengo solucionado. Su padre los cuidará por la mañana, y yo por la noche. Solo quedan dos días de cada ocho, en los que tendré que contratar a alguien para que los cuide cuando salgan del colegio. Será fácil.

Hannah asintió. Los turnos en la ambulancia eran de cuatro días seguidos de trabajo, y otros cuatro días libres. De esos cuatro días, dos de ellos eran en turno de mañana, y los otros dos de noche. Eran preferibles los turnos largos, de más de ocho horas, para poder disponer de cuatro días libres. Hannah no esperaba tener problemas. Su madre estaba más que dispuesta a ayudar.

Desde la muerte de su marido, hacía años, Norma Duncan había vivido en el campo. Para ella, resultaba demasiado solitario. Volver a vivir con su hija había sido como una bendición. Además de tener una nieta a la que cuidar, vivía de nuevo en Wellington, la capital de Nueva Zelanda. A sus cincuenta y nueve años, había encontrado una nueva dirección hacia la que encauzar su vida. Su entusiasmo por conocer a gente y por hacer algo positivo la había llevado a aceptar un trabajo de jornada partida como recepcionista en una consulta médica. A pesar de ello, estaba decidida a ocuparse de su nieta Heidi. Norma solo trabajaba por las mañanas, pero con el horario de ambulancia Hannah necesitaría una guardería.

–Tener niños jamás es fácil –alegó Jackie convencida–. Yo no pienso tenerlos. ¿Y tú, Hannah?

–Yo no creo que sea tan terrible –sonrió Hannah, deseosa de cambiar de tema de conversación–. Y tú, Derek, ¿por qué quieres ser oficial de ambulancia?

–Por lo mismo que tú –contestó él pensativo–. Como policía, me he encontrado muchas veces en situaciones difíciles, y siempre llegaba antes que la ambulancia. No me gustaba sentir que no podía ayudar.

–¿No os entrenaron en primeros auxilios?

–Sí –respondió Derek–, pero muy poco. Decidí que me gustaba más ese trabajo que el mío.

–Pero tú tienes niños, ¿verdad? –preguntó Christine.

–Sí, tres –confirmó Derek.

–Apuesto a que Adam no te ha dicho nada de que no puedas trabajar en una ambulancia teniendo niños –comentó Christine.

–Bueno, pero yo siempre he tenido un horario parecido –señaló Derek–. Mi familia está acostumbrada.

–Entonces es que Adam es machista –sacudió la cabeza Christine.

Hannah no dijo nada. No era esa la impresión que Adam le había causado. En realidad, había sido precisamente al contrario.

El descanso les había sentado bien a todos. Adam entró en clase a la una en punto.

–Vamos a dedicar la tarde a ciertos casos prácticos de fracturas, pero primero quiero revisar los exámenes y la práctica sobre los daños en la columna vertebral.

Michael abrió el libro de texto por la página indicada. Adam colocó una transparencia en el proyector. Ross y otros siguieron el ejemplo de Michael. Phil se reclinó sobre el respaldo de la silla, jugando con el bolígrafo. Jackie se inclinó hacia John.

–¿Puedes prestarme un bolígrafo?

–Yo tengo uno de sobra –ofreció Anne.

–Esto es un repaso, no hace falta que toméis apuntes –señaló Adam encendiendo el proyector–. ¿Cuál es la clave a la hora de hacer una valoración de un daño en la columna vertebral?

–El shock neurológico –se apresuró a contestar Michael.

–Dolor y parálisis –añadió Ross.

–Vamos a ver... –dijo Adam mirando a su alrededor–. ¿Jackie?

–Parestesia –sugirió Jackie–. O anestesia.

Era evidente que nadie había dado aún con la respuesta correcta. Adam dirigió entonces la vista hacia Anne.

–¿Cuál es el primer síntoma que puede hacernos sospechar un daño vertebral? –volvió Adam a preguntar.

–Umm... –Anne parecía nerviosa–. Supongo que precisamente lo sucedido.

–Exacto –sonrió Adam–. ¿Y qué es, Hannah?

–El mecanismo según el cual se ha producido la herida –contestó Hannah.

–Excelente –sonrió Adam. Hannah bajó la vista incómoda. En realidad no había sido ella quien había acertado–. ¿Y cuáles son esos mecanismos, por ejemplo?

–Compresión –contestó Michael–. Una caída desde cierta altura, o un golpe con un objeto contundente.

–Bien –asintió Adam–. ¿Qué más?

–Incisión –contestó Phil–. Por arma de fuego o arma blanca.

–Distracción –añadió Jackie.

–Colgamiento –añadió Phil.

Adam esperó a que se enumerasen todas las posibilidades y luego preguntó:

–¿Y por qué es tan importante la forma en que se produce la herida?

–Porque el paciente puede estar inconsciente –contestó Derek–. Es posible que no pueda decir qué síntomas tiene.

–¿Es posible tener una herida en la columna vertebral, y no tener ningún síntoma? –preguntó Adam. La clase quedó en silencio–. Hace poco asistí a un accidente de tráfico. Un coche chocó contra un árbol. Solo había una víctima, y cuando llegamos estaba de pie, frente al coche, en medio de la escena. Estaba muy preocupado por los daños del véhículo. Era de su empresa, y no estaba asegurado como conductor, de modo que tendría que pagar la factura de su bolsillo –explicó Adam pensativo, acariciándose la barbilla–. Insistía en que se encontraba perfectamente bien, y se negaba a que lo examináramos o lo lleváramos al hospital, pero yo me fijé en que se rascaba la nuca. Finalmente lo persuadí para que me dejara ponerle un collarín y llevarlo al hospital.

La clase escuchaba con mucha atención. Adam los observó en silencio y continuó:

–Tenía una fractura en la columna. De haber vuelto la cabeza, o haber estornudado, no habría tenido que preocuparse de la factura. Habría quedado parapléjico para el resto de su vida.

La clase quedó impresionada. El impacto de aquella historia quedó interrumpido de repente, sin embargo, por las notas de una melodía. Era el teléfono móvil de Christine que, incómoda, se disculpó y lo sacó del bolso. Adam se molestó.

–¡Oh, Dios! –exclamó Christine segundos más tarde–. ¿Se ha dado muy fuerte? –preguntó, con evidente preocupación–. ¿Y por dónde dices que sangra?

La clase intercambió miraditas. Hannah observó a Adam. Él no apartaba la vista de Christine. Su rostro permanecía inexpresivo.

–Voy a tener que marcharme –se disculpó Christine–. Robbie se ha caído de la bicicleta, quieren que vaya a recogerlo al colegio.

Adam frunció el ceño, pero no de preocupación.

–¿Qué harías si te sucediera esto durante las horas de trabajo? –inquirió con frialdad.

–No lo sé –contestó Christine.

–Pues piénsalo –añadió Adam–. Mañana hablaremos.

Todos se miraron. Hannah bajó la vista. Era evidente que Christine tenía un fuerte obstáculo que superar. Probablemente acababa de echar a perder su última oportunidad. ¿Era Adam demasiado duro con ella o, sencillamente, sería cierto que sus responsabilidades familiares interferirían en el trabajo? ¿Qué ocurriría si Adam descubriera la existencia de Heidi? Hannah trató de olvidarlo. Adam no lo descubriría. No, hasta después del examen, al menos.

Tras la marcha de Christine el ambiente se hizo más tenso. Adam se apartó el pelo de la cara y apagó el proyector. Puso sobre la mesa una bolsa enorme y buscó algo en su interior.

–Esto son collarines –dijo enseñándolos–. ¿Alguien ha puesto alguno alguna vez?

–Yo –contestó Michael.

–Y yo –añadió Anne.

–¿Algún problema?

–No –se apresuró a contestar Michael–. Recuerdo muy bien cómo se hace.

–¿Y tú, Anne? –preguntó Adam.

–Pues a mí me costó –admitió Anne–. La mujer a la que tuve que ponérselo llevaba el pelo largo, y se le enganchaba en el velcro. Se enfadó conmigo, y me puso nerviosa.

–Sí, por mucho que practiques en casa, es muy distinto hacerlo por necesidad –asintió Adam–. Hay cosas a las que no damos importancia, y que pueden suponer una dificultad. Por ejemplo, el pelo o pendientes largos –explicó Adam mirando a su alrededor–. Hannah, ¿te importa sentarte aquí, y soltarte el pelo un momento?

Hannah sacudió la cabeza. Anne y Jackie llevaban el pelo corto. Hannah se quitó la goma que le sujetaba la trenza y se pasó los dedos por el cabello.

–Escoge un collarín, Anne –dijo Adam sacudiendo el pelo de Hannah para que le cayera por los hombros–. Vamos a necesitar a dos personas.

Eddie se puso en pie tan deprisa que tiró la silla, y se dirigió hacia la parte delantera de la clase todo ruborizado.

–Sujeta la cabeza de Hannah recta –ordenó Adam a Eddie–. Y tú, Anne, colócale el collarín.

Hannah sintió los dedos temblorosos de Eddie sujetarle la cabeza. Anne le colocó el collarín sobre el pecho y lo subió hacia el cuello. De inmediato el pelo se le enredó en el velcro. Adam los dejó ensayando unos minutos, pero luego tomó el puesto de Eddie. Hannah sintió la profunda reverberación de la voz de Adam en la cabeza, que él sujetaba contra su pecho.

–Bien, sujeto la cabeza en una postura recta –afirmó Adam–. Anne se lo colocará y se lo cerrará.

Hannah se quedó muy quieta. Podía sentir cada uno de los dedos de Adam sobre su cabeza. Eddie sencillamente la rozaba, Adam la sujetaba con fuerza.

–En cuanto el collarín sujete mínimamente la cabeza –continuó Adam–, moveré esta mano para apartar el pelo –explicó rozando su nuca con los dedos–. Ahora Anne puede cerrárselo y ajustárselo.

Adam soltó el pelo de Hannah y lo observó caer sobre el collarín. Desde el principio había adivinado lo suave y sedoso que sería ese pelo plateado, pero no había podido anticipar la extraordinaria sensación de sus dedos al dejarlo caer. Adam animó a la clase a practicar mientras pensaba en otra cosa. Los observaba a todos, pero a Hannah en particular.

Adam reprimió un suspiro. Aquel interés comenzaba a ser demasiado intenso como para ignorarlo. Hannah no se había molestado en volver a hacerse la trenza. Se había hecho una coleta, pero los mechones se le iban soltando uno a uno por los lados. ¿Cómo no se había dado cuenta antes de que aquel tono plateado de rubio resaltaba sus ojos grises? La respuesta era que, sencillamente, hasta ese momento su interés por Hannah había sido solo profesional.

Desde la primera clase, Hannah le había llamado la atención. Era seria y capaz. Tenía que admitir que, durante el curso, solía mostrarse muy duro con las mujeres. El trabajo de oficial de ambulancia era principalmente para hombres, y por una buena razón. Era un trabajo muy exigente, en muchos sentidos: físico, mental y emocional. Y podía resultar peligroso. Las escasas mujeres que alcanzaban el éxito eran muy especiales, muy inteligentes, y tenían una gran vocación. Se requería fuerza física y emocional.

Hannah sobresalía de entre los demás. Hacía mucho tiempo que Adam no se interesaba por ninguna mujer. Cuando hubieran terminado el proceso inicial de selección, y ella se convirtiera en su colega, quizá pudiera tantearla y ver qué respondía. ¿Por qué no?

Capítulo 3

EL CUERPO no le respondía. Sus piernas hubieran debido sacarla de allí, cuando Michael y Ross decidieron marcharse a casa. Su mente hubiera debido aprovechar la oportunidad cuando John rechazó otro refresco y anunció que se iba. Por fin, mientras Derek se disculpaba, sus piernas seguían sin cooperar.

—Te llevaré a casa, Eddie —comentó Derek.

—No hace falta —contestó el chico sacudiendo la cabeza—. Tengo coche, pensaba llevar yo a Hannah a la suya.

—No puedes conducir —contestó Derek firme—. No soy ex policía en vano.

Eddie se sonrojó y dejó la jarra de cerveza vacía sobre la mesa.

—¡Pero si estamos celebrándolo!

—Naturalmente —sonrió Derek—, hemos aprobado.

—Sí, habéis aprobado —asintió Adam lleno de satisfacción—. Lo habéis hecho muy bien pero, Eddie, Derek tiene razón.

—No importa, Eddie, tengo coche —intervino Hannah—. Me iré enseguida.

—Bueno, entonces supongo que te veré la semana que viene —contestó Eddie molesto, añadiendo, satisfecho—. ¡En el trabajo!

—Bueno —convino Hannah—, pero me temo que no

estamos en el mismo equipo. A mí me han asignado el equipo azul.

—Yo estoy en el rojo —afirmó Eddie desilusionado—. Quizá pueda cambiarme.

—Lo siento —intervino Adam—, es imposible. No podéis cambiar de equipo durante los tres meses de prueba. A veces se cambia al pasar al Grado 1, depende.

—Voy a hacerlo lo mejor que pueda —respondió Eddie serio—. Quiero llegar lejos —añadió soltando un hipo y sonrojándose.

—Por ahora basta con que llegues a casa —señaló Derek poniendo un brazo sobre su hombro y obligándolo a salir.

—Se entusiasma demasiado —sonrió Adam sacudiendo la cabeza.

—Y yo —comentó Hannah riendo.

—Lo harás bien —afirmó Adam serio—. Si alguien va a llegar a alguna parte, esa eres tú.

Hannah bajó la vista con modestia. Había llegado el momento de darle las gracias a su profesor y seguir el ejemplo de sus compañeros despidiéndose, pero sus piernas seguían sin funcionar.

—Lo lamento por Jackie y por Anne. Les defraudó mucho no aprobar.

—Siempre pueden volver a intentarlo —contestó Adam poco conmovido—. Anne necesita más confianza en sí misma, y Jackie... bueno, necesita madurar.

—Christine también ha debido sentirse muy decepcionada. Tenía mucho interés.

—Pues no se ha presentado al examen —se encogió de hombros Adam—. Creo que piensa esperar a que sus hijos crezcan.

–Phil tampoco se ha presentado –añadió Hannah–. ¿Sabes? En cuanto supe que había aprobado corrí a casa a ponerme el uniforme y enseñárselo a mi madre. Estaba orgullosa.

–Debes estarlo –contestó Adam–. Has sido la primera en los test. Felicidades.

–Gracias –dijo Hannah sin poder desviar la mirada de sus ojos. Por fin sus piernas obedecieron y se puso en pie–. Será mejor que me vaya, se está haciendo tarde.

–Sí –confirmó Adam poniéndose también en pie.

Era tarde, no quedaba nadie en el pub. Los empleados limpiaban y recogían. De pronto se hizo el silencio. Hannah estaba en la esquina, y Adam le impedía pasar. Ninguno de los dos se movió.

–Tengo ganas de que llegue el lunes –comentó Adam en voz baja.

–Yo también. ¡El lunes empiezo a trabajar!

–Lo sé –continuó Adam observándola–. Yo también estoy en el equipo azul. Probablemente trabajemos juntos.

Adam sabía perfectamente que irían en la misma ambulancia. Se había ocupado personalmente de organizar los turnos.

–¡Ah! –exclamó Hannah mordiéndose el labio inferior.

–¿Desilusionada? –bromeó Adam.

–No, no es eso –se apresuró ella a contestar.

Adam estaba demasiado cerca de ella. Necesitaba marcharse antes de que él sospechara nada. Su cuerpo accedió a moverse, pero no tuvo éxito. Casi estaba tocándolo.

–Yo... eh... –Hannah tartamudeó y quedó callada.

–Es posible mantener una relación profesional al

margen del terreno personal –afirmó Adam con los ojos fijos en ella–. Me gustaría conocerte, Hannah Duncan.

Adam inclinó la cabeza hacia ella. Si se movía un milímetro, él podría considerarlo una invitación. De pronto Hannah sintió que la cabeza se le ladeaba y que los ojos se le cerraban, y segundos después sintió los labios de Adam rozar los suyos. Él volvió a apartarse casi de inmediato. Hannah abrió los ojos y lo encontró sonriendo.

–No estoy muy seguro de poder esperar al lunes –murmuró él–. ¿Quieres salir conmigo mañana por la noche?

–¿Te parece una buena idea? –preguntó Hannah considerando las dificultades potenciales que una relación íntima en el trabajo podía conllevar.

–Creo... –contestó Adam, volviendo a inclinar la cabeza sobre ella–... que es la mejor idea que he tenido nunca.

Aceptar la invitación de Adam había sido, probablemente, la mejor decisión que Hannah había tomado jamás. La idea de volver a verlo el lunes, añadida a los nervios por emprender un nuevo trabajo, la excitaba aún más. Hannah se miró al espejo satisfecha, con el uniforme. Camisa blanca, detalles en azul marino, y una etiqueta en la que se leía «ambulancia» en rojo. Pantalón azul, botas. Hannah se metió un bolígrafo en el bolsillo de la camisa y una linterna, unos guantes y unas tijeras en el cinturón.

Eran las seis de la madrugada, pero no podía esperar. Entró de puntillas en el dormitorio de Heidi y la besó. La niña se estiró. Hannah sintió remordimientos. ¿Hacía bien dedicándose a una vocación que le quitaría tanto tiempo para su hija?

–¿Va todo bien, hija? –preguntó Norma saliendo de su dormitorio–. No te preocupes por Heidi, se queda conmigo. Ya verás cómo le gusta ir a la guardería, la recogeré a la hora de comer. Iremos al parque, a dar de comer a los patos.

–Debería ser yo quien la llevara al parque –comentó Hannah–. Estaba tan ansiosa por comenzar el trabajo que ni siquiera me había dado cuenta de lo culpable que me sentía.

–Estás nerviosa porque sabes que vas a hacer exactamente lo que quieres. Tienes que vivir, Hannah. Tienes mucho que ofrecer, no puedes encerrarte en casa con Heidi. Además, así podré estar con mi nieta. Tú sabes cuánto significa eso para mí.

–No podría trabajar sin ti –afirmó Hannah abrazando a su madre

–Tú también haces cosas por mí –sonrió Norma–. No me había sentido tan viva ni tan necesitada desde que eras pequeña. ¿Quién sabe?, quizá algún día tengas que hacer lo mismo tú por tu hija –comentó Norma–. Aunque en otras circunstancias, espero. ¿Has desayunado?

–No podría comer nada, mamá. Estoy demasiado nerviosa.

–Todo irá bien –volvió a asegurar su madre mientras Hannah recogía el jersey y la chaqueta del uniforme del perchero–. ¿Sabes con quién te toca trabajar hoy?

–Mmm... con Adam, creo.

–¡Vaya! ¿Es el mismo Adam con el que estuviste hasta las tantas el sábado?

–Sí –contestó Hannah abriendo la puerta–. Adiós, mamá. Deséame suerte.

–No te hace falta –sonrió Norma–. Te las arreglas muy bien sola.

Norma no sabía nada. Hannah aparcó el coche en un hueco asignado a los empleados y observó el Jeep estacionado al lado. Era de Adam. Su gusto refinado la había impresionado. La casa de Adam, situada sobre las colinas dominando el valle de Oriental Bay, tenía vistas espectaculares sobre la ciudad y el puerto. Desde allí habían visto atracar al ferry al ponerse el sol, mientras las luces de la cuidad se iban encendiendo, compitiendo por su atención.

No es que hubieran estado todo el tiempo en la terraza. El hecho de que Adam la hubiera retenido hasta tan tarde el sábado era precisamente lo que la hacía sentirse incómoda. No había esperado conocerlo tan a fondo, tan rápidamente, en la primera cita. Ni jamás habría creído lo maravillosamente bien que se había sentido, lo perfecto que había sido... hacer el amor con él. ¿Cómo trabajar con un hombre que había pasado de ser su profesor a su amante con tanta celeridad? Nada más entrar en el garaje Hannah olvidó sus preocupaciones. Adam estaba de pie, delante de la ambulancia aparcada.

–Ve por un equipo salvavidas, ¿quieres, Hannah? Tenemos un aviso de prioridad 1 y somos la única ambulancia disponible.

Hannah corrió al almacén. Se acordó de meter baterías nuevas y electrodos de repuesto. Adam tenía el motor de la ambulancia encendido cuando volvió.

–Déjalo en el suelo, de momento –ordenó Adam saliendo del garaje.

Adam encendió las luces de emergencia de la ambulancia y Hannah vio reflejarse el azul y el rojo sobre los cristales de los edificios por los que pasaban. Al llegar a una zona de mucho tráfico Adam encendió la sirena.

–El aviso es en Riverside Drive, número 26 –gritó Adam–. Busca en el mapa y dime la ruta más corta. Creo que cruza con Clarence Road. ¿Lo encuentras?

–No –respondió Hannah, que solo había abierto el mapa por el índice para buscar la localización exacta de la calle.

Hannah levantó la vista y comprobó que circulaban por el carril de sentido contrario mientras los coches que iban en su misma dirección, parados en un semáforo, iban despejando el paso. Al aproximarse a la intersección Adam cambió el tono de la sirena, poniendo uno de pitidos cortos. Hannah buscó en el mapa. Había olvidado los números de referencia. De pronto sintió pánico. Su primera tarea, y fallaba. Segundos después gritó aliviada:

–¡Lo he encontrado! ¿Dónde estamos?

–En Clarence Road.

–Bien... entonces tenemos que torcer en la tercera a la derecha. El número 26 debe quedar al final de la calle.

Adam apagó la sirena al llegar a Riverside Drive. Apretó el botón del intercomunicador para notificar a la central de que habían llegado a su destino y apagó el motor.

–Se trata de una persona con dolor en el pecho –le informó a Hannah–. Recoge la botella de oxígeno y tu equipo de primeros auxilios. Yo llevaré el mío.

La puerta de la casa estaba cerrada. Adam llamó y gritó:

–¡Ambulancia!

–Es aquí –gritó una voz desde dentro.

–Puedes encargarte tú, si quieres –comentó Adam mirando a Hannah.

Hannah pasó por delante de Adam y entró en una cocina donde había un hombre sentado. Tenía el rostro gris y una mano sobre el pecho.

–Hola, me llamo Hannah. ¿Cuál es el problema?

–Me duele aquí –contestó el hombre llevándose la mano a la garganta–. Y aquí.

–¿Puede describir el dolor?

–Es como... como si tuviera un camión encima –contestó el hombre con dificultad.

–¿Tiene usted problemas de corazón? –preguntó Hannah observando un medicamento en spray, sobre la mesa, indicado para problemas de corazón.

–Sí, tuve un ataque hace dos años, y desde entonces tengo angina de pecho, pero jamás me había dado tan fuerte.

–Y ese spray de Nitrolingual, ¿le disminuye el dolor? –preguntó Hannah tratando de recordar todos sus conocimientos al respecto.

–Solo al principio. Ahora me duele más que nunca.

–En una escala del 0 al 10, siendo el 10 el dolor más fuerte que haya sentido nunca, ¿qué nota le pondría? –preguntó Hannah respirando hondo mientras Adam iba abriendo la máscara de oxígeno.

Tenía que haber sido ella quien lo hiciera, se reprochó en silencio. Debía haber sacado la máscara mientras hacía preguntas.

–Nueve –dijo el hombre–. No, diez.

–¿Cuándo comenzó?

–Hace una media hora.

–¿Y tenía más síntomas?

–Sí, me sentía enfermo... y comencé a sudar.

El hombre seguía sudando. No tenía buen aspecto. Llevaban en la casa unos minutos, pero Hannah sabía que debía hacer algo más que preguntar. ¿Habría olvidado algo importante?

–¿Quieres sacar los electrodos, Hannah, por favor? –sugirió Adam con calma mientras le ponía la máscara de oxígeno al paciente–. ¿Cuánto tiempo hace que utilizó usted el spray por última vez?

–Justo antes de que ustedes llegaran.

–¿Suele utilizar este medicamento, señor Crombie? –volvió a preguntar Adam tomando el spray de la mesa y leyendo el nombre del paciente en la etiqueta.

Hannah trató de desenredar los cables de los electrodos. ¿Cómo no se le había ocurrido mirar el nombre del paciente en el spray? Eso por no mencionar que había olvidado preguntarle por sus medicamentos habituales. Incluso había olvidado presentarle a Adam. Había demasiadas cosas que recordar.

–Voy a ponerle estos adhesivos, señor Crombie –afirmó Hannah–. Así podremos ver cómo se porta su corazón.

Hannah se concentró en la tarea. El electrodo blanco iba a la derecha, justo debajo del cuello. El negro a la izquierda, y el rojo a la izquierda también, pero debajo. Hannah buscó entonces el equipo de primeros auxilios. Adam estaba abriendo el suyo.

–Voy a ponerle una inyección, señor Crombie –comentó Adam–. Así podremos combatir el dolor. Hannah, ¿quieres tomarle la presión sanguínea, por favor?

–Claro –contestó ella, contenta de seguir órdenes.

–¿Has comprobado el ritmo cardíaco? –preguntó

Adam con toda naturalidad, como si aquello no fuera
una emergencia.

Hannah se mordió el labio inferior vacilante. ¿Se
trataba de una taquicardia ventricular, o de fibrilación? Ninguna de las dos cosas era buena, pero la fibrilación estaba a un paso del coma. La curva de la
pantalla era demasiado regular para que se tratara de
eso.

—¿Es una TV? —preguntó Hannah omitiendo las
palabras «taquicardia ventricular» para no asustar al
paciente.

—Sí —contestó Adam—. Voy a ponerle morfina y
lignocaína. ¿Qué tal se encuentra ahora, señor Crombie?

—No demasiado bien.

—¿Siente mareos?

—Un poco.

—La presión es de noventa y cinco sobre sesenta
—informó Hannah. No era de extrañar que el paciente
se mareara—. ¿Quieres que traiga la camilla?

—Sí, gracias —contestó Adam mientras le inyec-
taba.

Le costó sacar la camilla sola de la ambulancia.
Cuando llegó con ella a la cocina, Adam le adminis-
traba una segunda dosis de lignocaína y la pantalla
marcaba un ritmo cardíaco regular. El riesgo, sin embargo, era aún importante. Adam parecía apurado por
llevar al paciente a un hospital. Colocaron al señor
Crombie sobre la camilla y Hannah recogió el equipo
y lo cargó en la ambulancia.

Hannah se sentó atrás con el enfermo, vigilando
los monitores que indicaban la situación del paciente
y rellenando los documentos necesarios. Al llegar al
hospital los médicos de urgencias se hicieron cargo

del señor Crombie. Adam revisó los papeles y rellenó muchos huecos sin contestar.

–Tienes que adjuntar un diagrama del ritmo cardíaco –informó Adam–. ¿Reconoces las irregularidades de la curva?

–No estoy segura –confesó Hannah.

Adam le explicó el diagrama y Hannah lo estudió mientras él consignaba las cantidades de cada medicamento que le había inyectado. Luego firmó.

–Tienes que indicar cuántos litros de oxígeno le has administrado –señaló Adam–. E indicar el tamaño de la cánula. Aquí.

–¿Era de dieciocho?

–No, de dieciséis –la corrigió Adam–. ¿Has señalado en tu intercomunicador las horas?

–Ni siquiera me he acordado de encenderlo –contestó Hannah de mal humor–. Lo siento.

–No te disculpes, lo has hecho muy bien –contestó Adam quitándose su propio intercomunicador, enganchado al cinturón, para darle la información y terminar de rellenar los papeles.

Tenían que indicar la hora en la que se había recibido el aviso, la hora de llegada a escena y la hora de llegada al hospital.

–Ahora son las siete de la mañana –continuó Adam sonriendo–. Comienza tu primer día de trabajo. Buenos días. Debo añadir que me alegro muchísimo de verte, Hannah.

Hannah sonrió y apartó la vista. Mientras trabajaba, había olvidado la relación íntima que mantenía con su compañero. De pronto sus relaciones personales se ponían de relieve. Quizá, si pudiera olvidarlo de nuevo, se le haría más fácil de lo que había supuesto.

–Puede que nos dé tiempo a tomar un café antes del próximo aviso –sugirió Adam. Instantes después sonó de nuevo el intercomunicador–. Creo que me he precipitado. Es otro aviso de prioridad 1. Dificultades respiratorias. Vamos.

Adam subió la camilla a la ambulancia. Hannah montó en el vehículo. El nuevo paciente resultó ser una mujer de la edad de Hannah, más o menos. Adam le indicó cómo debía respirar y serenarse y los síntomas fueron cediendo paulatinamente.

–Tenía las manos paralizadas, los labios hinchados –se disculpó la mujer asustada.

–¿Y qué tal se encuentra ahora? –preguntó Adam.

–Como una tonta –contestó la mujer violenta–. No deberíamos haber llamado, pero Joe se asustó.

El marido había estado observando la escena con un niño en pijama en brazos.

–Toda la culpa es tuya, no deberías haberte puesto tan nerviosa –le reprochó mientras el niño se echaba a llorar, deseoso de ir en brazos de su madre.

–Ya pasó todo, cariño –lo serenó la mujer sentándolo en su regazo–. Mamá ya está bien.

–Sí, pero ¿cuánto durará? –intervino el marido disgustado–. Cath comienza hoy a trabajar en un nuevo empleo –continuó dirigiéndose a Adam y a Hannah–. Y no creo que pueda con todo.

Hannah sonrió comprensiva. Conocía bien los nervios del primer día.

–No es por el empleo, Joe. Estoy preocupada porque tengo que dejar a Peter en la guardería, y tú lo sabes muy bien –señaló la paciente en tono de reproche–. No creo que le guste.

Adam se encogió de hombros y comenzó a rellanar los papeles.

–Sí, y tú sabes que no podríamos pagar la hipoteca si no vuelves a trabajar –contestó Joe de mal humor–. No fue idea mía que te quedaras embarazada.

El niño se echó de nuevo a llorar al oír los gritos del padre. Hannah observó que Adam estaba tenso, por mucho que lo disimulara.

–Necesito que firme aquí, señora Harvey –pidió Adam–. Es para notificar que atendimos su llamada, pero no fue necesario el traslado al hospital.

Cuando el formulario estuvo completo, Adam se despidió.

–Siento mucho haberles hecho venir –se disculpó la mujer–. Les aseguro que no fue idea mía.

Hannah siguió a Adam hacia la puerta. Podía escuchar los gritos detrás de ella:

–Y supongo que tampoco fue idea tuya quedarte embarazada, ¿no?

–Pues no se puede decir que tú no colaboraras –contestó a gritos la mujer–. ¡Por el amor de Dios, Joe...! ¿es que no ves cuánto le afectan a Peter los gritos?

Adam cerró la puerta de la casa y musitó:

–Familias felices.

–A veces es difícil –contestó Hannah subiendo al coche–. Es difícil compaginar la maternidad y el trabajo.

–No lo sé –contestó Adam serio–. Y, desde luego, no tengo intención de descubrirlo. ¿Te imaginas todas las mañanas así? –preguntó presionando el intercomunicador–. Unidad 241 a Control.

–Adelante, 241 –respondieron inmediatamente.

–No ha sido necesario el traslado al hospital –informó Adam–. Estamos disponibles, en Cranford Crescent.

–Roger. Volved a la central, 241.

–Bien –contestó Adam volviendo a colocar el micrófono en su sitio–. Quizá ahora podamos tomar café.

Hannah observó el edificio de la central de ambulancias, en el centro de Newtown, un barrio nuevo de las afueras cercano al hospital. De modo que Adam no tenía intención de averiguar cómo era la vida de una madre trabajadora. ¿Qué diría si conociera la existencia de Heidi? Hannah no pretendía ocultar una parte tan importante de su vida pero, ¿deseaba terminar con aquella relación recién iniciada? La respuesta era un no rotundo, comprendió mientras sentía que se le hacía un nudo en el estómago. Quizá, sencillamente, a Adam no le gustaran los lunes. O quizá no le gustara el bullicio de los niños. O ser testigo de una disputa matrimonial. Aún tenía mucho que aprender acerca de Adam. Y, a la inversa, él también tenía mucho que aprender de ella.

Al final de aquel primer día Hannah quedó agotada. Era muy diferente de trabajar haciendo prácticas, como mero observador. La gente esperaba mucho de ellos, y eso suponía una enorme responsabilidad. Aquel había sido un día lleno de incidentes, solo habían descansado para comer. Los avisos habían sido múltiples y variados.

Hannah había cometido una serie de errores de menor importancia, pero Adam se había mostrado paciente con ella. La había animado, y ella soñaba con llegar a hacer bien el trabajo algún día.

–Vamos a tomar una copa –sugirió Adam al terminar el turno, tras recoger y limpiar la ambulancia–. Celebremos que has sobrevivido a tu primer día.

–No puedo –se disculpó Hannah, ansiosa por ver si en casa todo había ido bien–. Esta noche no.

–¿Es que tienes una cita? –preguntó Adam decepcionado.

–Claro que no –contestó Hannah–. Ya te he dicho que no salgo con nadie.

–Sí, solo quería cerciorarme –sonrió Adam–. Me has dado un susto. No me gustaría pensar que lo del sábado no va a volver a repetirse.

–No es eso, es que... estoy cansada –contestó Hannah–. Y mañana hay que levantarse pronto.

–Sí, muy pronto. Creo que te toca ir con Tom.

–Ah –contestó Hannah desilusionada.

–Quizá podamos citarnos este fin de semana –sugirió Adam sonriendo.

–Sí, es una buena idea.

–Sí, eso creo yo –continuó Adam inclinándose hacia ella sin tocarla–. Creo que es la segunda mejor idea que he tenido nunca.

–¿Y cuál fue la primera?

–La que tuve la noche del sábado, por supuesto.

Ambos sonrieron. No hacía falta hacer preguntas. Aquella sonrisa prometía una nueva experiencia en común que no desmerecía de la primera.

Y no desmereció. Hannah y Adam comprendieron, durante la noche de su segunda cita en casa de él, la importancia de aquella nueva relación que acababan de comenzar. Durante aquel segundo fin de semana la vida de Hannah pareció cobrar nueva vida. Había tres aspectos nuevos que la llenaban: la casa, el trabajo y... Adam.

La casa no era un problema. Heidi apenas se daba cuenta de que Hannah estuviera ausente. Y, si se daba cuenta, Hannah se lo compensaba haciendo que el

tiempo que estuvieran juntas fuera muy especial. El
trabajo iba siendo cada día más sencillo y llevadero.
Al final de la tercera serie de turnos, Hannah se había
familiarizado con los equipos y protocolos. Se había
ganado una buena reputación en el equipo azul. Se
decía de ella que aprendía deprisa, que era más com-
petente que la mayor parte de la gente en ese estado
de aprendizaje y que siempre estaba dispuesta a ayudar.

Derek, el ex policía de su promoción, estaba también en el equipo azul. Y también se estaba haciendo
popular. Ambos charlaron y estuvieron de acuerdo en
que les gustaba el trabajo, en que se les hacía más fácil de día en día.

A lo que Hannah, en cambio, no estaba acostumbrada, era a estar de nuevo enamorada. Había vuelto
a trabajar con Adam solo una vez más, pero a menudo se encontraban. Durante los turnos nocturnos el
personal charlaba largamente, tomando café. Después de medianoche, se les permitía acostarse en habitaciones preparadas, si no había avisos. Hannah y
Adam apenas usaron esos dormitorios.

Era extraño, pero, hasta el momento, les había
sido fácil mantener oculta su relación ante los demás.
Hannah se llevaba bien con todo el mundo, y si
Adam se acercaba demasiado a ella, nadie parecía
darse cuenta. Hannah no ponía en cuestión las razones que pudiera tener Adam para mantener en secreto
su relación. Ella hacía lo mismo e, incluso, en mayor
medida, al no hablar de su vida en casa con él. Eso
hacía más fácil el trabajo. Quizá Adam opinara lo
mismo que ella, que su relación era demasiado nueva
y preciosa como para airearla, de momento, entre los
demás.

La única persona a la que no podía ocultar lo que sucedía era a su madre. Una tarde de sábado, al final de la tercera semana de trabajo, Norma se sentó junto a su hija. Hannah había hecho un turno la noche anterior, y se había quedado dormida hasta muy tarde. Hacía sol, de modo que salieron a pasear al jardín botánico. Ambas charlaron mientras observaban a Heidi jugar.

–Estás más feliz que nunca, cariño –comentó Norma.

–Soy feliz, mamá –sonrió Hannah–. Casi hasta me da miedo.

–¿Por qué?

–Porque es tan maravilloso, que es imposible que sea cierto. No puede durar.

–Por supuesto que puede durar, incluso puede mejorar.

–¿Te parece? –preguntó Hannah mordiéndose el labio inferior–. Yo me conformaría con que todo siguiera tal y como está.

–No es solo por tu nuevo empleo, ¿verdad?

–No –respondió Hannah observando a su hija que se acercaba.

–¡Mira, mamá!

–Ya lo veo, cariño. ¿Es para mí? ¡Qué hoja tan bonita! –exclamó inclinándose para besar a su hija–. Ve a ver si encuentras otra igual.

–Entonces, ¿cuándo voy a conocer a ese tal Adam? –preguntó Norma.

–No lo sé, mamá. Hay un problema.

–¿Cuál? –preguntó Norma perpleja.

–Adam no sabe nada de Heidi –contestó suspirando.

–Oh... y... ¿hay alguna razón en particular por la que no quieras decirle nada?

–Mmm –asintió Hannah. No deseaba hablar de ello, pero tampoco podía seguir ignorándolo eternamente–. ¿Recuerdas que te hablé de Christine? Estaba convencida de que a Adam no le gustaban las madres trabajadoras. Según decía, las responsabilidades familiares interferirían en el trabajo. Por eso es por lo que no le he dicho a nadie que tengo una hija. Pensé que sería un riesgo a la hora de conseguir el empleo como oficial de ambulancia.

–Pero ahora ya tienes el empleo –objetó Norma.

–Lo sé, pero ahora tengo otra razón para no decírselo.

–¿Cuál?

–Que Adam detesta a los niños.

–¿Te lo ha dicho él? –preguntó Norma incrédula.

–No, me lo dijo Tom. Tom y yo atendimos una urgencia, y Adam vino a echarnos una mano. Teníamos que trasladar a una madre al hospital. No estaba tan grave, pero Adam se negó a que su hija fuera con ella. Era una niña de la edad de Heidi, y estaba realmente desconsolada ante la idea de que la separaran de su madre. Yo le pregunté a Tom por qué no podía ir, y Tom me contestó que Adam detestaba a los niños. Siempre bromean a propósito de ese tema en la central.

–¿Y crees que es cierto? –preguntó Norma.

–No estoy segura –confesó Hannah–. En realidad había tres niños, eran demasiados para llevarlos a todos en la ambulancia. Pero hay más indicios.

–¿Cuáles?

Hannah recordó el caso de la disputa matrimonial, pero se encogió de hombros y no se lo contó a Norma.

–Pues, no lo sé, mamá. Es solo una intuición, en

realidad. Adam hace muchas bromas a propósito de los niños, los llama ratas de alfombra y siempre hace mucho teatro cuando el aviso es pediátrico. Si no los detesta, desde luego finge muy bien.

Heidi volvía en ese momento con un puñado de hojas.

—¡Hola, Nana! ¡Mira, mami! Tengo muchas hojas.

—¿Quieres ir a columpiarte antes de volver a casa, cariño? —le preguntó Hannah sentándola en su regazo.

—¡Sí! —exclamó la niña levantándose de golpe y tirando las hojas—. ¡Vamos al columpio!

—¿Vas en serio con Adam? —preguntó Norma.

—Sí, mamá. Voy en serio, por eso me da miedo de que se eche a perder.

Hannah llevó a Heidi a los columpios y la subió sobre uno de ellos. La niña comenzó a gritar entusiasmada. Norma se había acercado también. Hannah empujaba el columpio una y otra vez.

—Jamás pensé que volvería a sentirme así, mamá. Quizá lo haya olvidado, pero no recuerdo haber sentido lo mismo con Ben. No estaba tan entusiasmada.

—Pues tendrás que decirle la verdad, antes o después.

—Sí, eso trato de hacer.

—¿No te ha preguntado él por qué no lo invitas a casa? —volvió a preguntar Norma.

—Le dije que vivía con mi madre, que está enferma y tiene muy mal carácter.

—Muchas gracias —rio Norma—. Esa no es la mejor manera de comenzar una relación, ¿sabes, cariño? Me refiero al hecho de no ser sincera. No está bien, si quieres que sea una relación profunda.

—Quiero, mamá —contestó Hannah deteniendo el columpio y preguntando—: ¿Quieres bajar?

–¡No, colúmpiame más! –contestó Heidi contenta. Hannah sonrió y siguió empujando.

–¿Y crees que Adam quiere lo mismo? –preguntó Norma.

–Eso espero. Anoche me dijo que me quería, y no era la primera vez –confesó Hannah ruborizada–. Sí fue la primera vez, sin embargo, que yo le contesté que yo también.

–Cuanto más tardes en decírselo –aseguró Norma preocupada–, peor. Más difícil te será.

–Lo sé –suspiró Hannah–. No te preocupes, lo tengo todo planeado. El jueves que viene, en el turno de día, me toca ir en la ambulancia con él. Entonces se lo diré.

–Si te quiere, no le importará –aseguró Norma sonriendo mientras Hannah sacaba a Heidi del columpio–. Todo el mundo adora a Heidi.

–Quizá deba presentársela antes de decirle nada –sugirió Hannah.

–No te lo recomiendo. Es mejor que se haga a la idea primero.

–Pues espero que no le cueste mucho hacerse a la idea.

–Bueno, tú díselo.

–Lo haré –prometió Hannah–. El jueves por la mañana, será lo primero que haga.

Capítulo 4

AQUEL jueves por la mañana, sin embargo, Hannah no tuvo oportunidad de contarle nada a Adam. Nada más llegar a la central había un aviso de prioridad 1. Se trataba de un dolor de pecho. Al llegar, encontraron al paciente tirado en el suelo. Una mujer se arrodillaba a su lado, llorando histérica.

–¿Qué ha ocurrido? –preguntó Adam.

–Hola, ¿me oye? –preguntó Hannah sacudiéndolo por los hombros.

–Dijo que le dolía el pecho –explicó la mujer a Adam–, y luego cayó redondo al suelo.

Hannah comprobó que el hombre no tuviera obturada la garganta y puso una mano sobre su abdomen.

–No responde, no respira –le informó a Adam tensa.

–¡Dios mío, está muerto!, ¿verdad? –gritó la mujer–. ¿Pueden hacer algo?

Adam abrió el equipo de primeros auxilios y Hannah sacó la mascarilla de oxígeno. Se la colocó y apretó la perilla para llenarle de aire los pulmones. Adam le rasgó la chaqueta del pijama. La mujer dio un paso atrás, gritando horrorizada.

–¿Es su marido? –preguntó Adam. La mujer asintió–. ¿Ha tenido problemas cardíacos alguna vez?

–No.

–No tiene pulso –informó Hannah sentándose sobre sus rodillas, con la cabeza del paciente entre las piernas, para comenzar a presionarle el pecho.

Hannah se lo oprimió quince veces y se retiró. Conectó el cilindro del oxígeno a la mascarilla encendiéndolo a plena potencia y volvió a colocarle la mascarilla. Adam, mientras tanto, preparó los electrodos y encendió el monitor.

–Espera, no le oprimas el pecho aún –ordenó.

Ambos observaron la pantalla. La curva había variado con la opresión. Había que esperar la respuesta.

–Fibrilación ventricular –murmuró Hannah, interpretando la curva enseguida.

–Sí –asintió Adam–. Sigue con la respiración.

Adam colocó los electrodos en el paciente y preguntó:

–¿Lista?

Hannah se retiró para no tocar al paciente con las rodillas y contestó:

–Lista.

Al recibir el shock, el paciente se sacudió. La curva de la pantalla, sin embargo, permaneció inmóvil.

–Sigue oprimiendo –ordenó Adam–. Yo recargaré mientras tanto.

El nuevo shock, de doscientos julios, no alteró la situación.

–Recargando a tres sesenta –dijo Adam–. Lo entubaremos y llamaremos para que vengan a ayudarnos.

Hannah asintió. Seguía oprimiendo el pecho del paciente, estaba sudando. Era una tarea dura, pero debía seguir haciéndolo hasta que Adam consiguiera que respirara, entubándolo o administrándole algún medicamento.

–Deja de oprimirlo. Apártate –ordenó Adam–. ¿Lista?

–Lista.

La sacudida del paciente horrorizó a la mujer, que gritó. Adam levantó la vista.

–Hacemos todo lo que podemos –aseguró mirándola–. Voy a meterle un tubo por la garganta para asegurarnos de que le llega el aire.

Hannah estaba a punto de oprimirle de nuevo el pecho cuando miró la pantalla y se dio cuenta de que el paciente reaccionaba.

–Mira, Adam.

–Sí, ha recuperado el pulso –añadió él tomándoselo en la nuca, satisfecho.

El paciente respiró por fin espontáneamente. Adam y Hannah se miraron. Aquel era su primer éxito, y el rostro de Hannah debía expresar vivamente la satisfacción. Adam sonrió. La respiración del enfermo fue haciéndose cada vez más regular. Hannah le quitó la máscara de oxígeno. El paciente gimió y se movió.

–Ponle otra vez la máscara, por si acaso –ordenó Adam–. Hay que asegurarse de que no deje de respirar.

Hannah le colocó la máscara y le pasó a Adam la jeringuilla intravenosa. Por primera vez llevaba a cabo su tarea con prontitud, sin fallar. Estaba eufórica. Rellenaron los papeles y trasladaron al enfermo a la camilla. Para entonces, había recuperado ya la conciencia y fue capaz de contestar a las preguntas de Adam.

–Solo tiene treinta y cinco años –comentó Hannah una vez que llegaron al hospital–, y siempre ha estado bien de salud. Ni siquiera fuma.

–Sí, no hay señal de que haya sufrido ningún infarto anteriormente –musitó Adam–. Puede que se trate solo de un fallo respiratorio. Luego iremos a preguntar.

–¿Crees que se pondrá bien? –preguntó Hannah con ansiedad–. Es tan joven.

–Me alegro de que pienses así, porque yo también tengo treinta y cinco años –sonrió Adam.

–Es mi primer éxito. Hemos logrado resucitarlo.

–Felicidades –contestó Adam sin dejar de sonreír–. Acabas de salvar tu primera vida –añadió orgulloso de ella.

Hannah limpió y recogió la ambulancia y se sentó delante, en el asiento del copiloto, a esperar a Adam. Él seguía en urgencias, hablando por el transmisor con la central.

–Tenemos que ir al aeropuerto. Hay que recoger una carga para un trasplante. De médula espinal.

–¿Sin prisas? –preguntó Hannah.

–Sí –asintió Adam.

Aquel trabajo era todo lo contrario del anterior. Podían ir despacio, no salvarían más vidas aquella mañana.

–Me encanta este trabajo –comentó Hannah de camino al aeropuerto–. Nunca sabes qué va a suceder.

–Sí, la vida está llena de sorpresas –convino Adam.

Hannah se mordió el labio inferior. Ella también tenía una sorpresa que darle, y aquel era tan buen momento como cualquier otro. Tragó nerviosa y sintió que el pulso se le aceleraba. Hubiera deseado haberle contado lo de Heidi semanas atrás. Quizá entonces hubiera sido solo una sorpresa desagradable, en ese momento sería un shock. Y tenía mucho más que perder. Hannah era perfectamente consciente de sus sentimientos hacia Adam. Trató de armarse de coraje. Cuanto más lo retrasara, más difícil sería.

–¡Eh! –exclamó Adam tocándole el brazo–. ¡Que acabas de salvar una vida!

–Ayudé a salvarla –lo corrigió Hannah–. La salvamos entre los dos.

–Así es –confirmó Adam volviendo la vista hacia ella–. Somos un equipo excelente.

–Desde luego.

Por un momento Hannah se dejó llevar por la satisfacción, regodeándose en la cálida mirada de Adam. Incitaba en ella algo más que deseo. Algo más, incluso, que amor. Hannah deseaba compartir con él toda la felicidad que pudiera depararle la vida. Adam volvió la vista hacia la carretera. Entraban en el túnel Mount Victoria.

–¿Sabes lo que le ocurrió a Eddie anoche? –preguntó Adam.

–No –contestó Hannah concediéndose un respiro, un instante de conversación, antes de contarle a Adam nada–. ¿Qué le ocurrió?

–Que se rompió la pierna.

–¿Cómo?.

–Se cayó de la parte de atrás de la ambulancia –explicó Adam con una sonrisa perversa–. Según parece, tenía tanta prisa por salir y atender a un aviso de prioridad 1 que, al abrir la puerta, tropezó.

–¡Dios! ¡Pobre Eddie! –exclamó Hannah sin poder evitar sonreír.

–Una fractura muy fea –añadió Adam serio–. En el fémur, por el centro.

–¿Y con quién iba?

–Con Gary. Tuvo que pedir refuerzos y atender a Eddie. Creo que Eddie no podrá volver al trabajo en un par de meses.

–¿Y el paciente?

–No era grave, gracias a Dios –explicó Adam–. Al final había tres ambulancias en la escena, y mucha gente curioseando.

–Eddie debe estar muy contrariado. Se perderá parte del entrenamiento, y está tan decidido a llegar lejos...

–Pues por el momento tendrá que ir despacio. Estará escayolado durante semanas.

–¿Qué tal le va a Michael? –preguntó Hannah, que había visto poco a sus compañeros de clase.

–Discutió con su compañero, Jim Melton. Michael estaba convencido de saber qué le ocurría al paciente, y según parece no estaban de acuerdo.

–¡Vaya! –exclamó Hannah–. ¿Qué ocurrió?

Adam terminó de contarle la historia de lo sucedido mientras se dirigían al aeropuerto. Un policía de seguridad los saludó y los dejó pasar.

–Justo a tiempo –comentó Adam contento–. Creía que tendríamos que esperar al menos media hora a que aterrizara el avión.

Hannah también lo esperaba. Tenía pensado aprovechar el rato para hablarle de Heidi, pero según parecía había perdido la oportunidad. Y era poco probable que se le presentara otra.

Tardaron más de dos horas en toda la operación, y cuando terminaron recibieron un nuevo aviso. Adam fue el primero en leer el mensaje.

–Prioridad dos –anunció, añadiendo con disgusto–: Se trata de una guardería. Agárrate. Seguramente se trate de una de esas ratas de alfombra.

Hannah no contestó. En lugar de ello, apretó los dientes. Un poco más, y sería imposible contarle nada sobre Heidi. Hannah leyó la dirección del aviso en el intercomunicador. Adam activó las luces de emergencia.

–¿Es en Rupert Bear's Pre-school? –exclamó Hannah segundos más tarde.

–Ya te lo he dicho –contestó Adam sonriendo–. Debe ser un niño y, teniendo en cuenta que es una guardería, será serio.

–¿Por qué lo dices? –preguntó Hannah atemorizada.

Heidi asistía al Rupert Bear's Pre-school, y probablemente estuviese allí en ese momento, porque aún faltaba tiempo para la hora de comer.

–Porque apenas hay medidas de seguridad en las guarderías –explicó Adam con desagrado–. Personalmente, yo no dejaría en ellas ni a un perro.

Hannah se retorció las manos y apretó los dientes. Jamás debía haber aceptado ese trabajo. Hubiera debido quedarse en casa, cuidando de su hija como había hecho durante los dos primeros años de su vida. ¿Y si era Heidi la herida? Hannah cerró los ojos por un momento, tratando de serenarse.

Lo que había dicho Adam sobre las medidas de seguridad no era cierto. Hannah y Norma habían puesto especial atención a ese tema cuando visitaron unas cuantas en la ciudad. La Rupert Bear's era una buena guardería. Las empleadas eran casi todas madres, y Hannah no había dudado en confiarles a su hija. De pronto oyó a Adam gritando.

–¡Vamos, despierta! ¡Necesito la dirección!

–No hace falta que la busque, sé dónde está –afirmó Hannah–. Tuerce a la izquierda en el siguiente semáforo.

–Gracias –contestó Adam sarcástico.

Adam estaba de mal humor, pero pronto lo estaría más aún. La mera idea de estar rodeado de niños lo desagradaba. Hannah se sentía incapaz de pensar en ese momento en las consecuencias que podría tener hablarle de Heidi. Estaba demasiado preocupada por su hija.

Cheryl, la directora de Rupert Bear's, los esperaba en la puerta.

–¡Gracias a Dios que han llegado! Por aquí, es uno de los niños.

–¿Quién? –preguntó Hannah saliendo del vehículo.

–¿Qué ha ocurrido exactamente? –preguntó Adam al mismo tiempo.

Cheryl los miró a ambos alternativamente, preguntándose a cuál contestar primero. Y enseguida reconoció a Hannah.

–¡Dios mío, pero si eres tú, Hannah! –sonrió la directora–. Casi no te reconozco con el uniforme.

–¿Cuál es el problema, señora? –preguntó Adam bruscamente.

–Es Shane. Tiene tres años –explicó Cheryl. Hannah respiró aliviada–. Se cayó de la cama y aterrizó con las manos. Quizá se haya roto la clavícula. Normalmente llevamos a los niños al hospital o llamamos a un médico, pero el pobre chico no hace más que quejarse. Por eso pensé que necesitábamos ayuda.

Mientras hablaba, Cheryl se dirigía hacia la puerta. Hannah caminaba aprisa a su lado. Casi habían entrado cuando llegó Adam. Iba muy despacio, y su falta de preocupación molestó a Hannah. Al menos había recordado recoger el equipo.

Shane estaba en brazos de Megan, una monitora. Le acariciaba el pelo y trataba de calmarlo, pero el niño no paraba de llorar. Adam se agachó.

–Eh, Shane, yo soy Adam –dijo alegremente.

Shane volvió la cabeza por encima del hombro de Megan. El movimiento le arrancó de nuevo el llanto, y Adam pareció alegrarse de no tener que preguntarle nada más.

–Quítale el jersey, Hannah. Utiliza las tijeras. Vamos a ver qué tenemos aquí.

Hannah sacó las tijeras del cinturón. No quería romperle el jersey, sabía lo orgulloso que estaba Shane de él. Su madre le había cosido un dibujo de los teletubby. Hannah se puso nerviosa y miró a su alrededor. Entonces vio la cantidad de madres, niños y profesores que los observaban. Muchas madres habían llegado a recoger a sus hijos para comer. Las empleadas comenzaron a repartir el almuerzo tratando de despejar la zona. Heidi y Norma no estaban entre ellos. Quizá se hubieran ido ya.

Adam se aclaró la garganta impaciente, esperando a que Hannah cortara el jersey. Tras aquella vacilante pausa, Hannah se puso a la tarea. Le cortó la manga del jersey y de la camiseta que llevaba debajo. Adam se apresuró a examinar al chico.

–Se ha roto la clavícula –afirmó convencido–, pero me preocupa más el codo.

Hannah observó la protuberancia del brazo de Shane. ¿Tenía el brazo roto, o solo dislocado? Adam lo palpó tratando de sentir el radio, pero Shane gritó y apartó el brazo.

–Hay que ponerle una intravenosa y darle algo para el dolor –declaró Adam con calma, volviéndose hacia Cheryl–. ¿Puede ayudarnos a sujetarlo, por favor? Tenemos que darle la vuelta. Hannah, agárralo con fuerza para que le coloque el brazo en su sitio. No le va a gustar, pero se pondrá contento cuando le demos un analgésico.

Hannah se echó a temblar. Adam le colocó el brazo en su sitio en un tiempo récord. Luego se lo vendó y le dio un sedante. Shane dejó de llorar. Estaba medio dormido, en brazos de Cheryl.

–Quiero que venga mamá –dijo el niño.

–Lo sé –murmuró Cheryl besándolo–. Mamá nos estará esperando en el hospital. ¿Quiere que lo lleve fuera? –preguntó dirigiéndose a Adam.

–¿Va a venir usted con nosotros?

–Por supuesto. No puedo dejarlo en manos de extraños. Apenas conoce a Hannah, y además, con uniforme, no la reconoce.

–¿En serio? –preguntó Adam guardando su equipo.

–Ven conmigo –intervino Hannah tratando de distraer a la mujer–. Te prepararé un lugar para que te sientes y puedas llevar en brazos a Shane.

Muchos niños habían terminado de comer y estaban fuera, jugando. Hannah dejó a Cheryl en la camilla y salió de la ambulancia para recoger el escalón de subida. De pronto una de las niñas que se marchaba a casa se soltó de la mujer que la acompañaba y gritó:

–¡Mami!

Era un grito de júbilo. El rostro de Heidi mostraba una enorme sonrisa mientras se dirigía hacia ella. Hannah esperó a su hija, y enseguida Norma las alcanzó. Adam también llegó en ese momento.

–¡Dios mío! –exclamó Norma–, pero si no te había reconocido.

–Sí, creía que os habíais marchado a casa –contestó Hannah desesperada, soltando a Heidi–. Ahora tengo que irme.

–¡Yo voy contigo, mami! –gritó Heidi abriendo enormemente los ojos.

–No, cariño. Lo siento, pero tienes que ir a casa con Nanna.

Adam no apartaba los ojos de Heidi. La miraba como si se tratara de un animal salvaje horripilante. Norma y Hannah intercambiaron miradas cómplices.

–Mamá, este es Adam Lewis –lo presentó Hannah.

–Hola, Adam –sonrió Norma amistosamente–. He oído hablar de ti.

–Es mi madre, Adam –continuó Hannah–. Norma Duncan.

–Hola, Norma –contestó Adam atónito–. Yo también he oído hablar de ti. ¿Qué tal la artritis?

–Mmm.... –Norma miró a Hannah sin saber qué decir.

–Luego nos vemos, mamá –se apresuró a decir Hannah, interrumpiendo el violento silencio–. Ahora tenemos que llevar a Shane a urgencias.

Norma recogió a Heidi. Adam hizo un gesto breve y cortés con la cabeza y pasó por delante de ella. Heidi sonreía. Y les decía adiós con la mano.

–Adiós, mamá.

–Adiós, cariño.

Hannah cerró las puertas de la ambulancia y se sentó detrás, con Shane y Cheryl. Adam arrancó. Hannah observó su rostro por el retrovisor. Jamás lo había visto tan serio. Suspiró, y comenzó a rellenar el formulario.

–Cuéntame otra vez lo sucedido, Cheryl.

Al llegar a urgencias, Hannah fue la encargada de entregar el informe.

–Se llama Shane Davidson, y tiene tres años. Se cayó de la cama, que está a unos quince centímetros de alto, y aterrizó sobre la mano derecha. Tiene fracturada la clavícula, y el brazo derecho o bien fracturado o bien dislocado.

La enfermera que había ido tomando nota saludó al niño:

—Hola, cariño. Tu mamá te está esperando. Vendrá enseguida.

—Le hemos puesto 1,5 miligramos de morfina y ha surtido efecto —añadió Hannah tendiéndole el informe.

—Gracias, mandaré a alguien a buscar a su madre.

—Yo iré —se ofreció Hannah—. La conozco.

Natasha Dawson caminaba nerviosa de un lado a otro. Hannah sonrió.

—Shane está bien, Natasha. Ahora está dormido. Se alegrará mucho de verte —añadió indicándole el camino.

—Sabía que ocurriría algo así —suspiró Natasha—. Estaba a punto de cerrar un trato para vender una casa cuando me llamaron, y te aseguro que a mis clientes no les ha gustado nada que saliera corriendo. Si pierdo esta venta, mi jefe se enfadará, pero, ¿qué podía hacer? Shane es mucho más importante para mí.

—Por supuesto, yo habría hecho exactamente lo mismo —convino Hannah.

—Yo no necesito trabajar —confesó Natasha—. No necesito el dinero, quiero decir. Pero me encanta mi trabajo. Si tuviera que quedarme en casa, sería muy desgraciada, ¿y en qué clase de madre me convertiría entonces? —Hannah asintió—. Además, a Shane le encanta ir a la guardería. Es hijo único, y le gusta mucho estar con otros niños.

—El accidente podría haber ocurrido en casa —afirmó Hannah poniendo una mano sobre su hombro–. No necesitas justificarte, nadie te acusa de ser una mala madre.

Excepto, quizá, Adam Lewis, pensó Hannah.

Hannah esperaba que hablaran del tema en cuanto estuvieran solos, pero Adam no dijo nada. En lugar de ello condujo en silencio hasta recibir un nuevo aviso. Era un caso de poca gravedad, un traslado de un anciano de una residencia a un hospital. Hannah buscó la dirección en el mapa.

–Sé dónde está –dijo Adam–. He ido miles de veces.

–Pues yo no, y me gusta saber a dónde voy. Es bueno practicar.

Adam no respondió. Hannah observó su perfil durante unos segundos. Estaba tenso. Y era evidente que estaba demasiado enfadado como para hablar. Tendría que esperar a que él decidiera el momento. Suspiró, y miró hacia la carretera.

De camino al siguiente aviso, Adam seguía sin hablar. Cuando finalmente llegaron a la central, él desapareció en el almacén. Hannah sabía que debía ayudarlo a reponer todo lo necesario en la ambulancia, pero no deseaba encerrarse con él en una habitación tan pequeña donde podía interrumpirlos cualquiera. Aquel no era el lugar más adecuado para discutir. De todos modos, había que cambiar el cilindro de oxígeno, así que Hannah se puso a la tarea. Cuando terminó recibieron el último aviso de aquel turno.

Una hora más tarde, después de hacer el trabajo, Adam condujo la ambulancia hasta una gasolinera para repostar. Hannah estaba convencida de que Adam, sencillamente, no tenía intención de hablar durante las horas de trabajo, pero tras marcharse de la gasolinera él detuvo la ambulancia en el arcén y apagó el motor. Desconectó la radio, cortando así el ruido de fondo de los mensajes entre central y ambulancias, y se hizo el silencio. Estuvieron así, sin hablar, un minuto. Hannah esperó. Por fin había llegado el momento. Fue Adam quien rompió aquel violento silencio.

—Así que... —comenzó a decir serio, de mal humor—... esa era tu madre, ¿no?

—Sí —contestó ella con la cabeza gacha, mirándose las manos sobre el regazo.

—La mujer que está tan enferma de artritis que no puede vivir sola —continuó Adam. Hannah no respondió—. La mujer que detesta a los extraños y tiene tan mal humor, ¿verdad?

Hannah se encogió de hombros. ¿Cuántas de sus mentiras iba a sacar a relucir? Bien, no había sido sincera, pero tenía una buena razón. Hannah se enfadó. Adam había pasado la tarde planeando aquel ataque. Si quería que la discusión resultase desagradable, no iba a ser ella quien cediera sin luchar. En último término, no estaba dispuesta a perder su dignidad.

—En realidad es una persona muy agradable —comentó Hannah con firmeza—. Me mudé a vivir de nuevo con ella cuando nació Heidi, y fue una decisión muy acertada.

—¿Heidi? —repitió Adam con desagrado.

—Mi hija —afirmó Hannah orgullosa. Nadie, jamás, volvería a hacerla vacilar a la hora de declarar que era madre—. Tiene dos años y medio, y es una personita muy especial —añadió mirando de reojo a Adam, cuya expresión la hizo vacilar—. Llevo tiempo buscando el modo de contártelo.

–Y te ha costado mucho, ¿verdad, Hannah? Has tenido semanas, no, meses, para decírmelo. Podías haberlo sacado a relucir en la conversación en cualquier momento. Mira a Christine, que no paraba de hablar de sus malditos hijos.

–¡Exacto! –exclamó Hannah mirándolo a los ojos–. Y tú estuviste metiéndote con ella durante todo el curso. No necesito ese tipo de presión, gracias.

–Yo no me metía con ella –contestó Adam en tono de advertencia.

–Sí lo hacías –lo contradijo Hannah–. Dejaste muy clara tu opinión, y no la dejaste en paz ni un momento. Suspendió el curso en el momento en que la llamaron por teléfono para avisarla del accidente de su hijo.

–Yo no la suspendí, ella no se presentó –se defendió Adam enfadado.

–¿Y quién la presionó? ¿Niegas que tengas prejuicios contra las madres trabajadoras?

–Pero tú no suspendiste, ¿no?

–Tú no sabías que yo era madre.

Adam apartó la vista y comenzó a tamborilear con los dedos en el volante.

–Podías habérmelo contado en cuanto conseguiste el empleo.

–Sí, claro. ¿Cuándo, exactamente?, ¿después de atender aquella llamada de la cual saliste jurando que no querías saber cómo era la vida de una madre trabajadora? –Adam continuó sin mirarla–. ¿O después de que llamaras a los niños ratas de alfombra? O quizá te parezca mejor momento tras exclamar tú que no dejarías ni a un perro en aquella guardería. Detestas a los niños, todo el mundo lo sabe.

Los dedos de Adam dejaron de tamborilear. El si-

lencio fue haciéndose más tenso, pero Adam continuó sin mirar a Hannah. Cuando por fin habló, su voz
sonó tan vacía y falta de modulación como su rostro
carecía de expresión.

–Creía que entre tú y yo había algo especial.

–Yo también lo creía –repuso ella sintiendo que se
le formaba un enorme nudo en la garganta.

–No, tú no lo creías –contestó Adam mirando por
fin a Hannah con una expresión tan desoladora que
ella se estremeció–. Me refiero a algo especial de
verdad, algo con futuro.

–Mi hija es parte de mi futuro, Adam. Es parte de
mí.

–Mi futuro no incluye niños. Ni míos... ni de nadie. Creía que lo sabías, Hannah. Sabías que esto ter-
minaría en cuanto descubriera que tienes una hija,
por eso no me lo dijiste.

Hannah no podía tragar. Hubiera querido llorar,
desahogarse. Pero no podía. Aún no.

–Sí, supongo que sí. No hay futuro para nosotros
dos.

–No, creo que no –replicó Adam–. Lo siento,
Hannah.

–Yo también lo siento –contestó ella observándolo
poner el coche en marcha–. Sabía que esto no sería
una buena idea.

–¿El qué?, ¿mentir?

–No –respondió Hannah tensa–, mantener una relación con un compañero de trabajo. No va a ser fácil
trabajar juntos, ¿no crees?

–Lo superaremos –respondió Adam con frialdad–.
Al menos, yo –añadió mirándola brevemente–. Son
cosas que ocurren, pero se acabó. No pienso dejar
que esto interfiera en mi vida, y tú tampoco debes ha-

cerlo. Nadie sabe nada de lo nuestro –continuó Adam mientras las puertas del garaje de la central se abrían.

Adam salió del vehículo convencido de sus propias palabras. Había vivido cosas peores. Olvidar a Hannah no sería realmente un problema.

Capítulo 5

ERA UN grave problema. Adam había subestimado la dificultad que supondría olvidarse de Hannah. Al principio, el enojo lo había ayudado. Adam trataba de alimentarlo siempre que podía. Hannah lo había engañado, lo había alentado y atraído físicamente hasta hacerlo enamorarse de ella. Había llegado incluso a decirle que la amaba, y eso solo se lo había dicho a otra mujer en toda la vida. Y sin embargo ella había callado, omitiendo reiteradamente decirle que no había futuro para ellos. Y eso sabiendo, sin ningún género de duda, que detestaba a los niños.

En el garaje, Adam le dirigió a Hannah la mirada más severa que pudo. Ella pareció no darse cuenta. Llovía con fuerza. Adam comprobó el motor de la ambulancia y el equipo de primeros auxilios. Hannah se ocupó de la bombona de oxígeno. Pesaba demasiado para ella, pero Adam reprimió el deseo de ayudarla.

Tom Bagshaw llegó entonces para hacer su turno de día con Hannah. Iba bostezando, pero eso era habitual en él aquellos días. Hacía un par de meses que había tenido su primer hijo, y estaba orgulloso de perder las mismas horas de sueño que su mujer. Adam lo miró de mal humor.

—Tienes ojeras y cara de cansado. Otra vez.

–Merece la pena, compañero –sonrió Tom.

Hannah volvió la cabeza hacia ellos al oír la voz de Adam, pero solo miró a Tom.

–Hola, Tom, ¿qué tal estás?

–Agotado –contestó Tom contento–. Esta noche me he levantado cuatro veces. ¿Quieres que te eche una mano con el oxígeno?

–No, puedo arreglármelas sola.

–Entonces me ocuparé del equipo –se ofreció Tom.

–Eso ya está hecho –contestó Hannah.

–¡Excelente! ¿Listos para marcharnos, entonces?

–Cuanto antes, mejor –contestó Hannah limpiándose las manos en la ropa–. Solo falta la revisión mecánica.

Adam cerró el equipo de primeros auxilios de golpe. Quizá Hannah creyera que era sutil, pero él se daba cuenta. La única razón por la que tenía prisa por marcharse era él. Tras la discusión del jueves anterior, los días siguientes habían sido muy tensos, por decirlo de una manera suave. Por suerte no les había tocado salir en ambulancia juntos. Durante los turnos de noche, tanto Hannah como Adam habían hecho uso de los dormitorios después de medianoche, saliendo solo cuando se producían avisos. Apenas habían coincidido. Adam había esperado que los cuatro días libres les sirvieran para disipar la tensión, pero por desgracia parecía ser al revés.

¿Por qué diablos había puesto tanto empeño en que Hannah ingresara en el equipo azul?, ¿por qué había dejado que aprobara el curso con tanto éxito? Adam dejó el equipo de primeros auxilios en la ambulancia y comprobó las mascarillas de oxígeno. Aún podía ver a Hannah. Estaba de pie junto al vehículo de al lado, haciéndole señales a Tom para indicarle que las luces de la ambulancia funcionaban bien. Luego comprobaron la sirena y las luces de emergencia.

Por supuesto que no había podido suspender a Hannah, debía estar contento de que estuviera en el equipo azul. Lo que no debía haber hecho, sin embargo, era dejar que su atracción por ella sobrepasara ciertos límites. Hubiera debido de mantener con ella una relación estrictamente profesional. Lo único positivo de aquella situación era que ninguno de sus colegas conocía su relación, de modo que nadie sabía lo estúpido que había sido. Matt, el compañero de Adam de ese día, llegó en ese momento y preguntó:

—¿No ibas a hacer tú hoy el tercer turno?

—Lo cambié —respondió Adam esperando que Hannah estuviera escuchando—. Con Tom.

¿Pensaría Hannah que había sido él quien lo había cambiado, en lugar del director de la central?

—Tengo suerte —comentó Tom.

—Ya sé por qué lo ha cambiado —le dijo Matt a Tom—. Es por el trabajo que hay que hacer a las nueve de la mañana.

—¿Qué trabajo es? —preguntó Hannah.

—Hay que ir a un colegio en Naseby Street —explicó Matt colgándose el intercomunicador en el cinturón—. ¿Os imagináis que mandaran a Adam a esa misión?

Tom se echó a reír. Hannah ni siquiera sonrió. Ni Adam, que se marchó en dirección al almacén.

—Creo que alguien se ha levantado hoy con el pie izquierdo —comentó Matt.

—Sí, solo de pensar en esos chicos se pone enfermo. Para Adam es una pesadilla.

Adam abrió la puerta del almacén y dejó que se

cerrara de golpe. ¿Por qué había permitido siempre que se extendiera el rumor de que odiaba a los niños? Quizá, si Hannah conociera toda la verdad, se daría cuenta del daño que le había hecho. Se daría cuenta de que no tenía derecho a estar tan enfadada como él.

Adam buscó las mascarillas y el resto del equipo que necesitaba. Nadie sabía la verdad. Aquella parte de su vida había quedado atrás el día en que se mudó a vivir a aquella ciudad y comenzó a trabajar como oficial de ambulancia. Habían pasado muchos años, el pasado estaba enterrado. Era el único modo de continuar. Adam había encontrado el modo de seguir adelante, y no iba a dar un solo paso atrás. Ni tenía intención de contarle nada a nadie. Ni siquiera a Hannah Duncan.

El primer aviso de Hannah y Tom de aquel día fue un traslado. Tenían que llevar a una anciana a un centro de rehabilitación tras una operación. Para cuando llegaron de vuelta a la central eran las ocho y media. La lluvia torrencial había cesado, y un fuerte viento se llevaba las nubes que quedaban.

–No vamos a llegar a tiempo al colegio –observó Hannah.

–No –contestó Tom pensativo–. Central, aquí unidad 225.

–Adelante, 225.

–Estamos de vuelta, pero no llegaremos a Naseby Street hasta las nueve y media. Quizá debáis mandar a la unidad 241.

Hannah abrió inmensamente los ojos y sonrió. Si Adam estaba en su vehículo, lo habría oído. No era más que una broma, pero Adam no era precisamente muy feliz aquellos días. ¿Por qué no dejarlo sufrir, como sufría ella? La semana anterior había sido un suplicio.

Bien, era cierto, había hecho mal en no decirle nada pero, ¿por qué la existencia de su hija tenía que significar semejante catástrofe para los dos? Si Adam la quería, debía aceptar todo aquello que formara parte de su vida. De haber sido al revés, y ser Adam quien tuviera una hija, ella no habría puesto pegas a la hora de continuar con su relación. La central tardó unos minutos en contestar a Tom:

–Negativo, 225. Naseby Street tendrá que esperar.

–Adam no ha picado el anzuelo –comentó Tom dejando el micrófono.

–¿Por qué odia tanto a los niños? –preguntó Hannah.

–No tengo ni idea –contestó Tom encogiéndose de hombros–. No lo entiendo. ¿Te he contado ya que Harry empieza a sonreír?

–Sí, me lo has contado.

–Creo que le va a salir un diente.

–Es un poco pronto, con ocho semanas –contestó Hannah–. A Heidi no le salió el primer diente hasta los ocho meses.

–Algunos niños nacen con dientes. Lo he leído en un libro –afirmó Tom.

Hannah asintió. Tom estaba encantado de ser padre. Su sorpresa, la semana anterior, cuando Hannah le contó que tenía una hija, había sido tal que, desde entonces, aprovechaba todas las oportunidades que se le presentaban para hablar de su hijo. Hannah, en cambio, hubiera preferido hablar de otra cosa.

–¿Cuánto tiempo hace que conoces a Adam?

–Cuatro años –contestó Tom–. Ya estaba aquí,

cuando llegué yo. Eso fue justo después de que me casara con Jane. ¿Sabes que nos costó tres años que se quedara embarazada?

–¿Sabes si Adam ha estado casado?

–No, ¿qué te hace penar eso? –preguntó él sorprendido–. ¿Es que te interesa?

–En absoluto –rio Hannah–. Es solo curiosidad. Jamás habla de sí mismo.

–Justo lo contrario que yo, quieres decir –sonrió Tom–. Hubo un tiempo en que se rumoreó que había estado casado, pero ya sabes cómo son estas cosas. Él jamás habla.

–¿Cuánto tiempo lleva trabajando aquí?

–Unos cinco años, creo, pero estaba ya antes en el servicio de ambulancias. Hizo el entrenamiento en Australia, y era oficial cuando vino a Nueva Zelanda.

–Creo que ha mantenido relaciones con mujeres una o dos veces desde que está aquí –comentó Hannah.

–Bueno, él no habla mucho –asintió Tom–, pero yo jamás lo he visto salir dos veces con la misma mujer. ¿Estás segura de que no estás interesada?

–Me gusta trabajar con él –admitió Hannah–. Y me lo pasé muy bien durante el curso. Como profesor, es brillante. Me sorprende que no esté casado.

Debía habérselo preguntado a Adam mientras aún se dirigían la palabra. Había tenido muchas oportunidades, pero el instinto le había aconsejado no hacerlo. De haberle contado Adam algo personal, ella se habría visto obligada a hacer lo mismo. Guardar silencio había sido mucho mejor para los dos. En casa de Adam no había nada que hubiera podido darle una pista, y no era que no las hubiera buscado. Simplemente no había una sola fotografía.

–Este horario de turnos puede resultar muy estresante para las parejas –comentó Tom–. Sobre todo para las familias jóvenes. Quizá Adam quiera evitar el agobio. No todo el mundo puede soportar la tensión de tener niños en casa, con sus horarios de biberón y cambio de pañales.

–Tú sí –sonrió Hannah.

–Cierto –asintió Tom orgulloso–. ¿Cuánto tiempo tenía tu hija cuando comenzó a dormir toda la noche de un tirón?

–Seis meses –contestó Hannah resignándose a hablar de bebés durante el resto del día–. Aunque, claro, cuando comenzaron a salirle los dientes, volvimos atrás otra vez.

El trabajo en el colegio de Naseby Street fue todo un éxito.

–Hannah es madre, y eso se nota –comentó Tom después a sus colegas aquel día–. Tenía a los críos hechizados.

–Quizá debieras haber sido maestra –sugirió Matt.

–Aún puede serlo –intervino Adam levantando la vista del periódico que había estado fingiendo leer–. Seguro que acaba harta de trabajar aquí.

–Ya he escogido profesión, gracias –contestó Hannah mientras preparaba café, volviendo la cabeza para mirar a Adam, de espaldas.

–Sí, Adam, no le des ideas –añadió Tom–. Nos gusta tenerla con nosotros.

–Además, en este trabajo también hay que tratar con muchos niños, ¿verdad, Adam? –insistió Matt, bromeando.

Adam gruñó y pasó una página del periódico. Tom se sentó en la mesa de aquella sala de empleados.

–Casi es la hora de marcharse a casa –comentó satisfecho–. ¿Qué tienes planeado hacer esta noche, Hannah?

–Lo de siempre –respondió ella–. Bañar a Heidi y leerle un cuento. Luego me dedicaré a hacer algo realmente aburrido, como lavarme el pelo.

Adam volvió a pasar otra página. ¿Por qué no encontraba un solo artículo interesante? Necesitaba borrar de su cabeza la imagen de Hannah acurrucada en un sofá, con el pelo recién lavado, y una niña pequeña abrazada a ella. Casi podía oír su suave voz contando un cuento.

–Voy a lavar la ambulancia –dijo Adam levantándose de su silla bruscamente.

Tener algo que hacer no sirvió de nada. No podía dejar de imaginar a Hannah lavándose el pelo. O, peor aún, peinándoselo aún mojado, mientras los rizos le caían por la espalda. Conocía la sensación de aquellos rizos entre los dedos. Casi podía sentirlos acariciándole la piel. Adam juró entre dientes, golpeó el cubo de agua sin darse cuenta y lo tiró.

Pronto podría marcharse de allí, y quizá fuera capaz de olvidarla si no la tenía delante. De camino a casa, compraría comida preparada y escucharía música con una copa de vino. O, mejor aún, leería un libro. Adam siempre había tenido facilidad para engancharse a la lectura con un libro de ficción, siempre había sabido olvidar sus problemas para centrarse en los de los personajes.

Pero en aquella ocasión no lo consiguió. Por alguna razón, su escritor favorito no lograba cautivarlo. Los personajes parecían de cartón piedra, no tenían ni idea de qué era el amor. El autor, probablemente, jamás se hubiera enamorado. No como él se había enamorado de Hannah. O quizá fuera él el que se equivocara, quizá no estuviera en absoluto enamorado. Había estado enamorado de Linda, se había casado con ella y, sin embargo, jamás había estado obsesionado como lo estaba con Hannah. Jamás se había puesto tan nervioso al verla como cuando veía a Hannah. Ni jamás había tenido que hacer tal esfuerzo de voluntad para no acariciarla todo el tiempo. Adam nunca había puesto en cuestión el amor o la relación que había mantenido con Linda. Hasta ese momento.

El libro que tenía entre las manos pareció cerrársele por sí solo, sin ningún esfuerzo. Había comenzado a recordar pero, por mucho peligro que eso supusiera, Adam no dio marcha atrás.

Linda. La callada y valiente Linda. Valiente porque tenía miedo a muchas cosas, pero no dudaba en enfrentarse a ellas. Por ejemplo a un difícil embarazo y a un parto interminable y fatal. Tras el nacimiento de la niña, apenas se había quejado. Había aceptado el pronóstico del médico sin más, en silencio. Linda había permanecido estoicamente en cama durante dos días, hasta que fue evidente que lo que tenía no podía ser gripe. Pero entonces fue ya demasiado tarde para luchar contra la galopante infección postparto. Linda había muerto a los dos días de nacer Madison.

Adam terminó la copa de vino y se sirvió otra. Ya no había vuelta atrás, seguiría recordando. Últimamente apenas se acordaba del pasado. Quizá, en aquella ocasión, no le resultara tan doloroso.

En aquellos años oscuros Adam no había recibido la ayuda de nadie. Su familia no hizo nada por él, y la de Linda lo culpó de la muerte de su hija. El caso había aparecido en los periódicos como ejemplo de escasez de personal médico y presión laboral, caso que había terminado en un diagnóstico apresurado y erróneo. Los padres de Linda habían puesto una demanda al hospital, pero Adam no había querido colaborar. Había preferido centrarse en su hija recién nacida, canalizando la pena hacia la única luz al final del túnel que era capaz de ver.

Tras la muerte de Linda, Adam había pedido un año sabático en su trabajo como oficial de ambulancia. Quería ocuparse de su hija. Madison dejó enseguida de ser una distracción para pasar a ser el centro de su vida. Tenía un precioso cabello rubio rizado, y sus enormes ojos marrones y su sonrisa cautivaban a todo el mundo. ¿Por qué la hija de Hannah tenía que parecérsele tanto?

¿O no se parecían? Adam apartó la copa de vino y sacó de la librería una caja con forma de libro. Guardaba dentro los preciosos recuerdos de los que no había podido separarse, por mucho que le doliera contemplarlos. Llevaba cinco años sin mirarlos, desde que había llegado a Nueva Zelanda a comenzar una nueva vida.

En la caja había un brazalete hospitalario de identificación, un par de botitas de lana y dos anillos de boda. Al fondo, certificados de nacimiento, de defunción y de matrimonio. Y fotos. Quince, por lo menos. Una de Adam y Linda el día de la boda, el resto de Maddy.

Adam sacó la foto del fondo. En ella Maddy tenía precisamente dos años y medio, la misma edad que Heidi. No eran tan parecidas. Los ojos de Heidi eran azules, y su cabello era más espeso y de un tono diferente. Acabaría siendo rubia platino, como su madre. Maddy, en cambio, no se parecía a Linda. Jamás había sentido miedo, y no era callada.

La imagen de la foto quedó borrosa por las lágrimas. Adam sintió los tentáculos del dolor aferrarse a su corazón. Aquella había sido la última foto que había tomado de su hija. Al día siguiente estaba muerta. Y la culpa era suya. Adam seguía preguntándose aún qué habría ocurrido si...

Si no hubiera decidido volver al trabajo, si no hubiera necesitado algo más en su vida, aparte del hecho de ser padre, y se hubiera sentido satisfecho dedicándose únicamente a su hija... Si hubiera podido pagar a una niñera en lugar de llevarla a la guardería, si no hubiera estado de servicio precisamente aquel día... Si no hubiera sido justamente él quien acudiera con la ambulancia al aviso, encontrándose a su hija inconsciente tras una caída... Madison no se habría caído del árbol si la guardería hubiera dispuesto de las suficientes medidas de seguridad. La niña ni siquiera llegó a recuperar la conciencia.

Adam volvió a dejar la caja en la librería, a dejar los recuerdos atrás. Le había costado menos de lo que esperaba, quizá incluso pudiera dormir sin pesadillas. Había hecho bien enterrando los recuerdos, apartándose de los niños sin dejarse embelesar por ellos. Jamás volvería a exponerse a semejante riesgo. Había construido una muralla en torno a su corazón, y así había permanecido en pie, durante más de cinco años, tras la desoladora muerte de Maddy.

Y, por la misma razón, también las mujeres quedaban al otro lado de la muralla. Evitando el peligro, jamás sentiría dolor. Por el momento la estrategia había funcionado. Una aventura ocasional de vez en cuando, algo de sexo... nada importante. Nada que pudiera dejar después vacío su corazón.

¿Por qué diablos no funcionaba con Hannah?

Capítulo 6

NO IBA a ser fácil. Hannah observó el horario sobre el tablón de anuncios de la sala de empleados. No cabía error. Le tocaba salir con Adam en la ambulancia esa noche, y tendría que soportarlo. Pero no sería fácil. Bastante difícil había sido ya coincidir con él en los descansos. Aquella noche compartirían la estrechez de la cabina del vehículo.

Y Adam, evidentemente, sentía lo mismo. No sonrió al saludarla. A los dos les llevaría tiempo. Hannah revisó el equipo y esperó a que Adam saliera del almacén para ir a buscar recambios. Era domingo, y se celebraba un partido de rugby. Un aficionado, al menos, resultaría herido. Probablemente más.

A las seis y media de la tarde la unidad 241 estaba lista. El aviso era de prioridad 3, así que tenían media hora para llegar. El paciente, en la sala de maternidad de un hospital rural a media hora de la ciudad, no estaba grave. Se trataba de un recién nacido que había que trasladar a cuidados intensivos.

—Parece que va a llover —comentó Adam tras unos cuantos minutos en silencio.

—Sí, hoy ha hecho frío —respondió Hannah.

—En septiembre siempre llueve mucho.

—¿En serio?

—Mmm.

Hannah miró a ambos lados. Adam mantuvo la vista

fija al frente. ¿Era a eso a lo que se había reducido su relación, a una conversación cortés a propósito del tiempo? Probablemente era mejor que el tenso silencio. Hannah vio de reojo que Adam tenía ojeras. Hasta el momento se había alegrado de que él sufriera tanto como ella. Preocuparse por él resultaba muy molesto. Hannah tomó las hojas del aviso y comenzó rellenarlas.

–¿Qué sabemos del paciente? –preguntó, ya que había sido él quien había contestado por el interfono.

–Que nació con treinta y seis semanas de gestación, hace unas dos horas. No respira del todo bien, así que el médico ha preferido mandarlo a cuidados intensivos.

Hannah escribió la dirección del hospital rural y rellenó la casilla sobre el motivo del aviso con las palabras «traslado». Al menos el bebé permanecería callado, en la incubadora, y no molestaría a Adam.

–¿Vendrá algún médico acompañante?

–Eso creo.

–¿Sabemos el nombre?

–Escribe simplemente bebé Mulligan.

–¿Mulligan?

–Es el apellido. ¿Qué tiene de malo? –preguntó Adam dirigiendo la vista por fin hacia ella.

–Nada –contestó Hannah mordiéndose el labio. No creía haber pronunciado el apellido con excesivo énfasis. ¿Cómo podía haberlo notado Adam? Él volvió a mirarla por segunda vez, y ella suspiró resignada–. Ese hubiera debido ser mi nombre, de haberme casado. Con el padre de Heidi –añadió tras una pausa.

–¿Y por qué no os casasteis?

–Él murió –respondió Hannah escuetamente–. A los pocos días de descubrir que estaba embarazada.

–Entonces, ¿pensabais casaros? –preguntó Adam tras una pausa.

–Claro, llevábamos dos años de novios. Nos conocimos en Londres, pero yo quería volver a Nueva Zelanda antes de casarnos. Nos queríamos –continuó Hannah en voz baja–. Y estábamos muy ilusionados con el bebé.

En aquella ocasión, el silencio que se produjo fue más prolongado. ¿Estaría Adam comparándose con Ben?

–Y... ¿qué pasó? –preguntó Adam de repente.

–Que se ahogó –contestó Hannah tensa, volviendo a suspirar–. Bueno, en realidad no fue así. Tenía un problema cardíaco congénito del que nadie tenía noticia. Se le paró el corazón y murió instantáneamente, solo que justo en ese momento se estaba bañando en el lago.

Casi habían llegado a su destino cuando Adam volvió a preguntar:

–¿Y tú...? –vaciló–... ¿trataste de salvarlo?

–Sí.

–Debió ser terrible –comentó Adam con ojos compadecidos.

–Sí –contestó ella escuetamente, negándose a aceptar su compasión.

–¿Sigues teniendo pesadillas? –preguntó Adam en voz baja.

Hannah volvió la vista hacia la ventanilla. Su respuesta no fue ni positiva ni negativa. Quería demostrarle que aquella pregunta era demasiado personal. Adam ya no tenía derecho a obtener una respuesta.

El silencio que siguió fue menos tenso. Adam no tenía ni idea de lo cerca que había estado de la verdad. Hannah había vuelto a tener la pesadilla esa misma noche, pero diferente. Peor. Porque en esa ocasión no había sabido distinguir el rostro del hombre que se ahogaba. ¿Era Ben, o Adam? ¿Cómo era posible que Adam hubiera podido derribar el muro que protegía su corazón?, ¿y cómo diablos volver a echarlo de él?

–No debería habértelo preguntado –comentó Adam en tono de disculpa–. Sé muy bien que hay ciertas cosas que es mejor no desenterrar.

–¿En serio? –preguntó Hannah dejándose llevar por la curiosidad.

–Yo... estuve casado... durante muy poco tiempo –explicó Adam–. Ni siquiera llegamos a conocernos bien. Mi mujer también murió inesperadamente. Y de la manera más tonta.

–Lo siento.

Hannah hubiera deseado hacerle más preguntas. Miró a Adam y trató de averiguar hasta qué punto se mostraría comunicativo. Aquella mirada de Hannah le hizo desear a Adam contárselo todo. Sin embargo sus mecanismos de defensa estaban a punto, recién apuntalados. Y ya había hablado demasiado, aquello era el máximo que podía dar en respuesta a las revelaciones de Hannah. Ella había salido del drama más entera que él, había tenido mucha más suerte.

–Pertenece al pasado, y allí es donde estar –suspiró Adam–. No debí preguntar. A mí, por lo menos, no me gusta que me pregunten.

Hannah volvió la vista hacia la ventanilla. De modo que la vida personal de Adam quedaba fuera de su alcance. Tanto como la suya para él. Era justo. Tampoco ella tenía derecho a preguntar. Al llegar a su destino ambos perdieron la oportunidad de recuperar la confianza mutua.

–Sacaré la rampa –se ofreció Hannah–. Hará falta para subir la incubadora, ¿no?

El viaje de vuelta se desarrolló sin incidentes. Los acompañaron una enfermera y los padres del bebé. Hannah observó al bebé, de cabellos negros como el padre, y comentó:

–Se ve que el niño ha salido a usted.

–Sí, es completamente irlandés –contestó la madre sonriente.

–¿Han decidido ya el nombre?

–Bueno, llevamos ocho meses llamándolo Paddy. Es pegadizo. Era el nombre de su abuelo.

–Los abuelos de mi hija también son irlandeses –comentó Hannah, consciente de que Adam la escuchaba–. Algún día la llevaré a Irlanda a que los conozca.

–¿Es morena también?

–No, es como yo –respondió Hannah tomando un mechón de su pelo–. Al menos no tendrá que preocuparse cuando le salgan canas. Nadie las distinguirá.

Los cabellos de Hannah no eran grises, sino plateados. Tenían un tono absolutamente único, uno entre mil. Aquella noche Adam fue muy consciente de la presencia de Hannah. Ella lo hizo todo, hasta limpiar vómitos, con eficacia y buen humor, como siempre. Había probado la amargura de la vida, y sin embargo seguía adelante, sin miedo, lista para afrontar lo que fuera. Como por ejemplo el amor. Adam sabía mejor que nadie lo que debía haber sufrido tratando de salvar a su novio.

Quizá también él debiera echar fuera de su corazón los demonios del pasado, compartir sus expe-

riencias negativas con otra persona por primera vez.
Y, de hacerlo, sería con Hannah. Pero no era posible.
Sería dar demasiado de sí mismo, hacerse vulnerable.
Porque en realidad Hannah no conocía lo peor que la
vida podía ofrecerle, no había perdido a su hija.

Quizá, con el tiempo, Adam acabara confiando en
otro ser humano. Quizá incluso pudiera arriesgar
todo lo que había conquistado en los últimos cinco
años. O quizá, una vez más, lo de Hannah no fuera
más que una obsesión. Quizá se cansara de ella, si la
conocía lo suficiente. Entonces volvería a ver las cosas bajo otra perspectiva, y no más negativa. Al contrario, estaría mejor, porque se habría librado de la
obsesión y de la constante frustración de no poder
acariciarla. Tenía que haber una salida para su situación.

Lo que Adam no esperaba era que esa solución se
la ofreciera Enid Packman, una mujer de noventa y
seis años. El aviso llegó a las tres de la madrugada.
Cuando llegaron a Spring's Orchard Retirement Village, la residencia de ancianos, Adam seguía tratando de olvidar el delicioso aspecto de Hannah al
salir del dormitorio de la central.

–¿Tú qué crees, Hannah?

–¿Dónde dice que le duele, señorita Packman?

–En la pierna. Es terrible, pero solo me duele
cuando la muevo.

–Probablemente se haya fracturado el fémur izquierdo.

–Le daremos un calmante y le pondremos almoha-
das entre las piernas antes de moverla –asintió
Adam–. ¿Qué estaba usted haciendo, para caerse de
noche?

–Levantarme a desayunar, ¿qué otra cosa iba a hacer? –preguntó la señorita Packman–. Dios sabe por qué ponen el desayuno a media noche, pero no seré yo quien proteste. Olí las gachas, así que me levanté. Y entonces me caí. Si vais a servir el desayuno a esas horas, al menos encended la luz –añadió en tono de reproche, dirigiéndose a una de las cuidadoras del centro.

Hannah apenas podía contener la sonrisa. Miró a Adam y vio que él también sonreía.

–¿Qué tal se encuentra ahora, señorita Packman? Aparte de la pierna, claro –preguntó Adam.

–Estoy enfadada –declaró la paciente–. Y tengo hambre. Quiero gachas.

–¿Le duele el pecho? –insistió Adam, que conocía la historia cardíaca de la enferma.

–No. Y que sea con azúcar morena y crema. Con poca crema. No me va bien para el corazón –añadió la paciente–. Además, tengo que cuidar mi figura.

–Claro –convino Adam sonriendo–. Está usted estupenda, señorita Packman. Ahora voy a inyectarle un calmante para el dolor. La llevaremos al hospital.

–¿Sirven gachas en el hospital?

–A montones –contestó Adam ajustando el torniquete al brazo de la anciana–. No es usted alérgica a nada, ¿verdad?

–No me gusta la mantequilla de cacahuete –contestó la señorita Packman mientras Adam le buscaba la vena–. Se me pega a los dientes. Aunque, en realidad, no son míos –añadió para Adam, en un aparte.

–Me refiero a medicamentos, señorita Packman –sonrió Adam–. ¿Ha tenido alguna reacción adversa a alguno, alguna vez?

–No, no se menciona ninguna alergia en su historial –intervino la enfermera de la residencia.

–Soy alérgica a los hombres –comentó la señorita Packman dirigiéndose a Hannah–. Por eso no me casé.

–Muy inteligente –sonrió Hannah.

–Sí, pero es que jamás conocí a nadie tan atractivo como tú –continuó la paciente señalando a Adam–. Ni tan amable. Apenas me has hecho daño.

–Es que aún no le he clavado la aguja –contestó Adam reprimiendo la risa–. Ahí va.

–Pues no he sentido nada. ¿No es encantador, este hombre?

Hannah le pasó el sedante a Adam. Sus miradas se encontraron. La conversación de aquella paciente, con su salero y buen humor, bastó para borrar todo rastro de ira entre Adam y Hannah. Ambos sonrieron.

–Prepara nueve mililitros de suero y uno de morfina, ¿quieres, Hannah, por favor?

Eran las cuatro y media de la madrugada cuando la unidad 241 quedó disponible de nuevo. Hannah cargó la camilla en la ambulancia y agarró la sábana para doblarla al mismo tiempo que Adam. Sus manos se rozaron, pero Hannah las apartó rápidamente. Se dirigió a los asientos delanteros, donde había dejado unos papeles para rellenar debajo de la almohada, y entonces chocó con Adam, que había tenido la misma idea.

–Lo siento.

–No lo sientas –contestó Adam con voz ronca. Al oírlo, Hannah levantó la vista. Sus miradas se encontraron. Ella no pudo apartar los ojos de él–. Te he echado de menos.

–Yo también.

–Me resulta muy difícil trabajar contigo, Hannah. Deseándote así –suspiró pesadamente, tomando un mechón de sus cabellos–. Creí que te olvidaría, pero cada día me resulta más difícil –Hannah permaneció en silencio, asintiendo con la cabeza–. ¿Sientes tú lo mismo? –continuó Adam en voz baja.

Hannah levantó la vista. ¿Debía confesar sus sentimientos? Probablemente no pudiera ocultárselos, por mucho que quisiera. Adam podía leer la respuesta en su rostro. Él levantó un dedo y acarició su mejilla.

–¿Qué vamos a hacer, Hannah Duncan?

–No lo sé –susurró ella–. No creo que podamos hacer nada.

–Tiene que haber una solución –afirmó Adam enérgico–. No puedo seguir viviendo así, sin que formes parte de mi vida.

–Formo parte de tu vida.

–Ya sabes a lo que me refiero.

–No tenemos futuro, Adam. Tú mismo lo dijiste.

–Pero tenemos presente.

–¿Es eso lo que deseas realmente, Adam?, ¿una relación que no va a ninguna parte?, ¿sexo?

–Podría conseguir sexo en cualquier parte, Hannah –repuso él–. Es a ti a quien quiero.

–Yo no estoy sola –le recordó Hannah–. Tengo mi vida hecha, y no voy a dividirme en dos para teneros a ti y a mi hija.

–Ni yo lo espero.

–¿Qué sugieres entonces, Adam? –preguntó Hannah tratando de reprimir la esperanza.

Quizá Adam estuviera por fin preparado para aceptar a su hija. Con el tiempo, era posible incluso que llegara a amarla.

–Quiero estar contigo –explicó Adam con pasión–. El pasado ya no importa, y el futuro está lejos. Tenemos el presente, el aquí y ahora...

La luz amortiguada y la estrechez de la parte trasera de la ambulancia acentuaban la intimidad del momento. Adam no iba a tocar a Hannah. No durante las horas de trabajo, al menos. Pero le resultaba increíblemente difícil comunicarle lo que quería decir solo con palabras.

–Mis sentimientos hacia ti son demasiado fuertes como para reprimirlos –continuó Adam en voz baja–. Y no van a desaparecer así como así. Tiene que haber una forma de solucionar este problema. Lo único que te pido es que lo intentemos. Por favor.

–Me gustaría mucho, Adam –contestó Hannah pensativa, tras una pausa que se le hizo muy larga–. Es una buena idea.

–Sí, es la tercera mejor idea que he tenido nunca –respondió Adam sonriendo.

Adam arrancó el coche con entusiasmo, sonriendo y recibiendo a cambio una cálida recompensa. Después de todo, no tenía que casarse con Hannah. Ni siquiera tenía que vivir con ella. ¿Cuántas mujeres arrastraban a sus hijos a una cita romántica? Probablemente no tuviera muchas oportunidades de ver a Heidi, y cuando lo hiciera, bastaría con hacer lo mismo que hacía cuando tenía que tratar con niños en el trabajo. Se había enfrentado a ellos miles de veces, dominaba la técnica.

Todo sería más fácil de lo que esperaba, reflexionó Adam. Heidi rompió a llorar en el instante mismo en que puso un pie por primera vez en casa de Hannah.

–Lo siento –se disculpó ella agarrando a la niña–. No está acostumbrada a los extraños. Además, está cansada. Enseguida la acuesto.

–Yo la acostaré, si quieres –se ofreció Norma.

–No, tú vete, mamá. No querrás llegar tarde a tu primera cita, ¿verdad?

–No es una cita –se quejó Norma cohibida–. Solo voy a acompañar a Gerry a la consulta.

–Gerry Prescott es uno de los médicos de la consulta donde trabaja mamá –explicó Hannah dirigiéndose a Adam–. Lleva dos años tratando de conseguir que mi madre salga con él.

–En realidad lo que le gusta es mi familia –explicó Norma–. Gerry nunca tuvo hijos, y le da envidia de mi nieta. Adora a Heidi.

–Espero que te lo pases bien –repuso Adam.

–Bueno, solo vamos a una charla sobre unos productos farmacéuticos y luego a un concierto –explicó Norma besando a su nieta en la cabeza–. Adiós, pequeñina. ¿Qué tal voy?

–Preciosa –afirmó Hannah–. Pásatelo bien. No te esperaré levantada.

–No pienso llegar tarde –repuso Norma–. Me alegro de verte, Adam.

–Y yo de verte a ti, Norma –sonrió Adam–. Hannah tiene razón, estás preciosa.

–Entonces, me marcho.

Nada más cerrarse la puerta y quedarse solos se hizo un incómodo silencio. Hannah trató de desembarazarse de su hija, pero esta se agarró con fuerza a su cuello.

–¡No!

Adam trató de sonreír, pero la situación le resultaba desesperante. Y Hannah debía haberse dado cuenta, porque parecía incómoda.

–Hay una botella de vino en la nevera –repuso Hannah–. ¿Por qué no la abres y sirves dos copas? Le leeré a Heidi un cuento y la meteré en la cama.

Adam esperó unos minutos dando lentos sorbos de vino, pero Hannah no apareció por la cocina. Entonces Adam deambuló por el salón. Había pruebas de la presencia de una niña por todas partes en la casa. Una mesa diminuta con sillitas en un rincón, una cesta de bloques y una casita de muñecas, una galleta mordisqueada sobre el brazo del sillón... fue precisamente la galleta lo que lo irritó.

Aquello ya lo había vivido. Maddy jamás se terminaba la comida o los tentempiés, cuando encontraba algo más interesante que hacer. Y los restos de aquellas chucherías aparecían por todas partes, en los lugares más insospechados. Como la galleta de chocolate derretido que encontró en una ocasión bajo la almohada, o las zanahorias crudas flotando en el retrete. Adam se dirigió al vestíbulo y oyó la voz de Hannah murmurando. Entornó la puerta y escuchó.

–Y desde entonces el osito de peluche siempre hacía ese ruido, porque siempre había alguien que lo abrazara.

–¡Haz que haga ese ruido, mamá!

Adam se detuvo delante de la puerta. Contempló a Hannah abrazar a su hija y lamentó haber abandonado la cocina. Aquel abrazo era tan tierno que resultaba casi doloroso. Adam dio un largo trago de vino.

–Pero no he hecho ruidito, mamá.

Hannah volvió a abrazar a su hija haciéndola cosquillas para que la niña gritara y riera de placer.

–Ya está, ya has hecho ruidito. Ahora a dormir –sonrió Hannah levantándose del sillón.

Adam dio un paso atrás. No quería que ella lo descubriera espiando.

–¿Se ha ido ya ese hombre?

Adam dio otro paso atrás más. La pregunta de Heidi revelaba que estaba tan molesta con su presencia como él.

–No, aún no, cariño –respondió Hannah–. Es un amigo de mamá. Ha venido a cenar conmigo.

–¿Y conmigo no?

–No –negó Hannah con firmeza.

Adam volvió a la cocina. Estaba sirviéndose otra copa cuando ella llegó.

–Lo siento, no esperaba tardar tanto.

–No pasa nada –aseguró Adam–. Este vino es muy bueno, voy por la segunda copa.

–Gracias –contestó Hannah tomando la que él le ofrecía–. Salud.

–Esta casa es muy interesante –comentó Adam–. Tenía la sensación de que no encajarías ni en un apartamento de ciudad ni en la típica casa grande de las afueras.

–Sí, estas viejas casas con terraza son únicas –convino Hannah–. Son diminutas. Es una lástima por Heidi, porque el jardín trasero es demasiado pequeño, pero nos gusta vivir en el centro, y estamos a tiro de piedra del jardín botánico.

–Es una casa con carácter –afirmó Adam sonriendo–. Además, está cerca de la guardería.

–Mmm –asintió Hannah, que prefería no seguir conversando a propósito de la niña.

–¿Qué tal está ese niño de la guardería? –preguntó Adam con falso interés.

–Bien. Su madre le ha pintado a los Teletubbies en la escayola. ¿Tienes hambre?

–Pues creía que no, hasta que olí lo que hay en el horno –contestó Adam alegrándose de cambiar de conversación–. De pronto estoy hambriento.

–No es más que un guiso –repuso Hannah con una sonrisa–. Carne con setas, nada especial.

–Pues para mí, que no sé cocinar, resulta de lo más especial –confesó Adam brindando–. Igual que tú.

–¿Es que yo también huelo?

–Vamos a ver –Adam le quitó la copa de las manos y la dejó, junto con la suya, sobre la mesa. Luego retiró el pelo de la espalda de Hannah con ambas manos y se inclinó para besar su cuello–. Sí, hueles... de un modo absolutamente delicioso.

–¿A guiso? –preguntó Hannah sin apartar la vista de él.

–No, a ti –contestó Adam, sujetando aún sus cabellos.

Adam volvió a inclinar la cabeza, pero esa vez para besarla en los labios. Luego dejó que cayeran sus cabellos libremente por la espalda mientras sus dedos le sujetaban la cabeza enredados en ellos. Hannah abrió los labios bajo los de él y sus manos enseguida se enlazaron en la nuca de Adam. El sabor de la boca de Hannah lo llenaba de deseo, de un deseo que había estado reprimiendo durante casi dos semanas. Finalmente Adam se apartó gruñendo de frustración.

–Será mejor que sirva la cena –comentó Hannah temblorosa.

–Sé muy bien qué quiero comer –contestó Adam cediendo a la debilidad.

–No podemos –objetó ella nerviosa–. Aquí no –añadió mirando por encima de su hombro.

Aquel gesto fue suficiente para recordarle a Adam que no estaban solos. A pesar de todo, él sonrió.

–Entonces tendré que conformarme con el guiso. ¿Cuándo vendrás a mi casa a cenar?, ¿mañana?

–Pero si no sabes cocinar –bromeó Hannah.

–Bueno, puedo comprar algo –contraatacó Adam inclinándose hacia ella una vez más–. Además, ¿quién necesita comer?

–Nosotros –se apresuró Hannah a contestar dando un paso atrás y agarrando un guante para abrir el horno–. Ahora mismo, antes de que nos distraigamos más. Puedo ir a tu casa mañana.

–Sí, tengo buenas ideas, ¿verdad?

Adam tenía buenas ideas. Fue él quien sugirió que llevaran a Heidi de excursión el jueves y a comer pizza a su madre y a su hija a la semana siguiente. Alternaban las salidas familiares con las escapadas a solas, a casa de Adam. La negativa de Hannah de quedarse a dormir la noche entera en su casa decepcionó a Adam, pero a ella también le decepcionó tener que esperar a que él le contara más cosas sobre su pasado. A pesar de todo, las cosas iban bien. El hecho de que Adam accediera a contarle a sus colegas que salían juntos era una buena señal. Matt y Tom estaban encantados. Heidi seguía mostrándose muy tímida, pero a Adam parecía no importarle. Hannah sospechaba que incluso lo prefería. Al menos Heidi no lloraba cada vez que lo veía.

Hannah trabajó dos turnos intensivos de cuatro días antes de volver a salir en la ambulancia con Adam. Estaba en el período de prueba de dos meses. En pocas semanas comenzaría un cursillo teórico intensivo tras el cual tendría que hacer un examen para alcanzar el grado 1.

–¿Vas a dar tú las clases del grado 1? –preguntó Hannah.

–No, por suerte –respondió Adam.

–¿Por qué, por suerte?

–Porque no podría darlas contigo sentada enfrente todo el día.

–Pero en cambio no te molesta que salgamos juntos en la ambulancia.

–¿No?, ¿quieres apostar? –preguntó Adam sonriendo–. Ahora mismo he olvidado por completo adónde vamos.

–A Gibraltar Crescent –le recordó Hannah–. Hay un enfermo en el número 209. Toma la siguiente calle a la izquierda y luego la primera a la derecha –indicó mirando el mapa.

–Eso de una persona enferma puede significar muchas cosas –musitó Adam–. A veces me gustaría que nos dieran más información.

–Bueno, así es más interesante –señaló Hannah–. Nos mantiene en vilo. Hay que estar preparados para cualquier cosa.

La mujer que les abrió la puerta no parecía enferma. Estaba pálida y tenía ojeras.

–No, no es por mí por quien he llamado, es por mis bebés. Por aquí, por favor.

–Yo soy Hannah –se presentó mientras la seguía por el pasillo–. ¿Y usted?

–Susan.

–Pues no tienes muy buen aspecto, Susan.

–Sí, no sé si me ha sentado algo mal o tengo gripe. Estos son Molly y Tyler. Están enfermos, no puedo conseguir que coman nada.

Molly y Tyler eran dos gemelos de seis meses. Ambos habían vomitado y necesitaban un cambio de pañal. Y los dos lloraban. Hannah se mordió el labio y miró aprensiva a Adam. No iba a disfrutar mucho de aquel aviso.

–¡Oh, Dios! Disculpadme –se excusó de pronto Susan, corriendo por el pasillo.

Adam y Hannah la oyeron vomitar.

–Ve a ayudarla –sugirió Adam–. Que se acueste. Tómale la tensión y ve haciéndole una historia. Y ayúdala a preparar una bolsa con las cosas de estos dos. Sospecho que se están deshidratando, y su madre no está en condiciones de cuidarlos. Tendremos que llevarlos a todos al hospital.

–Pero hay que cambiar a los niños –señaló Hannah–. Déjame a mí.

–Susan necesita lavarse. Yo cambiaré a los niños –alegó Adam–. No soy un inútil.

Hannah dejó a Adam con los niños. Susan terminó de vomitar y se sentó en el suelo, llorando.

–Todo saldrá bien, Susan –aseguró Hannah–. Te ayudaré a lavarte, enseguida te encontrarás mejor.

Hannah le tomó el pulso y la presión sanguínea y comenzó a hacer la historia.

–Vamos a tener que llevaros al hospital. Os estáis deshidratando. Los tres. Y eso es peligroso para los niños.

–No sabía qué hacer –contestó Susan–. Los dos últimos días me las he arreglado bien, pero esta mañana todos estábamos peor.

–Has hecho bien llamando. Voy a preparar una bolsa con cosas para los niños. ¿Les queda algo de ropa limpia?

–Sí, en la cesta de la ropa –asintió Susan–. No he podido ni guardarla. Siento que esté todo tan desordenado.

–No importa –aseguró Hannah mientras las lágrimas comenzaban a correr por las mejillas de Susan–. ¿Dónde tienes la cesta de la ropa?

–En el salón.

Los bebés seguían llorando. Adam se puso unos guantes y cambió a Molly. Hannah lo vio al dirigirse hacia el salón.

–Pásame algo de ropa limpia, si queda –pidió Adam.

Hannah obedeció y se quedó atónita al ver lo hábil que era Adam manejando bebés.

–¿Dónde aprendiste a hacer eso?

–Tengo muchos talentos ocultos –respondió Adam con una sonrisa, terminando de vestir a Molly–. Bien, vamos a ver si podemos calmar a esta niña.

Adam tomó a Molly en brazos y la niña se calló instantáneamente. Su hermano seguía llorando. Entonces él, sin soltar a Molly, alcanzó a Tyler con el otro brazo.

–¿Qué te pasa a ti, amigo?, ¿no te basta con llevar pantaloncitos limpios? –preguntó haciéndole cosquillas–. Eres un chico terrible.

Hannah abrió los ojos sorprendida. Tyler había dejado de llorar. Para tratarse de una persona que odiaba a los niños, Adam sabía demasiado bien qué hacer con ellos. La curiosidad afloró en ella y, por fin, una vez que los dejaron a los tres en el hospital, preguntó:

–¿Tienes muchos hermanos, o qué?

–No, era hijo único. ¿Por qué?

–Pues entonces debes tener amigos con hijos. Sabes perfectamente cómo tratar a un bebé. Y no se trata precisamente de un don natural, ¿sabes? Y menos en los hombres.

–Llevo mucho tiempo haciendo este trabajo –contestó Adam encogiéndose de hombros–. Hay que ocuparse de niños muchas veces. Vamos a ver si llegamos a la central a tomar café antes de que haya otro aviso –añadió arrancando la ambulancia.

Adam no iba a engañarla. El trabajo en la ambulancia jamás habría podido proporcionarle tanta práctica en el manejo de bebés. Al llegar a la central Hannah se lavó las manos. Esperaba que no le afectara el virus gástrico que debían padecer los bebés. Mientras se secaba, Katherine Gordon entró en los lavabos. Era una colega del equipo rojo, y no solía coincidir con ella.

–He oído decir que Adam y tú os habéis enfrentado hoy a una pequeña epidemia.

–Bueno, seguro que Adam le ha dado mucho bombo –contestó Hannah.

–Sí, le encanta decir que detesta a los niños.

–Pues yo comienzo a tener dudas al respecto –comentó Hannah–. No creo que los odie, en realidad.

–Claro que no –contestó Katherine–. Llevo mucho tiempo trabajando con él, y te aseguro que no es un tipo tan duro. No sé por qué razón quiere aparentarlo.

Mientras se servía café, Hannah observó a Adam. Su amor por él había crecido en las últimas semanas. No podía imaginar el futuro sin él. Pero aún tenía dudas. ¿Qué ocurriría si no llegaba nunca a aceptar a Heidi? Si solo fingía que detestaba a los niños, ¿por qué no era sincero con ella? No resultaba muy agradable que Adam levantara aquella muralla de apariencias también frente a ella.

Adam permanecía mudo acerca de su breve y trágico matrimonio. Hannah le había contado su historia con Ben tratando de darle una oportunidad para que él hiciera lo mismo sin sentirse presionado. Pero

Adam se había escabullido. Quizá hubiera deseado tener niños alguna vez, con su difunta mujer. Quizá la pérdida hubiese sido tan desoladora que le resultaba imposible formar otra familia con otra mujer. O quizá no hubiera encontrado aún a ninguna mujer comparable a ella. ¿Era ese el problema?, ¿callaba Adam por no herirla?

Apenas se había tomado el café cuando recibieron otro aviso de prioridad 1. Hannah corrió al garaje. Confiaba en que, con el tiempo, las cosas se solucionarían por sí solas. ¿No había sido Adam precisamente quien había dicho que el pasado, pasado estaba, y que el futuro ya se vería? La vida les sonreía.

Sí, la vida les sonreía. Adam veía a Hannah casi siempre que quería, y cada vez estaban mejor. En realidad eso lo preocupaba. Él esperaba que sus sentimientos menguaran o, al menos, se estabilizaran hasta el punto de no importarle que Hannah abandonara el lecho por las noches para marcharse a su casa. O hasta el punto de no sentir celos por que ella quisiera pasar un día a solas con su hija. Estar sin ella comenzaba a ser molesto, era como perder el tiempo. Adam comenzó a pensar en la posibilidad de vivir juntos.

Tener a Heidi revoloteando a su alrededor tampoco sería tan terrible. Era una niña mona, y no había traspasado la barrera emocional que Adam había levantado para protegerse de ella. Casi hasta disfrutaba de su presencia, una vez que Heidi dejó a un lado su timidez. Se parecía a Hannah, y eso lo intrigaba. Sin embargo no lamentaría que Heidi desapareciera. Era a Hannah a quien quería, pero si el precio era Heidi estaba dispuesto a pagarlo.

El sábado por la tarde habían pensado ir al jardín botánico, el parque favorito de Heidi. Hannah debía preparar la merienda, pero cuando Adam llegó a buscarlas se encontró con que todo había salido al revés.

–Lo siento –se disculpó Hannah–, no me encuentro bien.

–¿Qué te ocurre?

–Creo que tengo lo mismo que aquellos dos gemelos. He vomitado tres veces durante la última media hora –contestó Hannah.

–Siéntate, no tienes buen aspecto. ¿Heidi está enferma también?

–No, está por ahí, jugando. Me muero por dormir, pero tengo que vigilarla.

–¿Dónde está Norma?

–Ha ido a montar en bicicleta con Gerry Prescott –sonrió Hannah.

–Ve a acostarte, y procura dormir. Te encontrarás mucho mejor.

–No puedo –protestó Hannah.

–Sí, sí puedes –insistió Adam–. Yo vigilaré a Heidi. De hecho... la llevaré al parque –añadió sorprendiéndose a sí mismo–. Así podrás descansar.

–¿Estás seguro, Adam?

Heidi llegó corriendo con un juguete de madera que hacía mucho ruido. Tanto, que Hannah se tapó la cara con las manos. Era evidente que estaba demasiado enferma para soportarlo.

–Heidi, ¿quieres venir al parque conmigo?

–¿Y mamá?

–No, solo conmigo.

Heidi se metió el pulgar en la boca. Adam estaba acostumbrado a verla hacer ese gesto. Significaba que estaba considerándolo.

–Mamá no se encuentra bien –insistió Adam–. Tiene que descansar. Tú y yo iremos al parque, te montaré en el columpio.

Unos enormes ojos azules observaron atentamente a Adam. Heidi se sacó el pulgar de la boca y tomó una decisión.

–Sí, vamos a los columpios.

–Bien, enseguida –prometió Adam–. Vamos por tu abrigo y a meter a tu mamá en la cama.

–Ten cuidado con lo que dices delante de mi hija –bromeó Hannah.

–Sí, no estaría mal aprovechar la oportunidad. Pero prefiero a las mujeres sanas –sonrió Adam–. Te haré una taza de té. Necesitarás algo para el dolor de cabeza, me figuro.

–¿Y cómo sabes que me duele la cabeza?

–Te has tapado la cara al oír a ese ruidoso juguete de madera. Vamos, a la cama –insistió Adam tomándola del codo.

Heidi quiso llevarse el muñeco al parque. Fueron caminando, con el muñeco arrastrando. Al llegar a un semáforo la niña se agarró de la mano de Adam. La última vez que había llevado así a una niña había sido con Maddy. Adam apretó los dientes. Cuidaría de Heidi solo esa tarde.

El parque estaba abarrotado, y Heidi tuvo que esperar turno para subir a los columpios. Luego quiso escalar por los puentes metálicos en forma de arco, construir un castillo de arena y volver a los columpios. Para Adam aquel alboroto infantil resultaba agotador. Una hora después, estaba deseando volver a casa.

–No, yo quiero quedarme a jugar –declaró Heidi.

–Solo cinco minutos más –ordenó Adam–. Luego iremos a tomar un helado.

–Bien –contestó Heidi volviéndose hacia el puente para escalar.

Heidi se colgó del puente cabeza abajo junto a otro niño. Adam se quedó de pie con ella, con el muñeco de madera en la mano. Entonces una mujer le dirigió la palabra y él se volvió, perdiendo de vista a Heidi por unos segundos. Cuando quiso volver a encontrarla había desaparecido. Adam se asustó. Aterrorizado, buscó a su alrededor. No estaba en los columpios. El parque estaba tan lleno, y los niños se movían tan deprisa... Adam la llamó a gritos.

–¡Heidi!, ¿dónde estás?

–Aquí.

Adam miró para arriba. Heidi se había subido a lo más alto del puente, muy por encima de su cabeza. Adam tragó asustado. ¿Cómo había trepado hasta allí?

–Baja ahora mismo –ordenó Adam.

–Bueno –contestó la niña soltándose tranquilamente para saltar.

Adam no sabía que tuviera tan buenos reflejos. Tomó a la pequeña en brazos justo un segundo antes de que llegara al suelo.

–Eres muy traviesa –gruñó Adam–. Eso que has hecho no está bien –Heidi observó el rostro asustado de Adam y se echó a llorar. Adam respiró hondo–. Bueno, tranquila, no pasa nada. Pero tienes que prometerme que jamás volverás a hacerlo. Podrías haberte hecho daño.

Heidi lloró aún más. Al ver que el resto de adultos los miraban, Adam recogió el juguete del suelo y se llevó a la niña a un banco apartado. No podía llevar a Heidi a casa en ese estado. ¿Qué pensaría Hannah?

Heidi enterró la cabeza en su hombro. Adam se sentó y le dio golpecitos en la espalda. Entonces recordó los llantos de Maddy. Solían desvanecerse poco a poco, hasta quedarse callada. Con Heidi ocurrió igual. Adam se quedó absorto en medio del silencio, abrazando a la niña, tratando de no disfrutar de aquel calor. Ni siquiera se dio cuenta de cuánto tiempo estuvo así. Heidi se quedó dormida.

Adam pensó despertarla, pero parecía tan serena que le dio pena. Su diminuto rostro expresaba una perfecta paz. Por fin se le había pasado el susto. Adam sonrió. Heidi había confiado en él, en que él la agarraría. Y él había sabido responder. La niña estaba a salvo y volvería a confiar en él. Sin darse cuenta de lo que estaba haciendo, Adam inclinó la cabeza y besó a Heidi en la frente. La niña abrió los ojos y sonrió.

—¿Volvemos a casa? —sugirió Heidi.

Adam asintió. Heidi sonrió y lo tomó de la mano. Al sentir sus deditos agarrarse confiados, Adam comprendió que estaba perdido. Heidi había conseguido lo que él se había jurado que nunca permitiría. Se había ganado su amor. Desde aquel instante, su miedo a perder a aquella niña sería tan grande como su miedo a perder a Hannah. Las amaba a las dos. Y eso era demasiado para él.

Capítulo 7

ADAM estaba nervioso. Hannah no creía probable que se debiera al aviso de prioridad 1 que acababan de recibir. Se trataba de un accidente de tráfico, pero él tenía que haber visto miles. Además, estaba así desde primera hora de la mañana. Adam tocó el claxon pidiendo paso. Apenas podía oírse la radio. Hannah tomó el micrófono y contestó:

–Aquí unidad 241. Adelante, control.

El ruido y las interferencias le impidieron oír la primera parte del mensaje. Luego escuchó:

–Un camión y un trailer han caído rodando por la falda de la colina. Parece que ha afectado también a tres coches que iban en dirección contraria.

–¿Qué hay de los refuerzos? –preguntó Adam encendiendo la sirena.

–¿Sabemos el número de víctimas? –preguntó Hannah presionando el botón de la radio.

–Negativo –respondió control–. Seguramente más de cuatro. Dos en estado 0, según los testigos. Hay gente atrapada. Código 100.

Hannah miró a Adam. Estado 0 significaba que había pacientes en estado crítico. Posiblemente inconscientes, con dificultades respiratorias o hemorragias internas. Código 100 significaba que los bomberos estaban de camino. Tenían que sacar a las víctimas atrapadas. Aquello sonaba muy serio.

–¿Y los refuerzos? –volvió a repetir Adam.

–La unidad 225 va detrás de vosotros. También hay médicos de camino.

Adam asintió y aceleró. Los coches se apartaron a los lados. Hannah contuvo el aliento al pasar por en medio de dos autobuses. Adam, sin embargo, aceleró.

–Unidad 241, ¿me copiáis?

–¡Roger! –contestó Hannah presionando el botón de la radio.

Hannah miró por el retrovisor. Había luces de sirenas tras ellos. Seguramente sería el médico, que participaba en los rescates cuando el número de ambulancias disponible era escaso y la situación era grave. Hannah no se atrevió a mirar el velocímetro. Jamás había viajado a tanta velocidad. Ni jamás había estado tampoco en un accidente grave.

Adam se concentró en llegar cuanto antes, ella en recordar qué debía hacer: evaluar la situación, comprobar la respuesta de los pacientes, su respiración y su circulación. En ese orden. Sin embargo la teoría siempre estaba lejos de la realidad. ¿Qué encontrarían al llegar?, ¿gasolina derramada, con peligro de incendio y explosión? ¿Qué transportarían el trailer y el camión?, ¿materiales tóxicos? ¿Y si había más de una víctima en estado crítico?, ¿tendría que ocuparse sola de uno de ellos? Las palmas de las manos le sudaban.

–¿Te encuentras bien?

–Sí, estoy bien.

–Estás pálida –afirmó Adam–. No estoy seguro de que hayas hecho bien hoy, viniendo a trabajar.

–Estoy bien –aseguró Hannah–. Me pasé el domingo y el lunes en la cama, y ayer me lo tomé con tranquilidad. Estoy completamente recuperada.

–Pues estás pálida.

–Es que jamás había estado en un accidente de tráfico de este calibre –admitió Hannah–. Estoy nerviosa.

–Lo harás bien. Recuerda la lección.

Hannah asintió. Por fin salieron a la autopista, y el tráfico aminoró. Adam aceleró y la miró. Hannah sonrió. Era agradable que se preocupara por ella. Un coche de policía los adelantó con la sirena. Hannah comprobó que llevaba los guantes y el impermeable amarillo reflectante necesario para trabajar en la autopista. Al llegar a la escena del accidente, se tranquilizó. Adam sabía exactamente qué hacer.

La escena no era lo caótica que Hannah esperaba. El camión y el trailer estaban volcados a un lado, bloqueando la autopista. La policía había cortado el tráfico. Había un coche boca abajo, hundido en un pequeño dique en la cuneta. Otro más tenía el techo destrozado, bajo el trailer, y un tercero estaba al otro lado de la autopista, incrustado en un poste que lo había detenido en la caída.

Adam observó la escena. Entonces llegó el médico y detuvo el coche junto a ellos. Había mucho personal de emergencia. Ivan Moresby, el director del centro de ambulancias, recogía información de los testigos y coordinaba a los equipos de emergencia. Hannah y Adam se dirigieron hacia él.

–Aún no han llegado los bomberos, pero no creo que tarden. Tú y Hannah id al coche que está en el dique, el de la cuneta. Según parece hay al menos una persona consciente allí. Creo que tenemos a dos en estado 0 en el coche que hay bajo el trailer, pero tengo que confirmarlo.

Adam y Hannah corrieron al coche que les habían asignado. En medio del asfalto, sentada bloqueándoles el paso, había una mujer, la única ocupante del tercer vehículo involucrado en el accidente. No tenía dificultades para respirar ni sangraba. Adam le puso un collar a toda prisa y llamó a una policía para que se ocupara de ella hasta que llegara otra ambulancia. Luego corrieron al coche volcado en la cuneta.

Al acercarse, un transeúnte salió del dique. Estaba muy nervioso. Desde el coche, se oían gritos pidiendo auxilio.

–Las puertas están bloqueadas –dijo el transeúnte–. No hay manera de entrar.

Hannah escuchó el llanto de un niño, más débil que los gritos de la madre. Asomó la cabeza por la ventanilla y vio a un bebé en su sillita, pataleando. No podía verle la cabeza, oculta tras las orejas de la sillita. Hannah trató de abrir la puerta, pero no pudo. Adam dio la vuelta al coche para abrir la del piloto. La mujer gritaba histérica:

–¡No se vayan!, ¡por favor! ¡Sáquenos de aquí!

–Los sacaremos en cuanto podamos. Por favor, no se mueva –contestó Hannah asomándose por la ventanilla del conductor, donde estaba sentada la mujer.

–¡Mi hija, por favor, salven a mi hija!

–La ventanilla de atrás está un poco abierta. Voy a forzarla –afirmó Adam con creciente ansiedad–. Los bomberos llegarán en un momento.

Hannah trataba de comprobar el estado de la madre. Estaba colgada boca abajo, sujeta por el cinturón de seguridad. El pelo le caía suelto hacia el techo, lleno de sangre. Hablaba, gritaba y lloraba sin parar, de modo que no debía tener dificultades respiratorias. Movía las manos, pero tenía las piernas atrapadas bajo el volante. Abría los ojos inmensamente, horrorizada.

−¿Cómo te llamas? –preguntó Hannah.

−Trudy.

−Yo soy Hannah. ¿Te cuesta respirar, Trudy?

−No, no creo. ¡Quiero salir de aquí!

−Lo sé, lo sé. Estamos esperando a los bomberos. Ellos saben cómo arrancar la puerta. ¿Te duele el cuello?

−No lo sé, me duele todo. Excepto las piernas.

−¿Sientes las piernas?

−No –contestó Trudy agitándose, tratando de salir inútilmente–. Tengo las piernas atoradas. No puedo moverme.

Hannah trató de buscar el medio de calmarla. La sirena que oyó entonces ayudó.

−Esos son los bomberos. Ellos te sacarán de aquí.

−¡Mi hija... por favor!

Adam seguía forzando la ventanilla. Consiguió abrirla justo cuando el bebé comenzó a gritar más. Luego se inclinó metiendo los brazos y trató de alcanzar el cinturón de seguridad que sujetaba la sillita del niño. Pero no pudo. Apenas le cabían los brazos, los sacudía a ciegas.

−Déjame a mí –gritó Hannah–. Yo soy más pequeña.

Adam se apartó y Hannah se inclinó sobre el coche. Ivan Moresby se acercó entonces a ellos.

−Las dos víctimas del otro coche están en estado 0 –les informó.

Hannah parpadeó, desfallecida. Se arrodilló y metió dentro del coche toda la parte del torso que le cupo por la ventanilla.

−¿Qué tenemos en ese vehículo? –continuó preguntando Ivan.

−La conductora, Trudy, está en estado 3. No sangra ni tiene dificultades respiratorias. Está atrapada bajo el volante, y la puerta está bloqueada. No podemos sacarla. Hay un bebé en el asiento de atrás. Estamos tratando de sacarlo.

Hannah vio la carita sonrosada de la niña. Se inclinó un poco más y trató de llegar al cinturón de seguridad.

–Huele a gasolina –dijo de pronto Ivan.

–¿Dónde diablos está el código 100? –preguntó Adam a gritos–. ¡He oído la sirena!

–Tienen problemas para llegar. Demasiado tráfico. Los policías están despejando la zona –contestó Ivan asomando la cara por la ventanilla–. Hola, Trudy. Te sacaremos enseguida. ¿Tiene *airbag* tu coche? –preguntó enderezándose de pronto, nada más escuchar la respuesta, y mirando a Adam significativamente–. ¿Has oído eso?

Adam asintió tenso. Y sintió pánico. No por él, sino por Hannah. Alargó una mano y le tocó la espalda.

–Sal de ahí, Hannah. Es peligroso.

–Un segundo –contestó ella luchando con el cinturón de seguridad–. Casi lo tengo.

–Iré a interceptar a los bomberos –afirmó Ivan–. Hay que inutilizar ese *airbag* cuanto antes.

Adam observó marcharse a Ivan. Los gritos de Trudy se hicieron más intensos. El *airbag* podía saltar en cualquier momento, incluso una hora después del impacto. Y la electricidad que lo accionaba podía causar una explosión, si el coche perdía gasolina. Y olía a gasolina. ¡Hannah estaba dentro!

–¡Ahora mismo, Hannah, sal! –gritó Adam tomándola de la cintura.

–¡La tengo! –gritó Hannah girando la sillita del

bebé para que cupiera por la ventanilla y comenzando a echarse atrás.

La sillita tropezó y Hannah volvió a intentarlo. Adam la sujetó de la cintura.

–Vamos –dijo Adam tenso.

Hannah no había oído la conversación acerca del *airbag,* y se quedó confusa, mirando a Adam. Adam tiró de ella. Los bomberos acababan de llegar. La madre de la niña seguía gritando histérica, atrapada en el coche.

Un bombero se acercó corriendo y gritando hacia ellos. Llevaba un cobertor de seguridad para inutilizar el *airbag.* Adam se volvió. Apenas pudo ver a la ocupante del vehículo mientras el *airbag* se accionaba. El bombero agarró a Hannah del otro brazo, tapándola a ella y al bebé con su pesado abrigo de seguridad. Trudy dejó de gritar bruscamente. El repentino silencio resultó chocante, pero fue peor lo que siguió. La explosión desencadenó una fuerte onda expansiva. Hannah se tambaleó, aferrada a la sillita del bebé. Todos se volvieron al mismo tiempo para ver la espiral de llamas y humo que envolvía al vehículo.

–¡Oh, Dios mío! –exclamó Hannah soltándose de Adam y del bombero y dejando la sillita en el suelo.

No pretendía ponerse a salvo, corría hacia el coche. Adam la interceptó y la sujetó.

–Ya no puedes hacer nada, Hannah –dijo Adam obligándola a volverse hacia él, sosteniéndola y tratando de evitar que viera la escena–. Ya nadie puede hacer nada.

El equipo de bomberos se puso en acción, pero ya era tarde cuando lograron contener el fuego. Adam llevó a Hannah a la parte posterior de la ambulancia y la mantuvo ocupada con el bebé. La segunda ambulancia, con Tom y Derek, ya había llegado. Se ocupaban de la mujer a la que Adam había puesto el collar. Ivan había vuelto a la central. Apenas quedaba nada que hacer.

Nada más ponerlo en posición vertical, el bebé volvió a recuperar su color natural. La sillita lo había mantenido a salvo. Hannah lo sostenía en brazos, y por fin había callado. Ella contemplaba el coche ardiendo. Trudy seguía dentro. Alguien llamó a la puerta trasera de la ambulancia. Adam abrió. Era la policía a la que habían visto antes.

—Hemos encontrado al padre del bebé. Os verá en el hospital.

—Gracias. ¿Sabes su nombre?

—Freeman. John Freeman. La niña se llama Melissa.

—Enseguida vamos.

Adam observó marcharse a la policía. Aún tenía mucho que hacer allí. Hannah sabía que debía poner al bebé en su sillita para ir al hospital, pero era incapaz de despegarse de él. Melissa se agarraba a su trenza y sonreía. Hannah estaba a punto de llorar.

—Siéntate en la camilla, os ataré juntas a las dos —dijo Adam.

Adam condujo despacio, mirando de vez en cuando a Hannah por el retrovisor. Sentía un enorme peso en el pecho. Trató de calmarse. Seguramente se debía al estrés, pero había superado cosas peores que aquella.

Sabía cuál era el problema. La muralla defensiva que había levantado en torno a su corazón estaba llena de grietas, evidentes incluso antes de aquel espantoso accidente. Esas grietas las había causado su amor por Hannah y por Heidi. El miedo que había sentido al ver a Hannah en peligro, inclinada sobre el coche con medio cuerpo dentro, había ensanchado esa grieta. Solo de pensarlo se le ponía la carne de gallina.

—¿Va todo bien ahí atrás?

—Sí, estamos perfectamente —contestó Hannah ausente.

Adam suspiró y aceleró. Ante él se presentaba un peligro más. ¿Qué ocurriría si dejaba que esa muralla se desmoronara, si volvía a amar y permitía que lo amaran? No se trataba solo de un riesgo personal. Adam sabía que se debilitaría profesionalmente, que sería más vulnerable al estrés, al caos y al horror como el de aquel día. Y no se sentía lo suficientemente fuerte como para echarse esa carga sobre los hombros voluntariamente.

Tom y Derek llegaron a urgencias antes que ellos, y observaron a Hannah con preocupación. Hannah trató de sonreír, pero no pudo. Para ella era la primera vez. Debía estar preguntándose cómo podía haber creído que iba a poder realizar un trabajo como aquel. Hannah le tendió el bebé a la enfermera.

—El padre está en una de las salas de espera —dijo la enfermera—. Quiere hablar con alguien que haya estado en la escena del accidente.

Hannah se quedó helada, miró a Adam. Él la tocó el brazo y dijo:

—Yo lo haré.

Hannah asintió. Lo observó marcharse. No le quedaban fuerzas. Tom y Derek se marcharon, respondiendo a otro aviso, y Hannah se quedó sola, en la ambulancia. Se sentó en la camilla, enterró el rostro en las manos y se quedó inmóvil. Luego escuchó que se abría y cerraba la puerta, pero no levantó la vista. El colchón de la camilla se hundió con el peso de Adam al sentarse. Adam puso un brazo sobre su hombro y Hannah apoyó la cabeza sobre él.

–Lo siento –dijo ella con voz amortiguada–. No podré ser un buen oficial de ambulancia si me derrumbo así, ¿verdad?

–No te has derrumbado –contestó Adam apretando su hombro–. Es una reacción perfectamente natural a un accidente tan grave y estresante como el de hoy. Mucha gente tendría problemas para asimilarlo, por eso hacemos reuniones y disponemos de consejo psicológico –explicó Adam acariciándole la cabeza–. Has salvado a ese bebé. De haber sabido que el coche tenía *airbag*, ni siquiera te habría dejado intentarlo hasta no colocar el cobertor de seguridad. Podríamos haberlos perdido a los dos.

Hannah asintió. De pronto, deseó marcharse a casa más que nada en el mundo, abrazar a su hija.

–¿Se hace cada vez más fácil, con el tiempo? –preguntó Hannah en voz baja–. Me refiero a enfrentarte a este tipo de cosas.

–Sí, aprendes a distanciarte –respondió Adam–. Tienes que hacerlo, o no sobrevivirías. Pero eso no significa que te conviertas en una persona dura e insensible.

Adam respiró hondo y abrazó a Hannah con fuerza. ¿Era eso lo que le estaba ocurriendo a él?, ¿era eso lo que deseaba que le ocurriera? En ese momento lo que más deseaba era contarle a Hannah sus miedos, las razón de ese miedo. Ella lo comprendería. Y si se lo contaba, quizá las cosas cambiaran. Para mejor. Adam se aferró a esa esperanza con decisión. Se lo contaría. Pero no allí.

–Más tarde habrá una reunión –añadió Adam.

–¿Y qué se hace allí? –preguntó Hannah con poco entusiasmo.

–Bueno, nos reunimos todos los que nos hemos visto envueltos en el accidente. Hablamos de él y de nuestra reacción. Probablemente Ivan llame a un consejero, o a un psicólogo para llevar la sesión.

–¿Es obligatorio asistir? –preguntó Hannah, a quien no le gustaba la idea de exponer públicamente sus emociones.

–Es aconsejable, no obligatorio.

–Preferiría hablar contigo.

–Yo también quiero hablar contigo –sonrió Adam–. Hablar de verdad. Ven a casa conmigo esta noche –añadió acariciando su mejilla.

–No puedo, Adam. Mamá tiene clase, no puede quedarse con Heidi –suspiró Hannah pesadamente.

–¿Y no puede perderse la clase por una vez?

–Está aprendiendo a hacer ventanas de cuarterones. Está haciendo una para el baño, y la terminará esta noche. Es la última clase.

–¿Y no puedes llamar a una niñera?

Hannah sacudió la cabeza. De ninguna forma estaba dispuesta a separarse de su hija esa noche, pero no podía decírselo a Adam. Él también la necesitaba. No podía rechazarlo en favor de su hija, no después del accidente.

–Ven a casa conmigo –sugirió Hannah–. Meteré a Heidi en la cama y mamá no estará. A menos que...

La voz de Hannah se desvaneció. A menos que Adam estuviera interesado en algo más que hablar. O a menos que Heidi se hubiera convertido en un obstáculo demasiado importante para él.

Adam vio cambiar la expresión de Hannah. Sabía

qué estaba pensando. Por mucho que deseara abrazarla y hacerle el amor para reafirmar el lazo que los unía, había algo más urgente y más íntimo que compartir esa noche.

—Yo llevaré la cena –sonrió Adam–. Estaré allí a las siete.

Adam llegó justo a la hora. Hannah abrió la puerta y lo guió al salón.

—Siéntate, te traeré algo de beber.

—Será mejor que primero meta esto en el horno –contestó Adam señalando la comida preparada.

—Yo lo llevaré.

Hannah alargó la mano para tomar el paquete, pero se le escurrió. Por suerte Adam no lo había soltado.

—Tú siéntate, yo traeré algo de beber –sugirió Adam.

—Lo siento –rio Hannah–. Aún estoy nerviosa.

Hannah se sentó junto a la chimenea. No había conseguido calmarse. Estaba feliz de volver a ver a su hija, pero también nerviosa. Y el hecho de que Norma hubiera escogido precisamente ese día para comprarle una cama nueva a la niña no resultaba de mucha ayuda. Heidi había provocado un gran alboroto, consciente de que aquel era un símbolo de madurez.

—Espero que Heidi se vaya a la cama antes de que llegue Adam –había dicho Norma antes de marcharse.

—No importa, creo que Adam comienza a aceptar a Heidi como parte del trato, mamá.

—¿En serio? –preguntó Norma.

–¿Es que tú no lo crees? –Norma había sido la única que había visto a Adam volver del parque con Heidi el sábado anterior. De pronto Hannah recordó la expresión de irritación de Adam a primera hora de la mañana. Las piezas del rompecabezas comenzaron a encajar–. Tú no lo crees, ¿verdad, mamá?

–Claro, es solo que el sábado parecía tener prisa por marcharse. Eso es todo, cariño. Debió resultarle pesado cuidar él solo de Heidi.

–Bueno, esta noche no estará solo –sonrió Hannah.

Claro que debía haberle resultado pesado, era natural. Pero la experiencia tampoco había sido tan terrible. Desde entonces, Heidi no hacía más que hablar de Adam. Pero quizá Adam no se alegrara tanto como ella del cambio de actitud de la niña hacia él.

Hannah había acostado a la niña poco antes de la llegada de Adam, pero Heidi la había mirado con ojos brillantes y pícaros desde su nueva camita. Eso inquietaba a Hannah, pero aquella noche tenía demasiadas cosas en que pensar.

Por suerte Adam parecía tomárselo con calma. Él sabía cómo enfrentarse a un accidente, y la ayudaría a superarlo, a distanciarse y verlo con perspectiva. Hannah respiró hondo y sonrió al ver a Adam acercarse con una copa de vino. Él se sentó en un sillón frente a ella. Entonces una diminuta carita apareció en el dintel de la puerta.

–¡Oh, no! –murmuró Hannah.

Los ojos de Heidi brillaban con intensidad, tras descubrir que podía salir de su cama cuando quisiera. Llevaba un osito de peluche en la mano y se había metido el pulgar en la boca, pero no buscaba a su mamá. Observaba a Adam. Sacó el dedo y saludó:

–Hola –Adam se sobresaltó. Estaba de espaldas a la puerta, no la había visto aparecer–. Este osito suena.

Adam dio un largo sorbo de vino recordando la escena del parque. Más valía olvidarla, bastante tenía ya con lo que pretendía contarle a Hannah. Cada cosa a su tiempo. Apretó los dientes y se esforzó por sonreír. Hannah debía comprender que aquel no era el mejor momento.

–Vuelve a la cama, cariño –ordenó Hannah.

–Yo también quiero hacer ruidito, como el oso –dijo Heidi desobedeciendo y entrando en el salón.

Adam se desesperó. Había visto a Hannah abrazar y hacer cosquillas a Heidi. Sabía lo que quería la niña. Igual que Maddy. Adam se hundió en el sillón, pero Heidi siguió avanzando hacia él. Hannah se levantó.

–Te llevaré a la cama –dijo Hannah con firmeza–. Vamos.

–No, quiero hacer ruidito.

–Yo te haré ruidito –se ofreció Hannah.

–No, él.

–No –negó Adam tratando de sumar su autoridad a la de Hannah.

Unos diminutos brazos se agarraron a su pierna. Aquello era demasiado. Adam se puso en pie de inmediato. Heidi se soltó entonces sin querer y cayó hacia atrás, golpeándose la cabeza. Hannah gritó horrorizada. Agarró a Heidi y la abrazó más rápida que el rayo, y luego miró a Adam furiosa.

–¿Cómo te atreves a empujar a mi hija?

–Yo no la he empujado –la contradijo Adam con calma–. Ha sido un accidente –añadió alargando la mano para tocar el chichón en la cabeza de la niña.

–No la toques –gritó Hannah apartando a su hija.

–¡Por el amor de Dios, Hannah! –exclamó Adam ofendido–. No pretendía hacerle daño.

–Bueno, pero se lo has hecho, a pesar de todo.

–¡Es solo un chichón! –volvió a exclamar él desesperado, en su defensa.

Adam estaba irritado consigo mismo por haber perdido el control. Y Hannah reaccionaba de un modo exagerado.

–No me refiero al daño físico –afirmó Hannah–. La has rechazado.

–¡Por el amor de Dios! –volvió a exclamar Adam.

Heidi sollozó y se metió el pulgar en la boca, dirigiéndole una mirada dura, apoyando a su madre. Adam sacudió la cabeza.

–Todo esto no es necesario.

–No –convino Hannah–. Desde luego. ¿Por qué no te marchas, Adam? Déjanos solas.

Adam sintió que un soplo de aire helado invadía su corazón para morir instantáneamente, creando un silencio frío.

–¿Es eso lo que quieres que haga, Hannah?

–Nadie va a hacerle daño a mi hija, Adam –afirmó Hannah enérgica, pero con calma–. Ni física, ni emocionalmente.

–Pero no ha sido como tú...

–Vete –lo interrumpió ella–. Sal de aquí, Adam. Sal de mi vida. Sal de nuestras vidas –terminó Hannah estrechando a su hija.

Capítulo 8

LAS COSAS podían haber salido peor. Mucho peor. De haber continuado por ese camino, derribando por completo el muro que protegía su corazón, no habría tenido esperanzas de volver a reconstruirlo nunca. Había que ser fuerte para reconstruirlo. Tal y como estaban las cosas, apuntalarlo sería difícil, pero no imposible. Adam se había pasado la mayor parte de la noche intentándolo, y a primera hora de la mañana, al llegar a la central, estaba agotado.

Pero podía enfrentarse al agotamiento. En cierto sentido, el cansancio le distanciaba de las cosas, de la realidad, y eso le gustaba. Sus pacientes no lo notarían, por mucho que estuviera destrozado a nivel personal. Hannah no le importaba. Y no necesitaba que lo echara de su casa; estaba deseoso de salir de su vida. Para bien, en esa ocasión. Al pasar por delante del teléfono Adam respondió automáticamente.

–Aquí control.

–¿Podría hablar con Ivan Moresby, por favor?

–Aún no ha llegado –contestó Adam mirando el reloj–. Llame dentro de diez minutos o, mejor, déjeme el mensaje.

–Soy Norma Duncan, la madre de Hannah.

–Hola, Norma, soy Adam. ¿Qué ocurre?

–Hannah no irá hoy a trabajar.

–¿Y eso? –preguntó Adam aliviado y preocupado al mismo tiempo.

–Creo que aún no ha superado el virus. Anoche, cuando volví a casa, tenía un aspecto lamentable. No creo que haya dormido nada.

Adam escuchó indiferente. Hannah lo superaría. Después de todo, había sido su elección. De no haberse vuelto tan violentamente contra él habrían hablado. Y él habría tenido la oportunidad de explicarle por qué había reaccionado de un modo tan exagerado ante Heidi. En ese momento, sin embargo, cualquier explicación quedaba descartada.

–Y luego, cuando le he preparado el té esta mañana, ha empezado a vomitar. No puede ir a trabajar –continuó Norma.

–Claro –convino Adam–. Asegúrate de que descanse. Y si no consigues que tolere líquidos y que deje de vomitar, llama a un médico.

–Voy a llamar, de todos modos –respondió Norma–. Le diré a Gerry Prescott que venga a verla a última hora de la mañana.

–Yo avisaré a Ivan Moresby. Lo arreglaré todo para cubrir los turnos de las dos próximas noches. Hannah debe recuperarse.

–Bueno, no creo que eso le guste mucho. Seguramente estará bien mañana. La preocupa conseguir las suficientes horas de carretera antes del cursillo.

–Eso no será ningún problema –aseguró Adam–, y estoy convencido de que Ivan opinará lo mismo que yo. Dile a Hannah que no queremos volver a verla hasta la semana que viene.

Aquella enfermedad resultaba de lo más oportuna. Él se encargaría de ajustar los turnos en el equipo azul. Hannah no era la única que necesitaba tiempo para recuperarse.

Adam debía estar implicado en el cambio de turnos. Por primera vez desde que trabajaba como oficial de ambulancia, Hannah tenía asignado el cuarto turno. Su compañero sería un oficial de segundo grado llamado Roger Marks, un hombre que llevaba más de dos meses sin trabajar, recuperándose de un problema de espalda. Hannah no lo conocía, pero había oído hablar de él.

–Tendrás que conducir tú –fueron las primeras palabras que le dirigió a Hannah–, porque yo tengo que cuidar mi espalda. Eres nueva, ¿verdad?

–Llevo casi tres meses en ambulancias.

–Estas más verde que la hierba –sonrió Roger alejándose–. Espero que seas más fuerte de lo que pareces.

En aquel momento no se sentía muy fuerte. De hecho, solo llegar al trabajo le había costado un gran esfuerzo. El descanso en casa no le había servido de gran cosa. Casi hubiera preferido volver al día siguiente, enfrentarse a Adam inmediatamente después de lo ocurrido. Durante aquellos días de descanso, la ira había ido cediendo para dar paso a una batalla de sentimientos contradictorios en su interior: su amor por Adam, y su amor por su hija. Pero no iba a dejar que Adam le ganara terreno, no podía permitírselo. Una desagradable sensación de decepción envolvía su vida.

En realidad era pena más que decepción. El rechazo rotundo de Adam hacia su hija había sido definitivo, terminante. Hannah comprobó el equipo y reflexionó. Roger tenía más de cuarenta años, y según se decía jamás le había gustado el trabajo. Quizá todo fuera para bien. Hannah cerró el maletín de primeros auxilios. Aquella mañana había vuelto decidida a que su ruptura con Adam no le echara a perder el resto de su vida, y menos aún la satisfacción que le proporcionaba su trabajo. Abandonarlos ambos habría sido demasiado, tenía que aferrarse a su vocación.

Los avisos de aquel día parecieron conspirar con Roger para procurarle uno de los días más negros de su vida. Primero tuvieron que trasladar a un paciente de un hospital a una residencia. Roger alegó algo urgente que hacer y la mandó sola a cumplirlo. Hannah sospechó que simplemente quería tomar café.

Los dos avisos siguientes fueron también traslados, pero en esas ocasiones Roger la acompañó. Eso sí, quejándose continuamente de lo mal que conducían los taxistas, los conductores de autobuses, los viejos y las mujeres. Hannah se animó un poco cuando recibieron un aviso de prioridad 3, pero cuando llegaron a la dirección indicada se encontraron con que el médico había llegado antes. Roger no quiso perder el tiempo valorando de nuevo la situación, así que el aviso acabó convertido en otro traslado. La única diferencia fue que el paciente, en esa ocasión, estaba realmente enfermo. Se pasó el viaje vomitando. Al llegar al hospital, Roger quiso encargarse del enfermo y le asignó a Hannah la tarea de limpiar la ambulancia.

A la hora de la comida volvieron a la central, pero Hannah no se sorprendió al descubrir que no tenía hambre, así que se dirigió a la biblioteca. Quizá los libros lograran hacerla recordar por qué había escogido un trabajo así. Sin embargo el intercomunicador sonó antes de que pudiera abrir un solo libro. Leyó el mensaje. Otro traslado. Hannah atravesó la sala de empleados para dirigirse al garaje. Tom y Derek estaban allí.

–No tienes muy buen aspecto –la saludó Tom.

–Estoy bien, gracias –contestó Hannah tratando de sonreír.

Entonces sonaron más intercomunicadores y unos cuantos hombres la siguieron hasta el garaje.

–¡Prioridad 1! –exclamó Derek leyendo el mensaje de su intercomunicador–. Dolor en el pecho.

–¡Otra vez no, por favor! –exclamó a su vez Tom abriendo la puerta y cediéndole el paso a Hannah.

Las luces de la ambulancia de Tom se encendieron. Hannah atravesó el garaje sin hacer caso de otra ambulancia que entraba. Sabía perfectamente quién conducía la unidad 641. Al abrir la puerta de su vehículo, Hannah se encontró con Roger sentado en el lugar del copiloto.

–Tendrás que darte un poco más de prisa –le reprochó Roger–. No te pagan para dormir, ¿sabes?

Dormir aquella noche le costó. A la mañana siguiente besó a su hija antes de marcharse. Norma parecía preocupada.

–¿Estás segura de que quieres continuar con este empleo?

–Eso es precisamente lo que tengo que descubrir, mamá. Sería patético que dejara una vocación y un empleo que tanto me ha costado conseguir solo por un romance desgraciado.

–Adam Lewis es un estúpido –afirmó Norma–. Y te aseguro que no me importaría decirle lo que opino de él.

–No serviría de nada, mamá –suspiró Hannah–. Tengo que superarlo y continuar con mi vida.

–Esperemos que hoy tengas un día mejor –sonrió Norma tratando de animarla.

–No puede ser mucho peor –contestó Hannah sonriendo a medias.

A pesar de tener a Roger de nuevo como compañero, el día sí pareció al menos comenzar mejor. Nada más entrar, tuvieron un aviso de prioridad 1. Se trataba de un hombre que se tambaleaba en medio de la calle. Al llegar lo encontraron sentado en medio de una rotonda.

–Apenas puede andar –explicó un transeúnte que pasaba por allí–. Estaba gritando y jurando, se ha lanzado contra un coche, casi lo atropellan.

–Está borracho –dictaminó Roger de inmediato.

Hannah no estaba tan segura. No olía a alcohol, y el hombre iba demasiado bien vestido y limpio como para llevar toda la noche en la calle.

–¿Cómo se llama, señor?

–¡Déjame! –exclamó el hombre empujándola, articulando a duras penas las palabras.

Hannah se volvió hacia el testigo y preguntó:

–¿Se ha golpeado la cabeza?, ¿ha estado inconsciente en algún momento?

–Venga, vamos a llevarlo a la ambulancia –afirmó Roger tomando al hombre del brazo y tirando de él para que se pusiera en pie–. Estamos bloqueando el tráfico.

–Puede que se trate de una contusión –dijo Hannah agarrando al hombre del otro brazo para ayudarlo a subir a la ambulancia.

–Pues yo no lo veo –contestó Roger sujetando al hombre con firmeza, tras sentarlo en la camilla, de donde se quería levantar.

El hombre cayó en la camilla musitando incoherencias. Roger se apresuró a ocupar el asiento del conductor. Hannah sacó el instrumental para tomarle el pulso, pero el hombre la empujó, gritando:

—¡Vete, déjame en paz!

—¿Cómo se llama? —volvió a preguntar Hannah—. ¿Sabe dónde está?

La única respuesta que recibió fue un sonoro ronquido. Hannah sacó la linterna. En esa ocasión, al levantarle los párpados al paciente, este no la empujó. Las pupilas respondían y parecían idénticas, pero le preocupaba la progresiva pérdida de conciencia que mostraba el paciente. Le palpó la cabeza, pero no notó que tuviera ninguna contusión. Hannah le tomó la tensión y observó que tenía la piel húmeda y fría. Sacudió al paciente y preguntó:

—¿Me oye, señor? Abra los ojos —Hannah no obtuvo respuesta. Comenzaba a preocuparse seriamente—. Roger, creo que el paciente se nos va. Será mejor pedir refuerzos.

—Pero si estamos a diez minutos del hospital —protestó Roger molesto.

Hannah se balanceaba entre la camilla y el equipo, apenas podía trabajar con tanto movimiento. Agarró la máscara de oxígeno y rogó:

—Por favor, para. No me gusta el estado en el que se encuentra el paciente.

Por fin Roger, incómodo, se detuvo y pidió refuerzos. La idea de que fuera Adam quien acudiera a ayudarlos no desanimó a Hannah. Esperaba que fuera él.

—Ha perdido reflejos, y tiene taquicardia —informó Hannah.

—Utiliza un tubo de succión —ordenó Roger—. Y dale respiración asistida. Yo conectaré el monitor.

Hannah se sintió aliviada de ver que Roger respondía por fin, pero seguía preocupada.

–Está muy frío –señaló–. ¿Crees que debemos inyectarle glucosa?

–Dentro de un minuto –respondió Roger desenredando los electrodos.

Hannah le puso la máscara de oxígeno tras succionarle la saliva con un tubo. Por fin oyó la sirena de la ambulancia de refuerzo. De pronto se abrió la puerta trasera. La presencia de Adam resultó reconfortante.

–¿Qué ocurre?

–Lo hemos encontrado tambaleándose por la calle, jurando y vociferando delante de los coches –informó Roger–. Según los testigos, debe estar borracho.

–¿Qué nivel de azúcar tiene en sangre?

–Ahora mismo estamos tratando de averiguarlo –contestó Roger.

–Yo le pondré la intravenosa –dijo Adam tomando el equipo que le pasaba su compañero, Matt.

Le hubiera gustado ayudar a Adam, pero se vio atrapada en la parte delantera de la ambulancia, sin poder moverse. Con tres hombres, una camilla y todo un equipo desplegado, sencillamente no había espacio. Adam la miró brevemente.

–Cámbiale esa máscara y ponle quince litros de aire por minuto –ordenó.

Hannah obedeció y sacó suero para ponérselo al paciente, pero al darse la vuelta comprobó que Adam había sacado el suyo de su equipo y no lo necesitaba.

–El nivel de glucosa es de dos mililitros –informó Matt.

Demasiado bajo. El paciente tenía hipoglucemia.

–Trae glucosa –ordenó Adam conectándola de inmediato al catéter y abriéndolo al máximo–. En marcha. Matt, síguenos en la otra ambulancia. ¿Qué nivel de conciencia tenía cuando lo encontrasteis? –preguntó Adam dirigiéndose a Hannah.

–Poco, enseguida quedó inconsciente –respondió Hannah.

–¿Y no se te ocurrió medir el nivel de glucosa?

–Bueno, para empezar no se mostró muy cooperativo.

–¿Olía a alcohol?

–No –respondió Hannah mordiéndose el labio inferior–. Ni tenía signo alguno de contusión en la cabeza.

–Se tarda treinta segundos en medir la glucosa –afirmó Adam de mal humor–. Quizá, la próxima vez, te acuerdes de que es uno de los test más importantes. Aunque haya bebido alcohol, los síntomas pueden enmascarar un problema más importante –le reprochó Adam observando el monitor. La irregularidad de la curva parecía ceder progresivamente, pasando a estabilizarse–. Lo menos que podías hacer era monitorizarlo. Tienes suerte si esto no acaba en una denuncia.

Hannah no necesitaba aquella reprimenda. El tono de voz de Adam resultaba suficientemente desalentador. El hecho de que Roger, como oficial de más experiencia, no hubiera hecho su trabajo, no era una excusa. Trataría de hacerlo mejor. Y sería feliz, si el resto de avisos de aquel día eran solo traslados. Así no tendría que pedir refuerzos, y Adam tendría que descargarse con otra persona.

Las dos noches siguientes Hannah hizo el turno con Matt. Trató por todos los medios de evitar discretamente a Adam, pero Matt se dio cuenta enseguida.

–Ya sé que no es asunto mío, pero Adam es mi mejor compañero, y no me gusta verlo así –dijo Matt en un descanso, sonriendo a medias–. Trabajar con él es un infierno.

–Lo superará –contestó Hannah fingiéndose interesada por el documental que ponían en la televisión–. No había futuro para nosotros dos, Matt. Jamás debimos comenzar la relación.

Matt gruñó de mal humor. Evidentemente la explicación no lo convencía. Miró a Hannah y suspiró, resignado.

–Quizá tengas razón. Lo superará –musitó.

Por supuesto que Adam lo superaría. Y ella también... algún día. Tras el descanso de cuatro días, Hannah consiguió convencerse a sí misma de que las cosas se arreglarían por sí solas. Roger estuvo de baja de nuevo durante la semana siguiente, de modo que Hannah trabajó con Tom. Era agradable hablar de niños. Hannah echó mucho de menos a Heidi, y comenzó a preguntarse si aquel empleo merecía la pena. Quizá abandonándolo solucionara todos sus problemas.

A la semana siguiente Ivan la llamó a su despacho. Eso la alarmó. La única razón que se le ocurría era que Adam se hubiera quejado de ella por el caso del paciente con hipoglucemia. El hombre había recuperado la conciencia enseguida, poco después de llegar al hospital, e incluso había sido dado de alta aquella noche, pero quizá las quejas, la burocracia, llevara su tiempo. Hannah entró nerviosa en el despacho.

–Estoy preocupado por ti, Hannah –afirmó Ivan–. Empezaste muy bien. Todos los informes que recibía de ti eran muy positivos. ¿Cuánto tiempo llevas con nosotros?, ¿tres meses?

Hannah asintió y se retorció las manos en el regazo. Adam se había quejado, estaba segura.

–¿Se ha quejado alguien de mí?

–¡Cielos, no! No es esa la razón por la que te he llamado –contestó Ivan ajustándose las gafas en el puente de la nariz–. No pareces muy contenta. ¿Es que el trabajo no te resulta lo satisfactorio que esperabas?

–No sabía muy bien qué esperar –contestó Hannah aliviada–. Y sigo sin saberlo. Cada aviso es diferente. Eso es lo que más me gusta.

–Hmm... –murmuró Ivan pensativo–. No soy yo el único que está preocupado por ti, Hannah. Estás muy callada, nadie te ve nunca cuando estás en la central.

–Es que voy a la biblioteca –contestó Hannah comprendiendo que sus compañeros se habían dado cuenta de que evitaba la sala de empleados. Ivan debía conocer el motivo tan bien como los demás. Y seguramente no aprobaba que dos empleados mantuvieran relaciones–. La semana que viene comienza el curso para pasar al primer grado, pronto serán los exámenes. Pensé que me vendría bien estudiar.

–Muy loable –asintió Ivan poco convencido de su explicación–. Todos respondemos al estrés de forma diferente, Hannah. Este trabajo ejerce mucha presión sobre nosotros a nivel personal. Y tiene un coste emocional. Pero eso no debe afectar a los distintos aspectos de nuestras vidas.

–Mis relaciones personales marchan bien. Ya sé que últimamente he estado poco sociable, pero es que quería aprovechar el tiempo en la biblioteca. Tengo una hija pequeña, apenas tengo tiempo de estudiar.

–No pretendo inmiscuirme en tu vida privada,

Hannah —asintió Ivan suspirando—. Solo quería seña-
lar que, desde que atendimos aquel accidente de tráfico, hace unas semanas, estás distinta. No viniste a
la reunión, y era tu primer accidente de gravedad.
Pensé que quizá te hubiera afectado, eso es todo.
Quiero que sepas que una de mis funciones es estar
aquí, disponible, por si necesitas mi ayuda.

—Oh —exclamó Hannah—. Gracias.

—Aquel fue un caso muy estresante. Para todos.

—Sí —confirmó Hannah apartando la vista. Había
sido el día más negro de su vida desde la muerte de
Ben—, supongo que me obligó a replantearme ciertas
cosas.

—¿Y has cambiado de opinión en cuanto a tu vocación?

—No lo creo —contestó Hannah sin levantar la mirada—. Soy capaz de soportar el estrés.

—Eso espero. Sería una gran pérdida para el
cuerpo si decidieras retirarte —hubo un silencio—. ¿Te
gustaría cambiar de equipo? —preguntó Ivan inesperadamente.

—¿Por qué? —inquirió Hannah levantando la vista.

—Hay mucha gente a la que no conoces. Por ejemplo en el equipo rojo. Ellos cubren los turnos cuando
tú descansas, así que nunca los ves. Parece que Eddie
va a estar de baja algún tiempo, podría cambiarte por
él.

En ese caso jamás volvería a trabajar con Adam,
ni siquiera cuando pidiera refuerzos. Dejaría incluso
de verlo, y no tendría que replantearse la posibilidad
de abandonar el empleo. Era su oportunidad, y lo ló-
gico hubiera sido saltar de alegría. Todo sería mucho
más fácil. Superaría el abatimiento, olvidaría la sonrisa de Adam, su forma atenta de escucharla y su cos-

tumbre de pasarse la mano por los cabellos. Podría incluso olvidar las razones por las que se había enamorado de él. La distancia era la mejor solución, la más sensata. ¿Acaso era masoquista?

–Piénsalo –recomendó Ivan cansado de esperar su respuesta–. Pronto tendrás dos semanas de clase. Dame tu respuesta después.

Todo volvía a ser como antes. Los mismos compañeros, la misma clase. Solo que había algunos menos, y Hannah era la única mujer. Además, todos iban uniformados y eran más sabios, más expertos y más viejos que la primera vez. Hannah había visto a Derek a menudo, pero el cambio producido en el resto de compañeros la sorprendió.

Michael había perdido su aire de infinita confianza en sí mismo, estaba más callado y más atento a lo que decían los demás. Él y Ross habían estado en una central de un barrio de las afueras.

–Es un gran profesional –le contó Ross a Hannah–. Jim Melton, el instructor de esta clase, es compañero nuestro.

–Sí, es cierto. Vamos a aprender un montón –aseguró Michael.

–Ojalá fuera Adam quien diera el curso –comentó Eddie con sus muletas–. Aunque yo voy a suspender. Al menos, mientras no consiga reunir las suficientes horas de carretera.

–Pero has conseguido llegar aquí –respondió Hannah amable–. ¿Qué tal tu pierna?

–Va mejor. Voy a fisioterapia a diario –sonrió Eddie.

–Sí, he oído hablar de ti y de esa fisioterapeuta rubia –comentó Ross.

Eddie se sonrojó. Hannah sonrió y se sentó suspirando.

–Has adelgazado. ¿Has trabajado mucho? –le preguntó John a Hannah.

–Sí, tuve una infección, me la pegó un paciente. Me costó curarme. Tú, en cambio, tienes mejor aspecto que nunca –sonrió Hannah.

–Sí, estoy entrenando. Cuando termine el curso voy a ir a Hawai a una competición.

–¿En serio?, ¿te han dado permiso?

–No les he dejado opción –contestó John encogiéndose de hombros–. Para mí, las competiciones son tan importantes como este empleo –añadió sentándose al lado de Hannah–. A decir verdad, ya no me resulta una novedad. Estoy un poco harto de los traslados. Me estoy planteando si quiero seguir.

Hannah asintió. Para ella también había dejado de ser una novedad, pero a pesar de ello sabía que no quería dejar el empleo.

–Sí, pero a veces, cuando hay avisos importantes, recuerdas por qué estás donde estás –intervino Michael.

Sí, Hannah también necesitaba esos momentos para recordarlo. Resultaban alentadores.

–Pues yo no querría hacer otra cosa –repuso Ross.

El trabajo académico durante aquellas dos semanas fue intensivo. Estudiaron el estado clínico durante la primera y los problemas traumáticos durante la segunda. Hannah tomó muchos apuntes. El estudio en casa, con los libros de texto, consumía el resto de su tiempo.

–Pregúntame, mamá –le pidió a Norma una noche, una vez que Heidi estuvo en la cama.

–Bueno. ¿Cuáles son los tres procesos patológicos

que siguen a una obstrucción pulmonar y desembocan en un ataque de asma agudo?

–Espasmos bronquiales, que provocan dilatación de los vasos sanguíneos, producción de mucosa en las membranas de la pared bronquial y obturación de los bronquios debido a la secreción –contestó Hannah con los ojos cerrados, haciendo memoria.

Norma asintió y continuó preguntando:

–¿Qué enfermedades, aparte del asma, puede provocar una dificultad respiratoria?

–Fallo cardíaco, aspiración de cuerpos extraños, inhalación de humos tóxicos, embolismo pulmonar, reacciones alérgicas y... y... –Hannah se mordió el labio–. Se me olvida algo.

–Bronquitis crónica –dijo Norma.

–¡Eso es!, ¡maldita sea! Pregúntame otra.

–Ya es hora de dejarlo, cariño. Es casi medianoche.

–Solo una más –rogó Hannah.

–La última –afirmó Norma seria–. ¿Qué síntomas produce un ataque cardíaco?

–Desasosiego, confusión, dificultades respiratorias, respiración rápida e irregular. Mmm... elevación de la presión sanguínea y... –Hannah enterró la cara entre las manos–. Dios, no lo recuerdo. ¡Ojalá no estuviera tan cansada!

–Necesitas dormir –dijo Norma preocupada–. Estás trabajando demasiado, y no comes bien. No es de extrañar que siempre estés cansada –añadió mirando a Hannah y sacudiendo la cabeza–. ¿Sabes?, creo que aún no te has recuperado de ese virus.

–Pero si de eso hace semanas...

–Sí, pero llevas días vomitando, y desde entonces

no tienes buen aspecto. Quiero que vayas a ver al doctor Prescott.

–Estoy bien, mamá –suspiró Hannah.

–Mañana –declaró Norma sin posibilidad de apelación–. Te pediré una cita para las cinco y media. Para entonces ya has terminado la clase, ¿no?

–Si eso te hace feliz –se resignó Hannah–. Iré a verlo, pero me va a decir que estoy bien. Es una pérdida de tiempo.

–Deja que sea él quien juzgue eso –aconsejó Norma.

Gerry Prescott no creyó que Hannah estuviera perdiendo el tiempo. Hannah no puso objeción a los análisis y preguntas que él quiso hacerle en aquel chequeo general.

–Vengo por mi madre. Estoy bien, en serio –insistió Hannah mientras terminaba de vestirse, saliendo de detrás de una cortina y sentándose frente a la mesa del doctor–. Un poco cansada, claro, pero con el nuevo trabajo y todo eso...

–¿Sueles tener menstruaciones regulares? –preguntó Gerry Prescott con naturalidad.

–Sí, normalmente sí.

–¿Y cuándo tuviste la última?

–No lo recuerdo –confesó Hannah frunciendo el ceño.

–¿Es posible que haga más de dos meses?

–¡Oh, no! –negó Hannah convencida–. Jamás tengo retrasos tan largos. Debe hacer unos... –su voz se desvaneció–. Pero no es posible que...

–Definitivamente. Estás embarazada, Hannah –asintió el doctor Prescott–. De unas ocho semanas,

diría yo. Si quieres, te doy cita para hacerte una ecografía, así saldremos de dudas.

—Pero es imposible, se lo aseguro —negó Hannah
sacudiendo la cabeza.

—Tu madre me contó que has mantenido relaciones últimamente.

—Sí, pero tomamos precauciones —insistió Hannah—. No puedo estar embarazada.

—Ningún método es infalible, me temo —señaló el
doctor Prescott observando preocupado a Hannah—.
Ya veo que la noticia ha sido un susto para ti, pero te
aseguro que no cabe duda. Tanto el análisis de orina
como el examen físico han dado positivo.

—¡Pero no puedo estar embarazada! —exclamó
Hannah en un susurro desesperado, comenzando a
entrever las consecuencias de la noticia—. ¡No puede
ser!

Capítulo 9

NO PUEDES estar embarazada –negó Adam inexpresivo, con los rasgos endurecidos–. Tuvimos cuidado, tomamos precauciones.

–Lo sé –contestó Hannah mirando por la ventana del salón de la casa de Adam–. Por desgracia, ningún método es infalible. Me he hecho análisis y una ecografía. Estoy embarazada de ocho semanas.

–Entonces aún no es demasiado tarde.

–¿Demasiado tarde? –repitió Hannah volviéndose y elevando la voz–. Demasiado tarde, ¿para qué, Adam?

Adam evitó su mirada. Se sentó abatido en el sofá y se tapó los ojos con una mano. Sobre la mesa, junto al sofá, una bandeja con la cena sin terminar. Hannah había ido a verlo sin avisar.

–¿Demasiado tarde para nosotros? –sugirió Hannah fríamente, sin esperar respuesta. Luego suspiró–. Siempre fue demasiado tarde para nosotros, Adam.

–No era eso lo que quería decir.

–Ah, entonces es que prefieres que haga desaparecer nuestro problema, ¿no es eso? –preguntó Hannah comenzando a enfadarse por el hecho de que él ni siquiera la mirara–. Quizá sea yo quien deba desaparecer. Dejo mi empleo y desaparezco por completo de tu vida. ¿Quieres eso, Adam? –preguntó Hannah cruzándose de brazos–. Tranquilo, es probable que ocurra. No creo que pueda conservar mi trabajo estando embarazada. Y, aunque no lo estuviera, no estoy segura de querer trabajar cerca de ti.

Ni siquiera aunque tuviera al niño y aceptara la generosísima oferta de su madre de cuidar de sus dos hijos. Adam continuaba sin mirarla.

–¡Maldita sea, Hannah! –exclamó Adam dando un golpe en la mesa–. No esperaba que ocurriera algo así. Me aseguré muy bien de que no hubiera consecuencias –repitió levantándose–. Te dije desde el principio que en mi futuro no podía haber niños. Ni míos, ni de nadie. Especialmente míos.

La forma en que Adam la miraba era desoladora. Sus ojos expresaban tal angustia que Hannah comenzó a comprender lo profundamente afectado que estaba. ¿Cómo podía habérsele ocurrido la idea de que Adam aceptara a su hijo?, ¿cómo podía haber creído por un momento que su embarazo podía tener un efecto positivo sobre sus relaciones?

Hannah se enfadó. Estaba asustada ante la profundidad de las emociones que veía en él. No podía creer que el bebé fuera la única causa de esa desolación, pero fuera como fuera, Adam parecía incapaz de soportarlo. Si lo presionaba, quizá llegara a descubrir la verdad, pero se sentía demasiado débil, demasiado vulnerable como para cargar con los problemas de los demás. Bastante tenía con los suyos.

–No debería haber venido –afirmó con calma, apartando la mirada de Adam para darle la oportunidad de calmarse–. Pensé que tenías derecho a saberlo.

El silencio que siguió fue tenso, tenso por todas las palabras y las cosas que no se dijeron. Hannah volvió a mirar por la ventana. Fue Adam quien habló entonces, era su turno de decidir.

–Te quiero, Hannah –Hannah no contestó. Aquellas palabras la hirieron más que cualquier grito, porque sabía qué iba a decir Adam a continuación–. Es simplemente que... no estoy preparado para enfrentarme a esto.

–¿Qué quieres que haga, Adam? –preguntó Hannah volviéndose hacia él.

–Es tu cuerpo –declaró él encogiéndose de hombros–, la elección es tuya –añadió apartando la mirada–. No es la primera vez que te enfrentas a la idea de tener un niño sin padre.

–¿Cómo puedes siquiera compararlo? Con Heidi no tuve otra elección, tuve que seguir adelante sin su padre.

–Siempre hay una elección, Hannah.

–Yo amaba a Ben –repuso Hannah pálida–. Y quería a mi bebé. A nuestro bebé.

–¿Y a este?

Hannah apretó los dientes. No iba a confesarle que sus sentimientos hacia él eran aún más fuertes de lo que lo habían sido por Ben. Ni a decirle que incluso en ese momento, tras su rechazo de Heidi, era incapaz de mirar al futuro sin él. Aquel rechazo había servido para hacerle comprender lo difícil que sería superar el obstáculo, pero a pesar de todo Hannah no podía dejarlo marchar.

La batalla de sus sentimientos, con Adam de un lado y Heidi del otro, la había destrozado. No podía seguir soportándolo. En aquel momento, ni siquiera estaba segura de que sus sentimientos por Adam no hubieran cambiado. En todo caso, no quería añadir una tormenta emocional más a la situación.

–Tal y como has dicho, es mi elección –afirmó Hannah dirigiéndose hacia la puerta.

–Espero que sepas arreglártelas bien... sea lo que sea lo que decidas –dijo Adam siguiéndola hasta la puerta.

–Eso espero –contestó ella tensa–. Tú lo has dicho, tengo práctica criando hijos sin padre. Podré manejar uno más. Quizá no sea tanta la diferencia.

–Si puedo ayudarte en algo... económicamente, me refiero. Dímelo –continuó Adam incómodo–. He oído decir que la clínica Cambridge Terrace tiene el mejor departamento de maternidad de la ciudad, pero también que es muy caro.

Hannah salió de la casa. La clínica Cambridge era famosa por sus cuidados, pero también por proporcionar abortos rápidos y discretos. Hannah ni siquiera estaba dispuesta a contemplar esa posibilidad.

–Adiós, Adam –se despidió sin mirarlo siquiera.

–¡Hannah!

Hannah lo oyó llamarla, pero no hizo caso. No había nada más que decir.

A la mañana siguiente Adam dio un portazo al salir de casa. Estaba tan irritado que hacía las cosas automáticamente, sin darse cuenta. No podía olvidar ni por un instante el dilema en el que le había puesto Hannah la noche anterior. Aquel iba a ser un día infernal. El único consuelo que le quedaba era que no la vería, porque Hannah seguía asistiendo a clase.

Pero acabarían por discutir. La disputa de la noche anterior no había terminado, y eso lo carcomía por dentro. Había estado a punto incluso de llamar a Hannah a las cuatro de la madrugada.

¿Cómo había podido atreverse a sugerirle que abortara? Era impensable. Era una solución terminante, definitiva, fría e insensible para algo que, en realidad, ni siquiera debía ser un problema. Hannah y él se amaban. O se habían amado. ¿Podía un amor como aquel desvanecerse solo por el caos emocional al que había sido expuesto durante las últimas semanas?

Caos del cual el único culpable era él. Hannah no había hecho más que ofrecerle su amor y tratar de proteger a su hija. ¿Seguiría amándolo? La noche anterior ella no había dicho nada al respecto. Había hablado de su amor por Ben y por su hija, pero no del que sentía por él o por su hijo. Habían acordado que la decisión era de ella, y luego él la había dejado marchar.

Adam aparcó el coche y entró en el garaje. Estaba en el trabajo. Había llegado la hora de demostrar que su vida privada no le afectaría. Por suerte le tocaba salir con Matt, pero por desgracia el primer aviso fue por maternidad.

—Prioridad 1 —señaló Matt mientras ambos corrían a la unidad 241—. Una mujer a punto de parir. Gasgoine Street, 12B.

Conducir a toda velocidad lo distrajo. Tenía que emplear en ello toda su concentración. Tardaron solo cuatro minutos en llegar. Un hombre nervioso, de unos treinta años, abrió la puerta instantáneamente.

—¡Gracias a Dios! —exclamó al ver a Adam—. Tenemos prisa, no queda mucho tiempo —añadió poniendo una maleta en manos de Adam—. Tenga esto, yo iré por Pamela.

Adam y Matt se miraron frunciendo el ceño. Era inquietante tanta ansiedad. Primero había que valorar la situación, antes de ponerse en marcha. Adam dejó la maleta en el suelo y entró en la casa con el maletín de primeros auxilios. Siguió al hombre y lo encontró en un dormitorio, ayudando a la mujer embarazada a ponerse el abrigo.

—Esta es mi mujer, Pamela —explicó el hombre al ver a Adam en la puerta—. Estamos listos para marcharnos.

—Hola, Pamela —sonrió Adam—. Yo soy Adam. ¿Es tu primer parto?

Pamela sacudió la cabeza en una negativa y Adam enarcó las cejas. De ser primeriza, habría comprendido perfectamente los nervios.

—¿De cuánto estás embarazada?

—De treinta y seis semanas.

—¿Has tenido contracciones?

El hombre tomó a Pamela del codo y la ayudó a ponerse en pie.

—Ahora no hay tiempo para preguntas —dijo impaciente—. Tenemos que marcharnos. Esto es una emergencia.

—Preferiría conocer primero de qué emergencia se trata —alegó Adam con calma—. Puede que seamos mucho más útiles aquí que en carretera.

—Me mareo, Bruce —dijo Pamela con ansiedad—. Creo que voy a vomitar.

Matt entró en el dormitorio y dejó la maleta en el suelo. Adam corrió a ayudar a Pamela.

—Siéntate —ordenó Adam—. Este es mi compañero, Matt. Bruce, ¿podrías traer un barreño para Pamela, por favor?

—Tengo uno aquí —dijo Bruce soltando reacio a su mujer—. Tuvo ganas de vomitar antes, cuando comenzaron las contracciones.

—¿Con qué frecuencia las tiene?

—Cada dos minutos —informó Bruce—. Y duran

unos sesenta segundos, por lo menos. Por eso tenemos que marcharnos.

Adam le tomó el pulso a Pamela. Luego tocó su abdomen, que estaba duro como una piedra. Pamela se retorció de dolor.

—Ya vuelve —gritó—. Necesito empujar. ¡Voy a vomitar! —gritó segundos después.

Bruce sostuvo el barreño y Adam se volvió hacia Matt.

—No podemos llevárnosla así, el parto es inminente. Tendremos que hacerlo aquí y llevarlos después a los dos al hospital.

—¡Pero no puedes hacer eso! —gritó Bruce sosteniendo el barreño y a su mujer, por la frente—. Todo está preparado en el hospital. Necesitamos cuidados intensivos para el bebé.

—¿Es que esperan tener problemas? —preguntó Adam mientras Pamela caía exhausta en la cama y gritaba.

—Es demasiado tarde, Bruce. De verdad, tengo que empujar.

Matt estaba preparado para rasgarle la ropa a Pamela con las tijeras. Adam dobló una toalla y la colocó bajo sus caderas. Bruce tomó de la mano a su mujer.

—Tranquila, amor mío, ellos saben lo que tienen que hacer.

—¿Qué problemas esperan? —volvió a preguntar Adam.

—Los mismos que la última vez —jadeó Pamela.

La contracción había terminado, pero era demasiado tarde para llevar a Pamela al hospital. Adam podía ver casi la cabeza del niño asomando. Una contracción o dos más y tendría al bebé en las manos.

—¿Y qué problemas fueron? —volvió a preguntar Adam.

–Se trata de un desorden conectivo de las membranas. Es un síndrome muy raro, poco frecuente –explicó Bruce con más calma–. El problema principal es la anatomía del corazón y de los pulmones del niño. Es muy probable que tenga dificultades para respirar nada más nacer.

Adam respiró hondo. Matt había recogido más equipo de la ambulancia. Adam colocó el barreño limpio junto a Pamela por si volvía a vomitar. Luego conectó la máscara de oxígeno a la bombona y se puso guantes. Por fin comprendía la terrible ansiedad de los padres.

–¿Perdisteis al primer bebé en el parto? –preguntó Adam con amabilidad.

–No –respondió Pamela–. Bethany vivió seis meses. Mucho más de lo que esperábamos. Incluso pudo venir a casa con nosotros. Era un bebé feliz y precioso.

Adam se sorprendió. Aquello debía haber significado una gran pérdida para ellos. Aún peor con seis meses que recién nacido, cuando no hay tiempo siquiera de encariñarse con el bebé.

–¿Y sabéis que este bebé va a padecer lo mismo? –preguntó Adam.

–Sí, lo sabemos –asintió Bruce–. Al principio creían que era poco probable que sucediera una segunda vez, pero lo descubrieron en la segunda ecografía, cuando Pamela estaba embarazada de doce semanas.

Adam se quedó atónito. ¿Cómo era posible que hubieran seguido adelante, sabiendo que su segundo hijo padecería la misma enfermedad que el primero? Más aún, Pamela y Bruce parecían ansiosos por lograr que aquel segundo bebé sobreviviera al parto.

–¡Ya viene! –gritó Pamela aferrándose a la mano

de su marido y levantando la cabeza de la almohada para empujar.

Adam colocó las manos sobre el cráneo del bebé ejerciendo una suave presión, con cuidado de evitar la cara y la fontanela.

–Tiene el cordón umbilical enrollado al cuello –dijo dirigiéndose a Matt–. ¿Tienes unas pinzas?

Matt le pasó unas pinzas y Adam las colocó presionando el cordón, a unos centímetros de distancia una de otra. Luego cortó el cordón por en medio y sacó la cabeza del bebé, succionándole la mucosa de la boca y de la nariz varias veces seguidas. Con la siguiente contracción el resto del cuerpo del bebé salió. Adam lo tomó y lo dejó sobre una toalla limpia para volver a succionarle la mucosa.

Adam se ocupó del recién nacido, y Matt de Pamela, que volvía a vomitar y a gritar. Bruce se echó a llorar al ver a su hija. Aquello no resultaba de ayuda. Adam le hizo al bebé el test de Apgar de inmediato. Estaba azul. Le tomó el ritmo cardíaco, pero el corazón apenas latía cien veces por minuto. El bebé no mostraba síntomas de actividad, solo a veces parecía hacer esfuerzos por respirar.

Adam sacó la mascarilla infantil del equipo y se la colocó para procurarle oxígeno. De esa forma consiguió ventilarlo delicadamente, hasta dilatarle el pecho. Bastó con apretar la perilla una vez. Después de treinta segundos, volvió a tomarle el ritmo cardíaco. Tenía menos de ochenta pulsaciones por minuto.

Adam estaba muy serio. Colocó los pulgares sobre la parte baja del esternón del bebé rodeando su diminuto pecho y presionó. Lo presionó rápidamente, con una frecuencia de al menos ciento veinte presiones por minuto.

Unos cinco minutos después, volvió a realizarle el test de Apgar. Por fin el bebé estaba rosado, pero seguía teniendo las manos y las piernas azules. El pulso había subido a más de cien. El bebé movía los rasgos de la cara al respirar. Adam le movió un brazo. La flacidez había cedido en parte.

—Ya se mueve un poco —informó a Matt.

—Y la respiración va mejor —observó Matt—, aunque sigue siendo lenta.

—La mejoraremos, conseguiré que sea del doble —sonrió Adam por primera vez, desde el momento de llegar a aquella habitación. Luego miró a los padres—. En cuanto me asegure de que está bien, los llevaré a todos al hospital.

—Ya sale la placenta —dijo Matt.

—Ocúpate tú de eso —ordenó Adam volviendo su atención deprisa hacia la niña.

Adam presionó los pies del bebé y este lloró por primera vez. Pamela levantó la cabeza excitada y gritó:

—¡Está viva!

—Y es preciosa —añadió Bruce.

—Dentro de un minuto podréis abrazarla —le dijo Adam a Pamela, observando cómo Matt terminaba de sacarle la placenta—. Séllala en una bolsa, Matt. ¿Podrías traer la camilla hasta aquí tú solo?

—Claro.

Diez minutos más tarde, Adam realizó el test de Apgar una tercera vez y quedó satisfecho. Nueve sobre diez. Envolvió a la niña en una sábana y la dejó en brazos de la madre. Se los llevaría en cuanto hubieran puesto un poco de orden en todo aquel caos. Ambos pacientes requerían el cuidado de un especialista cuanto antes.

—Es exactamente igual que Bethany —susurró Pamela contemplando a la recién nacida–. ¿No te parece, Bruce?

–Como dos gotas de agua –convino Bruce.

Adam guardó las toallas sucias en una bolsa. ¿Cómo podía aquella pareja estar tan contenta y llena de júbilo, cuando sabían a qué se enfrentaban, cuando sabían que aquel bebé sobreviviría como muchos unos cuantos meses? Adam sabía qué se sentía contemplando a un hijo por primera vez. Sabía que en ese momento uno no podía evitar preguntarse qué sería de él, cómo sería cuando fuera mayor. Con cinco, con diez años. Igual que se lo había preguntado él con Maddy, igual que seguiría preguntándoselo el resto de su vida. Adam suspiró y guardó las cosas en el maletín. Le ocurriría lo mismo con el hijo de Hannah, fuera cual fuera su decisión.

–Esta es Bethany. Tenía tres meses –dijo Bruce ofreciéndole una foto a Adam mientras guardaba el equipo. Adam tuvo que mirar la fotografía. Parecía un bebé normal, feliz–. Ahora tendría cinco años. Muchas veces nos preguntamos cómo sería, de haber sobrevivido –sonrió Bruce débilmente.

–Lo sé, lo sé –repuso Adam amablemente–. No es fácil, ¿verdad?

Matt había preparado la camilla. Adam se aclaró la garganta.

–Vamos. Bruce, ¿puedes sostener a la niña mientras trasladamos a Pamela a la camilla?

Adam quería conducir, pero Matt llegó primero y ocupó el asiento.

–De ningún modo, colega –le dijo a Adam–. Tú la has ayudado a nacer, así que ahora rellena los papeles.

Durante el viaje al hospital, Adam se las arregló

para ocuparse de la madre, de la niña y de rellenar los papeles. Bruce se sentó a su lado en la camilla que quedaba libre.

–Probablemente pienses que estamos locos, decidiendo volver a pasar por esta experiencia otra vez –dijo Bruce de pronto, casi cuando llegaban al hospital. Adam sonrió y calló–. Después de lo de Bethany, no pretendíamos que Pamela volviera a quedarse embarazada, pero tampoco quisimos evitarlo, una vez que lo estaba. Se nos ofreció una oportunidad.

–Perder a Bethany fue lo peor que nos ha ocurrido en la vida –añadió Pamela–. Pero luego nos dimos cuenta de que los meses que pasamos con ella fueron los mejores de nuestra vida.

–Esta vez sabemos qué esperar –continuó Bruce, deseoso de hacerle comprender la situación–. Por eso sabremos disfrutar al máximo del tiempo que la tengamos con nosotros, y por eso estábamos tan preocupados por que el nacimiento fuera un éxito.

–Queremos aprovechar cada minuto con nuestra hija –añadió Pamela besando la cabeza diminuta de su hija–. Cada instante.

Adam estaba deseoso de llegar al hospital y pasar el caso a maternidad. Todos lo felicitaron por el éxito del parto, pero él tenía otra cosa en la mente. Se trataba de una emergencia personal, en realidad. Subió al asiento del piloto de la unidad 241 y esperó a Matt. Eran casi las cinco y cuarto. A esas horas Hannah habría terminado sus clases, estaría en casa. Adam sacó el teléfono móvil y marcó el número.

La línea estaba ocupada. Adam suspiró lleno de frustración. Necesitaba hablar con ella. De inmediato. No podía esperar. En cuanto llegó Matt, encendió el motor y soltó el freno de mano.

–¿Qué prisas tienes?, ¿es que hay otro aviso?

–No, es un asunto personal –explicó Adam escueto–. Y urgente.

Adam condujo hasta la casa de Hannah. ¿Cómo podía haber estado tan equivocado durante tantos años?, ¿cómo podía haber estado tan obsesionado con algo tan negativo? Pamela y Bruce tenían razón. El tiempo pasado con la persona amada era un tiempo precioso. Cada minuto. La pena y el dolor que causaba la pérdida de esa persona solo se producía precisamente por el júbilo y la felicidad perdida. Llevaba años negándose a reconocer la felicidad que había vivido con Maddy, con tal de evitar el dolor. Por fin comprendía la enormidad de su error, de lo que se había negado a sí mismo.

Adam sentía ya de hecho la pérdida de Hannah. Trataba de negarla también, cuando ni siquiera se había permitido a sí mismo gozar de toda la felicidad que ella podía procurarle. Felicidad que solo alcanzaría si aceptaba su amor y se confiaba a ella plenamente, con completa sinceridad, felicidad que solo alcanzaría si le confesaba cuánto deseaba tener un hijo de los dos.

Adam paró delante de la casa de Hannah y llamó a la puerta. Matt lo miró confuso, pero no preguntó nada. Lo miró más preocupado, sin embargo, cuando lo vio volver corriendo. En el porche, una mujer mayor y una niña los observaban.

–¿Qué ocurre? ¿A dónde vamos ahora?

–A la clínica Cambridge –contestó Adam–. Y esta sí que es una emergencia.

Capítulo 10

LA VERJA de hierro de la clínica estaba abierta, pero no había modo de entrar. Adam apretó el freno ante la línea de gente caminando en silencio delante de la puerta. Sus manos, unidas, formaban una cadena imposible de atravesar.

—¿Qué diablos...? —preguntó desconectando la sirena.

—Es una manifestación en favor de la vida —observó Matt—. Mira los carteles.

—¿Y qué diablos hacen aquí?

—Se dedican a bloquear todos aquellos lugares en los que se practica el aborto.

—¿Pero por qué aquí?, ¿y justo hoy?

—Aquí se hacen abortos —respondió Matt con sensatez—. Creía que todo el mundo lo sabía.

—¡Por el amor de Dios! ¿Y por qué crees que estamos aquí? —sacudió la cabeza Adam incrédulo—. Pero no solo se hacen abortos, ¿es que esta gente no tiene nada que hacer?

Un hombre de mediana edad se acercó a la ambulancia dándose aires de importancia. Golpeó la ventanilla y Adam la bajó.

—Lo siento, amigo, pero no podemos dejarlo pasar.

—¡Al diablo con que no pueden dejarme pasar! —gritó Adam—. Obligue a esa gente a moverse, es una emergencia.

–Todo son emergencias –asintió el hombre–. Por eso nosotros tenemos que hablar en defensa de aquellos que no pueden hablar. Estamos salvando vidas.

–¡Por el amor de Dios! –exclamó Adam elevando la voz–. ¡Muévanse! ¡Voy a tener un hijo!

–¿En serio? –preguntó Matt incrédulo–. ¿Vas a tener un hijo?

–¡Eso espero! –musitó Adam–, si es que no llego demasiado tarde. Si quiere usted salvar una vida, amigo, dígale a esa gente que se aparte del camino.

Adam volvió a encender la sirena y las luces. Comenzó a conducir despacio hasta llegar al primero de los manifestantes, y entonces la cadena se soltó. Adam aprovechó para acelerar. Matt seguía observándolo incrédulo.

–¿De verdad vas a tener un niño?

–No, claro que no.

–Entonces, ¿qué hacemos aquí?

–Hannah va a tener un niño –suspiró Adam–. Mi hijo. Es decir, si es que ha decidido seguir adelante.

–¿Quieres decir que está considerando la posibilidad de abortar?

–No lo sé –contestó Adam distraído, leyendo las señales que indicaban la dirección de los diferentes departamentos dentro de la clínica. Las posibilidades eran numerosas: hospitalización, consulta de pacientes externos, paritorio, quirófanos, preparación para el parto...–. ¿A dónde habrá ido? –musitó Adam tenso.

–Y el problema que habéis tenido, ¿ha sido porque ella quería abortar? –preguntó Matt confuso–. ¿No quiere tener un hijo tuyo?

–No, ella cree que yo no quiero tener un hijo.

–¿Y quieres?

–Por supuesto que quiero, ¿qué crees que hago

aquí? –preguntó Adam dando un golpe en el volante–. Pero tengo que decírselo.

–Puede que sea un paciente externo que va a consulta –sugirió Matt–. O que vaya al quirófano. Todo depende de lo rápidas que sean estas cosas. ¿Cuándo pidió la cita?

–No tengo ni idea. Yo me enteré ayer de que estaba embarazada, pero ya se había hecho las pruebas, incluyendo la ecografía. Puede que tenga la cita desde hace mucho tiempo. Probemos en el quirófano –decidió de pronto Adam girando a la izquierda.

–¿Y qué pasa si surge un aviso?

–Tendrás que acudir solo –contestó Adam–. Tengo que solucionar esto. Es una emergencia –repitió mirando el reloj–. De todos modos, enseguida acaba nuestro turno. Espérame aquí –añadió deteniendo el vehículo y abriendo la puerta.

Adam subió los tres escalones de una vez y abrió la puerta enérgicamente. La recepcionista se sobresaltó.

–¿Hemos llamado a una ambulancia?

–No, estoy buscando a una persona. Hannah Duncan. ¿Está aquí?

–¿Es usted pariente suyo?

–No –contestó Adam automáticamente–. Pero necesito encontrarla.

–Me temo que no puedo dar detalles de los pacientes sin permiso explícito. Su visita... ¿es profesional? –preguntó la recepcionista mirando la ambulancia.

–¡Claro! –mintió esa vez Adam–. Escuche, no necesito detalles. Solo necesito saber dónde está.

–¡Ah! ¿Qué nombre dijo?

–Hannah Duncan

–No está citada para hoy en quirófano.

–Entonces, ¿dónde puede estar? Su madre me dijo que estaba aquí.

–Esta clínica es muy grande. ¿A qué ha venido?

–No lo sé –gruñó Adam–. Eso es lo que estoy tratando de averiguar.

–Pregunte en información, entrando por la puerta de al lado.

Adam bajó las escaleras más despacio. El intercomunicador estaba sonando. Matt se había sentado ya en el asiento del piloto.

–Se trata de una prioridad 4, nada más. Un traslado. Trataré de que me acompañe una enfermera. Podré arreglármelas solo, y después nuestro turno habrá terminado, así que quedas libre.

–Gracias, amigo. Te debo una –respondió Adam dejando el intercomunicador en el asiento de la ambulancia.

–Ve a buscar a Hannah. Y soluciona esto –aconsejó Matt.

–Tranquilo, no me marcharé de aquí hasta que no lo haya solucionado.

La ventanilla de información estaba repleta de gente. Un enorme grupo de personas daba vueltas por la sala. Adam se acercó a preguntar.

–¿Ha venido usted a visitar la clínica, señor? Ahora mismo va a comenzar la visita guiada.

–No, estoy buscando a una persona, Hannah Duncan. No estoy seguro de a dónde puede haber ido, pero tiene una cita a las cinco y media.

–Son las seis menos veinte –señaló la recepcionista–. ¿Debía usted acompañarla a esa cita?

–Sí –respondió Adam, que comenzaba a acostumbrarse a mentir–. Es imperioso que esté presente. Soy su marido –sonrió complacido.

–Bueno, vamos a ver.

La recepcionista mecanografió el nombre en el ordenador. Entonces llegó una pareja que preguntó:

–¿Llegamos tarde?

–¿Para qué, señor?

–Para la visita guiada. Acabamos de enterarnos por el periódico. Annie está embarazada –añadió el hombre orgulloso–. Queremos elegir la mejor clínica de maternidad.

Adam apretó los dientes, tratando de dar a entender que tenía prisa.

–Enhorabuena, han venido ustedes al lugar adecuado. No llegan tarde. La visita va a comenzar ahora mismo –explicó la recepcionista señalando a la gente que esperaba caminando de un lado a otro por la sala–. Si se dan prisa, no se perderán nada.

–Gracias –contestó el hombre tomando de la mano a su mujer.

–Bien, ¿dónde estábamos? –preguntó la recepcionista mirando a Adam–. ¿Cuál era el nombre de su mujer?

–Hannah Duncan –contestó Adam viendo con el rabillo del ojo que se abría la puerta de los servicios de señoras. Era Hannah quien salía–. No importa, acabo de encontrarla –Adam corrió a unirse a ella–. ¡Hannah!

–¡Adam! –exclamó Hannah girando la cabeza y abriendo enormemente los ojos–. ¿Qué diablos haces tú aquí?

–Tengo que hablar contigo.

–Tendrás que esperar, llego tarde.

–No puedo esperar –afirmó Adam tomándola del brazo–. No puedo dejarte que hagas esto, Hannah.

–¿Hacer qué?

–Lo que sea que hayas venido a hacer –respondió Adam desesperado–. No te lo permitiré.

–Tú no eres quien para ordenarme nada –contestó Hannah soltándose el brazo–. Es mi decisión, ¿recuerdas? –añadió marchándose con el grupo que se disponía a hacer la visita guiada.

Adam pensó en otro plan de ataque. Hannah no parecía deseosa de hablar con él, pero no podía culparla. Y aquel lugar público no era el mejor sitio para discutir. Sin embargo no tenía otra alternativa, pensó alcanzándola.

–Quiero a este niño –afirmó Adam resuelto–. Aunque tú no lo quieras.

Annie, la mujer embarazada cuyo marido había interrumpido a Adam en información, estaba de pie junto a Hannah. Se volvió y miró a Adam atónita. En medio del silencio, sonó una voz de mujer.

–Como pueden ustedes ver, tenemos todas las facilidades para el parto, dentro de un hospital altamente cualificado. Camas dobles en habitaciones individuales para parejas que decidan quedarse juntos antes, durante, y después del nacimiento...

–Hannah, ¿es que no me has oído?

Hannah asintió en silencio. Escuchaba con atención a la mujer que guiaba la visita.

–En la sala de espera hay televisión, vídeo y equipo de música. Animamos a la gente a que se traiga sus discos. Hay baño completo en cada habitación, con bañera de hidromasaje.

–¡Debe costar una fortuna! –exclamó Annie.

–¡Hannah! –exclamó Adam en voz alta–. Yo puedo ocuparme de todo, puedo traer a nuestro hijo al mundo, si hace falta. Lo he hecho antes.

–¿Qué?, ¿de qué estás hablando, Adam? –preguntó Hannah, cuya atención había conseguido captar al fin.

–De Maddy, mi hija.

–¿Tienes una hija? –preguntó Hannah atónita, en voz alta.

Varias personas se volvieron para mirarlo con gesto de desaprobación.

–Tenía –la corrigió Adam en voz baja–. Murió cuando tenía dos años y medio.

Hannah estaba confusa y atónita. De pronto la guía parecía decir solo incongruencias.

–Pasemos a otra zona. Estoy segura de que los quirófanos les impresionarían...

–Es la misma edad que tiene Heidi –susurró Hannah.

–Por supuesto, seleccionamos a nuestros obstetras y ginecólogos de entre los mejores... –continuaba la guía tratando de acelerar la visita.

–Sí, se parecía mucho a Heidi –confesó Adam–. También dejaba galletas mordisqueadas por todas partes. Y le gustaba que le hicieran cosquillas.

La mayor parte del grupo se había marchado La guía los estaba esperando.

–Vamos, por favor, no tenemos mucho tiempo.

Adam y Hannah obedecieron caminando el uno al lado del otro detrás del grupo. La guía se adelantó y el grupo se detuvo.

–Me llamo Miranda –se presentó a sí misma la guía–. ¿Qué les parece la clínica?

–Es fantástica –comentó Adam con entusiasmo–. Nosotros pediremos una habitación con cama doble.

–Pasen y asomen la cabeza, por favor. Vayan pasando –sonrió Miranda–. Por supuesto, no podemos entrar en los quirófanos, porque están esterilizados.

–Por eso sabías cómo manejar a los bebés –dijo Hannah de pronto–. ¿Por qué no me lo dijiste antes?

–Jamás se lo he dicho a nadie. Nunca he querido confiar tanto de mí mismo a otra persona –confesó Adam tomando las manos de Hannah entre las suyas–. Hasta ahora.

La expresión de Hannah también había cambiado, parecía aliviada.

–Sabía que tenía que haber algo más, algo importante. No me atrevía a preguntar, pero sabía que si no confiabas en mí era porque no sentías lo mismo que yo.

–Te lo contaré todo –prometió Adam–. Además, tengo fotos.

Aún estaban agarrados de las manos, mirándose el uno al otro, cuando la voz de Miranda los interrumpió:

–Por favor, traten de seguir la marcha del grupo, tienen que ir con ellos. No puedo dejar visitantes perdidos por la clínica.

–Lo siento –se disculpó Hannah–. Vamos, Adam, no tardaremos mucho. Quiero ver cómo es este sitio.

–En esta zona los costes son mucho más reducidos –explicaba Miranda–. Viene a costar igual que la estancia en un hotel, solo que con todo el equipo médico incluido.

–Me he sentido tan mal –comentó Hannah con tristeza–. Me sentía dividida entre mi amor por ti y mi amor por Heidi. No podía separaros, pero tampoco uniros.

–Lo sé –contestó Adam apretando su mano–. Creía que lo conseguiría, que podría estar contigo y dejar de lado a Heidi. Y luego me llevé aquel susto en el parque.

–¿Qué susto? –preguntó Hannah asustada–. ¿Qué ocurrió en el parque?

–Pasemos al solarium –anunció Miranda–. Veremos la piscina y el gimnasio. Luego, saliendo por los jardines, llegarán ustedes a la entrada principal y a los aparcamientos. Tengo folletos informativos para todos aquellos que lo deseen.

Adam y Hannah volvieron a quedarse atrás. El corredor quedó en silencio al marcharse el grupo.

—¿Qué ocurrió en el parque? —insistió Hannah preocupada.

—Nada importante —sacudió la cabeza Adam—. Bueno, sí es importante, porque fue entonces cuando me di cuenta de que quería a Heidi tanto como a ti. Al principio no logré separaros, y después me dio miedo aceptar el riesgo que suponía admitirlo.

—¿Qué riesgo?

—El riesgo de perderte. A ti y a Heidi. Sabía a ciencia cierta cuánto riesgo suponía.

—No vas a perdernos —afirmó Hannah alzando una mano para acariciar su mejilla—. Esas tragedias solo ocurren una vez en la vida. Sé lo que es, en serio. Yo también perdí a alguien a quien amaba, y esta vez asumo un riesgo mucho mayor.

—¿Por qué?

—Porque mis sentimientos por ti son mucho más fuertes de lo que lo fueron por Ben. Ni siquiera sabía que se pudiera amar tanto a una persona.

Adam tomó la mano de Hannah, que acariciaba su rostro, y la presionó contra sus labios.

—Eso es exactamente lo que siento yo, por eso el riesgo me parecía esta vez mucho mayor.

—¿Y qué te ha hecho cambiar de opinión?

—Hoy ha ocurrido algo. Un aviso con un bebé. Ya te lo contaré más tarde.

Los tacones de Miranda resonaron por el corredor apresuradamente.

–¡Aquí están ustedes! ¿Querrían, por favor, venir por aquí? Estaba a punto de alertar a seguridad.

–Lo siento –se disculpó Hannah de nuevo–. Teníamos algo importante que discutir.

–Aún tenemos que discutir –sonrió Adam mirando a Miranda, que se ruborizó–. Vamos a tener un niño.

–¡Enhorabuena! –sonrió Miranda poniéndose seria de nuevo–. Por aquí, por favor. Espero que elijan la clínica Cambridge para el parto.

–Es muy probable –asintió Adam–. ¿No crees, Hannah?

–Sí, eso de la cama doble es muy tentador –comentó ella apretando su mano mientras pasaban por delante de la piscina y el gimnasio.

–¿Tienen ustedes el coche en el aparcamiento principal? –preguntó Miranda.

–Sí –respondió Hannah.

–No –respondió Adam al mismo tiempo. Ambas mujeres lo miraron–. La ambulancia tuvo que marcharse a hacer un aviso.

–¿Has venido en ambulancia? –preguntó Hannah sorprendida–. Claro, aún estás en tu turno de trabajo. ¿Cómo te las has arreglado?

–Cuando tu madre me dijo dónde estabas, encendí la sirena.

–¿Cómo, has venido con la sirena y las luces puestas? –sonrió Hannah.

–Claro, era una emergencia.

–No era para tanto –rio Hannah.

Miranda seguía esperando a que se dirigieran hacia la salida, pero en lugar de cooperar, Adam tiró de Hannah de pronto y la abrazó.

–Para mí lo era –dijo muy serio–. Una emergencia personal.

–Pues, según parece, ha resuelto usted esa emergencia, fuera la que fuera –comentó Miranda obser-
vándolos y escuchándolos con curiosidad.

–Bueno, es un comienzo –convino Adam guiñán-
dole un ojo a Miranda–. Aún queda algún que otro
problemilla.

–Ah, ¿sí? –preguntó Miranda sonrojándose–. ¿Y
cuál es?

–Que todavía no he convencido a Hannah para
que se case conmigo.

–¡Oh! –exclamó Miranda sonriendo–. ¿Y crees
que te llevará mucho tiempo? Es que se supone que
debo cerrar esta puerta.

–Bueno, eso depende de Hannah –contestó Adam–.
Es ella quien tiene que decidir.

–¿Qué dices tú, Hannah? –preguntó Miranda acla-
rándose la garganta, con una enorme sonrisa.

La voz de Hannah sonó amortiguada. Adam no
supo si reía o lloraba. Tenía el rostro enterrado en su
hombro.

–No, no creo que tarde mucho –declaró Hannah
levantando la vista–. Ya es hora de marcharnos a
casa, Adam. Miranda tiene que cerrar la puerta.

–Pero aún no has dicho que sí –intervino Miranda
bloqueándoles el paso.

–Es cierto –la apoyó Adam–. ¿Es que piensas
mantenerme en vilo?

–¿Y cómo voy a decirte que sí, si aún no me has
hecho la pregunta? –señaló Hannah.

–Eso también es cierto –señaló una vez más Miranda.

Adam suspiró teatralmente y le dirigió a Miranda
una mirada cómplice.

–¿Tengo que ponerme de rodillas?

–Hmmm... –Miranda consideró la cuestión. Miró a Hannah y sonrió–. Bueno, creo que podemos librarte de ese deber.

–Gracias –contestó Adam–. Miranda, ¿no es hora ya de que te vayas a casa?

–No me perdería esto por nada del mundo –afirmó la guía apoyando la espalda en la puerta–. Vamos, Adam.

Adam colocó las manos sobre los hombros de Hannah y la miró a los ojos con intensidad.

–Te quiero, Hannah. Quiero compartir el resto de mi vida contigo. Quiero aferrarme a cada instante de felicidad que puedas proporcionarme. Quiero ser el padre de tu hija y el padre de todos los niños que traigas al mundo. Y quiero estar contigo cuando nuestros hijos tengan hijos. Quiero darte tanta felicidad como la que me das tú, sin proponértelo –Adam respiró hondo y añadió–: ¿Quieres casarte conmigo, Hannah?

Los ojos de Hannah brillaron con las lágrimas. Asintió y contestó:

–Sí, Adam. Claro que quiero.

Miranda la observó decepcionada.

–¿Eso es todo lo que vas a decir, después del precioso discurso de Adam?

Hannah rio y se estremeció.

–Tengo muchas cosas que decirle, pero tenemos todo el tiempo del mundo. ¿Verdad, Adam?

Adam se inclinó y la besó en los labios.

–Desde luego. Tenemos el resto de nuestras vidas. Por fin se ha resuelto la emergencia.

Epílogo

JAMÁS se había sentido tan bien, y esa vez la felicidad que sentía Hannah Lewis no tenía nada
que ver con los rayos de sol aunque, desde la habitación de la clínica Cambridge, se filtraba la última
luz de aquella tarde de otoño. La cama doble estaba
hecha, la bañera de hidromasaje limpia, y podía descansar. No obstante, Hannah planeaba marcharse
cuanto antes.

Hannah abrió los ojos y sonrió. Aún no podía
creer que hubiera dado a luz en una ambulancia, ni
que hubiera sido su padre quien hubiera traído al
mundo al bebé. Matt había hecho todo cuanto había
podido por llegar a tiempo, pero la sirena de la unidad 241 había sido perfecta para darle la bienvenida
a su hijo.

Hannah contempló el rostro diminuto de Edward
James Lewis, profundamente dormido en su cunita.
Miranda le había recomendado que descansara y pro-
curara dormir hasta que Adam fuera a buscarlos para
llevarlos a casa, pero estaba demasiado nerviosa
como para conciliar el sueño. No quería desperdiciar
ni un instante de aquel precioso día con su familia.

Su familia, suspiró Hannah satisfecha. ¿Quién habría imaginado que podía crecer tanto en el plazo de
un año? El matrimonio de Hannah y Adam no había
sorprendido a nadie, pero el de Norma y Gerry Pres-

cott, pocas semanas después, sí que había sido una sorpresa. Por fin Heidi y Edward tenían abuelo, un abuelo tan ansioso por estar con ellos como su mujer. Norma y Gerry animaban a Hannah y Adam a volver al trabajo cuanto antes; tenían una gran familia por la que velar.

Gerry, además, se había retirado de su profesión de médico para dedicarse a una vieja pasión largamente olvidada, el cultivo de la uva. Norma y él se habían mudado al campo y habían comprado terrenos de cultivo a las afueras de la ciudad. Su generoso regalo de bodas para la joven pareja, cinco acres de ese mismo terreno junto al río, había añadido una nueva dimensión a sus vidas. Ambos habían proyectado la casa de sus sueños, y la construcción casi había finalizado.

Hannah observó las muestras de tela que había estado escogiendo en la tienda cuando le llegaron los dolores de parto. De alguna manera habían llegado hasta la habitación de la clínica, quedando abandonadas sobre la cama. Nada más ver la tela con ositos y arcoiris Hannah se había decidido. Estaba a punto de encargarla cuando rompió aguas, así que llamó a una ambulancia. Las muestras de tela cayeron al suelo al abalanzarse Heidi sobre la cama, nada más llegar.

–¡Mamá!

–Hola, cariño –abrazó Hannah a su hija levantando la vista para sonreír a Adam, de pie junto a la cama. La felicidad era patente en la expresión de ambos. Ninguno de los dos apartó la mirada. Adam se acercó–. He venido en la ambulancia de papá –añadió Heidi orgullosa–. Hay una cama detrás, para que vengas a casa.

–¿Has vuelto a traer la ambulancia? –preguntó Hannah sonriendo y besando a su marido.

–¡Tiene luces como las de Navidad! –exclamó Heidi apartándose de su madre–. Y hace muchísimo ruido.

–¡Pero Adam... ! ¿No habrás...?

–Solo por un momento –sonrió Adam sin el menor arrepentimiento–. Pensé que Heidi debía saber qué hacen sus padres para ganar dinero –explicó acercándose a la cuna para contemplar y acariciar al bebé–. Este, en cambio, es aún un poco pequeño para comprenderlo. Volveremos a casa sin tanto ruido.

–Pues la sirena fue lo primero que oyó nada más nacer –comentó Hannah–. Ahora necesitaré otra igual en casa, cuando quiera que se duerma.

Heidi se había acercado a la cuna y alzaba una mano para tocar a su hermano. Miró a su padre y comentó:

–Tiene el mismo pelo que papá. ¿Por qué yo no?

–Porque tú tienes el pelo de tu madre –sonrió Adam–. Como debe ser.

–¿Por qué? –insistió Heidi mirando a Adam–. ¿Es porque soy chica?

–No –contestó Adam con ternura–. Es porque tú eres Heidi, y eres perfecta tal y como eres.

Los ojos de Hannah se llenaron de lágrimas. Abrazó a Adam y se las enjugó, contemplando al recién nacido que ataría aún con más fuerza los lazos que unían a la familia.

–Se llama Edward –dijo Hannah dirigiéndose a Heidi–, porque así se llama su padre, de segundo nombre, y así se llamaba también su abuelo.

–Ed... Ed... –Heidi no sabía pronunciarlo–. Eddie. ¡Teddy! –exclamó triunfante.

–Mucha gente llama Teddy a los Edwards –rio Adam.

—¿Tiene cosquillas? —preguntó Heidi.

—Aún no —se apresuró Hannah a contestar.

—Cuando sea mayor —añadió Adam—. Hará ruidito, igual que tú.

—Y que teddy —puntualizó Heidi refiriéndose a su osito—. Papá...

—¿Sí, pequeñina?

—Quiero irme a casa.

Adam estrechó a Hannah con fuerza y la miró a los ojos con intensidad. La respuesta de Hannah a la pregunta que iba a hacerle era de la mayor importancia para él.

—¿Estás lista?, ¿te encuentras lo suficientemente bien como para volver a casa con nosotros?

—Y con Teddy —puntualizó Heidi—. Porque nos lo llevamos, ¿no?

—Por supuesto. Jamás me había sentido mejor —aseguró Hannah—. A casa.

Bianca®...
la seducción y fascinación del romance

No te pierdas las emociones que te brindan los títulos de Harlequin® Bianca®.

¡Pídelos ya! Y recibe un descuento especial por la orden de dos o más títulos.

HB#33547	UNA PAREJA DE TRES	$3.50 ☐
HB#33549	LA NOVIA DEL SÁBADO	$3.50 ☐
HB#33550	MENSAJE DE AMOR	$3.50 ☐
HB#33553	MÁS QUE AMANTE	$3.50 ☐
HB#33555	EN EL DÍA DE LOS ENAMORADOS	$3.50 ☐

(cantidades disponibles limitadas en algunos títulos)

CANTIDAD TOTAL	$ _____
DESCUENTO: 10% PARA 2 Ó MÁS TÍTULOS	$ _____
GASTOS DE CORREOS Y MANIPULACIÓN	$ _____
(1$ por 1 libro, 50 centavos por cada libro adicional)	
IMPUESTOS*	$ _____
<u>TOTAL A PAGAR</u>	$ _____
(Cheque o money order—rogamos no enviar dinero en efectivo)	

Para hacer el pedido, rellene y envíe este impreso con su nombre, dirección y zip code junto con un cheque o money order por el importe total arriba mencionado, a nombre de Harlequin Bianca, 3010 Walden Avenue, P.O. Box 9077, Buffalo, NY 14269-9047.

Nombre: _____

Dirección: _____ Ciudad: _____

Estado: _____ Zip Code: _____

Nº de cuenta (si fuera necesario):_____

*Los residentes en Nueva York deben añadir los impuestos locales.

Harlequin Bianca®

CBBIA3

No creía en el amor, ni en el matrimonio, por lo menos para ella. Para los demás, Kelsey Armstrong Waters organizaba las mejores bodas y les deseaba lo mejor. Pero los fracasos matrimoniales de sus padres la hicieron jurarse que nunca recorrería el camino hasta el altar. Hasta que conoció a Will Addison.

Llegó pidiendo ayuda para organizar la boda de su frívola hermana, y contra lo que le decía su instinto, Kelsey accedió. Él era guapo, sexy, un romántico que creía en el amor. Provocaba en ella sueños y sensaciones que creía que nunca experimentaría. Se le estaba olvidando la norma principal: "Recuerda, Kelsley, ¡tú nunca serás la novia en una boda!"

Amor para toda la vida

Melissa McClone

PÍDELO EN TU PUNTO DE VENTA

Nadie quería meterse en líos con Joe Sanchez.
Pero una delicia de mujer le hizo caer a sus pies. En
una noche mágica y llena de pasión, él tomó la virgi-
nidad de aquella muchacha bella y tímida, pero tras el
éxtasis ocurrió un desastre. Joe nunca había podido
olvidarla, y cuando Elena Maldonado apareció de
nuevo en su vida, en medio de una misión muy deli-
cada, ambos tuvieron que poner a prueba su firme
decisión de no enamorarse otra vez. Joe tenía el instinto y la cautela propios de un agente secreto, y
ahora estaban en alerta roja. Sentía el deseo a flor de
piel. Tenía que infiltrarse... en el corazón del enemi-
go.

PÍDELO EN TU PUNTO DE VENTA